HOME COOKIN'

BRIAN CLARY

Author of *Amicus Curiae*
and *Unfinished Business*

HOME COOKIN'

iUniverse books may be ordered through booksellers or by contacting:

iUniverse
1663 Liberty Drive
Bloomington, IN 47403
www.iuniverse.com
1-800-Authors (1-800-288-4677)

Because of the dynamic nature of the Internet, any web addresses or links contained in this book may have changed since publication and may no longer be valid. The views expressed in this work are solely those of the author and do not necessarily reflect the views of the publisher, and the publisher hereby disclaims any responsibility for them.

Any people depicted in stock imagery provided by Getty Images are models, and such images are being used for illustrative purposes only. Certain stock imagery © Getty Images.

ISBN: 978-1-5320-5380-1 (sc)
ISBN: 978-1-5320-5382-5 (hc)
ISBN: 978-1-5320-5381-8 (e)

Library of Congress Control Number: 2018909046

Print information available on the last page.

iUniverse rev. date: 08/27/2018

"You never really understand a person until you consider things from his point of view … until you climb into his skin and walk around in it."

— Harper Lee, To Kill a Mockingbird

Dedication: Those not touched by the ravages of cancer in some way, represent a fortunate minority. Cancer is color blind, gender neutral and holds no compassion for children or the elderly—but it can be defeated. It has been my privilege to serve as an officer and director for Golfers Against Cancer, an all-volunteer charitable organization dedicated to one goal—the eradication of cancer from humanity. Since GAC's inception in 1997, we have witnessed the fall of cancer death rates, the rise of remissions and much cause for optimism for the future. While great strides have been made toward the goals and aspirations of GAC, there's much more to be done. I dedicate this book and the proceeds from it to Golfers Against Cancer and ultimately for its use by the dedicated men and women on the front lines of this crucial research. I hope you will take a moment and read the inspirational words of Bob Spinetti, one of the stalwarts of this wonderful organization, and someone that I am glad to have called my friend for the past 16 years.

Brian Clary

About Golfer's Against Cancer-(GAC): As you peruse, enjoy, laugh and perhaps shed a tear reading *Home Cookin'* you will get a glimpse or perhaps a grim reminder of the tragedy represented by cancer. Dedicated to its Mission Statement to raise funds for research to cure cancer, GAC continues into its third decade. Despite GAC's phenomenal success, far too many are affected by this dreaded disease. Those diagnosed often experience despair and anguish, emotions shared with family and loved ones. It was through this agony and the desire to *do something about it* that formed the foundation of what would become Golfers Against Cancer. Through the inspiration and vision of the GAC founders, including Susan and Bobby Jones, Sally Roberts and Sarah Longpre, and for the concern for two friends diagnosed with cancer, GAC was formed. One of the afflicted, a man known as *The Colonel* was diagnosed with prostate cancer. The other, Mike Longpre a young Assistant Pro the Deerwood Country Club in Kingwood, Texas contracted Glioblastoma, a deadly form of brain cancer. Though each lost their battle their passing fueled the determination for the group to press on. The first year of fundraising featured a golf tournament at Deerwood. The results exceeded all expectations by raising $85,000, and with that success, the Group incorporated as a 501(c) (3) charitable organization. The following year, in addition to the tournament a Gala was held, complete with a dinner and auction. GAC expanded nationally and similar fundraisers were held across the country including Orange County, CA, Atlanta, Greensboro, New York, Boston, Denver, Dallas, and Bradenton, Florida. A Pro-am titled the *Mike Longpre Memorial Tournament* was added. To date, this grassroots organization has raised, including matching funds, $23.9 million. This level of success would not have been possible without the dedication of GAC's all-volunteer board and the generosity of its presenting sponsor – United Airlines.

From all of us at GAC, we thank Brian for his years of service to GAC and for dedicating the proceeds from this book to "the cause".

Robert Spinetti

1
CHAPTER

onsidering my proper upbringing, a good education and having been baptized in the Navasota River by Pastor Ralph Taney of First Methodist Church, I know what you're thinking: *How-in-the hell did I, Gertrude Allison Chase, end up in a jail cell in McLennan County, Texas.*

It goes without saying that what I did was done with the best of intentions, but we all know what the road to hell is paved with, now don't we? Sure, money was a part of it, but there was so much more in play than just that. It is a heck of a tale and I am still sorting it all out in my own mind, but if you are willing to listen the good Lord knows I have time to tell it.

The seeds that led to my bumper crop of complications were sown early in life. I was born on a dirt farm in an old wood framed shotgun house in the small community of Lost Prairie, Texas. I refer to Lost Prairie as a *community*, as I was once advised that for an area to qualify as a *town*, it had to have a minimum of a post office and a Main Street—Lost Prairie had neither.

Our lives changed dramatically in the late 1950s following a devastating two-year drought. My dad reluctantly sold the farm and we moved a few miles away to the city of Mexia. For clarity it is pronounced *me-hay-a* or as the old-timers say *me-hair*—a town whose motto is: *a great place, no matter how you pronounce it.* Compared to Lost Prairie Mexia, with a population of just under six thousand, represented *the big city* to me and my family.

My dad took a job with the City of Mexia in its Water Department and his initial assignment was reading water meters. Soon thereafter he joined a maintenance crew, worked his way up to foreman, and by the early-sixties he had risen to Superintendent—the top of the heap in that department. This title earned him better pay and a house for us to live in that was furnished by the city—appropriately referred to by us as *the city house.*

This was an era when many towns remained fully segregated. The area of Mexia where people of color predominated was euphemistically referred to as *the other side of the tracks* by some, and by more pejorative references by others. This area was comprised of mostly ramshackle homes occupied by the poorest of black families.

My first glimpse of this section of town was tied to my father's affinity to the great outdoors. As a prototypical tomboy, I shared that interest and enjoyed most fishing with him. There were two types of catfish indigenous to Central Texas and the ones we preferred were known as *channel cats,* and the others were called *mud cats* or *pollies.* The latter were edible, but barely so as they were fatty and not very pleasing to the taste buds. Nevertheless, dad kept the mud cats we caught, but would place them on a separate stringer.

When we would leave the lake dad would head straight to *the other side of the tracks.* He would drive the unpaved, shale topped, dusty roads of the black section of town past one decrepit house after another in search of takers. In that era air conditioning was a luxury that precious few could afford. Accordingly, all houses were built with porches and it was common for folks on both sides of the tracks to spend time on their porch during the day. At night many families pulled beds, cots or pallets out onto the porch to endure the oppressive Texas summer nights. Consequently, instead of knocking on doors dad would simply cruise the area until we reached a house with folks out on the porch or in their front yard, a circumstance not hard to find in the summer.

When we spotted potential recipients dad would stop, roll down the window and ask if they wanted some catfish. We were never turned down—not once—ever. My dad would meet them at the back of the car and pop the trunk or the *turtle hull* as he called it. I would watch on as the folks eagerly stripped the stringer into a bucket or a tow sack and I marveled at just how much it pleased them.

A major local employer was the Mexia State School, a facility that once served as a prisoner of war camp during World War II. My mother's only out of the home occupation was using her culinary skills at the state school's cafeteria for six and half years. During this time mom developed close ties with her fellow kitchen workers, most notably Bea Jackson and Wanda Fuller. The latter, Miss Wanda as I referred to her, was a kind, soft spoken black woman of Creole origin. She had a beautiful light brown complexion mottled with faint freckles on her cheeks and was the mother to Nelda Fay, a girl that would become my dear friend.

I recall vividly a day when I was walking home from the picture show and saw Bea Jackson's car parked in front of the Spindle Top café. As I passed I noticed that Miss Wanda was seated alone in the back seat. My mother and Ms. Jackson emerged from the café having lunched there and mom waved at me as she handed Miss Wanda a paper sack containing her lunch. Mom and I had a long discussion that evening.

My confused and vague notions on issues of race and segregation turned crystal clear one Saturday afternoon when a particular movie played the Mexia Theater. It was Harper Lee's *To Kill a Mockingbird* and I was awed by it and saw it two additional times before it left the theater. For Christmas that year I asked for only one thing and that was for my own copy of the book. I managed to behave well enough to get a hardbound edition and wore it out reading it from cover to cover countless times. It opened my eyes to many things and spawned my dream of becoming a lawyer.

Though few girls from Mexia ever attended as much as a trade school I was audacious enough to imagine completing college and continuing on to study law. However, the notion of graduating high school and pursuing higher education was not in accord with the ethos of our community or our family's financial reality.

I settled on attending a vocational institute to study *business*—a curriculum that amounted to training to be a secretary. I completed the course, received the certificate in the mail and used those skills to land a job with Samuel Nelson. Sam was a venerable and respected general practice lawyer and he wasted no time involving me in his practice. It was a tad intimidating at first, but I excelled at it and absorbed as much as I could about the law and litigation. As time passed we became busy enough to warrant hiring another assistant, and I recommended my friend Dorothy Swayne, or Dot as she preferred. Much to my delight Mr. Nelson brought her aboard and though I enjoyed working with Sam and Dot, in the end it was not lawyering and I knew it.

Considering Mr. Nelson's age at the time I took the job I should have anticipated it, but seven and a half years into my tenure there, I was taken aback by the announcement of his retirement. Fortunately for Dot and me, Sam was kind enough to make phone calls on our behalf in order to get us placed with a new firm. With his enthusiastic recommendation we received several offers, but only one that was willing to take the both of us. We accepted that offer and joined the law office of attorney Louise Barbour. Though the pay was less, Dot and I wanted to stay together and mistakenly thought that with hard work we would make up the salary difference in short order. It would take five and a half years of toiling for Louise to rise to the level of pay we were earning when we left Sam Nelson's employ.

Joining our squad in recent years was Guadalupe Maria Sylvia-Sotomayor. Since her name was a mouth full we settled on calling her *Lupe*, appropriately pronounced *Loopy*. Until then she had been the housekeeper for our boss and we later learned that Louise figured that there were fewer and less expensive things for Lupe to break at the office. Lupe—sweet, kind little Lupe, stands five-foot nothin', is very pretty, has a heart of gold and looks much younger than her age of thirty-four. She struggled to improve her English, but with effort Lupe slowly made progress. With that advancement, coupled with me knowing a little of the *español* we managed to effectively communicate, resorting only on rare occasions to a well-worn paperback English to Spanish and vice versa dictionary.

Lupe proved proficient at making sure the coffee was fresh and that the office was tidy, but initially that was the limit of her skill set.

Over time she began assisting us with some of the office tasks and Dot and I grew to adore her like a sister. She occasionally blundered, but when she did she was truly remorseful, would earnestly pledge to try harder, and could redeem any transgression by bringing us her homemade hot tamales. I could eat her pork tamales by the dozen—even after I learned how they were made—but let's not dwell on that part.

The deeds that landed me in the hoosegow here in Waco all started on a day that changed our lives on a dime. By then, Dot and I had worked for Louise a long time—eighteen years, five months and twelve days to be exact, but who's counting? When I arrived at the office that fateful morning, I heard Lupe in the back of the office working in the kitchen. I was transcribing a tape of Louise's dictated letters until I heard the front door open and close. I poked my head out into the hallway and though Louise did not see me, I saw her, and she looked terrible. Her hair was disheveled, her complexion was red and splotchy and below her bloodshot eyes were dark puffy circles. I was relieved when she entered her office without comment, and closed the door behind her. I was continuing my transcription and when Dot arrived she began perusing the opened and date stamped mail from the previous day.

"How is she?" Dot said.

"She looks pretty rough."

"Hungover?"

"I assume so, but whatever it is she's got it bad," I explained as Lupe peeked into our office.

"Good morning Lupe," Dot said.

"Mornin' Miss Dot—mornin' Miss Gertie."

"Hello sweetie," I said, "now ask me what I want to drink,"

"Te gustaría—"

"English please," I interrupted.

Lupe cleared her throat and said, "Would jou like … some coffee … this morning."

"I certainly would, thank you," I said, "is the coffee brewing?"

"Jes, it is ready and I bring jou a cup soon," she said grinning, then scampered back to the kitchen.

Dot glanced at her desk calendar, and said, "You do know Louise has a hearing tomorrow?"

"Yes, it's on Whizzer Henderson's divorce. Is there anything else set?"

"No."

"Good, this one will be about all that Louise can handle, assuming she gets up to speed on it."

"You know him pretty well, don't you?" Dot asked.

"Whizzer?" I asked, and Dot nodded. "Yes I know him, and his soon to be ex-wife Deborah too. We used to play hearts and pinochle together until we realized that Debbie is about half nuts. "

"I always wondered how he got the nickname *Whizzer*—do you know?"

"He earned it in elementary school and the story goes that it had something to do with his prowess in the boy's room at one end of a urinal trough."

"Oh my," Dot giggled, then said, "What are we going to do about the hearing?"

"Let's wait and assess how Louise recovers. Perhaps she'll be in better sorts in the afternoon and we can get with her on it."

"And if she's not?"

"Then we have to cancel it and notify Whizzer and the other side," I said. "This is a custody hearing and it's too important to let Louise go down there without being lucid and prepared."

"Miss Gertie, me worry 'bout *Señora* Barbour—she *muy* sick, no?" Lupe asked, handing me my coffee mug.

"Don't worry about Louise," I said. "She'll be better once you get her some coffee."

"I no go there," Lupe declared firmly while shaking her head rapidly.

"Shhh—keep your voice down, we don't want to rouse her," I said, and noticed that the poor girl was trembling. None of us wanted to bring Louise her first cup of coffee, especially on mornings like this, but to console Lupe, I added, "Maybe she's napping and won't ask for any coff—."

"Where's my damn coffee?" Louise's raspy voice resonated from behind her closed door.

Dot retreated to the bathroom and Lupe took cover by positioning herself behind my desk chair.

"It's all right Lupe, get it ready and I will take it to her," I said.

"*Gracias*—I mean thank you, Miss Gertie," she said with relief.

"*No es nada,*" I said.

"Damn it to hell, didn't any of y'all hear me?" Louise yelled and Lupe cringed.

"We are getting it right now," I responded and followed Lupe down the hall, into the kitchen and over to the coffee brewer resting on the Formica countertop. I watched as she lifted the heavily used coffee pot, which was blackened with carbonous residue on the bottom from being left on the brewer too long with too little coffee. I could not discern whether it was the weight of the near full pot or Lupe's nervousness that had it shaking from side to side. She struggled to steady it and finally managed to pour the dark steaming Folger's into Louise's monogrammed ceramic mug.

Louise was very particular about her coffee and demanded it be prepared the same way each day. Once poured, it was to receive one level teaspoon of creamer and one heaping spoon of sugar. Then came a pinch of salt to kill inevitable bitterness from the old pot, and one ice cube to dull the heat. I watched from behind as Lupe used her trembling hand to measure out the ingredients, but since more of the condiments were finding the counter top than the coffee cup, I said, "Hand it to me, Lupe."

She eagerly relinquished the plastic spoon, but considering that an undetermined amount of the creamer had made it into the coffee, I thought it prudent to start from scratch. I emptied the cup into the sink, re-filled it with coffee and carefully measured out and added each ingredient. Once done, I finished it off with the ice cube which brought the coffee level close to the rim. Careful not to spill any I lifted the mug and walked gingerly back down the hall and toward Louise' office.

"Well?" Louise yelled, and it startled me enough to slosh the hot coffee out of the cup, across my fingers and dripping down to the hardwood floors.

"Coming right up," I said through gritted teeth just as Dot emerged from the restroom. Seeing my dilemma, she reached out to take the cup and I handed it off to her trying not jeopardize her own hand.

"Are you all right? Dot whispered, as Lupe came up from behind and handed me two sheets of paper towels.

"I think so," I said and used one of the towels to lightly dab my fingers and handed the other to Dot, "Just place the paper towel on my desk and set the cup on it."

She did so and then joined me in examining my fingers. "They're red, but I don't see any blistering—how do they feel?"

"They're throbbing a little, but I think the ice cube helped."

Lupe stared on anxiously, sniffled, and said, "Sorry you hurt, *qué es mi culpa.*"

"It's not your fault sweetheart and I'm all right," I said wiping the coffee streams off the outside of the cup before lifting it. I took a deep breath and continued down the hall and once at Louise's door, I put my free hand on the nob. I turned it slightly to assure that it was unlocked and tapped on the door before easing it open.

I entered and Louise was seated at her desk, but she had laid her head on her folded arms in front of her. This was not at all unusual so I placed the cup on a coaster and gently said, "Here you go, Louise." She did not stir. "Louise?" I said louder, but still received no response. "Louise?" I said urgently, and gently shook her shoulder, and noticed beads of sweat on the nape of her neck. I put my right hand on her arm, but my throbbing fingers were incapable of detecting the nuances of skin temperature. I placed the back of my left hand on her neck and it felt clammy. I leaned over to the other side of the desk to get a peek at her face and found it was ashen, and though her eyes were fully open they had a fixed gaze and did not blink.

I yelled the girls into the office and used Louise's phone to dial 911. When the paramedics arrived they tried, unsuccessfully, to resuscitate Louise and she was declared dead at 10:36 A.M. The EMTs lifted her limp body from her chair and placed it on a gurney. They covered her from head to toe with a sheet and pushed her out of the office, down the sidewalk to the street, and into the ambulance. When they drove away and the gawkers in the street disbursed, the girls and I returned inside. We each took seats in the reception area and all I could muster was, "I guess we need to pass Whizzer's hearing."

2
CHAPTER

Perhaps you are curious as to what led to the untimely demise of the matriarch of our small town law firm. Louise Barbour's fall from grace was years in the making and bearing witness to it was like watching a slow-motion train wreck. Most employees would never be privy to intimate details of the life of their boss, but reluctantly I was. Louise often had me stay at the office after hours, without pay I might add, while she drank vodka and bared her soul. Though she never offered me a drink, and I would have turned it down if she had, she held me over on the premise that *only alcoholics drink alone.* Louise spent countless hours regaling me with endless tales from her past. Many were very personal and should have never been told, but in retrospect they provide a perspective.

She was born into a family that did not have a pot to pee in or a window to throw it out of. That all changed one day when word came from a seismologist that their bottomland family farm just happened to be sitting atop one of the richest natural gas reserves in all of North Texas. Louise was just a teenager when her folks struck it rich and in an instant they went from the outhouse to the penthouse—literally.

As the drilling crews descended upon their property her family traded their meager farm house for a high rise in Highland Park, the uppity part of Dallas. Once there, they began hobnobbing with some big time socialites and titans of the boardroom. They were rednecks acting as blue bloods and were likely regarded by most denizens of Highland Park as the proverbial turd in the punch bowl—a Waterford crystal one of course. To their credit though, Louise's parents sought the advice of estate planners and accountants and had the good sense to place a large portion of their fortuitous wealth in a series of well-managed trusts each dedicated to the couple's offspring and their descendants.

Once Louise completed college she applied to, and was accepted by, one of the most prestigious private law schools in Dallas, proving that money talks and you know what walks. She managed to graduate, but failed the bar exam on the first two go-arounds. She squeaked by on the third try and took her oath becoming a bona fide *attorney at law* and set up shop in downtown Dallas.

During this time Louise met a fellow at a wedding reception for a mutual friend and they started dating. His name was John Rutledge, and after learning of Louise's wealth it was love at first sight—sight of her financial statement that is. According to Louise, Mr. Rutledge lured her into matrimony by convincing her that he was financially well off in his own right. He claimed to hold an advanced degree and was a self-described *philanthropist*—devoting much of his wealth to the benefit of others. Louise would later learn that Mr. Rutledge's alleged degree was actually a certificate from the Baldwin Vocational Institute certifying him as a lawn mower mechanic. The beneficiaries of his *philanthropy* were two ex-wives with each receiving court ordered monthly child support stipends enforced by the office of the Texas Attorney General.

Once married they had a child right away, but the wedded bliss did not endure. Louise struggled, unsuccessfully, to build her Dallas law practice and to lose the weight she gained during her pregnancy. The only thing she succeeded in losing was money, and a lot of it. She explained on one vodka-aided evening that her law practice brought in sufficient money to run the household, but John Rutledge had, and I quote, *battleship desires and a row boat income*. The two lovebirds rapidly grew disenchanted with each other and the marriage became unsustainable.

Louise had abused alcohol all of her adult life, but as the marriage crumbled she admitted that the frequency and quantity of her consumption increased and she really began to let herself go. She expanded greatly on her post-natal weight and with that, along with her erratic mood swings, even her money could not keep John Rutledge on the reservation. They split the sheets and he got his freedom from her and Louise got custody of their son Clarence.

Louise continued to struggle with her law firm and eventually threw in the towel and shut it down. She answered an ad in the bar journal for a position with the Limestone County District Attorney's office. She landed the job, bought a nice home here in Mexia, and drove the fourteen miles each day to the county seat of Groesbeck. She began on the lowest rung of the ladder trying misdemeanors, but after a couple of years in the courtroom, she tired of convicting first time drunk drivers, shoplifters and joy riders.

She decided that with her connections in the community and the county government, that she would take another stab at private practice—this time in Mexia. She purchased the office building, hung out her shingle and became something she could never achieve in Dallas by becoming a big fish in a very small pond. Soon thereafter she hired Dot and me and though our paychecks never reflected it, Louise thrived in private practice. She managed to create a steady stream of cases and became skilled at handling them, but one skill Louise could not master was how to avoid getting married.

When she met a gentleman named Brandeis Vanderbilt at a continuing education course in Fort Worth, she relapsed. Mr. Vanderbilt likewise came from oil money, but unlike Louise and her family he knew how to play the part of one occasioned with such wealth. Brandeis, or *Brandy* as Louise referred to him, was an older gentleman and somehow fell for Louise despite the fact that by that time she had become about as predictable as a Texas twister.

Louise's escalating alcohol abuse exasperated her already erratic temperament. With the added calories from the drinking, her poor diet and lack of exercise, she developed buttocks the size of a fifty dollar Valentine. Despite all of that Brandy was smitten and proposed to her, not considering that by asking for her hand, he also got her mouth, her butt, and Clarence.

Once married, Louise took the Vanderbilt surname and filed the paperwork to change Clarence's last name to it as well. Brandeis kept his mansion in Fort Worth and with the aid of his private jet he split his time between there and Mexia. He seemed convinced that he could change Louise and learn to like Clarence, oblivious to the fact that neither were possible. Louise was never going to change and Clarence is, was and will always be, rude, lazy and shiftless.

Louise's growing inattention to her work was directly proportional to her increased drinking. By necessity, this escalated the involvement of both Dot and me in the day-to-day handling of the cases. Word was that the tippling was much worse at home, so much so that things began to disintegrate there as well. Eventually, her drinking and the torment represented by the presence of Clarence caused the distinguished Mr. Vanderbilt to flee back to Fort Worth—never to return to Limestone County.

They divorced and Louise reclaimed her maiden name of Barbour, but encouraged Clarence to keep the Vanderbilt moniker. Dot and I figured that Louise insisted on that in order to cut down on the number of people that associated him with her. An alternative theory was that by him keeping the name Clarence would sound like high society to the locals. I was sure that most folks in Louise's circle of friends associated the name Vanderbilt more with fancy, overpriced, blue jeans, than a figure from the Industrial Revolution.

Despite all the advantages afforded by his birthright Clarence was a twenty-nine year old underachiever that managed to do less with more than any other human being I have ever known. He had never held a job—at least not a legitimate one and the closest he came to having a vocation was acting as a bookie for some of his college fraternity buddies. Clarence was a lot of things—mostly bad things— but he was no dummy. He was naturally intelligent and held a degree from a froufrou university in California. He must have learned a lot while there considering it took six and a half years to earn the diploma. Highly educated? Yes, but prime proof that you can't polish a turd.

I fully expected Clarence to rapidly overcome any grief and swoop in to try to capitalize on his mother's passing. In anticipation of that I was prepared to urge him to, with our help, select another area attorney to take over the caseload. This way the three of us could remain employed and with any luck we would be in the charge of a normal boss, but we would soon learn that Clarence had other designs.

When Louise's graveside service concluded, and as soon as the bottom of her casket hit the vault, Clarence made a beeline to Carl Peckham, the law firm's CPA. He cornered Carl under the shade of a spreading oak and I surmised that it was to ascertain what he could milk out of the firm. Monday morning Clarence rose at the crack of noon, strutted into the office and I met him in the reception area. I was drawn to his scraggly blonde beard that showed unkempt and greasy and his matching hair which was pulled back into a ponytail. He stood slouching as he perused a spreadsheet outlining the firm's financials with one hand and picking his nose with the other. Due to his habitual disregard for personal hygiene, I always tried not to stand too close to him, especially indoors and watched on at a reasonable distance as he analyzed the document.

Clarence lowered the papers and declared that he was *now in charge* and that our office was now *his building*. He instructed that we go through all the firm's files and farm them out to other lawyers, making it clear that our office would no longer operate as a law firm. I was further advised that once the files were reassigned and all the monies collected, the building was going to be converted into a *vape shop*—whatever the hell that is—and video game arcade. He afforded us two weeks with pay to get the firm's business wrapped up and thereafter we were instructed to vacate.

When he left I conveyed his edict to Dot and Lupe and they, like me, were devastated. We all wondered what we were going to do to make a living in Mexia considering that the price of oil had fallen by half since the first of the year. This plummet created a ripple effect in the local economy and we knew plenty of people that were out of work including some in the legal biz.

"I figured he would pull something like this," Dot said.

"So did I, but I did not think it would be so immediate."

"Two weeks to straighten out all of this is insane," Dot said, pointing at the long row of metal file cabinets lining the walls of our shared office.

"Problem is, he knows from Mr. Peckham what the accounts receivable are and realizes that every day we work means less in his pocket."

"Fine, but we have to get the filing caught up before we can even consider approaching the other firms."

"You can't explain that to Clarence, plus he doesn't care. He has made his decision and this is our fate, and us three and the clients be damned."

"This reminds me of an old western I watched where the Sherriff made the condemned prisoners build their own gallows," Dot lamented. "I have half a mind to walk out of here and let him figure out all of this out."

"That thought crossed my mind too."

"Why don't we? That'll teach him a lesson."

"Jes, teach on him, Miss Gertie!" Lupe said angrily, and stomped her foot for emphasis.

"First of all, Clarence can't be taught a lesson. Plus, if we did that he would just keep the money that comes in, walk away and the only people that would get impacted would be our clients."

Dot sighed. "You're right of course and we know most of them personally and some are our friends."

"That's why we have to see this through—I just hope we get paid for the effort."

"Do you think there is a chance Clarence will stiff us?"

"I would hate to think that he would, but I will take that up with Mr. Peckham. Perhaps he would be willing to fund the payrolls in advance before a dime goes to Clarence."

"I hope he will, but he is working for Clarence now," Dot said and glanced at newspaper splayed opened on my desk with blue ink circles around two listings. "I see you are already hitting the want ads."

"Yeah, I've been getting my ducks in a row, how about you?"

"I've been looking, but there's not much around here."

"Tell me about it," I said. "The closest I have seen worth considering is one in Waco and another in Corsicana."

"I saw those too, but I would hate to drive that far back and forth to work. Plus, if you are interested in either of those I will back off."

"Let's you and I coordinate our searches," I said. "I don't want to try for a job that you are interested in."

"But Gertie you should—"

"Dot, I have a husband and you don't."

She glanced sympathetically at me, and said, "True, but Jack is disabled."

"He still works some and gets a disability check."

"I know that, but I also know how meager it is."

"It's something though," I said. "I say let's get you hired first and then I will work on my situation."

"You are a true friend Gertie Chase," Dot said, then we heard a whimper and each turned to see the quivering lower lip on Lupe's face.

"Lo siento Lupe, I should have explained this up front," I said. "Tengo trabjo por tu—I have a job for you."

"Job … for me?" she said with excitement.

"Sí—yes," I said

"Dondé?"

"En mi iglesia—at my church. Mr. Jack found you work there like you do here," I said, then explained in Spanish that my hubby had discussed her with Sonya Thomas, our church Secretary. She agreed to use Lupe to clean the church and help with serving at functions in the fellowship hall. Though it would be part-time, and only paid the same as she earned with Louise I hoped it would tide her over until something better came along. As a precaution though, Jack did suggest to Sonya that she pack up the glasses in the fellowship hall and replace them with Solo Cups for the time being.

Saturday morning I rose early and reached the office ahead of the others. Despite our looming unemployment, I found it refreshing to unlock the door and enter knowing that no matter what happened that day I would not be yelled at, threatened, or have to stay after hours to attend a one-sided happy hour. I began reviewing the files and once Dot and Lupe arrived we got down to business.

"Clarence is supposed to be checking our progress this morning, so let's begin with these," I said pointing at the stack of files I had already pulled. "They are from the top drawer of the first file cabinet, and we can start with them and make our way through until we are done or get kicked out—whichever comes first."

"I know what will come first," Dot said.

"Me too," I said, and handed Dot a copy of a document I drafted. "I compiled this list of Limestone County law firms and a couple from out of the county. Included next to each are their phone numbers and what type of cases they handle."

"So we are looking to some firms outside of Mexia?"

"I think we will have to in order to get as many of them placed as we can, but do I favor keeping them as local as possible."

"What about the retainers?" Dot said, referring to the fees fronted by clients on the hourly billed cases. "Anyone we contact will want to know that figure."

"Good point. Let's put a stickie note on the outside of each file and write down the type of case and the amount left in trust, if any, and include all immediate deadlines. As we find each file a new home we need to contact the client and get their permission to transfer the case."

"I didn't even think about that, but reaching out to every client is going to add a lot of time to the process."

"I realize that, but we have to do it," I said.

We were plodding along nicely when we heard the front door open and close. I walked toward the front and into the reception area expecting to find Clarence, but discovered instead my husband Jack and his good friend William Howard Taft Highsmith. Though not the sharpest knife in the drawer and possessing the decorum of a *pull-my-finger* joke, Bill had at all times been a kindhearted, hardworking, decent man and his wife, Shirley, remains one of my closest friends.

"We dropped by to see if we could help out," Jack explained.

"That's awfully nice fellas, we just might need a little muscle power around here," I said, and turned to Highsmith. "Have you lost weight?"

"Not voluntarily," Bill said. "Shirley's been starvin' me on some powdered drink diet she saw on the TV."

"How much have you lost?"

"Well, as of today, and after my morning constitutional it's eleven and a half pounds."

I smiled, and said, "Congratulations."

Bill blushed. "Aw hell, a guy my size, losing an amount like that is like lock washer rattling off a bull dozer."

"I think you look great—maybe we should try that diet," I said glancing to Jack, and his expression showed panic. "I'm just kidding honey."

Jack exhaled with relief, and said, "That's good since with a little luck we may be hosting us a fish fry tonight."

"You guys have the trot lines out?" I said.

"Yeah, they're strung at Potter's pond."

Between moving files, boxing some of them and unsticking stubborn file cabinet drawers the men sat drinking coffee and telling war stories—literally. They each shared the distinction of having served honorably in Viet Nam and routinely told or retold stories from their respective experiences there. I had endured these accounts for years and Lupe was out of earshot in the conference room and would not have comprehended much if she could hear them. Dot, on the other hand, was privileged not to have been exposed to these tales and the vulgarities that seemed a requisite in relating them. I was worried about that but kept my focus on the tasks at hand.

"This one here is almost completed," I said displaying a divorce file to Dot. "I say let's send it over to Chuck Blackmun to finish up."

"Why Chuck, he's terrible isn't he?"

"He's a decent man, but couldn't pour pee pee out of a boot with the instructions written on the heel. Considering there is only one hearing yet to be done and only ninety-five bucks in the trust account, Chuck is perfect for it. He could use the money and it is so close to the finish line that even he can't screw it up."

Dot laughed, noted the transfer choice on the file, and then showed me another file label. "What about this one?"

"We should offer that one and the Hunt file to Johnny Jay, but make sure that—" I said until rudely interrupted by an outburst of laughter from our two uninvited visitors. "Jackson Chase!"

"Ma'am?"

"We're trying to work back here, plus Clarence is supposed to be here any minute."

"We ain't worried about that tub of lard, besides he's busy," my husband replied. "I seen Clarence leave Mr. Peckham's office a while ago and I asked Carl about it. He said that they had discussed finances and that Clarence was heading downtown to meet with a travel agent."

"A travel agent? In Mexia?" I asked.

"It's that lady that runs that fancy dress shop," Jack said.

"Martina?"

"Yes, and she does the travel stuff on the side right there out of her store. She has connections and supposedly gets good discounts on trips. Carl explained that Clarence is going morn his mom's passing by going on one of them Caribbean cruises."

"That's none of your affair Jack," I said, and returned my attention to the files. "As I was saying, let's send these two to Mr. Jay, but we have to make sure he can get to work on the Hunt file right away. I am putting a note on here that he needs to hire a shrink to analyze Ms. Hunt. She is as nutty as a fruit cake and the client is fighting for custody."

"Got it," Dot said.

While reading through the next case, we heard the boys discussing Clarence's vacation plans.

"I just can't picture ol' Clarence on a cruise ship," Jack said.

"Me neither, have you ever been on one?" Highsmith asked.

"Bill, the only cruise I went on was when your fellow swabbies sailed us gyrenes over to Nam."

"Well, someone had to do it," Highsmith said.

"Ah, yes—the U.S. Navy—the water taxis for the Marines."

"Yep, and that's why I picked them," Highsmith said. "My recruiter told me that Marines go up the hill, the Army goes near the hill, the Air Force flies over the hill and the Navy don't go nowhere near the hill."

"He was damn sure right about that, but I wasn't given a range of options."

"You went to the wrong recruiter?" Bill said.

"If you'll recall, my entry into the beloved Corps was ... let's say ... a little less than voluntary."

"That's right," Bill said, "I forgot you won Uncle Sam's grand lottery."

"Yes sir, a winning ticket straight to the hill and by the way sailing on a World War II-era destroyer was no pleasure cruise."

"You're telling Noah about the flood," Bill said, "but I'm sure with this windfall Clarence will have a vessel with a little more luxurious accommodations."

"Do you reckon the cruise line will charge that fat bastard the same as any other customer—I mean don't they offer all you can eat?"

"Yes, me and the missus went on one a while back, and they damn sure do," Highsmith said.

"Did the cruise line charge more for you than they did Shirley?"

"What's that supposed to mean?"

"I don't mean anything by it, but it's just a matter of risk assessment," Jack said. "It's like the restaurants know old folks and kids eat less so they get a break on price while guys like us pay full boat. Then there's the airlines, I hear some charge you twice if your gut spills over too much into the seat next to you. Since the cruise line offers all you can eat, I just thought weight might be a factor in the pricing."

"Since I didn't pay for the cruise, I can't say for sure, but I don't recall a weigh-in or providing my girth on any of the forms we filled out, but I did eat until I was about to pop."

"The ship puts out a spread, huh?"

"Yes, and nonstop too. Do you know that Ranchero Vista steak buffet over in Fairfield?"

"Know it? Hell, I've almost been banned from the place," Jack said.

All a cruise ship amounts to is one big—floating—Ranchero Vista buffet and they'll damn sure regret letting Clarence's ass on board."

"Guys! He could be here any minute," I warned.

"Yes dear," Jack said. "Say Bill, I once saw an ad for one of them a cruise lines in the Sunday paper. It was in the Parade magazine, I think—anyway there were fellas pictured on deck wearing swimsuits that looked … well … like panties."

"I know exactly what you're talking about Jack, and they call them speedoos, or something like that."

"Can you imagine Clarence sunbathing in one of them Speedoos all splayed out for the world to see?" Jack said.

"I refuse to go there, Jack. It ain't healthy for the brain to conjure such images."

"By golly, I think you're right," Jack agreed. "So Bill, how did you come to get a free cruise in the first place?"

"Back when I was working at the cotton mill we had a production contest and the winner got to go on one of those ships leaving out of Galveston. I messed around and placed first and me and the missus drove ourselves down to the port. After I had looked at the ship I thought the second place winner might have gotten two cruises."

"What was wrong with it?"

"It was a real old ship, kinda raggedy on the outside—not a lot different than the destroyer I served on except for the color, of course. It was an old ocean liner that they had converted into a cruise ship, but on board, it was pretty nice."

"What'd y'all do when you got on?"

"The first challenge was finding our room and that alone was its own journey. There wasn't a soul we encountered that spoke English well enough to direct us, but we eventually managed to find it. We unpacked our carry-ons, endured a muster drill and when we got back to the room our luggage had arrived. We slipped on our swimsuits and went topside to attend what they call the *departure party*. It was held on the pool deck and when we found our way up there it was crowded as hell and very loud. This Hindu lookin' dude in a Hawaiian shirt, Bermuda shorts with a lei around his neck approached us. He was holding a tray of tall tropical drinks with slices of fruit on a plastic sword. He asked if we wanted one and me and the bride weren't about to turn that down, so she picked a red one and I chose a blue."

"Sounds nice," Jack said.

"It was real nice—until I got a bill for it."

"They weren't free?"

"Hell no—they were over six bucks a pop plus a mandatory fifteen percent gratuity."

"No joke?"

"It was a joke all right, and it was all on me, but I didn't make that mistake again."

"So the drinks ain't free?" Jack asked.

"Things like coffee, iced tea and punch were, but cokes and anything with alcohol you pay through the nose for."

"Did any of the men on your ship wear those speedoos?"

"Yeah, but very few thankfully, and those that did had European accents—mostly French."

"They came all the way across the ocean to take a cruise out of Galveston?"

"I guess so," Highsmith said, "and they sure stood out amongst the local demographic."

"I figure to wear one of those skimpy speedoos you have to be packin', if you know what I mean?"

Dot giggled, and I intervened, "I know what you mean Jackson Chase and you stop it!"

"Sorry, hon."

"It ain't true, Jack," Highsmith confided in a muffled tone, but not so low that Dot and I could not hear. "A couple of them seemed about standard, but nothing to brag about."

"Kinda like that statue of David?" Jack asked.

"Yeah, how'd you know about that?"

"I saw a PBS show on the old-timey artists and they included that statue."

"I saw that too and one of those Europeans would've actually envied David."

"Not packin'?" Jack asked.

"No—not packin' at all, and when he passed by me in his speedoo exiting the buffet I thought he had smuggled a mushroom from off the salad bar," Highsmith said.

"That's enough of that," I said, trying to conceal my own amusement.

"Sorry dear," Jack said. "Come to think of it, wasn't that statue of David chiseled by a Frenchman?"

"Naw Jack, if I recall correctly David was done by that Michael Angeles fella. He's the same one that did the sixteenth chapel and I'm pretty sure he was I-talian."

"By Golly, I think you're right," Jack said. "Tell me about the grub."

"I ain't lying when I say they lay it out nonstop. They put out a full breakfast spread starting at the crack of dawn. For lunch, they set out another buffet, plus you can also go to a sit-down lunch in the main dining room. In the afternoon they fire up bar-be-que grills and ovens out by the pool and hand out free hamburgers and fries, hot dogs, link sausage and pizza. For the evening meal, just like lunch, you can do the buffet or go to the dining room."

"Which did y'all do?"

"As you know I'm partial to the *all you can eat* format, so the first couple of nights we did the buffet. On the third night, we tried the dining room. When we passed some of the tables the first thing I noticed was that the portions were kind of scrawny—you know like they do in fancy restaurants?"

"I've seen that on the cookin' channel. They make it look real pretty, but it ain't enough to fill-up a half-grown man," Jack said.

"Right, but the food was better in the dining room so I was torn between quality and quantity, at least until I learned a very important fact. You see, I overheard a man at the next table tell his waiter that he was trying to decide between the Peking duck and the rack of lamb. The Indian waiter said he could have both and that was a useful piece of information and I sure took advantage of it."

"So you turned the good food into all you can eat?"

"I damn sure did," Highsmith boasted. "Though it embarrassed the old lady, I got seconds on the entrees and desserts and didn't have to get off my ass to get it either. The only energy I expended in the dining room was loosenin' my belt at the end of the meal."

"I always heard no one goes hungry on a cruise ship."

"It's the truth Jack, and one night they even had a midnight buffet."

"Did you go to that?"

"Uh huh. You know I don't like to stay up that late plus I was full as a tick from supper."

"But don't you have to tip the waiters if you eat in the dining room?"

"You gotta do that whether you eat in there or not. They got it rigged where you have to tip the waiters and your house boy no matter what and that's why I put them through the paces in the dining room."

"What do you mean by *houseboy?*"

"Every room has one assigned to it and they make the beds, clean up the cabins and bring you ice and stuff like that, but they don't barge in on you. Somehow they mysteriously know when you're gone, and when you do leave your room weird things happen, and I'll give you an example. One afternoon, me and the old lady went up to the pool deck for pizza and when we got back to the room, everything was changed. The first thing I noticed was that some of our clothes were gone, but when we investigated we found it all either folded neatly in the drawers or hung up in the closet."

"That is weird," Jack said.

"Yeah, and one night we got back from watching the magic show and the dude had come in and twisted the bath towels into animal shapes. They were realistic too and Shirley's was a chimpanzee, and fittingly mine was an elephant."

"So he never walked in on y'all in the room?"

"No, not once," Bill said. "I'm tellin' you they got a way of knowing when the passengers leave."

"You reckon they have cameras in the rooms and that's how they knew y'all left for the show?"

"I'd hate to think they did, but if so, me and the bride gave them a show or two of our own—if you know what I mean."

"Quit bragging!" I said.

"But there is a downside to all of the eating," Highsmith said, ruefully. "It's the old what goes in—must come out thing, and the head in the stateroom was a real problem. You see, the whole restroom ain't much bigger than a phone booth and first time I entered and saw the commode I thought it was the kiddie model. I looked around for an adult toilet—but that was it."

"Tiny, huh?"

"Yes, and I couldn't sit straight on it like normal as my knees hit the bulkhead. I had to squat cockeyed on it in order to … you know … take care of business. On top of that they have a strong vacuum flush system and one day Shirley messed around and elbowed the button while seated and it dang near gave her a hysterectomy," Bill said and Dot and I covered our mouths to muffle our chortling.

"Sounds dangerous," Jack said, "but what's there to do when you ain't eaten'?"

"Oh hell, there's lots of stuff. Some people swim and sunbathe on the pool deck, but except for getting the free burgers and pizza I tried to stay out of that area."

"How come?"

"First of all, it was a reminder of the tropical drinks rip off, but I likewise didn't want to catch a dose of the skin cancer. There ain't a lot of shade on that deck and they wanted a fortune for sunscreen at the gift shop. Then there were these Jamaican dudes with these long braids in their hair. I think they call them Ralph Starfarians and they are out there constantly playing loud assed calypso music."

"You didn't like it?" Jack asked.

"It was fine … I guess, but I learned the first day that if you expose yourself to it long enough you spend the night lying in bed hearing steel drums banging in your head."

"What else is there to do?"

"You can see movies in the theater during the day and in the evenings they have the live entertainment there, like that magic show. Then there's also a full casino, stores for the ladies to shop in, and a library and a spa. Speaking of that last one, do you want to hear somethin' funny?" Bill asked lowering his voice, and Dot and I listened closer.

"Sure."

"As a part of the package I got from the cotton mill me and Shirley each got a free spa treatment."

"Spa treatment?" Jack asked dubiously.

"Yeah, and Shirley picked what they call a seaweed wrap and I took—"

"A what?"

"A seaweed wrap," Bill repeated.

"What the hell is that?" Jack said.

"I ain't exactly sure, but I think they lay you out on a table and wrap your body in seaweed. I believe it's supposed to open your pores or something—hell I don't know," Bill said.

"Did you let them do that to you?"

"Hell no," Bill said emphatically

"Guys," I said, "both of you need to cut out the language."

"Tone it down Bill, I know when Gertie's gettin' miffed," Jack warned, then asked, "So what did you pick?"

"Since I didn't want that wrap thing and doubted they that had enough seaweed for the both of us anyway, I chose me a Swedish massage."

"Sweetish?"

"No Swedish, as in Sweden," Bill said.

"You really got one, huh?"

"Yep, it was either that, a facial, or the seaweed, so I didn't have a lot of choices."

"None of the above is a choice."

"Believe me, Jack, I considered that, but I hate to pass up on anything free," Bill said. "Besides, have you ever had a massage?"

"No—at least not since Vietnam, but I doubt that's the kind you're talking about—if you know what I mean."

"I do, and it wasn't like that, but what do you expect for free?" Highsmith said. "You see, these massages are a little more ... let's say ... on the up and up and they work on just about every area, *except* where they do in Saigon."

"Last warning guys," I scolded. "Dot and I don't care to hear about your lewd escapades through Southeast Asia."

"Yes ma'am," Jack responded, then asked Bill, "So what was it like?"

"First off, I got lost trying to find the place and nearly missed my appointment. When I did locate the so-called *Neptune Spa*, I showed them my voucher and they asked me to take a seat in this room full of leather lounge chairs. When I did, I noticed the joint kinda stunk—like Bengay or something. I ignored the smell and filled out some paperwork and just waited. Before long they took me to a locker room where you take your clothes off and put on a bathrobe. Though they gave me the largest robe they had in stock it weren't quite big enough, so I had to clinch it tight in the front of me as I walked back into the waiting room."

"Embarrassed?" Jack asked.

"Unlike those Europeans, I ain't got nothing to be ashamed of. I did feel out of place there, but the other customers seemed like they was just sitting at home, or in the waiting room of a doctor's office. Some walked around sipping ice water from this large glass jar with slices of lemon floatin' in it. Others thumbed through magazines while I just sat clinching my robe and waiting."

"How do they do a massage with a bathrobe on?"

"Aw dummy, you don't keep the robe on during the deal. You go into this tiny room with a weird bed in it. You take off the robe, lie down on a table and they put a towel on your nether regions."

"Sounds a little like Saigon," Jack said. "Did you have a man or woman masseuse?"

"They sent a dude in there at first, but I put a stop to that right away. I sent his ass out and said that wasn't happening—even for free."

"So they got you a woman?"

"They damn sure did and she wasn't from around here, I can tell you that. She was a Scandinavian looking gal and had a strong accent. I could hardly understand what she was saying, but didn't really care to, if you get my drift," Bill said with a lecherous chuckle.

"So what happened?"

"Well sir, she went to work on me and began rubbing, poking, and prodding first one spot then another. Though she had the hand strength of a blacksmith and could mash real hard it felt pretty relaxing. Then about halfway through she had me roll over on my stomach. She put the towel on my backside and placed my head in this oval cushion with a hole in it."

"What for?" Jack asked.

"Beats me, but I guess your head has to go somewhere," Bill said. "She first worked on my neck and shoulders, then she started in on my back. When she got about half way down she mashed real hard with both hands putting a lot of pressure on my stomach. Well ... I guess I ought not to have made the extra trip through the Mexican lunch buffet."

"Why is that?"

"I ripped one," Highsmith confessed.

Dot spontaneously erupted with laughter, and Jack said, "Did you really?"

"Yes, I'm sad to say."

"What did the massage lady do?"

"I don't know considering I couldn't bring myself to look at her. I just got up and ran out of there as fast as I could."

"Why? I'm sure that's not the first time someone has broken wind in front of her."

"I'm sure you're right considering she had on a wedding ring, but I didn't think about that. All I wanted was out of there fast so I bolted out the door and into that room with the leather chairs. It was then that I realized that I had left without my robe and was standing there naked as a jaybird in front of that whole damn waitin' room."

"How'd the other customers react?" Jack asked.

"Let's just say that they were no longer lounging nonchalantly, and knew I weren't one of those Frenchmen"

"Quit bragging," I said.

"What did you do then?"

"I cupped my hands over myself, backed pedaled to the massage room door and knocked. That Swedish gal opened the door and held out my robe with one hand and the poor thing was pinching her nose with the other. I snatched the robe, put it on and I ran back to the locker room. Once there, I grabbed my clothes, dressed and got the hell out of there and never looked back."

"What're y'all doing here?" An obnoxious voice resonated from the front and I knew Clarence had arrived.

"Well hello to you too," Jack said, and I jumped to my feet and scampered toward the reception area.

"I mean it—what are you doing in *my* building?"

Jack sighed, and said, "Me and Bill are helping the ladies, and we was just having a cup of coffee between tasks."

"This isn't a coffee shop," Clarence said.

"Are you telling us to leave?" Highsmith asked.

"We are getting a lot done here Clarence," I intervened, "but from time to time we need a hand from the fellas."

"Fine, I just don't want them getting in the way or drinking up *my* coffee," Clarence demanded. He was wearing a pair unhemmed cut-off blue jeans, an L.A. Lakers basketball jersey—two sizes too small and flip-flops adorned his bare feet. Atop his head sat a backward facing red cap with a bright green marijuana leaf on it. It was a warm and humid September morning and Clarence stood sweating and breathing heavily, with a white paper bag in his right hand.

Jack downed the last sip from his coffee cup, pulled a crinkled one Dollar bill from the hip pocket of his jeans and sat it on the butler's table in front of him. "Here, six bits ought to cover two cups, and you can keep the change."

Clarence responded by storming off down the hall and into our office and I followed.

"Hi, Clarence," Dot greeted, in as friendly a tone as she could muster.

"Why are all these files stacked up in here?" he asked.

"They are the ones that we have updated and reviewed and each stack represents a particular firm that we hope will agree to take them," I explained. "Though we have made some progress this is just one half of one cabinet."

"Look at all the others we have left," Dot added, pointing the metal cabinets. "We started with the A's and even with all of this progress we are only on the C's."

Clarence said, "Seems like y'all need to speed things up."

"We are doing the best we can as fast as we can," I said.

"Where's that Mexican girl? If I'm paying her I expect her to be working."

"Her name is Lupe and she's Guatemalan," I advised. "At the moment she is in the library catching up the filing."

"Good—did any checks come in?" he asked as he pulled a large éclair from the white bag and bit into it. Crumbs and flakes from the dark icing dislodged with some nestling in his beard while others landed on the front of his shirt or fluttered down to the floor.

"There were none yesterday and today's mail hasn't gotten here," Dot said.

"Keep up the work—the clock is ticking," he said then waddled back down the hall toward the reception area and I tailed him in order to maintain the peace.

"Say, Clarence, what's the line on tomorrow's Cowboys' game?" Jack asked.

"They are getting four and a half and the over and under is—" Clarence blurted, until he realized by my husband's expression that he had posed the question only to prove Clarence was still bookmaking.

"Speaking of betting lines what're the odds on you getting a job anytime soon?" Highsmith said.

"I don't see y'all working," Clarence sneered.

"I put in thirty-four years at the cotton mill and Jack here was exposed to Agent Orange fightin' for your freedom. He's certified disabled from it and even with all that he still works more than you— so what's your excuse?"

"I don't owe you an excuse," Clarence said, "but I'll have you know that I am starting my own business and this place will soon be a vape shop."

"Glad to hear it," Bill said.

"Really? You mean it?" Clarence said, hopefully.

"Sure, a town can always use another bait shop."

Clarence barked, "I said *vape* shop, you idiot."

"What's a vape shop?" Jack said.

Clarence pulled his e-cigarette from his hip pocket, displayed it to the men, and said, "It's where you get these."

"What is it?" Highsmith asked.

Mistakenly sensing that the fellas were truly interested, Clarence commenced a tutorial. "Vape is short for vapor and you put e-fluids in these electronic cigarettes. It is battery operated and when activated it makes vapor that you can actually inhale."

"What for?" Highsmith said.

"To get the taste and nicotine like a cigarette."

"Sounds like a lot of trouble to me, why not just smoke a cigarette?" Jack asked.

"You two old fools will never understand this, but I'm a millennial, and we do things different than y'all did back in the Stone Age," Clarence said, then turned and stormed out through the front door.

Once Clarence was out of earshot, I said, "Guys, I have enough of a challenge dealing with him without you two jerking his chain."

"Sorry hon," Jack said contritely, "but with y'all already on your way out what can he do to you now?"

"First and foremost, I want to make sure we get paid for the next two weeks. I believe Mr. Peckham has our back on that, but I don't want to take any chances. Secondly, it's impossible for us to wrap up all of this in the time allotted. At some point I am going to need to approach him for an extension and don't want him ticked off when I do."

"We'll behave," Jack said. "Do you need anything else from us?"

"I don't think so, but thanks for what you two did do."

"All right then, Bill and me are going to head down to the pond and I'll let you know how it goes."

"Are you able to run the lines?" I asked. "You've been moving a little gingerly this morning and I don't want you falling out of the boat."

"I'm all okay," Jack said. "I took a pill when we got here and it's kickin' in."

The guys left for Potter's pond and I got back to the files. Except for a quick lunch of my homemade seafood gumbo, we all worked diligently, file by file, well into the afternoon.

"I've never heard of this one," Dot said.

"Which one?"

"This one," she said displaying a thin file folder to me. "The tab reads in Louise's handwriting *Nelda Fay Blatchford-PI case.*"

"A personal injury case for Nelda?"

"It seems so—do you know her?" Dot asked, handing me the file.

"Sure, and so do you," I said. "I knew her mother, Miss Wanda, and have known Nelda Fay my whole adult life."

"How do I know her?"

"You two met several years ago at that decoupage class at the Teague civic center."

"Oh yeah, I recall her now that you mention it," Dot said. "She's a real nice pretty black woman with the wonderful skin and brunette hair."

"I would still kill to have her flawless complexion, but as for the hair, there's not a lot of brunette left."

"I empathize," Dot said.

"Me too, but since we've been through the B's, how did we miss it?" I asked.

"It wasn't in the B's, I found it in the C's."

I opened the file and leafed through the first few pages. "I bet Louise stuck it in there because the case involves Nelda's husband, Clifford."

"You're probably right, she had a habit of filing by first names."

"Is it a live case?" I asked.

"Beats me, but I'll check," Dot said, and perused the firm's case list. Once done she looked up at me curiously, and said, "I don't see it in the active B's or C's, nor is it on the list of closed files. Did her husband have an accident like car wreck or something?"

"No, not that I recall, but Clifford is deceased, he died of cancer a couple of years ago."

"Oh no, that's terrible."

"It was tragic and Nelda was really tore up about it."

"Hmm, I wonder why Louise would sign it up and never have us work on it."

"It doesn't seem like the type of case we would handle in-house so perhaps she referred it out," I said, and not wanting to slow our progress, I placed the file in my handy souvenir PBS tote bag and we continued with our work.

3
CHAPTER

As luck would have it the boys found heavy lines at Potter's Pond. With that haul, coupled with the fish stored in our freezer we had plenty to share. Jack and I asked several friends over to our house that evening and the invitees included the Highsmith's, the ladies from the office, a few folks from our church and several vets from the VFW post. A dry front had blown through Central Texas that afternoon sweeping away the sultry dead air of the morning. In its place arrived cooler temperatures and lower humidity resulting in ideal outdoor conditions.

Fish fries were events where Jack assumed the entire cooking duties and his large kettle was fired up and ready to go. Since he could not stand for long stretches without paying a heavy price, he positioned a high bar stool next to the kettle. From there he delivered one load after another of the cornmeal coated filets plunging into the bubbling hot peanut oil. Also within arm's length of his stool was a tapped keg of draft beer and a table with condiments and stacks of plastic cups.

Dot and Lupe drove over together and were the first to arrive. Next came the Highsmith's and once in our backyard Bill made a beeline to the keg. He grabbed a cup, placed it under the tap at an angle, and pulled the handle until it overflowed.

"My cup runneth over," he said cheerfully and sloshed some of the sudsy head from the cup and down to the grass below. He then topped it off, raised the cup high into the air and, toasted, "Here's to you Jackson Chase for buying my favorite beer."

Shirley glanced at the unlabeled keg, and said, "How do you know Bill, it don't even have a brand on it?"

"Because my favorite beers are *free* and *free lite* and this must be one of the two," he said and took his first gulp.

Other guests trickled in and each enjoyed the music, the libations and most of all the food. Later in the evening and after having had one or two or twelve more beers, Bill decided to regale those remaining by performing his droll, Henny Youngman like routine. Adopting our raised deck as his stage he lead off saying, "I've been married thirty-nine years, and it's been the best seven years of my life. Shirley once told me *you're gonna drive me to my grave* and I said, I'll start the car." Shirley frowned, but Bill took another swig and was only warming up. "I just returned from a pleasure trip—I took my mother-in-law to the airport. I take my wife everywhere—but she always finds her way back home. Speaking of trips, Shirley asked me to take her somewhere she'd never been before, so I led her into our kitchen. Jack Chase, asked me the other day, *Bill, when did you start wearing women's bras*, and I said ever since Shirley found one in my glove compartment." That was the way it went until he ran out of beer and material. Bill then teetered down the steps of his makeshift stage, and Shirley intercepted him between the deck and the keg and ushered him to their car.

I was never much of a drinker, and as the quintessential lightweight when I did partake I had to monitor my consumption carefully. One sure sign I was close to the edge was when I commenced speaking less English and more Spanish. As a result, when Jack asked from his stool if I wanted another beer and my response was *si—una mas por favor* I thought it was time to taper off. As the evening turned into night, Dot, Lupe, and several others had departed. That was fortuitous since some of the remaining guests were getting playfully rowdy and mildly vulgar—a condition not likely to improve.

Having had my fill of fried food, beer, and crass entertainment, I found myself thinking about Nelda Fay's case. I retreated to the house, pulled the file from my tote bag and began perusing it. I first read Louise's handwritten notes which included Nelda's full name, address and Social Security number. Next to that, she scrawled *cancer* and below that, Louise added the words *smoker* and *black* and underlined each multiple times. I then turned to a section marked *medicals* and found among the handful of pages a report reading:

Pathology Consult

Patient: Clifford Blatchford

On January 11, this 68-year-old man underwent a right side lung biopsy for suspicion of a malignant neoplasm. I reviewed the frozen sections of the tissue preserved from this procedure. Microscopic examination of the slides reveals that the tumor is consistent with an epithelioid malignant mesothelioma. This diagnosis is made based on my pathological analysis and this unfortunate patient's reported history of occupational exposure asbestos fiber.

/s/ Scott Strong, MD

I had heard the term *mesothelioma* countless times in those lawyer commercials on television, but knew little about it. I likewise knew nothing about the status of the case and decided to phone Nelda. I explained that I had a matter to discuss with her and she agreed to meet me at the office the following day—after church of course.

I arrived before Nelda that Sunday afternoon and started a pot of coffee. Once brewed I poured myself a cup and returned to the front of the building. Considering Louise's computer was the only one with unrestricted internet access I took a seat at her desk and powered up her desktop. As it booted I found myself ill at ease with sitting in the chair Louise died on. I rose, pushed her chair to the corner, walked to my desk and rolled my chair into its place.

I took a seat and once online I keyed *mesothelioma* into the search engine and was taken aback by all of the law firm websites that popped up. I perused several and each described awful things about asbestos and this terrible form of cancer. It was then that I remembered a friend at church whose daughter worked for a big law firm in Dallas. I seemed to recall her firm doing this type of litigation and was searching for her contact information when I heard knocking at the front door.

I walked into the reception area, unlocked the door and in walked Nelda Fay. We hugged in the entry and when we ended our embrace I took a step back. I stood staring at her and marveled at just how much she resembled her mom—Miss Wanda.

"You look wonderful," I said.

She smiled and eyed me up and down. "So do you and just how do you stay so thin?"

"Thin? You just might be overdue for an eye exam," I joked.

"Oh, please," Nelda scoffed, "you truly look healthy and fit and that makes me very happy."

She declined my offer of coffee so I lead her into Louise's office and she took a seat across the desk from me. I noticed a tense expression on her face, and said, "Are you okay?"

"It's just a little nerve-wracking coming to a lawyer's office, that's all."

"Nelda, it's not the IRS or the dentist—it's just me," I said. She nodded, but still seemed edgy so I eschewed the business for the moment and opted for small talk. "How are you and the boys?"

"We're all fine—I got another grandbaby on the way."

"That's great," I said enthusiastically, "that's the second, right?"

"The third, don't forget the first were twins."

"Of course, how could that slip my mind?"

"Because it has been way too long since you and I have caught up with each other, that's how."

"You're right about that," I said.

"How are Jack and Levi?"

"Jack is his same old ornery self, but hanging in there and our boy is a foreman on a drilling crew in Tulsa."

"That's good to hear, it sounds like Levi is doing pretty well for himself."

"He is and we are really proud of him."

"Still not married?" Nelda asked.

"Still not re-married, don't forget little Miss you know who."

"How could I forget that—now we're even," she said with a chuckle. "How's Jack's muscular problems?"

"Not so good, I'm sad to say. He doesn't complain, but I watch him closely and know he hurts. He gets tired quicker, but he's on a new medicine that seems to be helping."

"I'm glad to hear that last part, but am sorry about the rest," Nelda said. "So why did you want to meet with me?"

"While going through the case files we found this one," I said, passing the thin folder across the desk to her with the fee agreement on top.

She looked at the contract, handed the file back to me and said, "I haven't thought about this in quite a while. After Cliff passed on I started noticing those asbestos lawyer ads on the TV, you know the ones I'm talking about."

"Oh yes, you can't get through a commercial break without one of those ads, or a one for the male dysfunction pills."

"That's right, but they got me thinking about poor Cliff and his work down at the foundry. You know I am not the suing type, but the commercials said that you could get compensation without going to court. Since money was tight then and it still is for that matter, I thought it was worth a try. I called up here one Saturday morning expecting to leave a message, but to my surprise, Ms. Barbour answered the phone and we talked for quite a while."

"I'm curious, why did you call here instead of one of those law firms from the commercials?"

"The main reason was all that fine print at the bottom of the screen. Plus, some of the lawyers were from as far away as New York and I did not want to get tangled up with some long distance law firm. Heck, I saw one ad for a firm in Houston and wouldn't call them either. If I was going to pursue this, I wanted to keep it local."

"Did you know Louise?"

"I knew of her, God rest her soul."

"So you know about her passing?"

"Yeah, I read about it … what a pity," Nelda said, shaking her head, "but since I knew you worked here I chose to call her. When I did I explained everything I knew about what Cliff had gone through and she wanted me in right away and I agreed."

"Louise had you come in on a Saturday?"

"She sure did and seemed very enthused and said I just might have a good case. So I located the records I could find, drove straight here and we met."

"How did it go?"

"When Ms. Barbour opened the front door she looked at me real funny. It was as if she was not expecting me—causing me to wonder if I had misunderstood her. I introduced myself, handed her my materials, and she led me in here and we talked."

"What did she say about the case after that?"

Nelda darted her eyes away from me for a moment, then said, "Let's just say she did not seem as excited as she did on the phone. Nevertheless, I signed those papers you just showed me and have not heard a thing since."

I found this perplexing until a thought struck me. Louise harbored a lifelong bias against certain ethnicities, a mindset that was only hardened during her years at the DA's office. She would occasionally accept an hourly billing case for a person of color, but only if they could fund the retainer—in full—up front. She would rarely accept a minorities' case on a contingency fee basis and never took one pro bono.

"I too think you have a good case—perhaps a *real* good one," I explained. "I likewise know that in Texas you have limited time frame to bring injury suits. Based on the date of that medical report in the file, that deadline is nearing fast, do you know if Louise filed suit?"

"She wasn't supposed to."

I stared at her curiously. "I don't understand."

"I made it clear from the get-go that I wanted no part of a lawsuit, much less a trial. Ms. Barbour explained that the case would not have to go to court and that she was going to hand it off to someone that could get it settled for me—just like the commercials said."

"Who was she going to send it to?"

"I assumed it would be someone around here, but I don't know for sure."

I explained, "Since we can't run with it here I will see if I can find someone to take it and get moving on it right away."

"Why can't y'all handle it?"

"Nelda Fay—the only lawyer in the firm is dead."

"You and ... what's that nice ladies' name that works with you?"

"Dorothy, but we call her Dot."

"Yes, of course," she said, "so you two can do that part, right?"

"No we can't, we are not lawyers," I said.

"You might not have fancy documents like these," Nelda said, pointing to Louise's framed diplomas and certificates adorning the wall, "but everyone around town knows you girls run this office. Besides, you've always been the smartest person I've ever known."

I blushed, and said, "I don't know why you would say such a thing."

"Because it's the truth—that's why. What with you being top of the graduating class, excelling on the debate team, being the high school spelling bee champion. You're still one of the few people I know personally that went to college."

"It was a two-year program at a vocational school," I said.

"That's more than most do from around here, and I know in my heart you could have gone to a big time college and on to law school, if you had the resources."

"Thank you for that, but I didn't and this place is no longer going to operate as a law office?"

"No one's taking Ms. Barbour's place?" she asked, and I shook my head. "Why not?"

"Louise's boy has other plans."

"I am uh ... I'm real sorry Gertie ..." she said empathetically. "You've been here a long time haven't you?"

"Yes, and this has been a quite a blow to all of us. We have been asked to go through all the files and place them with other firms and that is how we happened across your case."

"What are y'all going to do?"

"We are looking for work, but the employment scene is pretty grim. Jack hasn't said anything about it, but I know he's worried. For years we have made ends meet off of what I earn here and then there's the health insurance issue. Jack can go to the VA to see a doctor, but I have to find coverage until Medicare kicks in."

"I sure hope this works out for y'all," Nelda said, "but I really want you all to settle my case."

"I am humbled by your vote of confidence, I truly am, but I have to get this to someone qualified before the time runs out. I will start searching in the morning, but I need your permission to send this out to another firm."

"A firm here in Mexia?" she asked.

"I promise to try, but if there's no one here I am comfortable with I may need to look elsewhere."

"Oh … I don't know," Nelda said, frowning.

"This is what we are doing on all of the firm's cases. Every file has to go to another lawyer, including yours and I doubt any lawyer around here does this kind of work."

"What about Groesbeck?"

I smiled, and said, "I consider that *around here* dear."

"But it's the county seat," she said, as if that upped the likelihood of finding a qualified candidate.

"Sweetie, this isn't a car wreck or trip and fall case," I explained. "I am going to start in Dallas—I may have a connection there."

She shook her head. "I would just as soon let that limitation thing run out as to mess with anything like that."

"Dallas really too far for you?"

"Yes it is. I do not want you to send me to some city slicker lawyer in some big giant office building. That is going to cause me to have to travel there and cost me a fortune to boot."

"Don't worry about the costs," I said. "I checked the contract and it is a standard contingency fee agreement."

"I recall Ms. Barbour using that term, but what does it mean?"

"Essentially it means you don't pay anything up front."

"I can't pay up front and I can't pay on the back end either," she said anxiously.

"What I mean is, whoever handles the case pays all of the expenses upfront and only collects those and the attorney's fees out of the settlement or a trial verdict."

"Gertie—I don't want no trial," Nelda stressed.

"I understand, but I know for a fact that most civil cases settle out of court. You said, yourself that Louise was going to send the case to someone to do just that, and that's all I aim to do too."

"All right—I feel better now," she said. "I trust your judgment, so go ahead and do whatever you think is best. While I do not want a trial I do want something done about Clifford. I know for certain he was eat up with the cancer because of his work at that filthy foundry."

"Based on the records in the file I believe that to be true. So let me make some phone calls and I will see what I can come up with."

Nelda nodded, rose to leave, and said, "I'm having the kids over for fried chicken this afternoon if you and Jack would like to join us. I haven't see Jack in ages and y'all can spend the afternoon with us."

I looked at her slyly, and said, "Will you let me help prepare the chicken if we do?"

She stared back at me suspiciously. "Are you scheming to get the secret to my seasoned breading?"

"That, and your marinade."

"I thought so, and I am willing to divulge both in exchange for your collard greens recipe."

"You know I can't do that."

Nelda wagged her finger at me, and said, "Then you ain't getting' mine sister."

I laughed and said, "Thanks for the invite. I would love to accept, but I have a lot of work to do here this afternoon. Louise's boy, Clarence, is putting heat on us to get these files moved ASAP."

"Clarence … gosh, I haven't thought of him in years. Is he still as worthless as a—"

"Yes," I said.

Nelda grinned and thanked me, and I showed her to the door. Though I worked on several thick files that afternoon my mind kept drifting to Nelda's little thin folder.

Monday morning I arrived at the office ahead of Dot and Lupe and decided to locate my Dallas connection, Iredell Vinson. Since I struck out with locating her firm online my only alternative was to reach out to her mother, Ethel Vinson. Through church, and my long friendship with Ethel, I knew Iredell when she was just a little girl. Back then she was a freckle-faced redhead, a characteristic we shared and though I was much older than her it formed a bond between us. Not wanting to wait until the following Sunday's church services to speak with Ethel I opted to phone her. We chatted for a while, then I explained Nelda's situation and she gladly gave me Iredell's office number.

I dialed her firm and when the receptionist transferred my call, Iredell answered and sounded just as I remembered—bright, cheerful and upbeat. I was gratified that she remembered me and my cooking and the potluck picnics and revivals we once enjoyed together. We spent several minutes catching up with each other and reminiscing before getting down to business.

"I need some advice on something and was hoping you can help."

"Sure thing Miss Gertie, what can I do?"

"Doesn't your firm handle asbestos injury cases?"

"Yes, we do quite a lot of it in fact, why do you ask?"

"I have someone close to me with an asbestos case that needs to be pursued."

"Sorry to hear that, who is the poor soul?"

"It involves a friend of mine here in Mexia and you may know her," I said. "Do you recall Nelda Fay Blatchford?"

"Sounds familiar, but I can't place it—is she the one that's sick?"

"No, it was her husband, Clifford. He was diagnosed with that mesothelioma cancer."

"Oh no—that's a horrible disease and very difficult to treat," Iredell said.

"The doctors sure didn't do much for poor Clifford."

"So he has passed on?"

"Yes, unfortunately, and quite a while back too. We need to get this case moving and I was wondering if your firm would handle it for her. You see, my boss Louise Barbour took the case, but died suddenly last week."

"You are just full of good news—now aren't you?" Iredell said.

"Ain't it the truth," I said, "so do you think you all can help?"

"Miss Gertie, we don't handle the victim side of the lawsuits, we represent the companies that are sued by them."

This was not at all what I wanted to hear. "What do you suggest I do?"

"You'll have to find a plaintiff's asbestos lawyer and believe me there are a lot of them that would be eager to handle it."

"I found a jillion of them online, but most seemed to be out of state. I am at a loss as to which one to contact and Nelda is very particular about this. It has to be someone who will do a good job, one she can trust and they need to be local."

"There are a couple of firms here in Dallas that will do it."

"She is not going to agree to just any Dallas firm. I called yours thinking that I could cajole her into it due to our mutual acquaintance. No, picking a random firm there is likely out of the question."

"You could just find some local firm to file the suit," Iredell said. "These cases are complicated, but they almost always settle. In my seven plus years here I have only seen a couple of them even get close to a trial."

"Only a couple—ever?"

"Ever," Iredell confirmed, "and even then, it was only because the other side was bluffing and asking for way too much money."

"Are these valuable cases?"

"God yes," she said emphatically. "Miss Gertie, they are a gold mine and the partners here complain constantly that they are on the wrong side of the litigation."

"I don't understand."

"The hourly billing side is no match for taking percentages of these asbestos cases, but if we got caught taking one it would cause an uproar with the insurance companies that hire us to defend the cases. If I were you, I would find someone experienced around there that will file the suit and the defendants will eventually want to negotiate."

"It's that easy, huh?"

Iredell laughed. "I may have oversimplified it some, but it's essentially true. The firm you select will need to work it up, and then it's time to settle."

"It sounds pretty straightforward, but I still need to find someone in this area to carry the water on it. Do you have any recommendations?"

"There's a firm in Waco and one in Center that are on the asbestos docket, but they are also on the defense side. They might *want* to take your friend's case, but for the same reason the lawyers here can't take it—they won't either."

"Sorry I'm so thickheaded about this, but I'm confused. They want to do the victim's side because they would make more money, but won't do it because they may not get any more of the cases that pay less?"

"It sounds crazy when you put it that way, but it's true," Iredell said.

"If the suit is filed in or around Limestone County do you think that firm in Waco or the one in Center will defend it?"

"It's possible, but I doubt it. Odds are it will be defended by a firm from here in Dallas or one from Houston."

I thanked Iredell for her help, hung up the phone and the gears in my head were turning.

That night, as was our routine, Jack and I were lying in bed watching a re-run of the Carol Burnett Show. After Carol sang her closing song and tugged her ear I used the remote to switch off the television. Jack turned off his bedside lamp and the room fell dark except for the moonlight creeping through our bedroom window blinds. I closed my eyes, silently said my standard nightly prayers, added a couple of extras and then laid still. I stared upward at the moonbeams dancing on the whirling blades of the ceiling fan above us and decided to broach the topic of Nelda's case.

"Honey?"

"Yes, Gertie," Jack yawned.

"I want to discuss something with you."

"Thought you might," he said rolling over on his side to face me. "You were pretty quiet during supper and didn't laugh at all at the show—even during the *momma's family* part."

"I am burdened," I said, and described the whole dilemma presented by the discovery of Nelda's file and my conversation with Iredell.

"What're you going to do?"

"Hear me out on this Jack, and don't prejudge it. According to Iredell these cases always settle and I am seriously considering handling it for Nelda."

"I think you should," he said.

"Really?"

"Sure, if Louise would have bothered to handle it you and Dot would have done all the legwork on it anyway."

"That's true," I said. "We will just be doing what we would do on any other case."

"So Dot's in on it too?"

"I haven't said anything about it, but I would like her to be involved and Lupe too. According to Iredell if we settle it for Nelda it could bring in a tidy sum, but Jack, you need to know up front that the expenses to work it up will be all ours."

"Ours as in you and me?"

"Yes, and preparing a case like this can be very pricey," I said. "I can't ask the girls to kick in on it—they don't have that kind of money—so we would be the ones taking the risk."

"What kind of expenses are we talking about?" Jack asked.

"There is the expert retainers, court reporters bills, filing fees, and such. I looked through two of Louise's medical malpractice cases, and the expenses on one was eighteen and the other was just under twenty-two."

"Hundred?"

"No ... thousand," I said, and tensed.

"You do realize that if this doesn't pan out it could gobble up a sizable chunk of our savings."

"I know that and that's why I am so burdened."

"I'm all for helping Nelda being that she's a widow and all, but we've got potential money problems of our own coming down the pike."

"That's why I want to lay all the cards on the table and not sugar coat it. If I do this and fail we do lose our money, but if it settles it just might remedy those future money worries."

"So you and the girls will take a percentage?"

"Yes, but it is a big risk though and if you say no I won't blink an eye and will walk away."

"If you don't help what happens to Nelda's case?" Jack said.

"It will likely just fade away."

Jack switched his lamp on. "You've really thought this through, haven't you?"

"Yes I have, so what do you say?"

He propped himself up on his elbow and grasped my left hand, and said, "Gertie, you have worked hard, lived meagerly and done without, and that's the main reason we have that money to even risk. I trust your judgment and believe in you more than I do the damned ol' stock market. If you believe this is a risk worth taking I'm behind you a hundred percent."

"Thanks, Jack," I said wiping tears on the sleeve of my nightgown.

"I do have a question though," he said. "Since you're not a lawyer how can this work?"

"You are sleeping with another woman tonight," I said grinning.

"Who?"

"Louise Barbour."

4
CHAPTER

"We need to have a meeting," I said when the Dot and Lupe arrived the office the following morning. I lead them into Louise's office and took my chair at her desk. I motioned them into the client seats and stared across the desk at a pair of concerned expressions. "Dot, do you remember that Blatchford file that we looked at on Saturday?"

"Sure, the PI case."

"That's right. I met with Nelda and it turns out that Louise signed it up one weekend and never lifted a finger on it. I think it's a good case and it involves Nelda's husband getting cancer from asbestos materials he used at the foundry."

"The Morrison foundry?"

"Yes, don't you know Waite Morrison?"

"Somewhat," Dot said. "He goes to our church some, mostly on the big days like Easter, Christmas Eve, and for dinner on the grounds."

I explained the details of Nelda's meeting with Louise and added, "She had Nelda sign the contingency fee agreement and was supposed to refer it out, but Nelda hasn't heard a peep since."

"Louise didn't refer it, did she?"

I shook my head. "It doesn't look like it and it is three months from the statute of limitations expiring."

"Why would she do that? This case has a lot of potential," Dot said.

"It could be she did not realize the value, or she did and something soured her on the case."

Dot stared quizzically at me, and said, "Like what?"

"Nelda's husband smoked cigarettes in his younger days and in Louise's notes she included the word *smoker* and underlined it twice. She also included the word *black* and it was underlined four times."

"Oh no ... do you really think Nelda's race played a part?"

"Who knows for sure, but we all remember how Louise was," I said. "She must have stuck the file haphazardly in the cabinet and by the time we arrived on Monday the case was a distant memory."

"Did you explain the racial part to Nelda?"

"I didn't have the heart to and when I showed her the file I made sure she did not see the notes," I said, "but I'm not going to let Louise get away with this—my friend's case will be handled."

"Hmm, so who are we going to send it to?" Dot said.

"Listen carefully," I said in a confidential tone, causing Dot and Lupe to lean forward in their seats. "When I met with Nelda she asked that we work up the case and resolve it for her."

"Us as in us?" Dot said, using her index finger to alternate pointing toward her and me.

"Correct, and Lupe you're in too if you want."

"*Gracias*, Miss Gertie," Lupe said eagerly, oblivious to what she was committing to.

"Have you thought about the fact that we aren't lawyers?" Dot said.

"Of course, and I reinforced that very point with Nelda."

"What did she say?"

"The darnedest thing, that's what. She said that we run the show here and she regards us as capable of handling it as Louise."

"That's nice, but how did you leave it with her?"

"I told her we couldn't take it, and that I would find her a lawyer that would."

"Oh, thank goodness," Dot said fanning herself, "I thought for a moment you had gone off the deep end."

"Hold on now. Since then I've done a lot of research and cogitating on this and I think we can do it," I said, but Dot's expression showed skepticism. "Come on Dot, think about what Nelda said. Though you and I aren't technically *lawyers* haven't we been doing the true *lawyering* here for a real long time?"

"Well … I …um …" Dot stammered.

"You know it's true and I can prove it," I said, then challenged, "would Nelda's case get any better quality of preparation if Louise worked it up or us three did it?"

"Us, but that's not much of a standard and all the more reason to get it farmed out to a qualified firm."

"I have tried, but Nelda does not want a big city firm working on it. She would just as soon abandon the case as to do that."

"There are some talented personal injury lawyers in and around Limestone County," Dot said.

"True, but none that handle this type of case."

"You researched that too, huh?" Dot asked, and I nodded. "Fine, we work it up for her and then what?"

"We settle it," I said. "I'm going to tell Nelda exactly what we're doing, and I expect that she will agree and we will file the lawsuit."

"Shouldn't we try to settle before filing suit?"

"We are way too close to the limitations expiring to sit on it, and if the deadline runs the case has zero value. No, I think we have to file it to preserve her rights and deal with it from there."

"And if it doesn't settle?"

"Then we dismiss it, Nelda will have to agree to that up front. That said, I have it on good authority that these asbestos suits almost always settle and when they do they fetch a lot of money."

"Fine, but we are still going to need a lawyer involved on some level—I mean who's going to sign the pleadings, for god's sake?" Dot asked.

"Louise Barbour, that's who," I said and Lupe gasped and started panting. *"Lo Siento Lupe, voy a ser ella—*I will act as if I am her."

Lupe asked, *"Que no hay fantasma?"*

"No fantasma—there are no ghosts," I said, and Lupe calmed.

"How is this supposed to work since she's dead?" Dot said.

"The firm on the other side won't know that."

"How can you be so sure?"

"My source predicts that the case will likely be defended by a firm from Dallas or perhaps Houston."

"Fine, but the people around here will know and so will the court personnel in Groesbeck."

"I realize that, and that's why we won't file it in Limestone County."

"Are you thinking Freestone?"

I shook my head. "That's still too close, and Louise practiced there some too. No, I am thinking Waco."

"McLennan County, huh?"

"I can be talked out of it, but that's where I am leaning. It's close enough to pacify Nelda and big enough and far away enough to avoid detection," I said. "Although, I am a little worried about the *home cookin'* if a Waco firm defends it."

"I heard Louise use that reference, but I never understood what she meant by it."

"It's a term meaning that home teams get favoritism from judges and referees. When Louise had to appear in an unfamiliar court, she often felt the local lawyers got preferential treatment. When that happened, and things did not work out so well, she would say she *got a taste of the home cookin'*."

Dot nodded and said, "This is all very interesting, but if you don't mind me asking who is this source you keep mentioning?"

"I don't mind saying, and just know I was not trying to keep it a secret. It is Ethel Vinson's daughter—Iredell."

"Oh yeah, the cute little red-headed girl."

"That's the one, but she's not a little girl anymore. She's all grown up and working for a big-time law firm in Dallas. They actually handle these type of cases and I wanted them to take it, but unfortunately, they only defend these type of suits."

"She really thinks it will settle?" Dot asked, and I nodded. "I'm sorry to ask so many questions."

"You should ask questions, and you're only doing to me what I have been doing to myself for the last twenty-four hours. That said, I have thought this through carefully and I really think we can do it."

Lupe chimed in, *"Ustedes cuidar de archivos—no me."*

Dot looked to me for translation and I explained, "She says that you and I work on the cases and not her." I turned to Lupe, and added, "Necesitamos tu, también—we need you."

"Gracias, Miss Gertie, I need jou too."

"Thank you dear," I said and turned back to Dot. "We will handle the pleadings and discovery like we always have. After all, Louise just signed them and rarely made a single change."

"That's true, sober or not our work almost always held up."

"All we have to do is our jobs and with any luck, Nelda will get her money and in the process, we will make some too."

"How do we get paid out of this?" Dot asked.

"We are going to take a portion of the fee. The percentage will be less than what Louise would have gotten, but we three will share in the proceeds."

Dot said, "What about the costs?"

"Jack and I will front the case expenses."

"I see … what about Clarence?"

"I thought about him too and we can't just hide this from him."

"Why not?" Dot said. "After all the case isn't even on the firm's active list."

"Clarence has open access here and likes to snoop. It is too risky to get neck deep into this only to have him find out and ruin everything.

"Good point, but why would he ever go along with this?"

"I am working up an incentive plan for him that in exchange for it, we get to handle my friend's case to conclusion. To do that he has to give us access here for an additional sixty days beyond his deadline. As long as we have access to the office we have the computers, the copier-scanner, and we will look like a law firm to whoever defends the case."

"Won't Clarence be concerned we're not lawyers?"

"All he cares about is money, food, video games, and betting odds."

"You want Lupe and me to work that extra two months too?"

"I am hoping y'all will and here's the plan for that. As soon as we go off payroll we will file for unemployment—after all we are being fired *without cause* aren't we?"

"Yes, but won't that hack off Clarence?" Dot asked.

"It's possible, but I doubt it. Think back to that afternoon when Louise pitched a fit and fired us all. We went on unemployment then and though the pay was less than our normal salaries the checks came from the state and not the firm."

"That's because of the unemployment insurance and I recall Louise griping at us because it ran up her premiums," Dot said.

"It did and it was all her fault, but that won't impact Clarence since the firm is essentially dead."

"What if we don't settle the case within the sixty days and get kicked out of here?"

"We will switch to a P.O. Box for the mail and the rest of this can be handled out of my house."

"About the fees, how is that going to work?" Dot asked.

"Nelda's contract provides for a forty percent contingency fee provision, but that's too high. Since this is her money and we are just helping her get it, we will work it up for twenty-five percent of whatever results. Out of that twenty-five percent, I propose to split it fifty-five percent to me, thirty percent to you Dot, and Lupe you get fifteen percent."

"Money come to me?" Lupe asked.

"I sure hope so," I said, then explained my game plan and the percentages to her in Spanish. "*Es bueno*-is that good?"

"Jes Miss Gertie."

"Good. So, when you are not working at my church, *tu nos ayudarás*—you will help us with the case, right?"

"Jes, Miss Gertie."

"How about you Dot, are you in?"

"Sure, it all sounds very fascinating."

"I'm glad to hear it. What about my fee split proposal—do you think that is fair?"

"Absolutely," Dot said. "It's fair to Nelda and fair to us. After all, you're the one putting up the money and all I'm risking is my time in a jobless market."

"That's great guys," I said. "I think this has a chance of working out well for all of us."

"What do you think the case is worth?" Dot said.

"Iredell explained that some of these cases go for a ton of money, but that's for jury verdicts. If we simply settle out of court I am sure it will be a fraction of that."

"Even at a fraction it could be a lot, right?"

"I believe that to be true or I would not be doing this."

With the team now assembled the next nut to crack, no pun intended, would be getting Clarence on board. One thing he understood was money, not earning it, but rather getting it and spending it and it would take a little Texas horse trading to get the deal done.

Late that afternoon Clarence skulked into the office to snoop for checks and to assess our progress. I met him up front and saw that he was working on a foot long Philly cheesesteak sandwich. I took a deep breath, assumed a stance near him, but not close to him, and seized the opportunity to discuss my proposal.

"How are you, Clarence?"

"I'm hungry," he mumbled between chews and I noticed that some of the caramelized onions and au jus from the sandwich had streamed down his chin and coming to rest in his scraggly beard. It was all I could do to ignore it as I laid out my game plan.

"What do you mean by keeping a file for yourself?" he said, gnawing at the crusty end of toasted bun.

"The client is Nelda Fay Blatchford—a longtime friend of mine. Your mom had her sign a fee contract but never did a thing on the case. Her inattention dang nearly let the statute of limitations expire."

"Big deal," he said dismissively.

"It is a big deal, Clarence. If it had expired Nelda would lose her case and she could sue the firm for malpractice. If she won, which by the way would be a slam dunk, she would have been awarded a judgment against the firm."

"How does that affect me?"

"With that judgement, my friend could take all of the funds in the firm's operating account, the proceeds coming in through the mail and the very building we are standing in," I explained and succeeded in wresting his attention away from his sandwich. "My friend just wants her case to get moving before it's too late and if we don't handle it she's going to take it to someone else."

"Can she do that since she signed a contract?"

"Sure, no court would hold her to the fee agreement in the face of this level of neglect."

"What kind of case is it?"

"It involves asbestos," I explained, "her husband got sick from it and died."

"Sounds like a good case—why should I let y'all take it?" he muttered as he returned to the sandwich and bread crumbs fluttered to the floor like little brown snowflakes.

"One reason is Nelda wants me to."

"So?"

"Don't you see Clarence, it's leaving one way or another."

"What's the hourly rate on it?"

"It's not an hourly rate matter—it's on a contingency fee basis," I said, and watched as more juice dribbled from the corner of his mouth. "Can I get you a paper towel or something?"

"What for?"

"Never mind," I said.

"Explain that contingency thing," Clarence asked, as he placed his fist to his sternum and belched out loud.

"It means that the client grants a percentage interest to the one handling the case," I said piquing his interest, but quickly added, "but that same person has to front all of the expenses."

"Like what?"

I gave him a rundown of the likely expenditures and the estimated dollar amounts. "It's easily going to be thousands of dollars and if the case is lost then there is no fee and you do not recover the expenses."

"Screw that, but why not refer it to another firm like the others cases?"

"No one around here handles this type of case."

"Oh, and you do, huh?" he smirked.

"Leave that part to me and besides I've got something to sweeten the deal."

"I'm listening," he said between chews.

"First things first, we simply cannot complete all the remaining work on your mom's files in the time you have allotted. After all of our work so far we are only on the J's. The other girls and I have agreed to work beyond the two weeks, all the way until we are done, and will do it off of your payroll. In exchange, we want full access to the office for an additional sixty days to finish up the files and to work-up my friend's case."

"Two months, huh?"

"That's all, and since it costs you nothing you'll be pocketing the money that comes in."

"All of it?" he said, perking up.

"Just about, I mean, you still need to cover things like the utilities and insurance, but you will be paying those anyway."

"Doing this delays my vape shop plans."

"Not really," I said. "You're not likely to get money for it from the trust funds and can't do anything with the building until the probate court reconciles your mom's estate. That won't happen for quite a while—even with us helping."

"Y'all will help with mom's estate?"

"As a part of the deal, we will prepare all of the paperwork and won't charge you a dime for it."

"Y'all know how to do that?"

"Sure, we've done plenty of them, so what do you say?" He nodded, but wanting more in terms of confirmation, I asked, "Do we have a deal?"

"Yes," he said, and extended his greasy right hand and taking one for the team, I shook it.

"So, we'll have until late-November to vacate the office, right?"

"Fine by me, considering I booked a cruise for then."

I fought any attempt to picture him in a speedo, and said, "That's nice Clarence—I'm happy for you."

He shoved the last bite of the sandwich into his mouth and spied an opened envelope sitting on the butler's table, and asked, "What's in that?"

"It's a nice check, Clarence. It came in yesterday and it's for over a thousand bucks," I said, lifting it from the table and handing it to him.

He removed the contents, gazed at the check, and said gleefully, "This gives me gambling money for my cruise."

"Aren't you glad you don't have to fund my friend's case expenses out of that?"

"Hell yeah, but explain this," he said pointing.

"This is the fee bill the client paid with that check. It's for the Victor Reed divorce and it is for four point two hours of your mom's time and next to each entry is the hourly rate."

"Momma was charging two hundred and fifty dollars per hour?"

"On this case she did."

"Damn," he said and belched again. "That makes me really miss her."

I wanted to throat punch him, but curbed my urges in favor of the deal. He waddled out the front door happy as a clam and I watched out the window as he crossed the street. He was lumbering toward the bank and it dawned on me just how Clarence's gait was similar to that Bigfoot captured ambling through the brush in that Patterson film.

5
CHAPTER

phoned Nelda and gave her an overview of our plan, and she agreed to come in the next morning following her weekly hair appointment. Knowing from experience what we would need to prepare the case I asked her to bring some specific items. Among my requests were for Cliff's driver's license and Social Security card—if she still had them, any additional medical records and bills and some family photos.

When I saw her pull up out front I asked Lupe to get us some coffee. I met Nelda at the door and she entered carrying a brown grocery sack, and I ushered her into Louise's office. Nelda set the sack on the floor and took a seat on one of the client chairs and Lupe placed the two coffee cups and condiments on the desk.

"Thank you," Nelda said.

"No *problema, Señora* Nel—"

"Lupe, English please," I prompted.

"Okay, uh … No problem … Miss Nelda," Lupe said, then scampered back to the kitchen.

"Looks like you brought me some goodies," I said pointing to the paper bag.

"I brought all I could find on short notice," she said, and reached into her purse and handed me Cliff's driver's license and a photocopy of his Social Security card. "In the bag, are two photo albums, one with old pictures and the other has more modern shots. I have others, but they are boxed in the attic and the kids have some too."

"I am sure these will work and thank you for bringing them."

"You're welcome, but I must say it wasn't easy," she said as tears welled in her eyes. "I had not cracked those albums since Cliff ... um ... you know."

"Lots of memories, huh?" I asked, and she nodded and dried her eyes with a tissue. "By the way, your hair looks nice."

"You don't think she cut too much off the sides?" Nelda said while running her fingers around her temples and above her ears.

"No, I actually think it is perfect," I said, and she smiled. "I asked you here to fill you in on where we are on your case. As I mentioned in our call, I have discussed it with the ladies here and we are willing to handle it if you still want us to."

"Of course, I think that's terrific news."

"Good, but you must listen to me *very* carefully," I said in a tone that made her fidget in her chair. "Since we are not lawyers this ain't exactly kosher."

"I realize that, and I already said I trust you with it."

"And I appreciate it, but now that we are actually contemplating doing this we need to hash out a few things. Just because you want us to handle the case does not make it legit. I feel certain that the State Bar would not condone this in any way, shape, form or fashion."

The skin on Nelda's forehead furrowed, and she said, "You know I would never ask you to do something that could land you in trouble."

"I know you wouldn't and I am going into this with eyes wide open. I have done a lot of pondering on how to go about this and to do it I am going to have to pretend to be Louise Barbour."

"Oh ... I see," Nelda said, placing her hand over her mouth.

"Does that bother you?"

"No ... I uh ... I actually find it kind of amusing."

"Let's discuss the fees," I said. "The contract you signed was for the firm to get forty percent of the recovery plus expenses, and that's going to need to change."

"I understand that y'all would need more, considering this is your first time, and all."

"No Nelda, we're cutting it from forty percent down to twenty-five."

Nelda processed the comment then began shaking her head. "Why would y'all do that—after all I made a deal?"

"Your deal was with a lawyer," I said.

"So?"

"Since we can't take the case to trial, all we can do is attempt to settle it. Being in a settlement posture only I am sure means a reduced outcome."

"The plan all along was to settle," Nelda reminded.

"I get that, but with us amateurs handling the case, it seems to me that it cheapens the value. If a licensed lawyer is worth forty percent, then twenty-five for us seems abundantly fair."

"Oh, I don't know ..." she said fretfully.

"That's the deal Nelda. I have discussed it with Dot and Lupe and we insist," I said.

"I don't know what to say," she said

"I would take *we have a deal*."

"We have a deal," Nelda said emphatically. "So where do we go from here?"

"I recommend getting the suit filed ASAP."

She frowned, and said, "Why would you sue when you know I don't want that?"

"We have to stop the limitations clock from ticking, and filing suit is the only way. This plan will only work if we timely file the case and work it up some."

"I understand," she said leaning back in the chair.

"Once we file suit and the foundry's lawyers enter the case, they will undoubtedly send a document request and a set of interrogatories for us to respond to."

"What's the latter?" she asked.

"Written questions that will likely focus on you and Cliff, including your background together, his work history, and illness. Dot is our resident expert on this and she has a form containing most of the commonly asked questions. If we can fill in those answers now, when we do get served with the discovery we can create a draft for you to review, okay?"

"That's fine," Nelda said and returned her fingers to feeling the hairline around her ears.

I called out for Dot, and she entered with a clipboard in hand bearing her comprehensive questionnaire. She took the chair next to Nelda, and said, "Hello Ms. Blatchford, do you remember me?"

"Sure I do Dorothy," Nelda said cheerfully. "We met in at that decoupage class and please call me Nelda."

"Sure thing Nelda and I am Dot."

I added, "We discussed what we have to do here so we might as well dive right in."

Dot shifted in her chair to face Nelda, and said, "We will simply start at the top and work our way down until we're done."

"All right," Nelda said with a tinge of apprehension in her voice.

Dot lifted her pencil and covered the questions one by one eliciting Nelda's comments and making notes. Most wrenching to Nelda were the topics involving Cliff, but she kept on responding and Dot kept up the jotting. This is the way it went for the better part of two hours, and once done I capped it off by asking her about witnesses.

"We are going to need to list some people that can testify about Cliff's work at the foundry."

"Why? Aren't witnesses only for trials?" Nelda asked.

"Yes, but in order for us to position ourselves for a settlement, we have to prepare as if we are ready to try the case. Having witnesses is a big part of that, and whoever defends the foundry will have a right to know who they are. Most important to that equation is designating someone to describe what Cliff did at the foundry and how that work had him breathing the asbestos stuff."

"The doctor already said Cliff's cancer was caused by breathing it."

"We will need that too, but we have to establish that Cliff was exposed to it at the foundry."

"He wouldn't have gotten sick if he wasn't exposed there," Nelda countered, and I could tell she was getting upset.

I smiled sympathetically, and said, "I understand dear, but we will need proof of it."

"Though Cliff rarely discussed his work, after his diagnosis he told me all about using asbestos insulation and how dusty it was."

"I believe you, I truly do," I said, "but they won't just take our word for it, we'll need evidence."

"Can't you list me to testify as to what Cliff and I discussed?"

"We could, but the defense will consider that *hearsay*," Dot intervened and I was impressed.

"I've heard that term on *Matlock*, but what exactly does it mean?" Nelda asked.

Dot pondered then said, "It's ... uh ... like when ... uh—Gertie?"

"It essentially means you are not allowed to testify about what someone else told you. There are some exceptions to it, and I don't know all the ins and outs of those, but that's the gist of it. Bottom line is we need to list people that actually worked with Cliff."

"That may be a problem considering the pipefitters handled separate assignments," Nelda said.

"The pipefitters did not work together?" I asked.

"No, not usually. They were each assigned a couple of laborers to assist and worked on their own projects. The only exception might be on shut-downs, but that's about it."

"What do you mean by shut-downs?" Dot said.

"The foundry had a maintenance schedule and would shut down all or part of the plant to redo pipes, change out equipment, and re-insulate it all."

"Do you know the names of any of Cliff's fellow pipefitters from uh ... let's say ... the nineteen-seventies?" I asked.

"I might could come up with a name or two, but if any are alive they would have to be pretty darn old."

"I'll take any pipefitter still breathing," I said, as Lupe entered with the coffee pot and began topping off our cups.

Nelda cogitated, then said, "One was T. Wilson James."

"I know he's dead," Dot said.

"How do you know that?" Nelda said.

"We handled his probate estate."

"Oh," Nelda uttered, grimly.

"Does someone else spring to mind?" I asked.

"Tommy Johnson, but he moved out of state, Colorado I think, and I haven't heard anything about him in ages."

"Any others?"

"Not that I can think of," she said.

"I see ... hmm ... how about the laborers?" I asked.

"I'm afraid that's going to be tough too."

"How so?" Dot said.

"Part of the problem is that most of them did not speak English, at least very well."

I asked, "No Caucasian laborers?"

"No Gertie, in fact, all of Morrison's non-management level personnel were black or brown."

"Why is that?"

"Word was, it was because minorities were difficult to unionize and would work hard for less pay."

"Was that last part true?" I asked.

"Cliff always felt he was paid fairly, but perhaps that proves the point."

"Do you know the names of any of the laborers?" Dot said.

"Some, but they mostly went by their first names or nicknames."

"Can you tell me any?"

"Oh, Lord ... um ... let me think. There were two brothers, Tito and Chico. Then there was one they called *Beanbag* and I don't know why. There was a nice young man named Jesus with a last name beginning with a 'C'. Then ... uh ... there was *Speedy* and they called another fella *Nacho Man*."

"That one funny," Lupe giggled.

"Anyone else?" Dot asked while scribbling.

"Yes, there was another they called *teapot*."

"How did he get that moniker?" I asked.

"Because he was *short and stout*," Nelda said.

"Of course," I chortled. "Do you know any of their surnames? For example, do you think Speedy's last name was Gonzales?"

"That would make sense, but I really don't know."

"You're right—we are not likely to locate any of those folks with the phone book," I said and turned to Lupe. "We are going to have to poke around and see what we can find, puedes ayudar con eso—you can help with that, right?"

"Si Miss Gertie—I help," Lupe said enthusiastically.

"That's a good start on the fact witnesses, but we're also going to need to list medical experts," I explained. "Ideally, I would like to use one of Cliff's doctors, especially the one that linked his cancer to his work."

"Cliff's doctors were very good and kind to him, so perhaps one of them will help," Nelda said.

"What if that doesn't pan out?" Dot asked.

"I've been pondering plan B. Do you remember the medical suit we handled for Doris Breyer?"

"The hospital case?"

"That's right," I said. "Doris had a hip replacement surgery at Immaculate-Mercy in Warrensville and she dang near died of infection."

Dot said, "I remember that and recall Doris saying that the place was anything but *immaculate* and the patients had to beg for *mercy* to get out alive."

"I've heard awful things about that place," Nelda added. "There's a reason it's only a block away from the funeral home."

"Why did you mention her case?" Dot said.

"Didn't we hire a doctor from some sort of litigation expert service?"

"That's right, he was an infectious disease hired gun out of Houston."

"If we can't get a treater to help we may have to resort to something like that."

"That sounds expensive," Nelda said.

"Working up a case like this can be *very* expensive and some experts charge hundreds of dollars per hour."

"Oh no Gertie, I don't want you doing anything like that," Nelda said.

"Don't fret about it," I said. "I am willing to honor the contract."

Nelda moved to the edge of her chair. "I know what the contract says about fronting expenses, but I'm worried about you and Jack."

"I have discussed this with him and we are willing to do it."

"Fine, but I feel like I should kick in something," Nelda said anxiously. "I still have my beanie baby collection and I could get one of my boys to sell them on eBay. Some are supposed to be very valuable and they still have their tags."

"Thank you for that honey, but that's not necessary. We have some money set aside and will front the expenses and get it back when the case settles."

"What if it doesn't settle?"

"Nelda ... I'm trying real hard not to think about that, but if it doesn't pan out, it's our loss."

"No Gertie, no," Nelda implored. "I don't like any of this including all of these expenses, having to answer all of these personal questions and dredging up all these bad memories. It all makes me very nervous and it just started. I would be content if we just stopped this now before it gets out of hand."

"Trust me on this, it's going to turn out okay. We are going to resolve the case, the foundry will own up to what they did, and in the end, we will all be rewarded for the effort."

Nelda stared hopefully at me. "Do you really think so?"

"Of course I do."

We left it at that, and I walked Nelda to her car. When I returned to the office I collapsed on the couch in the reception area. "That wore me out girls."

"Mi tambien, I wear out too," Lupe said, then her eyes teared up.

"What's wrong?" Dot asked.

"Estoy triste," Lupe sniffled.

"English please," I urged.

She wiped her nose with a tissue, and said, "I sad."

"I am sad," I corrected.

"You too?"

"No Lupe, I was just ... I mean ... Never mind," I stammered. "Por Que estas triste—tell me why you are sad—in English please."

65

"Why I get money for Señora Nelda's case? She need it and I no do nada."

I placed my hand on her shoulder, and said, "Tu ayudas mucho—you help a lot—right Dot?"

"Of course, you're very helpful Lupe."

As tears streamed from her eyes, she asked, "¿qué pasa sí no puedo."

"Sé que puedes—I know you can help," I said.

"Jou think?" she sniffled

"Sure, you will a lot. You are bilingual … kind of … and you know the Spanish community as well as anybody. Tu buscar un testigo—you'll find us a witness, won't you?"

"Jes miss Gertie, I find weetness," she said perking up. "Mi padre es un labor worker you know."

"Padre as in a church pastor or padre as in your dad?" I asked.

"Ambos."

"Both?" I said, and Lupe nodded. "I remember your father being a lay preacher, but he was also a laborer?"

"Jes—for long time."

"I bet he will know other laborers," I said.

"Si, algunos van a su iglesia."

"Some laborers go to your dad's church?" I asked, and she nodded. "See Lupe, I knew you would be a big help," I said and she beamed with pride. "Now you need to get out there and talk to as many of them as you can."

"Jes Miss Gertie," she said eagerly, and the sparkle returned to her beautiful eyes.

I explained in Spanish that the whole case may well depend on her finding someone that worked at the foundry. I made a photocopy copy of Cliff Blatchford's old driver's license, handed it to her, and said, "You take this and show it around, okay?"

"Jes Miss Gertie," she said, but her expression changed when she stared at Cliff's DMV photo.

"What's wrong?" I asked.

She whimpered, "I sorry *Señora* Nelda *esposo* die."

"Me too," I said patting her shoulder. "Now let's all join together and do something about it."

The girls and I went about the task of finishing up the firm's business by day and I used the evenings to prepare the documents necessary to initiate Nelda's lawsuit. I spent considerable time tailoring the pleadings to our facts and named only one defendant—the Waite Morrison Foundry. Once completed, I signed the petition as Louise, calculated the amount of the filing fees and the cost to get the paperwork served on the foundry. Since I dared not send it with a personal check I included the precise amount in a cashier's check and mailed it and the suit papers to the McLennan County District Clerk.

Thirteen days later FedEx delivered a large, stuffed to the gills manila envelope. I unsealed it and the first item I removed was the thirty-two page written appearance from the lawyers representing the foundry. I read it all and at the end, I noticed it was signed by Alexander S. Shiras, from the firm of Bloom, Taylor, Shiras, and Black. I looked them up online to see if they were a big firm and quickly learned that they were a *very* big firm. Their website boasted a roster of three hundred and seventy-seven lawyers occupying multiple offices spread out across the country and abroad. Their locations included Chicago, Dallas, Washington D.C., Los Angeles, London, New York, Philadelphia, and one in Paris, and I don't mean Paris, Texas. Iredell was right in that Mr. Shiras was based in their firm's Dallas office. Since my opponent was not a Waco lawyer I felt we just might have avoided the *home cookin'* after all.

The lengthy appearance did not arrive alone, and as anticipated I found among the other materials a thick set of interrogatories and a daunting document request. Dot had answered hundreds of sets of discovery, but never one thicker than the Mexia phone book and when I handed it off to her, she nearly fainted. She held the stack in her right hand and fanned through the pages with her left then dove right in. With the benefit of Nelda's questionnaire, Dot began answering the questions that she could and marking those requiring further input from Nelda. Once finalized, signed, and notarized, the responses were filed with the court with a copy to the lawyers for the foundry. Feeling the need for guidance concerning our next steps, I phoned Iredell.

"So you guys found someone to take the case?" she asked.

"Yes, but I have a confession to make," I said taking a deep breath. "The girls and I at the office are the ones that took it."

"Took it—as in handling it?"

"That's right. I tried hard to get it placed, but as you predicted, no one around here handles this type of case. So we are going to work it up right here in Mexia and I did not feel right leaning on you for advice and not coming clean on that."

"I appreciate that Miss Gertie and I admire your grit."

"You don't think I am crazy?"

She laughed and said, "A little ... I suppose, but I'm also a tad envious."

"Knowing this are you still willing to help?"

"Of course," she said eagerly. "After all, us girls have to stick together—especially the redheads."

"Thank you ... that's a big relief," I said. "The game plan is to try to settle it for Nelda, but we need witnesses to get us to that point. I'm afraid that if we don't list the right ones the other side will sense we are not prepared."

"Your concern is valid. These cases are fact and expert witness driven and the opposing firm is going to concentrate on that. Do you know who's going to defend it?"

"I do, his name is Alexander Shiras."

"Ouch," was her response.

"You know him?"

"I sure do. He is with a mega firm and they have a sizable office here in Dallas. He's very good, but obstinate, a little tricky and a *real* snazzy dresser."

"Snazzy, huh?"

"Oh yes. He dresses to the nines and the partners here call him *the popinjay*," she said with a giggle.

"I'm not familiar with the term, is that a bird?"

"It does mean a parrot, but it also refers to a vain person, one that likes to dress like a dude or a dandy. Attire aside, Mr. Shiras is a very formidable lawyer and if you don't do enough to show you've got a good case—one that poses a risk to his client—he won't take it seriously."

"You didn't mention being taken *seriously* when we talked before," I lamented.

"Sorry Miss Gertie, but it sounds like you're on the right track. Though you are not going to court look at everything through the prism of trying the case—that's what we do here every day. Your goal is to convince them that you can meet your burden of proof. If you don't make the grade they know that at the end of your case they can make a *motion for directed verdict*. If the judge grants it—it's game over."

"They can win without putting on their case?" I asked.

"It's certainly possible."

"This is a tad overwhelming, but I appreciate your guidance more than I can express."

"I'm pleased to do it—so where are you on the case?"

"They have answered and we responded to their discovery. We are seeking co-workers that can testify about the work that went on at the foundry. I'm feeling pretty good about that, but what kind of experts will we need?"

"Expensive ones," Iredell said.

"I figured you'd say that—how expensive are we talking?"

"We have used this pathologist from California on some of our cases. He's really good, but his bill for just for reviewing the case materials and drafting the written report has been as much as twenty-five thousand dollars." I struggled to catch my breath and Iredell reacted to the silence by saying, "Hello? Hello? Are you there Miss. Gertie?"

"I'm here—I think—I'm just a little floored, that's all."

"I certainly understand, maybe one of the treating doctors will testify."

"We are looking into that too, but what if they won't?"

"You can always subpoena one to appear for a deposition, but fat chance on the doc being very friendly if you do. No, winning a treating doctor's cooperation is your best bet."

"You know so much about this I wish you could have taken the case."

"Thanks for that, but these are complicated cases and there is plenty I do not know. Here's what I'll do, tell me where to mail it and I will send you a little care package that should be helpful."

"You're a peach," I said, gave her the office address, and I added sincerely, "I *really* want to do something to repay you for your kindness."

"Well … now that you mentioned it, I'd settle for your collard greens recipe."

"Ha, you know I can't do that," I said.

"It was worth a try," Iredell chortled. "You don't owe me anything Miss Gertie, but if you are so inclined I would settle for your fillet gumbo recipe and you hugging my mom's neck for me at this Sunday's church services?"

"Consider it done."

A few days later a large box arrived at the office and I recognized from the label that it was Iredell's *care package*. Not wanting to slow our progress on the file reassignments, I loaded the box in my car and at the conclusion of our work week, I dedicated my weekend to perusing its contents.

Saturday morning Jack left to mow and trim the church grounds and I opened the box. On top laid a handwritten note from Iredell reading: *Got your email with the gumbo recipe-thank you. Burned it on the first go, trying again tonight. Good luck Miss Gertie.* I smiled, put the note in my pocket and began removing the materials. Once splayed out on our kitchen table I found several hard copy deposition transcripts. Also included were three videotaped expert depositions and an example of a plaintiff's standard witness list. Her stickie note on the latter instructed me to include on my list all of the fact witnesses we find and every doctor and hospital mentioned in Cliff's medical records.

I started reading one of the transcripts and learned more about asbestos in one morning than I ever wanted to know. I discovered it is what is known as a *naturally occurring mineral* and that it is present in most of the air we breathe. I learned that its use spans back to the beginning of recorded history and that most of the asbestos used in North America came from Canada. Other types were exported from Europe and other countries including South Africa.

There was a time when asbestos was used in just about everything including some hair dryers, certain siding shingles, electrical cords, theater curtains, work gloves, bowling balls and a wide range of the construction products. Most important to me was the fact that asbestos was incorporated into materials used in industrial plants, including the insulation Cliff Blatchford would have used at the Morrison foundry.

I knew that if I was going to make an impression on the foundry's lawyers, I had to speak their language. This not only required me to acquaint myself with the terminology, but to also learn how to pronounce it all. To that end, I watched the videotaped deposition of one of my opponent's designated experts. His name was Brockholst Livingston and he spoke with an English accent which I always felt made people sound smart, even when they were as dumb as dirt. Brockholst was no dummy though, and his pay rate validated that at a whopping three hundred and fifty bucks per hour.

He possessed more degrees than a thermometer and proudly recounted the schools and universities he had attended. Included was completing prep school at Eton College and Brockholst made a point of stating that Ian Fleming, George Orwell, and Prince Harry were likewise educated there.

He testified to giving speeches all over the world, writing an array of published papers and claimed to hold a commission, whatever that is, from the Queen of England. Ever heard of ten dollar words? Well, some of his were worth at least twenty-five and it was my charge to learn them. As I viewed the video I paused it occasionally to make notes and to write down the difficult terms phonetically. The longer I watched the more I realized that if I studied hard I could handle questioning a rascal like this.

I watched the video to its conclusion and learned one undeniable truth—lawyers love themselves some objecting. Each side lodged plenty and did so to all manner of questions and responses. I jotted down several of the frequently used objections to assure that if the time came for a deposition my opponent would know I was prepared.

Monday morning Dot and I were working on the files when Lupe bounded in grinning from ear to ear.

"What are you so happy about?" Dot inquired.

"I have weetness! I have weetness!" Lupe repeated eagerly.

"You found a co-worker?" I asked.

"No—me have dos!" she said, waving a folded piece of paper in her hand.

"Two witnesses?" I asked and she nodded vigorously and passed the note to me. I unfolded it and saw two names written in pencil, *Romeo Catron* and *Jesus Cardozo*. "These are their names?"

"Jes, this is them and ellose saben Sénor Blatchford."

"They both recall Mr. Blatchford?" I asked.

"Jes, from the foun … found …" Lupe stammered.

"Foundry?" I said, handing the note to Dot.

"Jes, por mucho anos tambian and they help jou."

Dot looked up from the note, and said, "Romeo … and … Jesus—really?"

"Don't you worry about their names Lupe," I said flashing Dot a disapproving glance. "When can we talk to these fellas?"

"Whenever jou want," Lupe said.

"That's fantastic—you did a real nice job, Lupe," I said and she beamed with pride. "Did they work with Mr. Blatchford?"

"Senor Cardozo say jes."

"Great, what about Romeo? Did he work side by side with Mr. Blatchford?" I asked.

"No side to side like Jesus," Lupe said. "Senor Catron know Senor Cliff, but Romeo work in … how do you say … el almacen."

"A warehouse?"

"Jes, Miss Gertie."

"I guess we have to take what we can get," Dot said.

Lupe slumped her shoulders, hung her head and whimpered, "Jou no like mi weetness?"

Dot rolled her eyes, but I rose and gave Lupe a robust hug. "Of course we like them. I am certain they will help and thank you *very* much for finding them. Puede ganar el caso—they just may win the case."

"Jou mean it?" she said, raising her hopeful eyes toward me.

"Absolutely, yo I nececita Jesus' domicilio—I need his address because I'm going to put him on our weetness ... I mean witness list, okay?"

"Jes Miss Gertie," Lupe said, and traipsed out of the door like she was walking on air.

Once out of earshot, Dot asked, "Do you really think this is helpful?"

"Maybe, but who knows how much."

"What about Romeo, why are you not putting him on the list?"

"You heard what she said, he only took care of a warehouse."

"Well Gertie, if nothing else you made Lupe happy—have you ever seen her so thrilled?"

"No, and I'm glad for it. She tends to get down on herself and can use some encouragement," I said. "I do feel like all of this is all coming together, don't you?"

"I'm very impressed with how you have taken charge of this case. Louise would have never done anything like you have for Nelda," Dot said, then her expression soured. "You're doing great work, Lupe came through with witnesses, but I'm not pulling my weight. I can't in good conscience take a share of the money if I'm not contributing."

"You've done plenty so far," I said.

"Like what?"

"Like taking the laboring oar on the file reassignments and you got the unemployment checks coming in. You also prepared the answers to that monstrous discovery for Nelda, and I'm going to need a lot more from you going forward."

Dot said, "What else can I help with?"

"Reach out to both of Cliff's treating doctors and politely ask them to contact us. Let them know that we are the Blatchford's lawyers and that we need to discuss his treatment."

"Will do, what are the doctor's names?" she said, with pencil and legal pad in hand.

I grabbed the witness list and said, "The surgeon was Souter S-o-u-t-e-r, last name Patel, and the pathologist was Eugene S. Strong."

She stopped writing and stared at me. "Doctor Strong?"

"Yeah, why?"

"That's great," Dot said.

"Do you know him?"

"We both do," she said. "I am fairly certain that's Chap Strong's boy."

"Chap's son, Scotty?"

"I think so."

"Little Scotty is a doctor?"

"Yes, he went to medical school in Houston."

"He won't remember me, but how well do you know him?"

"I haven't laid eyes on Chap or Scotty in many years, but they used to go to my church and I actually taught Scotty Sunday School."

"If you're right this could be a game changer—assuming he will help, that is."

"I'll see what I can do."

That evening Jack and I invited the Highsmith's over for dinner and dominoes. I prepared a meal consisting of seasoned pork chops, fresh purple hull peas and a batch of my collard greens. The men sat in the living room watching a college football game and having a beer while Shirley and I were in the kitchen enjoying conversation and wine coolers. Once the meal was ready to serve, Shirley set the table and inquired of the boys as to what they wanted to drink with dinner. Jack chose sweet tea and Highsmith opted for another beer.

"Bill, I don't want no repeat of your behavior at the fish fry," Shirley scolded.

"Oh hell Shirl, I ain't had but two."

"Two here, and one before we left the house."

"That first one don't count," Bill said, "it was over an hour ago and has surely been processed by now—besides you're drivin'."

"Getting home is not what I'm worried about. It's your poor

dominoes playing and vulgar language that's weighing heavy on my mind."

"He's fine," Jack defended. "He ain't told a single joke—at least not yet. Besides, you two have run through a fair amount of those wine thingies y'all drink."

"I've had one and a half," Shirley said, "and though I don't know how many Gertie has had, she ain't said or sang a single word of Spanish."

A pleasant dinner ensued and when we were all done the plates were clean enough to skip washing them. I did so nonetheless and Jack dried them, while the Highsmith's set up the card table. Soon the dominoes were out of the box and Bill was shuffling them and Jack and I joined the couple and the games began.

"Gertie, you outdid yourself with that fine meal," Bill said, as he shoved the dominoes to the center of the table for the taking. "The greens were excellent as always and the purple hulls were as good as I ever had."

"Ditto," Shirley added.

"Thanks, guys," I said.

"I sure hope you liked the peas," Jack said, "I shelled every one of 'em, and it dang near took all the hide off my fingertips."

"Why bless his little pea picking heart," I said facetiously, "put Jack's name in for the purple-hull-heart medal."

"I sympathize, Jack—shelling peas is as tough on your hands as cleanin' catfish and crappie," Bill said. "But back to the collards Gertie, what gives them that extra kick? Is it a spice or a—"

"Save your breath Bill," Shirley intervened. "I've been trying to pry that out of her for nearly a decade."

We played dominoes well into the evening and decided to end our couples match with an amicable tie. Once the dominoes were back in the box I started a pot of coffee. While it brewed I turned on our old console stereo, put on my *Best of Conway Twitty* album, and it played soft and low in the background.

"Is that who I think it is?" Shirley said as I passed the card table on my way back to the kitchen.

"Sure is," I said with a wink as Conway's *I See the Want in Your Eyes* played.

"Conway Twitty ... what a handle," Bill scoffed. "Who the hell would do that to their kid?"

"That's not his real name, silly," Shirley explained. "His name at birth was Harold Lloyd Jenkins and the story goes he was named after some old comedian."

"Harold Lloyd—the old silent movie actor?" Jack asked.

"I think that's right," she said.

"I remember him," Jack said fondly. "He was a real funny dude."

"He sure was," Bill agreed. "He wore those round glasses and would nearly get run over by cars and trains."

"Yeah, did that and he hung off of tall buildings by the hands of a clock and other funny stuff like that," Jack added.

"Wow ... sounds real entertaining," I said facetiously.

"Women just don't get *real* comedy," Bill said.

"Oh?" Shirley said. "Like what—The Three Stooges, Monty Python, and those dopy Pink Panther movies you two insist on watching?"

"Those are all great, aren't they Jack?"

"I sure like 'em, and don't forget Benny Hill."

I intervened, "Jack, you watched Benny Hill just for those half-naked *Hill's Angels*."

"They definitely didn't drag the show down," Jack said bobbing his eyebrows up and down.

"If he wasn't born Conway Twitty how'd he get the name—did he lose a bet or something?" Bill said.

"The story goes he looked at a map and threw darts at it, or something like that," Shirley said. "Anyhow, he ended up hitting near Conway, Arkansas and Twitty, Texas. He combined the two and the rest is history."

"I would have re-thrown the damn darts," Bill said.

"It could've been worse," Jack said. "He could've wound up with *Ding Dong-Cut and Shoot*."

Bill roared with laughter, and said, "We've all heard of Cut and Shoot, but is there really a Ding Dong, Texas?"

"Damn sure is. I've driven through it and it's not far from Temple," Jack said.

"Well I'll be damned, truth *is* stranger than friction."

"It's fiction Bill, not *friction*," Shirley corrected.

"I prefer me some friction if you know what I mean," Bill said salaciously while patting Shirley on the thigh.

"You're a cad," Shirley responded, as the final bars of Conway's *Lay Me Down* wafted through the stereo speakers.

Bill said, "You call me a cad, but what about this record y'all are listening to."

"What about it?" I said.

Bill turned to my hubby, and said, "Did you hear that last song and the one playing now?" Jack nodded. "You know why gals like these two swoon over ol' Mr. Twitty?"

"I doubt it was that goofy hair of his," Jack said.

"Mmm ... the hair," I purred and Shirley nodded her concurrence.

"Fine, you like his hair," Jack said, "but is it the pompadour of the fifties or the curly permanent wave era?"

"Yes!" Shirley and I said simultaneously.

"The hair might be part of it, but I bet the clincher is that most every song he sang was about fornicatin' with some ol' gal," Bill said, and Jack looked perplexed. "Think about it, that last one was—*Lay Me Down* and before that it was *I See The Want in Your Eyes*, then there's *You've Got a Way of Doing Little Things That Turn Me On*."

"By golly, I think you're right," Jack said, reaching for the album cover and perused the titles. "He also did *You've Never Been This Far Before*, *Rest Your Love on Me* and *Slow Hand*.

"*Slow Hand*, what the hell," Bill carped.

"Don't forget his *Tight Fittin' Jeans* and I don't just mean the song," I said.

"Gertie's right about that," Shirley said, then added, "and Bill, if you don't quit talkin' about the subject matter of Conway's songs, you may start somethin' you can't finish."

"Oh I can finish it all right—I ain't had that much beer," Bill said.

"The point is it ain't acceptable for normal, human, Christian married women to swoon over such things."

"I agree," Jack said. "After all, y'all are the ones that refuse to see an R-rated movie when it's me and Bill's time to pick, but then you turn around and listen to these X-rated song?"

"X-rated—really?" Shirley said.

Bill added, "Absolutely, I say it is phonographic pornography, and believe ol' Mr. Twitty just might have been one of those nephromaniacs you hear about."

"The word is nymphomaniac," I corrected.

Shirley added, "No matter how you say it, I can only hope he was one."

"You see! You see!" Bill protested. "He's cast a spell on them that endures from the grave."

"It's just classic country music for Pete's sake," Shirley countered.

"No, it's not," Bill said, shaking his head defiantly. "Country and western songs are supposed to tell a story for the common man—you know—normal life experiences that regular folks can relate to."

"I can relate," Shirley said.

Fed up with the accusations, I posed a question to Bill. "So if Conway sang songs about Vietnamese massage parlors or farting on cruise ships it would be okay?"

Highsmith kicked me under the table and I winced. Shirley glanced at me curiously and Jack laughed under his breath. Bill looked terrified so I let it drop. I rose and walked to the coffee maker and returned to the card table toting a tray with four steaming cups and the condiments.

We sipped and talked and all was pleasant until Bill said, "So Jack tells me that asbestos at the Morrison foundry is what did in poor ol' Cliff Blatchford."

"It seems so," I said, without elaboration.

"I knew he had some form of cancer, but what kind was it?" Shirley asked.

"It was that mesothelioma cancer you here about on TV," I said.

"I sure know about that one," Bill added. "I keep up with my shipmates on a website dedicated to the USS John Archibald. Several fellow sailors have caught it and I wouldn't wish that disease on anyone—not even a lawyer."

"That last part's good since I'm married to one now," Jack said.

I could not believe my ears and it was my turn to employ some under the table messaging. In deference to Jack's compromised legs, I opted to apply the sole of my right shoe on his left instep. It was not enough to do harm but was enough to make him flinch. When he did, he bumped the table causing the coffee to slosh out of the cups.

Shirley instinctively rushed to the kitchen for some paper towels and I stared at Jack, and said, "Ixnay on the awyerlay."

Despite having a lifelong struggle with the King's English, Bill proved fluent in pig Latin, when he said, "Gertie, are you studying the law?"

"We are supposed to be keeping this under wraps," I muttered, glancing urgently toward Jack.

He hung his head, and said, "Sorry honey—I should've known better."

"It's all right," I said, as Conway's *Hello Darlin'* played and Shirley hummed along wistfully as she sopped the spills. "I think we can trust the Highsmith's and thanks for the clean-up, Shirley." She nodded, and I explained the situation I discovered after Louise's funeral, and our plan to work up the case in her name.

"I think that's great and just know that your secret is safe with us, right Shirl?" Bill said,

"Of course," She said, "and I agree with Bill—it's a nice thing you're doing for Nelda Fay."

"Thanks, guys," I said. "Say, Bill, you mentioned your buddies that got sick—didn't Navy ships have a lot of asbestos on them?"

"They were full of the stuff," Bill said, shaking his head ruefully. "Once my buddies started going public about getting sick I read up on it. I learned that the Navy was one of the largest purchasers of asbestos in history. The WWII era Fletcher class destroyer I served on had tons of insulation on board. We called it lagging and it was all over the hotlines that ran throughout the ship."

"Hotlines?" I asked.

"Yes, since the ships back then were steam driven they had a lot of steam pipes on board. They had to be insulated to retain the heat and to keep the men from getting burned by accidentally brushing up against the pipes."

"They were that hot, huh?" I asked.

"Yes they were, and they needed to be kept that way for the ship to run. That's why it was mandated that the pipes have asbestos lagging and block insulation was required on the outside of the boilers," Bill said, and I sensed that the discussion was making Shirley nervous.

"Did you work with it, Hon?" she asked.

"Thankfully no—at least not directly. It was the guys that worked down in the fire rooms that got the worst of it," Bill said.

"Is that where the boilers were?" Jack asked.

"That's right, and the Archibald had fire rooms forward and aft. Each had a large boiler that made the steam to turn the screws that propelled the ship. There were also steam turbines there to make the electricity. It was hotter than hell down there and was close to the bilge so it smelled awful. Unfortunately for the guys working there screwing with insulation was a part of their daily routine."

Jack added, "The insulated piping was throughout that ship I sailed on and one ran right above my bunk."

"Steam lines were where the sailors slept?" I asked dubiously, and both men nodded. I had never heard that from Jack and now two wives were concerned. "Jack, do you think you were exposed to it?"

"It's hard to say."

Bill explained, "Jack only had the one voyage and if he was exposed at all it was very minor."

"You had two voyages, right?" I said.

Jack shook his head. "I sailed over to Nam, but flew back."

"Jack, was it dusty on board?" I asked.

"That was a long time ago, but I don't recall there being much dust."

"The lagging was pretty stable unless you bumped it and a little dust would come out," Bill said. "It was when we did war games that it got real bad."

"War games?" I asked.

"Yeah, every now and then while at sea, we would practice combat. They would set up billboard-size targets or use an old mothballed ship for us to attack. When they fired the 5-inch guns the ship would pitch, roll and vibrate like hell. The dust from the lagging would fill the air and get all over everything. So no, I didn't work with it, but everyone on a ship gets a snoot full to one degree or another. That's why the Navy continues to monitor us swabbies with X-rays and breathin' tests."

"The more you talk, the more *the hill* sounds better than the ship," Jack said.

Bill chuckled. "Maybe, but many on *the hill* didn't come back at all. At least for the poor souls I knew that got sick it took decades to develop."

Shirley asked. "You've never talked about this before—does it worry you?"

Bill shrugged as he stared down at his coffee cup. "Some ... I guess, but considering those fifty-two thousand that never made it home I just focus on the time I've had and the time they didn't have, and consider myself lucky."

"Do you believe Cliff Blatchford got sick from working at the foundry?" I asked.

"I most certainly do. Cliff's experience there wouldn't be much different than what I described on the ship."

"How so?"

"Gertie, I know for a fact they've got boilers down at Morrison's and most if not all of the pipes there would be been insulated. The foundry needed it for the same reason the Navy did."

"Thanks for sharing your experience," I said. "You sure know a lot about it, and I just might list you as a witness."

"Does it pay well?" Bill asked facetiously.

Shirley rubbed Bill's shoulder, and said, "I don't mind him being a witness, but I don't want my little Conway becoming a plaintiff."

"Hey—what do you mean by *little* Conway," Bill asked.

"Take it easy, honey."

Jack said. "Speaking of getting paid, tell them how much that British dude fetches for testifying," Jack said.

"What dude?" Bill said.

"Jack's referring to Brockholst Livingston. He's one of my opponent's experts and gets paid three hundred and fifty Dollars per hour."

Shirley gasped, and Bill blurted, "That's crazy."

"Hang on now, he is highly educated and did go to Eton," I countered.

"I wish I could get paid for goin' to eatin', I'd be a millionaire," Jack said, and Bill laughed.

"I can attest to that," I said, "but it is Eton E-T-O-N. It is a prestigious school in London and guess what famous people went there?"

"Bond—James Bond," Bill said in his poor attempt at a Sean Connery impersonation. Shirley and I stared at him incredulously, and he added, "He did go there, didn't he?"

"Bill, James Bond ain't a real person," Shirley said.

"You're close though," I said, "Ian Fleming, the author of the James Bond books went there as did Prince Harry and George Orwell."

"Say, didn't Albert Einstein go to school there and flunked math or somethin'?" Jack asked.

"I've never heard that and I doubt it considering he was German," I said.

"By golly, I think you're right," Jack conceded.

"That reminds me of an ol' boy that worked under me at the cotton mill named Philo Bradley," Bill said. "He was a nice guy, but was as thick as the steam off a winter turd."

"Bill!" Shirley scolded.

"Sorry dear, but it's true," Bill said. "You see, Philo had a habit of falling asleep at his desk and was thought be one of those narco-epilectrics or whatever it's called. The brass kept calling him on the carpet and threatening to fire him if he didn't quit snoozin' on the job. Since he couldn't help it, he got real down on himself, so one day I tried to cheer him up. I described a documentary I watched about Einstein and it seems ol' Albert used to do the same thing. So I told

Philo, *even Einstein would sit at his desk and take short naps throughout the day*. Philo pondered, then said, *Einstein huh … Einstein … He must've got fired before I started here."*

"Did he end up getting fired?" I asked.

"Technically speaking, no, but that's only because he quit first so as to not have a pink slip on his record."

"Considering his snoozing problem where did he end up?" I asked.

"Last I heard he was an air traffic controller."

"Is that true Bill?" Jack said, dumbfounded.

Shirley shook her head, and said, "No, Bill's just funnin' you."

"So this high priced Eton man is testifying for Morrison's?" Bill said.

"He's on their list," I said.

"Bill, didn't you used to hang out with that big wig from the foundry?" Jack asked.

"Yeah, I know the stutterin' fat bastard."

"Bill! You stop it!" Shirley chastised.

"Sorry, but it's the truth. He does stutter and he's three hundred pounds if he's an ounce."

"That don't matter, you still shouldn't say things like that, and just who are you talking about anyhow?"

"Waite Morrison, the grandson of the guy that built the foundry. His dad, Waite junior, was a good, decent and smart man. Waite the third or the *turd* as we call him is living proof that the acorn *can* fall far from the tree. He's as dense as a blacksmith's anvil, and never seemed right in the head to me."

"Fine, but you ought not to belittle the man for having a speech problem," Shirley said.

"It's a problem all right. When Morrison was in our poker rotation, he was a big pain to have at the table since it would take him forever to utter his bet. He became an easy mark though, once we realized he stuttered most when he was lying, nervous or had a good hand. Since he was too miserly to ever bluff, when he would stutter a raise it would take him forever to say it and when he managed to get it out, we'd all fold. Gertie, if you get to question Trey Morrison you'll have your way with him and if he doesn't own up to the insulation being there, I'll personally call him out on it."

"How can so you so sure about that part—have you ever been inside the plant?" I asked.

"No, but they have those giant furnaces there and they don't plug them into a regular 110 wall socket. Plus, haven't you noticed those two large brick smoke stacks on the back side of the foundry?"

"Sure, you can see them long before you get to town."

"Right, and that means they have a power plant to make their own juice to run the furnaces. Like the ships, they need large boilers and generators to make the electricity. Most everything associated with that would be insulated, from the boilers, pipes, pumps, valves, and probably the furnaces themselves. Girl, I think you got yourself a hell of a case."

6
CHAPTER

The next day's mail delivery included an envelope from the foundry's lawyers containing a notice to take Nelda Fay's deposition. They had, without consultation with me, selected a date for it to occur and scheduled it to take place at their office in Dallas. I thought it was awful of them to make Nelda answer more questions, but I knew from experience that they had every right to do so. I likewise knew that we had a right to have it occur at our office, but I did not think it was wise to demand that and have that wily Dallas lawyer hanging out in Mexia. As a consequence, I favored traveling to Dallas, but in order to coax Nelda into the concept I needed a plan and had to gather all of the particulars in advance.

I started by checking the rates for some of the hotels in downtown Dallas, but they were higher than a cat's back with many asking well over two hundred dollars per night. I placed a call to a hotel in Arlington, a town situated between Dallas and Fort Worth. It was a property Jack and I had used in the past when taking Eli to Six Flags or to see the Texas Rangers play. Their rates were higher than I was comfortable with, but considering that they were far less than the Dallas hotels, the fact that I knew how to get to it, and that the deal came with a free breakfast—I booked it.

I phoned Nelda and laid it all out for her and initially, she was none too pleased. However, the more I explained the trip including the plan of heading up there a day early and us staying in the hotel, she warmed to the prospect. Though she made me answer some curious questions about the size, layout, and location of the hotel, I did not think too much about that and in the end, she agreed to go.

When the day came to leave, we hit the road early afternoon and as we drove out of Limestone County, I put in my best of Willie Nelson CD. Appropriately Willie's *On The Road Again* played in the background as I discussed the do's and don'ts of depositions—at least as I understood them. On occasions, I had sat in on sessions when Louise prepped clients for their testimony and recalled some of her training tips. Accordingly, I urged Nelda to make sure she understood any question asked before answering it. I explained that if she did not understand a question to make Mr. Shiras re-ask it until it was clear in her mind. I warned her to listen carefully to the questions and to only answer what was asked and not add to it. She seemed unnerved by just discussing it, but the longer we talked and the more she understood, her tension seemed to ease.

Halfway through the trip, the Willie CD began to repeat so I traded it for Johnny Cash-live at Folsom Prison. I ceased the deposition coaching and we sang along to the songs, except for *cocaine blues*—I skipped that one, and as hoped the trip took on the feel of a vacation.

It had been quite a while since I had ventured to the big city and even longer for Nelda and as we drew within a few miles of Dallas the sight of its skyline took our collective breaths away. The line of tall buildings rose high and foreboding on the horizon and served as an ominous reminder of where we would be the following morning.

We veered onto interstate twenty west and I drove it until taking the Arlington exit. I steered us to the hotel, pulled on to the parking lot and I chose a slot closest to the entrance. With our bags in hand we walked through the sliding glass double doors and over to the front desk. Finding no one manning the counter I availed myself of the silver desk bell, giving it a couple of dings. I sensed movement from behind an ajar door to our left and a young man emerged through it, straightened his necktie, and asked, "Can I help you?"

"Yes sir, I have a reservation under Chase."

"Hmm, let's see here," the man said as he leafed through a box of white envelopes with handwriting at the top of each.

While the desk clerk searched I snagged a free USA Today off of a stack on the counter, then turned and noticed Nelda exploring the lobby. She was pacing about and glancing around, not like someone exploring unfamiliar surroundings, but rather as one would attempting to locate something or someone.

"Oh, here it is," the man said, lifting one of the envelopes. "I'll need a credit card and a picture ID."

I handed him both and was startled when Nelda blurted from just over my left shoulder, "What floor did we get?"

I explained that I did not know and we both stood staring at the desk clerk. He returned my credentials and handed me the envelope, and said, "I have you on five and there are two keys inside."

I heard a slight squeal from behind me, and Nelda asked, "Do you have something on the first floor?"

The man shook his head. "They're all either booked up or reserved for our handicapped guests."

"I'm handicapped," Nelda said.

I wheeled around to face her. "You're what?"

"Never mind," she said. "How about the second floor?"

"Let me check," the clerk said and made several punches on his keyboard. "It looks like we have three suites open on two."

"We'll take one," Nelda said, having seized the dominant roll concerning our lodging.

After the man re-swiped the keys, I thanked him, turned and Nelda motioned me into the breakfast area. At her insistence, we bypassed the elevators and I followed her up a set of stairs connecting that area to the second floor. After we settled into our suite and refreshed ourselves, we opted for an early supper. I considered splurging by ordering room service but abandoned that notion once I located the menu in the nightstand drawer. I sat on my twin bed astonished to read that they wanted nine dollars and fifty cents for a hamburger and fries. I showed the menu to Nelda, and she was likewise taken aback. I tipped my hat to that idea, rose and opened the window drapes and conjured Plan-B. I convinced Nelda to walk with me an extra two blocks over to a nearby restaurant named Mighty-Burger.

She and I strolled together as the sun waned to an orange glow on the western horizon and we each enjoyed the cool breezes and lower humidity of North Texas. Once inside the burger joint, we ordered and when it was all said and done we both ate for just over ten dollars, did not pay a fifteen percent delivery fee or a tip, and I must say it was delicious.

When we returned to our hotel room we washed and treated our faces and changed into our bedclothes. Knowing that we had a big day ahead of us we decided to hit the hay early.

When I switched off my bedside lamp the room went dark, and moments later, Nelda said, "Gertie?"

"Yes?"

"Thank you for taking the case, if it weren't for you all it would have just withered away."

"You're welcome dear, and thank you for trusting us with it," I said, staring straight up at the ceiling and reflecting back on my theory as to why her file had been neglected in the first place. "Nelda?"

"Yes, Gertie."

"I want to get something off my chest."

"All right," she said, apprehensively.

"I can't prove it mind you, but I believe the reason Louise lost interest in your case was ... um because ... of uh—"

"Of my skin color," she finished.

I rolled over on my side, and asked, "How did you know?"

Nelda sighed, then explained, "It was the meeting at your office that Saturday morning. When Ms. Barbour opened the door to let me in I saw *the look*."

"The look?"

"That's right. It starts with me not speaking like a lot of black folks do. It is not uncommon when I meet someone in person for the first time that until then I have only spoken to by phone, they're often surprised, sometimes pleasantly so ... sometimes not."

"Louise was a *not?*" I said.

"Correct, and I sensed right away that it lessened her interest in helping me, but I never dreamed she would just abandon the case."

"I would like to think she didn't consciously do that," I said, and leaned back onto my pillow. I laid still and tried to divert my mind, but I had opened a dialogue that I could not ignore. "Nelda?"

"Yes, Gertie."

"My dad sometimes used the N-word."

"So did mine, and on occasions, I have too—so what about it?"

"It's different when someone from your race says it."

"It most certainly is not," she said firmly. "It's a bad word no matter whose mouth it comes from. Besides, I knew your folks well and they were very kind to me and my family. To the extent your dad used that term, I know it was just the way things were back then and he meant nothing by it."

"It certainly was the way folks talked back then, but that's no excuse," I said. "My father should have known it was wrong and set a better example."

"Words are just words Gertie—that's all. I have always judged people by their acts and deeds more than the comments they say or the jokes they tell. Neither of your folks had a racist bone in their bodies and I can prove it."

"How?"

"They raised a girl that befriended the likes of me at a high school that was integrating."

"That was no great feat, you and I hit it off right away."

"From where I stood it was certainly a feat—I was terrified to enter the building that first day. You not only became my friend you made it acceptable for others to do the same, and let's not forget how fond our mothers were of each other."

"My mom adored Miss Wanda," I said.

"And mine loved and admired your mom, and they never exchanged a cross word, did they?"

"That's true."

"As for your dad, I remember vividly how he would, sometimes with you and him, come to our area of town to bring us or our neighbor's fish he had caught."

"It was the fish we didn't like to eat," I said.

"My family sure liked them," she said. "Your dad could have just chunked those pollies on the bank to die and let the buzzards eat them so they would not reproduce. Instead he took the time to keep them and bring them over to our neighborhood."

"That's another thing, all of y'all down there lived in dilapidated shotgun houses with tin roofs, no indoor plumbing, and no electricity. I know for a fact you had no running water because when my dad was busy I personally collected the five cent payments for barrels of it from the water department."

"We were glad to get it and besides, was the living conditions you just described much different than what y'all had on that Lost Prairie dirt farm?"

"No ... but we moved."

"So did we, now cut it out," Nelda admonished, yawned and the room fell silent.

"Nelda?"

I heard long sigh, followed by, "What is it now?"

"I once did eenie meenie miney mo to see who would be *it* in freeze tag and I um ... uh ... I didn't say catch a *tiger* by the toe."

"How old were you, Gertie?"

"Oh my," I said, pondering. "It was way back, I was just a little girl."

"Did any of the other kids around there say it that way?"

"They all did, I'm sad to say."

"Then you were just repeating it the way you heard it, and just did not know any better."

"I guess you're right, but I still feel bad about it."

Nelda issued her penance saying, "Say three Hail Marys and go to sleep."

"You know I am not Catholic."

"Neither am I, but what else do you want me to do?"

"I would like to square the deal somehow," I said.

"Fine—eenie meenie miney mo, catch a *cracker* by the toe. Now there—we are even."

"I'm not bothered by that term."

"Gertie, what makes you think I'm bothered about something you said a half century ago?"

"All right ... I'll let that one go, but I have something else to confess," I said, and flinched when Nelda's nightstand light switched on.

"Gertrude Chase! For a Protestant, you sure seem determined to turn this hotel room into a confessional."

"I know and I am sorry, but I am burdened and they say confession is good for the soul."

"I am certain that your soul is intact, but if you insist ... have at it."

I took a deep breath, exhaled, and said, "Shortly after we moved to Mexia I saw my mom and Ms. Jackson coming out of the Spindle Top cafe. They had already eaten their meals inside and my mother handed yours a paper sack containing her lunch to eat it in the back of Miss Bea's car."

"Those were the rules back then and your mom and Bea Jackson didn't make them. I bet both women hated that it was like that then."

"My mom was sure sickened by it, but I feel like she should have done something."

"Like what? Defy the law and get fired at the State School and risk your dad's job with the city?"

"But it was so wrong and I—"

"Gertie, two white women in the nineteen-sixties south had a colored woman in the car with them. For heaven's sake don't you know what courage that alone took?"

"I guess you're right, but why did it have to be that way here?"

"It wasn't only here," Nelda said. "Do you recall that cousin of mine that went into the insurance business after he left the service?"

"The one that lived in New Jersey?"

"That's right, he lived in East Orange and because he lived both here in Texas and up there, he had a perspective on this. Most everything was segregated up there too, perhaps not so much by law or policy as much as custom and practice, but that's the way it was. He was treated poorly there, often more so than when he was here."

"Really?"

"Yes indeed. According to him people up there talk a good game about tolerance and advancing race relations, but they are far less likely to be seen around minorities, much less associate with one. He once made an observation and I quote: *in the north, they love the race, but despise the people, and in the south, they despise the race but love the people.*

"Pigmentation should never be a basis for liking someone or not."

"In a perfect world that's true, but it also cuts both ways," Nelda said. "Make no mistake about it, white people have no monopoly on bigotry. Folks have a tendency to associate with people that are like them and colored folks are no different. It's only natural and it's not always done out of ill motives. If you want to see for yourself just go to a black-owned business and see how many white people are working there. Truth is, there are some from my race that are just as prejudice against whites as a Klansman would be about one of us. Things aren't perfect now and they never will be, but no matter how much things improve for my people some insist living in the past."

"The past can be hard to ignore," I said.

"I get that, but the past can be a key or a shackle and it's up to the individual which they reach for."

"I guess you're right."

"Is there anything else, or can we go to sleep now?"

"I feel better," I said, and laid my head down.

Nelda reached over to her lamp and returned the room to darkness. "You're a good woman Gertie Chase, and I love you."

"I love you too."

The next morning I awoke before Nelda and used a wet washrag to wipe a layer of cold cream from my face. I showered and dressed for the day and when I exited the bathroom I saw that Nelda had arisen. While she took her shower I had designs on working the crossword puzzle from my complimentary newspaper. I was far too preoccupied for that, so I opted instead to sit at the small desk in our suite, sipping coffee and reading over my notes. The next time I looked up Nelda was standing in front of the full-length mirror brushing her hair.

"You doing okay girl?" I asked.

"Let's just say you are lucky we had twin beds, I tossed and turned most of the night."

"Same here," I said.

"How are you feeling today?"

"A tad nervous, but I feel prepared for this, and am armed with my objections," I said pointing to my notes.

"Objections?" she asked and walked to my side as she continued her long steady strokes with the brush.

"Yes, that's what lawyers do at depositions. I jotted some down when I read and watched those samples Iredell sent. When Mr. Shiras is asking his questions it is my job is to listen carefully and lodge certain objects along the way," I said, displaying the list to her. "As you can see there are several, but the main ones are *hearsay*—that's the biggie we discussed at the office. Then there is *asked and answered*, *calls for speculation*, and *assumes facts not in evidence*."

"What does that last one mean?"

I thought for a moment, and said, "I'm not quite sure, but it's in the rotation to be on the safe side."

"You're really going to do some?"

"Sure, I have to make Mr. Shiras follow the rules, or he won't think I'm much of a lawyer."

Once packed and dressed for the day we headed out of our suite with our packed bags in hand. We made our way through the hallway and took the steps down to the first-floor dining area. We selected a table just off the stairway, sat our bags down, and then explored the options for our free continental breakfast. We made our plates, took seats across the table from each other, and silently said grace. We ate knowing all that separated us from the *show time* was the short drive to the big city and the seriousness of the day manifested through our mutual silence.

We finished our meals, discarded our plastic utensils, cups and plates and checked out of the hotel. We loaded my car and I steered us out of the parking lot and back to the freeway. I took the up ramp and merged into the traffic heading east toward Dallas. Despite driving the speed limit I was nevertheless being passed by other motorists at breakneck speeds. Some honked as they passed while others offered colorful gestures, but as we neared the city the chaos ceased when we reached the downtown traffic. We were now creeping along on an elevated portion of the highway and I glanced to the dashboard clock to check the time. I was nervous and addled and was watching the cars around me, while searching the signs for a way down to ground level, when Nelda screeched, "Downtown exit to the right!"

I took a quick look toward her and saw that she was pointing to a green sign with white writing. I whipped over in the right-hand lane, and my maneuver drew more honks from my fellow commuters. We exited onto a sweeping down ramp and I glanced in my rearview mirror and noticed a large delivery truck only inches from my back bumper. Accordingly, I dared not touch my brakes as we spiraled rapidly downward. The centrifugal motion took on the sensation and insecurity of a carnival ride until it delivered us safely to street level. I glanced back at my mirror and saw the truck no longer posed a threat but also noticed that the tall buildings of the Dallas skyline were shrinking as we drove.

I consulted the compass inset on my rearview mirror and said, "Crap, we are heading in the wrong direction."

"How could that be, we took the exit for downtown?" Nelda said.

"There was a big truck tailgating me and I probably missed another sign," I said, and made a U-Turn in the median and headed back east toward town. When we reached Commerce Street we were finally driving in the shadows of the skyscrapers, but I knew we were running short on time.

"I need your help finding Shiras' office. He's in the Ellsworth building located on North Akard, A-K-A-R-D," I said, alternating glances between the street signs and traffic lights, all the while trying not to collide with the bustling pedestrians. I turned down first one street and then another, and each time I thought we needed to go in a particular direction we reached a street that was *one way* in the opposite direction. When we proceeded as required, I could not turn to get back toward the direction I thought we needed to go. Some of the streets dead-ended into buildings causing us to shear off in undesired directions thus starting the process over.

Despite my best efforts, my mental navigation must have been awry, as I knew that we had passed some of the same buildings and landmarks multiple times. One such false turn took us on a tour through Dealey Plaza, and according to the signs we were on the exact route President Kennedy's motorcade took in sixty-three. When we passed the storied School Book Depository it seemed a little ironic to me, but I set that aside and stopped my car at the next intersection.

I struggled to ignore the horns blaring from behind us which only intensified when I rolled my window down. I asked a couple of gentlemen on a corner the way to the Ellsworth building. As the symphony of honkers reached a crescendo the two fellows did their best to direct us. They barked out a series of turns, but only the first two registered with me. I felt that to be a good start, thanked the men and proceeded onward.

Moments later I felt a measure of relief when I happened upon Akard Street. In proof that broken clock is right twice a day, I then spotted the Ellsworth building, but what I did not see was a place to park. There were metered parking spots along the curb that ran down the side of the building, but each were taken. The only unoccupied spaces had signs reading *no parking* or *loading zone only*.

I again resorted to rolling my window down and asked a passerby in a business suit if she knew where we could park. The nice lady directed us to a large parking garage catty-corner to the office building. I thanked her and wheeled us over in that direction and noticed that the garage alone was larger than any building I had ever been in. I pulled into the entrance and sat in front of this machine that automatically produced a ticket. When I pulled the ticket from the slot this orange and white striped wooden arm in front of us rose. This allowed us to pass under it and as I moved forward I noticed, for the first time, the sign listing the parking rates.

"Hold on to your hat, Nelda," I said pointing. "Parking, twenty-four dollars minimum."

"Oh lord," she gasped. "Could that be right?"

"I guess so, I just want to rent a space for an hour or two, not buy one."

We proceeded deeper into the interior of the garage and started up a steep ramp that lead to more ramps. We passed only spaces that were either occupied or marked *reserved* as we rose higher and higher through the cavernous space. It was creepy and dark inside the garage, so much so that my automatic headlights switched on, as did those on many of the cars now following us.

Like a NASCAR pace car, we were leading the field of other drivers up the ramps making left turn after left turn. This yawing made me a tad dizzy and I glanced at Nelda. She looked worried, but sat eerily quiet and staring straight ahead. I rechecked my mirrors and noticed that the car directly behind us was now so close to mine that I could not see its headlights, and wondered, *Lord, why is everybody in this town in such a doggone hurry.*

I alternated my attention between the jerk behind me, looking for available spaces and negotiating my next turn without striking any of the garage's large concrete support pillars. When one of us spotted a space that appeared to be available I would slow as safely as I could. Each time I did, it turned out to be a false alarm due to the presence of a subcompact, a double-parked car, or a motorcycle.

When I finally happened upon a fully unimpeded open slot I hesitated to take it, since doing so would require me to brake hard and risk calamity from behind. Over Nelda's protest, I ceded the space to my tailgater in hopes that it would make the remainder of our search less nerve-wracking. It worked, and the sedan from behind whipped into the slot, but just as quick the next car from behind filled the space. We continued upward and rose so high that I wondered if we would run out of building before finding a parking space.

It was not until we reached the twelfth floor that I found an open spot, one that was safe to access. Once securely parked we exited my car and I grabbed my purse and tote bag. As the parade of vehicles continued unabated, our next mission was to find our way from the garage to the Ellsworth building.

As we walked, I saw a metal sign in the shape of an arrow that read *to elevators*. I guided Nelda in that direction and when we reached the elevator bank, I punched the down button and stood awaiting the arrival of the next car. Soon, a bell rang, the doors eased opened and Nelda grasped my arm—hard.

"What's the matter?" I asked.

"Elevators," she blurted and goose bumps appeared on her bare forearms.

I turned back toward the open elevator door and noticed its occupants staring impatiently at us. "It's all right, y'all go on ahead," I told the folks and when the doors closed, I asked, "What about elevators?"

"I'm scared to death of them, that's what," she said, and mercifully eased her grip on my arm.

"Really?" I said, and she nodded vigorously. I could tell by her expression that this was no small matter, and asked, "Since when?"

"Since forever, and it's only gotten worse over time," she said.

"How could I not know that after all these years?"

"It's not something you publicize, plus there were only four public elevators in Mexia back in the day and even now there's only six."

"You've kept an inventory of them?"

"Yes, there were five until the Roller Hotel closed and it went down to four. The new bank building has one bringing it back to five and the expansion of City Hall has another—raising it to six. There is one at Brookshire Brothers grocery store, but it's in the back and not for the public use so I don't count that one."

"Didn't the notion of getting on an elevator cross your mind when you agreed to come to Dallas?"

"Of course it did and I immediately regretted agreeing to come. Since then I have been more petrified about elevators than I have the deposition itself. I held out hope that the foundry's lawyers would be in a small one-story office like yours, or perhaps on the first floor of a larger building or at least low enough that we could take the stairs. That's why when we checked into the hotel yesterday I asked if they had something on the first floor."

"They didn't and when we got offered a room on the second floor you took it."

"That's because while you were registering I scoped out the breakfast area and saw the stairway."

"I wondered what you were doing, but thought you were looking for snacks," I said.

"I was doing that too, but mission number one was finding those stairs."

"All hotels have fire exit stairs you can take," I said.

"I know, and if that's all they had I would have likely done it, but those make me nervous too. Those metal doors are hard to open and they always make a loud racket when they close and I am very afraid of getting locked inside one."

"If that did happen you could simply use your mobile phone."

"Have you seen the cell signal in one of those?" she asked and I shook my head. "It's awful, one bar maybe two at best—there is too much metal around."

"Maybe Shiras is on one of the lower floors," I said.

She asked urgently, "You don't know the floor?"

"No, I only paid attention to the street address."

"Oh, no," Nelda said clutching her hands at her breast.

"Look—I'm sure it will be fine, but first things first. How do you want to get out of this parking garage?"

"What are our options?"

"As I see it, it's either the elevators or those stairs," I said pointing to the brown metal door next to the elevator bank.

"That's it?"

"Barring sprouting wings and flying out of here, I think that's the full range of options," I said and checked my watch.

"How about walking back down the ramps?"

"You may not have seen from the passenger seat just how fast those cars are whipping around corners and into spaces, but we would risk our lives doing that. No, I think we have to take the elevators," I said and she closed her eyes and shook her head.

I was becoming disillusioned with the practice of law—if this was what practicing law was like, but I kept my focus on the mission at hand. Struggling for calm, I said, "We are already running late Nelda, so you need to pick elevators or stairs and I *strongly* recommend the elevators—so what do you say?"

"Stairs," she muttered.

"We're twelve floors up for Pete's sake."

"Can we take them down, for Nelda's sake?"

"All right ... we will take the stairs," I conceded.

"Bless you, Gertie. Do you want me to carry your tote bag?"

"Take my purse, it is lighter," I said, handing it off to her as others were now gathering around us awaiting the arrival of the next elevator. I pointed to a sign on the wall and said, "If I'm reading this right we need to take the stairs down to the second floor and use a crosswalk to get into the building."

"Oh no—a crosswalk?" she said.

"Is that a problem too?"

"I don't know ... what is it?" she said as the elevator car arrived and those around us began to enter.

When the door closed I said, "I'm not exactly sure, but there's only one way to find out," I said, and began tugging hard on the handle of the scratched and rusty door to the stairway. It was stubborn and I used all of my might and leveraged my weight until it gave way enough for us to enter. I struggled to hold the door and coaxed Nelda through the opening and into the poorly lit stairwell. I immediately noted the dampness and the musty smell that had a hint of urine and Nelda cringed when the rusty door slammed shut behind us. We stood side by side on the landing and stared down at the first flight. We each took a deep breath and proceeded arm in arm downward—stair by stair—floor by floor. As we walked I lifted my cell phone from my tote to check the cell signal—it was one bar.

"Told you so," she muttered.

"While the stairs are fine for going down that won't work coming back up," I said.

"I realize that."

I look over to her. "What are we going to do about that?"

"I don't know," Nelda said, "let's just take things a step at a time."

No pun intended I thought, then said, "I have an idea, when we are done with the deposition and leave Shiras' building, you can wait on the sidewalk in front of the garage. I will ride the elevator up to twelve, drive my car back down and pick you up there."

"Oh, thank you, Gertie. I feel so much better, and I am sorry to be such a burden."

"You're not a burden, and I'm happy to do it."

We made it down to the second floor and I shoved opened that metal door. Passerby's stared curiously at us as we emerged from the stairwell and fell in with a stream of mostly well-dressed men and women.

We walked with them en masse until I saw what I was sure was the crosswalk. It was a tunnel suspended thirty or so feet above the street and signs confirmed that it connected the parking garage to the Ellsworth building. The walkway was lined on each side with thick transparent panels, each providing a bird's eye view of the surroundings. We paused for a moment to stare out and watched as the cars, buses and pedestrians passed right under us. I then glanced upward and was struck by just how tall Shiras's building was. It was a skyscraper to be sure, and the impressively large parking garage now seemed minuscule in comparison. I was jolted back to reality when I saw the time on a clock tower atop an adjacent building.

"We've got to get going, it's past the top of the hour," I said.

Nelda nodded and we hot-footed it through the remainder of the cross-walk and into the building. I looked down to the large ground level lobby and it reminded me of a European cathedral I once saw on the National Geographic channel.

Finding Shiras' office was our next and most urgent challenge, and to do so we needed to go down one level to the lobby. Elevators and a long escalator were the only options and I wondered what phobias moving stairs represented to Nelda. Fortunately, she harbored no such fears and we took the escalator down toward the first floor. Once there we walked the lobby until we found a uniformed security guard sitting behind a black marble desk.

"Can I help you ladies?" he asked, as we neared.

"I hope so," I said, "we're trying to find the office of a Mr. Alexander Shiras."

"What company is he with?"

"Oh goodness, it's a law firm with a string of names and his is one of them," I said perusing a board listing all of the building's tenants.

"I found it," the guard said.

"Oh good, can you tell us what floor is he on?" I asked, and braced myself.

"He's on the sixtieth, ma'am."

"Oh no," Nelda gasped, and staggered backward three steps and fearing she was going to faint I took her by the arm to steady her.

"Is she all right?" the guard asked.

"She's fine," I said, "so where do we go to get up there?"

The man pointed the way and I guided Nelda by her shoulders in that direction. She stared at the marble floors as we walked and I could feel her muscles trembling through her blouse. We reached the elevator area, a room that had more doors than the set of *Let's Make a Deal*. Each provided access to a separate elevator and I noticed that three of the four walls of each elevator car mimicked the skywalk by featuring clear glass panels. The cars were moving silently, but rapidly, up or down and two of them were descending toward us. Others cars packed with passengers lurched upward and I could see through the glass that some were occupied with reading newspapers, while others were enjoying the views provided by their ascent.

"Oh god," was Nelda's response when she ventured a glance upward. She began panting, shaking her head rapidly and said, "Gertie, I just can't do this."

"You *have* to," I implored.

"Can't we take the stairs?"

"Nelda, you heard the man. The firm is on the sixteenth floor, and to walk it we would have to have started yesterday and packed a lunch."

She nodded, then asked, "Reckon he would come down here to ask his questions?"

"You know I am not an expert on all of this, but I am pretty sure we can't do a deposition in the lobby."

"Maybe he could come down to the second or third floor and do it there," she suggested hopefully.

"Where? In the hallway?"

"I know I'm being silly, but I just can't do the elevators."

I repositioned myself to face her, stared squarely into her eyes, and said, "Sweetie, we have no choice. We are already late and need to do this and do it now, and here's the plan," I said offering the crook of my elbow and she took it. "I am going to wait for the next elevator to arrive and when the door opens just hang on to me. When you step inside keep your eyes closed and imagine you are just entering your walk-in closet at home."

"Closets don't move fast, shake and rattle."

"I understand, but just pretend," I said, and noticed that the area around us was swelling with others each eager to reach their own destinations. Many were staring upward trying to handicap the arrival of the next elevator and they jockeyed to position themselves near the corresponding door. As luck would have it, an elevator car close to us arrived. When the doors slid apart and as the passengers emptied out, I asked, "Are you ready?"

"I guess so," she said, with her eyes already clenched shut.

When the last passenger exited I wasted no time in guiding Nelda inside the space and facing her toward the back of the elevator—the only side with no transparent wall. The elevator filled, the door closed and before I could press the button for our floor it took off like a rocket. The velocity was enough to cause my knees to buckle and for Nelda to shriek, and as we rose higher and higher the people on the first floor got smaller and smaller until they looked the size of ants. I then discovered another problem. The elevator's highest floor button was for forty-five, and thought *Oh lord, if I got us on the wrong elevator and have to go back down and start over Nelda is going to lose it.*

Next to me stood a distinguished gentleman in a business suit. He was occupied by a Wall Street Journal until I tapped him on the shoulder. I explained what floor we needed and he informed that we had to get off on the forty-fifth floor and take another elevator from there up to the sixtieth. Nelda overheard the exchange, but managed hold it together and endured the journey up to forty-five. When the doors opened I led her off and followed the other passengers to the next set of elevators. There were only two doors there, and we entered the first elevator car we could and I punched the button for the sixtieth floor.

"Look—it could've been worse," I whispered, and pointed to the button for the eighty-sixth floor. Nelda squinted to read the number, nodded, and returned them shut.

When the elevator opened on the sixtieth I positioned my hand to stop the doors from closing. I wanted the least amount of elevator time as possible so I poked my head out the door and into a foyer to assure we were on the right level. I confirmed it was Shiras' floor by the string of names in large block letters on the wall opposite the elevator.

I summoned Nelda, and then and only then, did she fully open her eyes and eagerly exit the elevator. I led the way through the foyer and into the firm's reception area, a room that alone was larger than our entire office back in Mexia. I glanced around at the furnishings and admired the paintings, the fancy oriental rugs and bronze statues.

I looked to my right and noticed a pretty lady sitting at a large, horseshoe-shaped granite desk wearing a headset with a microphone like Garth Brooks wears on stage. I explained who we were and our reason for being there and she asked us to make ourselves at home in the waiting area. Nelda and I eased over to one of the leather couches, took a seat and I gazed at the coffee table in front of us. It had a glass tabletop resting on a hand-carved wooden base and atop it sat rows of neatly arranged current magazines and fresh newspapers.

We were not seated long when a woman emerged through a side door and identified herself as Alex Shiras' secretary. We introduced ourselves, and she escorted us through the same door and down a long hallway toward the conference room. We saw it before we got to it, as it was fronted with a long wall of frosted glass with the law firm's name etched into it.

She opened the door and led us inside and I noticed first that the room had the most beautiful dark wood paneling I had ever seen. Filling the center of the room was a large conference table, mahogany I think, and it was about the length of a school bus. There must have been forty high backed chairs encircling the table and each were as wide as Jack's rocking Strata Lounger at home. Matching porcelain vases with fresh cut flowers embellished the table, with two shallow versions on each end, and a deep one occupying the middle. At the end closest to where we stood sat a digital recorder and a court reporter machine attached to a tripod.

Our escort directed our attention to an antique oak buffet positioned against the wall. She advised that we were welcome to the items displayed atop it, which included more magazines, a variety of snacks, coffee—regular and decaf, and iced down soft drinks, juices and water. She advised that Mr. Shiras would join us shortly and excused herself. Now alone in the room, Nelda and I stood surveying the buffet. Considering our free hotel breakfast, our jangled nerves from our morning odyssey and the impending commencement of the deposition, neither of us were particularly thirsty or hungry. Nevertheless, I placed two Diet Cokes in my purse figuring that it would save us a Dairy Queen stop on the way home.

"Look," Nelda said pointing to the buffet, "they have coasters with the name of their firm burned into them."

"I'll be dog," I said, lifting one and examining it front and back.

"Are they real leather?"

"I think so," I said, then glanced at the wall above the buffet. Hanging there was a wide, impressive, gold-framed photo portrait depicting several men and one woman. All were in business suits and they posed side by side on the steps of a courthouse. "They must be some of the big wigs in the firm."

"I bet you're right," Nelda said.

"Look at that dude there," I said pointing to one of the smartly-dressed men. He sported more of a smirk than a smile and had kinky white hair, matching eyebrows and dark beady eyes.

"He looks like a buzzard," Nelda said, and I grinned.

We took a seat at the table and waited with an awkward silence until a well-dressed lady entered and greeted us. She introduced herself as Jenny Day and explained that she would be our court reporter. She seemed very nice and we introduced ourselves to her, and I added, "I'm sorry we were late—we had some difficulties getting here."

"No worries, I get paid by the hour," Jenny said smiling.

"Good for you," I said with a chuckle, "but at least we beat Mr. Shiras here."

Jenny's cheerful expression waned, and she said, "Um ... you should know that he has popped in here twice looking for y'all."

We chatted with Jenny until the conference room door opened and I looked up to see none other than the *buzzard* from the framed portrait entering. It was Alexander Shiras and Iredell was right about his *snazzy* appearance. He walked to the table on shiny black wingtips and was clad in a gray suit. His jacket pocket displayed a silky red and white handkerchief that matched his perfectly knotted necktie.

"You're late," he said, as he placed his briefcase on the table, unsnapped the two latches and opened it.

"Sorry, but we had some travel issues," I said.

"That happens, but all the more reason to budget time for such contingencies, and a call sure would have been nice," he added.

We watched as he removed his suit jacket revealing his snow-white starched shirt with monogrammed French cuffs, gold cufflinks and a gold Rolex adorned his left wrist. He laid the jacket neatly on the back of the adjacent chair, extended his right hand to me, and said, "Ms. Barbour?"

"Who?" I asked in a momentary lapse.

"You are Louise Barbour, aren't you?"

"Oh—yes of course," I said, taking his hand and noting his perfectly manicured nails and the effeteness of his grip, one which was more fingers and less palm.

I released his hand, and said, "This is my client, Nelda Fay Blatchford."

"Good to know you," Shiras said, and added in a perfunctory manner, "I speak for me and my client in saying we are sorry for your loss."

"I appreciate that," Nelda said meekly.

With the introductions out of the way, it was time to get down to business. As Jenny had Nelda swear to tell the truth I unfolded my objection list and had it resting on my lap.

Shiras led off with, "State your name for the record."

"Objection," I said.

Shiras asked, "What's the nature of your objection?"

"Um ... you haven't laid a foundation for that question and it assumes facts not in evidence."

"Are you saying I have to establish that she has a name before I can ask her what it is?"

"I just want you to follow the rules and keep it clean, Mr. Shiras."

"Keep it clean?"

"Do what you have to, but I am going to make my objections."

"Whatever," he said dismissively, then addressed Nelda. "Ma'am, do you have a name?"

"As a matter of fact, I do."

"Huh, what a surprise," he smirked. "Would you mind telling me what it is?"

"Objection, asked and answered."

"I asked it all right, but you didn't let her answer," Shiras said. "Plus you told me her name just before we got started."

"Then you're being ... uh ... you're being ... hang on," I said peeking down at my list, "repetitive and harassing."

Shiras glared at me. "Ms. Barbour ... I *have* to identify the witness."

"Why? You just said you know who she is."

"It's for the record—she has to be identified for the court reporter."

"Jenny knows her name, she was introduced to Nelda before you came in," I said, then turned to Nelda. "Go ahead and tell your name ... *again* ... if it makes him happy."

"I am Nelda Fay Blatchford."

"Good—I just wanted to make sure it had not changed since three minutes ago," Shiras said. "Where do you live Ms. Blatchford?"

"Objection."

"What's the matter now?"

"It assumes facts not in evidence," I said.

"Is it that I haven't established she is alive, so I can't ask her where she lives?"

"Well ... um ... that's part of it, but my other objection is that it's an invasion of privacy and ... uh ... it violates her due process."

"Are you taking the position that I am not allowed to ask for her street address?"

"Why would you? Are you planning on visiting her?"

"No, but I have to—"

"That's good, considering she's *my* client and is a widow to boot."

"Forget about it, I'll move on," he sighed. "You have two sons, right?"

"Objection."

Shiras hung his head. "I give—what is it this time?"

"You're leading the witness."

"She's not my witness," he said, his voice rising an octave or two. "She's *your* witness and since we are on the opposite side of the case the rules allow me to treat her as a *hostile witness.*"

"I'm not the one who is hostile, sir," Nelda said.

Shiras raised his hands and said, "Hang on now, let me rephrase my question. Do you have any children?"

"Why yes I do. I have two grown boys," Nelda said proudly.

"Good, I think we're making progress," Shiras said. "Now, you have been married, right?"

"Objection," I barked. "I don't know how they do things here in the big city, but in Limestone County people walk down the aisle and *then* start a family—so of course she has been married. Plus, haven't you read your own file? We are all here because of her deceased husband for goodness sake."

"Let me ask it this way," Shiras said pulling our discovery responses from his briefcase and thumbing through them. "Okay—here it is. Ms. Blatchford, I understand from your sworn interrogatory responses that you married your husband Clifford on the twenty-third of March in nineteen sixty-nine."

"That is correct," Nelda said.

"When was the first of your two sons born?"

Nelda hesitated, turned to me, and I urged, "Go ahead, I have no objection to that one."

She uttered sheepishly, "October."

"Of what year?"

Nelda glanced to me anxiously. "Do I really have to answer that?" I again consulted my objection list, and finding nothing to rely on, I nodded. "That uh ... that um ... was also in nineteen sixty-nine."

"Nelda Fay," I yelped.

Shiras smirked, and said, "Hmm, I guess in Limestone County you just need to be married by the time the child arrives."

"Was Clete a preemie?" I asked.

"No, in fact, he was a week and a half late and weighed over nine pounds—it was like giving birth to a bowling ball."

"Does Clete know?"

"No, he's never been worth a hoot at math."

Shiras resumed by questioning Nelda about her relationship with Cliff and their life together. He asked about Cliff's health and that of his parents and siblings, and the incidence of cancer in his family. He covered Cliff's smoking history, every one of his injuries, and each disease for which he had been treated.

He then turned to Cliff's work history, culminating in his time at the foundry. Since Nelda had visited the plant only on rare occasions to bring Cliff his lunch box when he left home without it, she admitted that she had no firsthand knowledge of what he did there.

Shiras took Nelda through the onset of Cliff's illness, the diagnosis, his decline in his health and ultimate death. Discussing this upset her greatly, but Shiras covered the topics with no more emotion than one would if asking her to describe what she had for breakfast.

"What do you want out of this lawsuit, Ms. Blatchford?" Shiras inquired, as he closed his file and returned it to his briefcase.

"Justice ... I guess."

"What's justice to you—a whole bunch of money?"

"Not necessarily, but I do believe that people ought to be held responsible for what they have done. My husband is dead only because day in and day out for decades he did everything the foundry told him to do. That work killed him Mr. Shiras and I want that known, and I want the foundry to be held accountable."

"Objection, nonresponsive," Shiras said. "That's all well and good ma'am, but your lawyer did not sue for so-called *accountability* she sued for money, right?"

"How else does the law make companies accountable?" I intervened.

"Oh, there's plenty of ways. There are agencies such as OSHA, the EPA, and the National Labor Relations Board, but no, you chose the courthouse, now didn't you Ms. Barbour?"

"No," Nelda said. "I chose it, and we are going to win this case, Mr. Shiras."

He grinned, and said, "We will see about that—pass the witness."

We all began packing our belongings and once Shiras snapped his briefcase shut, he offered to validate our parking. Wanting to make a statement, even if it cost me twenty-four bucks, I said, "I can handle my own parking fees—thank you very much." Then, in a further act of defiance, I reached into my purse, removed both Diet Cokes and set them on the table. "And you can keep these too."

We bid Jenny goodbye, exited the conference room, and backtracked to the elevator foyer. Though unnerved by it, Nelda braved the two elevator trips to the ground floor. We walked out the front door of the building and across the street, and to the entrance of the parking garage. As agreed, Nelda waited by the garage cashier, while I, in turn, rode the elevator back to the twelfth floor.

When I reached my car I backed cautiously out of the parking spot and spiraled my way slowly downward until I reached the bottom floor. I paid the ridiculous parking fee, then spotted Nelda biding her time on the sidewalk to my left. When the wooden gate rose I pulled forward, stopped to let Nelda in, and as a parting gift the car behind us honked.

I followed the signs out of downtown and toward Interstate 45. Once the Dallas skyline was shrinking in my rearview mirror, I glanced to the passenger seat and could tell Nelda was exhausted. With the exception of a coke and potty break at the Dairy Queen in Ennis, Nelda slept all the way home.

7
CHAPTER

The following morning Lupe brought me the mail that she had already opened and stamped and as I sifted through the stack I happened upon a letter from the McLennan County District Clerk. I read it and learned the court had issued a scheduling order providing a trial date, a list of deadlines to be met in advance of the trial, and an offer to refer the case to mediation. The latter was exactly what I wanted to see, but I would soon learn that Mr. Shiras did not share my enthusiasm for mediating. He fired off a written response informing the court that he and his client were of the opinion that doing so would be, and I quote, *not fruitful.*

I decided to write a letter of my own, one favoring mediation, and sent it to the court with a copy to my opponent. Mr. Shiras's protests notwithstanding the judge sent an order demanding that all parties attend a mediation and included a roster of McLennan County area mediators.

I reviewed the list and decided to make my selection according to price and commenced calling the various offices. I quickly learned that there were several factors involved in the cost, the first being the length of the mediation with most offering full and half-day options. From there the amount was dependent upon the experience of the mediator—including whether or not they were a former judge and the value of the case which some referred to as *the amount in controversy.*

I was floored by the results considering that most ranged from a $1,000 to $1,500 per party for a full day to as much as $800 to $1,200 for a half day. In the end, I settled on attorney Bernard Van Devanter in the small town of Lorena. He was a bargain at $300 per party for a half day and for Nelda's peace of mind I confirmed that there would be no elevators involved. I ran the selection by Shiras and considering he did not want to mediate in the first place, he agreed to the choice and a date was set.

Over the years I had accompanied Louise on a handful of mediations, usually when the client requested my attendance or when Louise knew so little about the case facts that she needed me there. Consequently, I had some familiarity with the process, including that each side got a chance to make their case and the mediator, who is neutral, would work both sides to common ground and toward settlement. However, my most enduring memory of the process was the abundance of free food and beverages offered for the taking to all participants. I began rehearsing my spiel hoping that with a good presentation, coupled with the influence of the mediator, we just might put Nelda's case to bed once and for all.

When the day arrived I met Nelda at her home and drove us out of Mexia and into McLennan County with Ronnie Milsap's greatest hits playing in the background. We traveled directly to the small town of Lorena situated eighteen miles south of Waco, and I turned left on to the street for the mediator's office. I drove slowly while glancing to each side of the road in search of his building, but all I saw were houses. When I reached a dead-end I pulled into a driveway and turned my car around, then eased back down the street. As I neared the road we had turned off of without spotting an office I had Nelda hand me the letter I received from Mr. Van Devanter. I stopped the car and dialed the number on the letterhead and when a lady answered, I recognized her voice as the person I spoke to when booking the mediation.

"Good morning ma'am, we are mediating there this morning and I—"

"You must be Ms. Barbour," she said, in her deep East Texas accent.

"Yes ma'am, that's me all right," I said, and Nelda chuckled under her breath.

"We have you right here on the calendar dear," she said, cheerfully.

"That's good to know, but we're on your street … I think … but all I see are houses."

"That's because we're in a house," the woman said. "The address is twenty-four and it's a yellow wooden one story with green trim."

"I think I see it," I said glancing past Nelda and through the passenger side window, "is there a black Lincoln Towne car parked in the driveway?"

"Yes, ma'am that's …um … let's see here," she said and I heard her rustling through some papers, "that's Mr. Shiras's rent-a-car."

I thanked her and pulled into the driveway and parked behind Shiras' elegant rental. I grabbed my purse and tote bag and walked with Nelda along a sidewalk and to a set of concrete steps leading us up to a wood planked covered porch. It was there where we encountered a sign next to the front door reading:

LAW OFFICE OF BERNARD VAN DEVANTER, ESQUIRE
Howdy, y'all come on in!

I turned the brass doorknob and the rusty hinges screeched as I eased it open. Once inside I closed the door behind us and saw a rather large bleached blonde sitting at a small desk playing solitaire—not the computer game—but rather with a deck of cards.

"You must be Ms. Barbour?" she twanged while extending her hand toward Nelda.

"No … uh … that would be me," I said taking her hand. "This here is my client, Nelda Fay Blatchford."

"I see," she said, and addressed Nelda, "I saw the name and thought it was French-Creole and figured with you being a … uh … well never mind that. It's a pleasure meeting y'all, and I'm Sandra Van Devanter, Bernie's wife, and you can call me Sandy."

"Good to meet you, too," I said, "are you from here in Lorena?"

"No, ma'am. We've been in this office for the last seven years, but I'm originally from Marshall."

I grinned and said, "I thought so, I have kinfolk in Longview."

"Oh, okay," she said. "Now—while y'all are here we want you to make yourselves at home, but I need you to know upfront that we do things a little different than other mediations you may have gone to," she said, and swiveled her rolling desk chair around and directed us to the kitchen area across the room. "As you can see, we have goodies laid out for y'all, like powdered do-nuts, potato chips, Twinkies, pork rinds, pretzels, peanut butter and crackers, cheese and crackers and moon pies. In the fridge you'll find, bottled water, canned fizzy waters, soda pop, Yoo-hoos, and a pitcher of grape Kool-Aid. You'll also find some beer in there, but that's Bernie's private stock."

"This is precisely what I am used to, so what's the difference here?" I said.

"We charge for it all," she said blushing.

"Oh … so you sell the beverages and snacks?"

"Yes ma'am and here's a price list," she said handing us each a yellow sheet of paper with a list of items and their corresponding cost. "We hate to do it, but we charge so little for mediatin' that we can't afford to … you know … just give snacks away. Now, not included on that list are my breakfast tacos which I make to order for a dollar a pop."

"'Mornin' ladies," a voice boomed and a man emerged from an adjacent room and approached us. It was Bernard Van Devanter and he was a cheerful, curly-headed man, wearing a powder blue polyester blazer, navy slacks, and eel skin cowboy boots. Dangling below his chin was a bolo tie cinched at the top by a silver ring featuring a large, inset, piece of turquoise.

After the introductions, he turned to Nelda. "Ms. Blatchford, I read the stuff y'all sent and I want to say up front that I'm as sorry as I can be for your loss."

"Thank you, Mr. Van Devanter."

"Please, you two call me Bernie, alright?" We nodded and he added. "Now, we're goin' to start with brief openin' session. Once we're done with that we will caucus in separate rooms and negotiate this thing to conclusion—any questions?"

I looked to Nelda and she shook her head, and I said, "I think we're ready to get started."

"Great," he said loudly, and slapped his hands together and rubbed them vigorously. "Come along with me and we'll get this show on the road."

We followed Bernie toward the space that had he just emerged from and when we entered I noticed that the room served as a library and conference room. All walls were lined with bookcases, except for the presence of two windows on the outer wall which provided most of the room's ambient light. Mr. Shiras was seated at the oak conference table atop which sat a can of Pledge furniture polish and boxes of Kleenex were placed on each end. Plastic drink coasters dotted the table's shiny surface and the centerpiece was a wicker basket of artificial daisies.

While I found the surroundings quaint and homey, in contrast, Shiras sat looking completely out of place in his finely tailored pinstriped suit. On the table in front of him sat sections of the *Dallas Morning News* and next to that was a wadded piece of paper that I knew from the color was Sandy's snack price list. He was clearly slumming in his mind and was not at all happy about being there. We exchanged awkward greetings, then Mr. Van Devanter shut the double doors and asked us to be seated.

Nelda and I took chairs at the opposite end of the table from Shiras and Mr. Van Devanter took a seat near the midpoint. Bernie kicked off the proceedings saying, "You two veteran lawyers know the drill, and Ms. Barbour I am sure you've filled your client in on what we're going to do here today. Considering that and the fact this is only a half day mediation, I think we should dispense with the boilerplate mediator mumbo jumbo and get down to the brass tacks—agreed?" We all nodded. "Good, now I recognize that this is an important case for each side and I am sure that both parties have come here in good faith to try to resolve their respective differences, right?"

"We certainly have," I said and glanced over to Shiras who sat silent and stoic.

"What says you, Alex?" Van Devanter prompted.

"I guess it depends on how you define *good faith*. As we discussed before these women arrived, we resisted mediation. They unilaterally forced the issue so here we are. I was going to save this for my opening statement, but my client and I believe this case has no merit. Mr. Waite Morrison, the CEO and third generation President of this family owned business, takes umbrage at the allegations lodged in this suit. We have every expectation that we will prevail at trial, and do so in such a convincing way that the impeccable Morrison family reputation will be fully vindicated. That said, I am here as ordered by the court and will participate," Shiras concluded, then raised the business section of his newspaper and read it.

"He kind of went out of turn Ms. Barbour, but do you have an opening statement you'd like to make?" Bernie asked.

"I don't guess," I said, abandoning all my preparation.

"Ms. Blatchford, do you have anything to say about your case?"

"I don't suppose, but I do have a question if that's allowed," Nelda said putting me on the edge of my seat.

"Certainly—fire away," Bernie said.

Nelda leaned forward in her chair, and said, "Why isn't Mr. Morrison here?"

"Good question—what about that?" Van Devanter said, turning to Shiras.

Shiras' face emerged from the stock quotes and his dark beady eyes narrowed. "I am here on Mr. Morrison's behalf."

"At the risk of provoking the man that stands between us and a settlement, Nelda has a point," I said. "The court's order required *all* parties to be present."

Shiras smirked, folded his newspaper and addressed only the mediator, "We saw no reason to take Mr. Morrison away from running his business for the likes of this."

"So, he's too busy?" I asked.

"Yes," Shiras said tersely.

I turned to Mr. Van Devanter for his reaction, but he punted by asking, "Anything else folks?" Receiving no response he said, "All right, Alex why don't you get Sandy to show you to your room, and I'll meet with the ladies in here first."

"Fine," Shiras said, rising from the table. He snatched up his newspaper sections, tossed the price list into the garbage can and abruptly closed the doors behind him as he exited.

Mr. Van Devanter moved down to our end of the table and tossed Shiras' business card on it. "Hell … I didn't need a card from him to know he was a Dallas lawyer."

"He's a rascal," Nelda said.

"I had another term in mind, one consistent with his initials," Bernie said wryly, "but look on the bright side, since he's from Dallas you won't get a taste of the ol' home cookin'."

"Does our judge favor local lawyers?" I asked.

"Let me see which one you drew," he said opening his file. "Oh, you're in Judge Cushing's court, and he's a fair, but no-nonsense jurist. He has some members of the local bar he is partial to, including me I'm glad to say, but odds are he won't cotton to the likes of Mr. Shiras."

"I hope you're right," I said.

"As you know Ms. Barbour, what happens in mediation is confidential. Even the judge himself can't compel me to disclose what we discuss here, but I am damn sure going to make Judge Cushing is aware that the CEO didn't bother to show."

"Thank you, Bernie," I said.

"You're very welcome, but the problem we have here is the other side doesn't seem to think a lot of your case."

"Do you think he means it," I asked.

"He could be bluffing in order to demoralize y'all, and lower expectations, but we won't know what they *really* think until y'all make a demand."

Nelda spoke first. "I would like to demand that he stop being so ugly to us."

"I understand, but you can't change the spots on a Dallas leopard," Van Devanter chuckled, "but I was referring to a *settlement* demand. What do y'all put as the value for this case? I read up on the verdict stats and the bar journals and know that these meso … mesothelio— whatever you call it cases, can fetch large sums in settlement. Some have resulted in staggering verdicts, including a few here in Texas."

"Frankly, you seem to know more about the value than I do,"

I said, then confessed, "you see, this is the first case like this I have handled."

"Oh ... I see ... well, that may be part of the problem," Bernie said somberly. He began flicking Shiras' business card with his fingers, causing it to spin on the polished tabletop. "I'm sure you're a fine lawyer in your own right, but these are hyper-technical cases and take a long time to master. This is Shiras' specialty and he knows well that preparing a case like this will be a real challenge for you."

"What do you recommend we do?" I said.

"You still have a death case, one involving a sixty-eight-year-old man. Hell, I can remember a time when I thought that was old," Van Devanter said shaking his head. "As I see it, you've got nothing to lose by making a high settlement demand and see what happens."

"What about his comment about winning the case?" Nelda said.

"Forget all of his huffin' and puffin'," Bernie said. "I say make the hefty demand and let's see what he does."

"My concern is that by doing that it just might run him off," I said. "You see Bernie, we *really* want to settle this case today. We don't want to give it away mind you, but I have always believed that pigs get fat and hogs get slaughtered."

"I understand, do you want me to leave you two alone to talk it over?"

"Nelda?" I said.

"I don't see a need to discuss it alone unless you do."

"I'm fine with it," I said, and pondered for a moment. "What about opening with ... um ... say five hundred thousand?"

Van Devanter shook his head, and said, "No, no, no, that's way too—"

"I'm sorry," I interjected, "how about two hundred and fifty thousand?"

"No, you're way too low with both of those figures. That range might be in the neighborhood of a suitable settlement number, but I'd start higher—a lot higher in fact."

"What do you suggest?"

"First off, I favor uneven numbers in negotiations—it makes them seem more ... let's say ... calculated," he said as he stared up to the ceiling and cogitated. Moments later, he lowered his head and said, "Let's do two point eight five million."

"Dollars?" Nelda gasped, and I sat with my mouth agape.

"Yes," Bernie said, but quickly added, "I ain't sayin' the case is worth that or that they would pay even a fraction of it, but it gets the ball rolling so to speak—so what do you say?"

I turned to Nelda, she nodded, and I said, "Let's do it."

Bernie excused himself and left the conference room to meet with Shiras leaving us to only to sit, wonder and hope. It wasn't long though until he returned, and with one glimpse at his expression, I knew he arrived with no good news.

"Just know that I do have an offer for y'all, but before we get to that, I would like to describe my conversation with Shiras," he said almost apologetically, as he dropped his notepad on the table and flopped down in his chair.

I said, "Isn't that confidential?"

"It is, but Alex specifically authorized me to tell you part of our conversation. The first thing I asked him was, *why all the bravado* and his response was akin to what he said in here. I asked why he felt that way and if it involved an ironclad defense, like a statute of repose or limitations or something along those lines. Shiras said it was nothing like that, but he did say he has a couple of *aces in the hole* that just might blow up the case."

"I don't suppose he authorized you to reveal spots on those aces, did he?" I asked.

"One of 'em is locked up tighter than Fort Knox," Van Devanter said.

"And the other?" I asked anxiously.

"Part of the reason for their confidence is something that ... well uh ... perhaps you and I should discuss alone," Bernie said, staring straight at me.

I looked at Nelda and back to Bernie, and said, "Nelda is not just my client, she's also my good friend—you can say whatever it is in front of both of us."

"If you insist," Bernie sighed. "He says the case ain't worked up right, and the deadlines to fix these problems have already passed or it's rapidly approaching. Shiras doesn't believe you're up to the task of handling a case like this."

"Don't believe it, Gertie," Nelda blurted, then placed her hand over her mouth.

"Gertie?" Van Devanter said.

"Yes ... uh ... I just," Nelda stammered.

"It's just a nickname," I said.

"That's right," Nelda said, "it is Gertie with a D—like the steel girders used on skyscrapers—her spine is every bit as strong as one of those beams."

"That's interesting, and I like it very much," Bernie said, smiling.

I marveled at Nelda's resourcefulness, and asked, "So what was Shiras' response to our demand?"

"I suppose y'all can blame me for that, but he actually laughed out loud at it."

"You did mention that he had an offer, though," I reminded.

He nodded and flipped through his notepad until he reached a page with his handwriting on it. "Shiras said he was going to *cut to the chase*. He explained that the foundry's insurance company asked him to estimate the cost of defending the case from now through the end of a trial. Alex estimates that the future attorney's fees, expert costs and other out of pocket expenses to be thirty-six thousand six hundred and seventy-seven dollars, and that's the offer."

"I guess he likes uneven numbers too," I sighed, and turned to Nelda, "so what do you think?"

"That's not a lot, but it's a good start, right?" Nelda said hopefully.

Van Devanter shook his head. "It's a start and a finish. I should have explained this up front, but that offer is take it or leave it."

"Should we lower the demand significantly, and see what he does? I mean he must realize that figure won't get it settled," I said.

"Maybe or maybe not, but I don't think he cares. If you take it, he's a hero to his client and the insurance company. If it doesn't settle, a large portion of that money ends up in guess whose pocket?"

"Now, I think we should talk alone," I said.

"Sure thing, but y'all hang on for a moment," Van Devanter said, and dashed out of the conference room. He quickly returned with two cans of diet coke clutched each hand, placed them on coasters, and said, "These are on the house ladies—y'all take your time."

He left the room, and Nelda said, "I'm sorry Mr. Shiras said those things about you—it's not true."

"Thanks, dear, but I'm afraid it is. I am not a lawyer and apparently, I don't play one very convincingly."

"Nonsense. I think you've done a *great* job, and I meant what I said about you having a strong spine."

"How did you come up with the *steel girder* thing?" I said with amusement.

Nelda laughed. "It was my slip up, and I felt obliged to make it right, and that was the first thing that popped into my head."

"Very imaginative, especially under pressure," I said popping the top on my complimentary soft drink.

"It may be imaginative, but it's also the truth. Gertie, I asked you to do this for me because I have the utmost faith in you."

"Do you still have faith after all of this?"

"Now more than ever," Nelda said without hesitation.

"I thought the Kleenex boxes were for the clients," I said, retrieving tissue. As I dabbed tears, I asked, "What do you want to do about their offer?"

"The reason I came to Louise in the first place was because I wanted something done about my Clifford. Money was certainly a factor, but I would have been satisfied with an apology. I just wanted them to own up to what they did to my husband, and to make sure they don't let it happen to anyone else. I didn't know what to expect coming over here today, and don't know what's fair or not, but I will tell you one thing that infuriates me to no end," Nelda said, and her jaw clenched. "You and I took the time to come all the way over here to settle my poor husband's case and that big shot, Waite Morrison, is too busy to even show up?"

"I don't blame you. It ticks me off too, and I am glad Bernie agrees," I said. "But, what do you want to do about their offer?"

"It's nothing to sneeze at and I could certainly use my share of it. At the same time it's not an amount that will change the lives of anyone involved, is it?"

"That's true," I said. "Once the expenses come out and the fees are deducted, your share would be somewhere between twenty and twenty-five thousand."

"That's not enough to buy a decent used car these days," she lamented. "A part of me wants to call his bluff, walk out of here and see if they come up with more money down the road. At the same time I realize you are the one putting in your time and risking your own personal savings. It's easy for me to march us on to war and have you fight to the last drop of *your* blood."

"The expenses haven't been too bad—at least so far."

"Oh—how does that three hundred dollar coke taste?" Nelda asked.

"It's only one fifty since we got two," I said with a chuckle, then added in a serious tone. "You mentioned calling his bluff, but you do know that if we turn this down they may never offer it, or anything like it again?"

"I realize that, but if you work it up and prove to them that you are capable of doing this like I know you are, who knows maybe they will up the offer—perhaps by a lot."

"I am truly humbled by the vote of confidence, but if we try this and it doesn't work out, you know we'll have to dismiss the case and walk away?"

"Why?"

"Why what?" I asked.

"Why dismiss it?" she said, flashing a wry grin.

I stared at her suspiciously, and said, "What are you getting at, Nelda Fay?"

"Why not finish working it up and if it does not cause them to cough up more money, then let's take it all the way?"

"To trial?" I asked, and she nodded. I stared at her with raised eyebrows searching for signs that she was jesting, but she sat steadfast. "You're serious aren't you?"

"Serious as the business end of a shotgun," she said. "But since it is your money at risk, I regard this as much your call as it is mine. I would be at peace if you accept the offer, but if you want to go all the way, I am with you."

"You said repeatedly you did not want a trial."

"True, but I am exercising my prerogative as a woman," she said. "If you are willing to do it, I'm fine with it—come what may—regardless of the outcome."

"Even if we end up with nothing?" I asked, and she nodded. "Nelda, my impersonation of a lawyer ends at the courthouse steps. I know very little about what goes on in a trial and have never even sat on a jury."

"You can figure all that out, can't you?"

"How? By watching Matlock re-runs?" I asked.

"Okay, then let's take it to the courthouse steps and see what happens," she said.

I said, "I have always heard that a lot of cases settle on those steps."

"Well there you have it," Nelda said. "Let's take it that far and see what they do."

I pondered for a moment, took a deep breath, and said, "This isn't a decision I can make on my own." I grabbed my cell phone and called Jack. I explained the events of the morning, answered all of his questions, then sat my phone on the table. "We are willing to push this to the brink if you are."

"I am," she said resolutely. "Let's tell the mediator that the *steel girder* will meet Mr. *too damn busy* Morrison at the courthouse!" she said, and we rose and hugged each other.

I poked my head out of the library door and saw Bernie helping his bride with the hand of solitaire from over her shoulder. I summoned him back into our room and informed him of our decision.

"Alex didn't give y'all much choice, now did he?" Bernie said.

"No—not really," I said, as I counted out the cash for the mediation.

"Just make it two hundred," he offered. "Y'all didn't even use half of your time."

"No sir," I said, "you blocked out the time and I owe it."

"Have it your way, just settle up with Sandy and she'll give you a receipt," he said, bid us farewell and departed to deliver the news to Shiras.

We tossed our empty drink cans into the trash, grabbed our belongings, walked out of the conference room, and over to Sandy's desk. I handed her the stack of twenties and she shoved the playing cards aside and placed a small lockbox on her desk. She counted the money, placed the bills inside the box, closed the lid and spun the combination dials.

"Ladies, my flour tortillas are gonna go spoil if I don't use them," she said. "Please let me make y'all a couple of breakfast tacos on the house. I don't aim to brag, but the people rave about them and I can wrap them up for you to take on the road."

"That's very kind of you, and I certainly wouldn't mind having one," I said turning to Nelda.

"Same here, I haven't had a thing since last night."

"Fine, it'll just take five to ten minutes—salsa and jalapenos?"

"Yes," we said simultaneously.

Sandy smiled, paced over to the kitchen and we waited patiently at her desk as she placed a skillet on the stove and lit the fire. As she began work on our tacos, we heard a door open from down the hall, followed by rapid footsteps, and I overheard Shiras say, "If I leave now, I can turn in my rental and have a chance at the earlier flight."

"We have your check so you're free to go," Bernie said, "have safe trip back."

The two men emerged from the hallway and Shiras slowed his determined gait only to glare at me with his *who farted* expression as he passed. He flung open the front door, exited and slammed it behind him.

"You do remember your car is blocking him, don't you?" Nelda whispered.

"Yes."

"Aren't you going to do something?"

"Eventually, but aren't we waiting for our tacos?" I said, with a wink and Nelda placed her hand over her mouth.

It was not long until we heard the sound of wing-tipped dress shoes romping on the wood-planked porch. The door flew open and Shiras poked his head through the opening, and said, "You have me blocked in."

"Oh … I do?" I said coyly.

"Yes," he snapped and checked his Rolex.

"Just bear with us, we are waiting on breakfast tacos," I said. Shiras commenced tapping the sole of his right shoe on the floorboards, Sandy was busy scrambling eggs, and Bernie stood by the conference room door watching on with amusement.

Moments later, Shiras sighed and stared past us and into the kitchen. "How much longer is it going to be?"

"Three or four minutes hon, give or take," Sandy said, "since I have everything out do you want one too—they're free?"

"I don't have time for that," Shiras said, pointing urgently to his watch and then addressed me, "Can you just move the car, while the *mediation firm* prepares your breakfast?"

"Sure, I would be glad to, but first let me find my car keys," I said, and I plunged my hand into my faux Gucci purse. I commenced groping around in it, though I knew well that my keyring was in my tote bag. "Be patient, more things have been lost in here than in the Bermuda Triangle."

"Just hurry, will you?" Shiras demanded.

While I continued my fruitless rummaging, Ms. Van Devanter handed Nelda the bag containing the tacos, and I asked, "Sandy, reckon there's a locksmith nearby?"

"I can check the phone book if you like," she offered.

"Locksmith? You got to be kidding me," Shiras said through gritted teeth, and Nelda could hardly contain herself.

Figuring I had played it out long enough, I said, "Nix the locksmith—I bet the keys are in my tote bag," I said and redirected my search.

Shiras again glanced at his watch. "Might as well take your time now, I can't make the—"

"Here they are!" I said lifting the keys from my purse and proudly displayed them.

We bid farewell to the Van Devanter's and Nelda and I walked together out of the office and to my car. We loaded our things and I swapped out the Milsap CD for a Haggard and started my car. I glanced up through my windshield and saw Shiras standing at the driver's side door of his Towne Car. He stared straight into my eyes, then simply shook his head as I eased back down the driveway.

The tacos lived up to their billing, and once back in Mexia, I dropped Nelda off and drove straight home. When I entered our home, I yelled, "Jack, I'm back from the mediation."

"Are we rich?" he responded from the back of the house.

"Yes, but not in a monetary way," I said, and followed the sound of his voice into the hallway.

"So you turned down the money and they didn't offer any more?"

"I'm afraid so—where are you?" I said.

"Soakin' in the tub."

I walked through the bathroom door and saw him laid back in the bath water with his eyes covered by a wash rag.

"Are you all right?" I asked.

"No," he said and removed the rag from his face. He struggled to sit up, then opened his eyes and blinked several times to adjust to the glare of the bathroom lights.

"Is it your legs?"

"Yes, they're really sensitive to the touch today, and my feet are also hurting."

I pulled my vanity stool next to the tub and took a seat. I grabbed his washrag and rubbed his back and neck with it. "Did you take your medicine?"

"I did and took another in about half the time I'm supposed to."

"Is it working?"

"A little—I think, but won't know for sure until I stand. Would you pull the stopper and help me out of here?"

"Of course," I said and reached into the soapy water and felt around until I found the stopper chain and tugged on it. As the water gurgled and whirl pooled down the drain, I helped Jack to his feet and immediately noticed how wobbly he was. I held his right arm as he eased his right leg over the tub wall and down to our furry powder blue bathmat. He followed with his left foot and I grabbed a towel and began drying him off. I started with his hair, then applied the towel to his back and down to his calves before handing it off to him. He leaned against the vanity and continued drying himself, and asked, "So Nelda's willing to take the dice roll, huh?"

"She is, and I hate that you called it a dice roll, but I guess that's what it amounts to," I said, and handed him his underwear, and held his arm while he slipped them on.

"How do you rate the odds?"

"Another gambling reference?" I said playfully.

"Sorry dear, but how do you feel about all of this?"

"I was enthused at the mediation, but not so much now. I'm scared Jack, I really am. I had a chance to bow out of this gracefully, get our expenses reimbursed and actually make a few bucks for everyone, and I passed on it."

"Do you reckon Dot and Lupe will be upset you turned it down?"

"I don't think so. Since you and I are funding the case, they told me to do whatever I thought best—are *you* upset that we didn't take the settlement?"

"No, it wasn't a fair offer," he said. "They take a man's life and then want to buy it for what amounts to a year's salary?"

"That's what Nelda and I thought, but it's a big risk to us."

"We knew that going in. Just go forward and make 'em feel the heat. I bet they'll eventually come around."

"I hope so."

8
CHAPTER

Now permanently out of our office and committed to working up the case, I transitioned our operation into our home. At our makeshift law firm, Dot worked at the card table and I set up shop at the breakfast table. With the permission of her pastor Dot was now doing our copying at her church, and she performed her legal research at the law library at courthouse in Groesbeck. When not working at our church, Lupe came to the house and kept the coffee flowing and performed case related tasks as needed. Our P.O. Box was established and Shiras was notified in writing to send future communications to it.

The jumping off point for preparedness was complying with all of the court's upcoming deadlines and one of those was providing our final expert witness list. I followed Iredell's advice and included every doctor, nurse, and Tom, Dick and Harry that saw Clifford from Mexia, all the way to Temple. Five days later I received Shiras' final witness list and accompanying it was a less than cordial letter demanding a date to depose our medical expert.

"Crap," I said, as I walked over to Dot's table.

"What's the matter?"

"It's Shiras, he's demanding to take the deposition of our doctor," I explained, and displayed the snarky letter to her. "Have you reached out to Doctor Strong?"

"I left a message for him, but his nurse said he was on a mission trip in El Salvador."

"Just my luck—when's he due back?"

"I'm sorry, but they didn't say."

"I really don't want to hire a litigation expert if we can avoid it. If Scotty is willing to testify, I am sure he will charge a lot less."

"I will follow up with his office," Dot said.

"Thanks, if he agrees to do it we need a deposition date from him ASAP."

The following Tuesday morning Dot came through big time. Not only did Dr. Strong agree to meet with me and give his testimony, he refused to take a dime for it—don't the Lord work in mysterious ways? We sent the defense a date to question Scotty and Shiras wasted no time in firing off a deposition notice. At the doctor's request, it was scheduled to occur at a conference room at the hospital in Temple.

When that morning arrived, I dressed for the day and dared to think that with a good showing, Shiras just might want to sweeten the settlement pot. I drove alone out of Limestone County with the soulful voice of Gene Watson playing in the background. I had always been a fan of his music, but it was not until I bought his Best of CD that I realized just how depressing his songs are. After the sultry *Love in the Hot Afternoon,* it was all downhill from there with heartbreak, betrayal, and misery. This was no atmosphere for a day like this, so I removed the CD, and as an antidote, I traded it for Ray Stevens.

I arrived at the hospital early in order to meet with Scotty beforehand. I parked and strolled through the front entrance and into the sterile environment of the multi-story building. As directed, I took the elevator to the sixth floor and was glad not to have Nelda with me on this particular venture.

When the elevator doors opened, I walked over to a nurse sitting behind a long counter. I asked her for directions and she kindly pointed the way to the conference room. When I reached it I saw that the door was ajar, knocked and eased it open. Sitting at the far end of the conference table was the handsome Scotty Strong in his blue scrubs and cap and a white lab coat with his name embroidered on it.

I reached out my hand and said, "Dr. Strong, I am Louise Barbour and it is certainly nice to meet you."

"My pleasure," he said, standing and shook my hand.

"I *really* appreciate your doing this for us—especially without charging."

"I am happy to do it," he said returning to his seat and offering me the chair next to him. "Miss Dorothy was like my second mom and Mr. Blatchford did not deserve to die the way he did."

"You are so right about that, it is just plain awful what happened to him," I said. "So are you up for this?"

"Sure, I've been deposed plenty of times."

"This is a pretty tricky fella on the other side."

"I can handle it. After all, the truth is the truth and that's all I plan to give."

"What is the truth in this case?"

"Let's start with the chart, I made you a complete copy of it," he said, handing me a thick file folder. "The truth is that asbestos exposure causes mesotheliomas. It says right in Mr. Blatchford's history that he was exposed to it on the job and that disease caused his death."

"That simple, huh?"

"It is to me," he said.

"So that you don't have to come to the courthouse, after my opponent is done with his interrogation I am going to ask you some questions of my own. When I do, I will want to start with your background and qualifications."

"I thought you would so I also brought this," he said handing me a thick set of bound papers titled *Curriculum Vitae*. "This is essentially my resume and it includes my educational background, associations I am a member of and the articles that I have published."

I perused his countless qualifications and achievements, and said, "This helps a lot, and by the way it is mighty impressive."

"Thank you very much," he said smiling, "so where did you attend law school?"

I struggled to compose an answer, and opted for, "It wasn't at a school you would be familiar with—I like to say that I am a graduate with honors from the school of hard knocks."

"I like that, life's struggles can be the best educator."

Together we leafed through the chart, and he explained, "This has all of Mr. Blatchford's medical records including the nurse's notes, lab reports, doctor's assessments and narratives, and the bills for all of his treatment from all of his healthcare providers."

Scotty was patiently answering my questions until we heard a knock, and I sprung to my feet. The door opened and in barged Shiras with his legal assistant followed by Jenny, the court reporter. Shiras passed me by without acknowledgement, placed his brief case on one of the unoccupied chairs and walked straight to Scotty.

"Alex Shiras, Baylor law school," he said shaking the doctor's hand. "I saw from my research, that you are also a Baylor grad."

Scotty explained, "I received my MD at Baylor College of Medicine in Houston, not Baylor University in Waco."

"What about undergrad?" Shiras asked.

"Sam Houston State."

"Oh … I see … well that's too bad," Shiras said, then removed his suit jacket and took a seat at the table. He thumbed through his file and reviewed his notes while Jenny set up her equipment. Once done, she swore in Dr. Strong, and Shiras commenced his questioning. He took Scotty through his background, including his education which was far beyond *the school of hard knocks*. After Shiras covered Scotty's specialty in pathology he delved into his treatment of Clifford.

"You were just one of Mr. Blatchford's doctors, right?"

"That's correct," Scotty said.

"You were not his admitting physician, were you?"

"I was not, Dr. Souter Patel was the admitting."

"You were not his attending doctor either."

"I was his pathologist."

"Right, but you yourself never performed a physical examination on Mr. Blatchford, did you?"

"Pathologists do not typically do physical exams, but I did review the slides from Mr. Blatchford's biopsy, and met with him and his wife."

"Objection, nonresponsive," Shiras said. "Doctor, please just answer my question. You were not his attending physician and you did not examine Mr. Blatchford, true?"

"I was not his admitting doctor, but I did examine his pathology."

"Admit it doctor—you did not do a physical examination on the plaintiff," Shiras pressed.

"I did not."

"Thank you," Shiras smirked. "You mentioned that you met with the Blatchford's—what was that for?"

"Dr. Patel and I broke the bad news of my findings to the couple."

"And what was that news?"

"That Mr. Blatchford had a rare form of lung cancer."

"What was his reaction?"

"I'm sure he was shocked by it, but he was fairly stoic as I recall. Ms. Blatchford on the other hand broke down sobbing."

"What did you tell them about your diagnosis?"

"That as a malignant mesothelioma, it would be very tough to treat, and it was likely caused by his occupational exposure to asbestos."

"Did you provide a prognosis?"

"Dr. Patel delivered that particular bad news," Scotty said. "He explained to them that the disease was currently incurable, and that Mr. Blatchford only had a matter of months."

"A matter of months to live?" Shiras said.

"That's right—six to nine as I recall."

"Did either of you offer any treatment modalities?" Shiras asked.

"Dr. Patel explained the chemo options and the side effects, and the patient declined."

"Patel again, huh?" Shiras said rhetorically. "Doctor Strong, it sounds to me like we should be getting his testimony instead of yours."

"That's between you lawyers, but make no mistake about it, I am *very* qualified to testify about Mr. Blatchford's assessment, diagnosis, the cause of it, and his treatment."

"We'll see about that," Shiras said. "Were any other treatments offered?"

"No, radiation would have been ineffective and we had him

assessed for an extraplueral pneumonectomy, but unfortunately he was not a candidate."

Shiras said, "For the jury's edification, the pneumonectomy is a surgery where the diseased lung and pleura are removed, correct?"

"It's a tad more complicated than that, but you captured the essence."

"Why was Mr. Blatchford not a candidate for the procedure?"

"Primarily because his mesothelioma was staged at three," Scotty explained. "He likewise had some lung function insufficiency and cardiac issues that made it too risky."

"Are you aware that Mr. Blatchford smoked cigarettes?"

"Yes, he had a remote prior history of cigarette use," Scotty said.

"That cigarette abuse could well have contributed to those insufficiencies you just mentioned."

"That's true."

"Then Mr. Blatchford's cigarette abuse contributed to his death, right?"

"Not true," the doctor said. "Cigarettes are certainly bad for you, but he ceased the habit many years before his diagnosis—decades in fact. Also, smoking does not cause mesotheliomas."

"We all breathe asbestos fibers on a daily basis, don't we?"

"Most people do, especially in urban areas," the doctor agreed.

"You are familiar with the mucociliary escalator, aren't you?"

"Sure, it's a defense mechanism where contaminants that are inhaled into the lung get caught in the sticky mucus. Then the ciliary tract brings it back up to the throat to be cleared from the body."

"Do you agree that cigarette smoking impairs the function of the ciliary escalator?" Shiras asked.

"It can."

"If a cigarette smoker had asbestos fibers in their lungs, from any source, those fibers would be more difficult to clear from the body via the escalator, true?"

"That's possible."

"So cigarette smoking increased Mr. Blatchford's risk of mesothelioma."

"No," Dr. Scotty said firmly, "only inhalation of asbestos fiber did that."

At this point I felt like a wallflower. These two men were having a conversation on a level that I could hardly comprehend. As such, I sat quietly and completely abandoned my objection list.

"Are you familiar with the term idiopathic mesotheliomas?" Shiras asked.

"I am."

"Tell us what that is?"

"It refers to mesotheliomas that occur with no known asbestos exposure. In that instance, it is often considered *spontaneous* or *idiopathic*."

Shiras asked, "Sometimes they just occur, right?"

"I believe that there are always causes, but we just don't know them all at this point."

"Mr. Blatchford's tumor could have been idiopathic, couldn't it?" Shiras pressed.

"It's possible, but not likely, considering his history of occupational exposure to asbestos."

"Didn't Mr. Blatchford have X-rays taken of his chest?"

"Yes, and an MRI as well," the doctor said.

"Were there any underlying markers of asbestos exposure on those films?"

"Like pulmonary fibrosis?" Dr. Scotty asked.

"That, or the presence of pleural plaques or calcifications?"

"No, but I do seem to recall a reference to some pleural thickening."

"I didn't see that," Shiras said, "but if there is such a reference that thickening could be caused by a wide range of things beyond asbestos inhalation, correct?"

"That's right," the doctor said.

"So the plaintiff had no underlying markers evidencing asbestos exposure."

"Other than his mesothelioma, that is true."

"Wouldn't you need those markers in order to diagnose this as an asbestos-related lung malignancy?"

"Perhaps for a person with another type of lung cancer, but not for a mesothelioma."

"You mentioned the decedent's occupational exposure to asbestos—what is your basis for that?" Shiras asked.

"I would refer you to Dr. Patel's narrative assessment, specifically, the section marked *occupational history*. It reads plainly that Mr. Blatchford was exposed to thermal insulation materials at the foundry at which he worked."

"Doctor, just how much do you know about industrial thermal insulation?"

"Enough to know that some of it contained asbestos—mostly amosite."

"You said *some* insulation contained asbestos," Shiras said, "are you likewise aware that some did not?"

"I believe that is true, at least at some point in time."

"Do you know that point?"

"Not specifically, but I assume it was in the seventies—sometime around or after the OSHA regulations took effect."

"Doctor, do you have any firsthand knowledge that the insulation the plaintiff encountered at the foundry contained asbestos?"

"I only know what is reflected in the occupational history. Mr. Blatchford said it contained asbestos and I have no reason to doubt that."

"Fine, but you don't know the veracity of plaintiff's assertion, do you?"

"No, other than him seeming to be a reliable historian and the knowledge vested in him as a trained pipefitter."

"Your only basis is that Clifford Blatchford said it was so, right?"

"That's true," the doctor conceded.

"You are not an industrial hygienist, are you?" Shiras asked.

"I am not."

"Epidemiologist?"

"Nope."

"Are you trained as a materials expert or geologist?"

"No, but I had a rock collection when I was a child," the doctor said, winking at me.

"I object to the non-responsiveness for everything after *no*, and pass the witness," Shiras said smugly, clasped his hands behind his head and leaned back in his chair.

It was now my turn and despite the doctor being a friendly witness I found myself staring anxiously at my notes while mustering the nerve to speak.

"Any questions?" Shiras intervened, impatiently.

"Excuse me?" I said.

"Are you going to question the witness?"

"Oh ... yes of course," I murmured, cleared my throat and said, "Doctor, let's start with the ... uh ... the diagnosis. What was done to arrive at it?"

"Doctor Patel performed a biopsy and removed tissue from Mr. Blatchford's right lung. The lab stained the tissue, cut frozen sections and made the slides. I examined each of them carefully and found, unfortunately, that he had a classic—textbook—epithelioid mesothelioma."

"What is the main cause of mesothelioma?"

"In North America, it is asbestos."

"Are there other causes?

"Nothing germane here," he said. "There is a mineral in Turkey that is thought to cause it. Some therapeutic radiation regimes may be a culprit, but there is nothing in Mr. Blatchford's history that would bring either of those into play."

"In your expert opinion, Clifford Blatchford's mesothelioma was caused by exposure to asbestos at the Morrison foundry."

Shiras blurted. "Objection, leading and foundation."

"Yes," was the doctor's response.

I then asked, "Did the mesothelioma cancer cause Mr. Blatchford's death?"

"Sadly, it did."

I spent the next few minutes covering the medical records and Scotty chronicled the progression of Clifford's disease. He discussed how Cliff's health failed and what was done to combat the pain and make Cliff comfortable during his final days. I then covered the bills with Scotty and as required for use in court, he testified to their *reasonableness and necessity.*

"I'm done," I said, feeling I had advanced the ball as far as I could.

"I have one follow up," Shiras said. "If this case does involve an idiopathic mesothelioma then my client, the Morrison foundry, is not at fault, true?"

The doctor explained, "I leave matters of *fault* to judges and juries."

"So do I," Shiras sneered. "Pass the witness."

With nothing further from me, the deposition concluded. When Shiras and his entourage packed up and exited the conference room, I excused myself from the doctor and followed them out into the hallway.

"Pardon me," I said.

Shiras stopped and turned in my direction. Not wanting to have this discussion in front of his assistant and Jenny, I motioned him back toward me. He seemed put out by it, but nevertheless sat his briefcase on the floor and walked toward me.

"Yes?" he said, now standing uncomfortably close.

"Don't you think we should try to settle this case?"

"We did try—don't you recall the mediation?"

"Of course I do, but I think we should—"

Shiras held up his hand and shook his head. "I made it clear to the mediator that my client's offer was *take it or leave it.*"

"Bernie told us that, but we would like to rekindle the negotiations."

"That's out of the question," Shiras said tersely.

"Come on now, be reasonable. Can't you at least contact the insurance company and ask?"

"They have made their one and only offer."

"Fine, then we accept it."

"You would need a time machine to do that."

"I don't get you," I said.

"It's off the table—you should have taken it while you had the chance."

"Look—since it was based on cost of the defense going forward you could not have spent much since then. Just deduct out what has been expended, make a new offer and I will talk to the client," I said hopefully, but he simply stared at me. "Come on, can't we try to come together?"

"Sure," he said, and a wave of relief washed over me until he added, "we are going to *come together* all right. It will be at the courthouse and I am going to win this case for my client."

Shiras abruptly turned, walked away, retrieved his briefcase and I watched on as he and the two ladies entered the elevator. I returned dejectedly to the conference room where I offered the doctor my heartfelt appreciation for all of his help.

"I was glad to do it," he said, as I gathered my belongings, "but I do have a question for you."

"Oh?"

"Yes, just one if you'll indulge me."

"By all means."

"You do realize you are dead, don't you?"

I stopped packing and slowly turned my head toward him. "Do you mean I am going to lose the case?"

"No, in fact, I think you should win the case," he said.

"Then what do you mean?"

"You are dead, as in deceased—long gone—bought the farm—*Ms. Barbour.*"

I stopped packing, and said, "How did you know?"

He smiled, and said, "I still read the Mexia Daily News online from time to time, and saw the obituary announcing your untimely passing."

"Oh ... I see, did you know Louise?" I said to the conference table.

"No, not really. Several years ago I consulted with her on a traffic accident and that's the only reason her obit caught my eye. Plus, I would know you anywhere—Miss Gertie."

"You remember me?" I asked dubiously.

"Remember you? I used to worship you," he said.

"I don't understand."

"I was just a kid when you would generously donate pies for my Boy Scout troop's spring fundraiser. Since my mom had passed on by then, and my dad was no baker, he made sure to outbid all comers each year to win those pies. It was like Christmas in April for me."

"I am very glad to hear that," I said, and provided him a rundown of what the girls and I were up to. "I am sorry for the deception—I had no idea that a man of your stature would remember the likes of me."

"No worries," he said, rising to give me a hug. "I've learned in my life and career to trust an alumnus of the school of *hard knocks* over a grad from any Ivy League university."

I fought back tears, thanked him again, and promised to bake him the pie of his choice. When I laid out my repertoire he was torn between chocolate, pecan, and mincemeat. He chose pecan, but on my drive back to Mexia I decided to bake all three.

When I arrived home that afternoon, I saw Dot working away at the card table, and I asked, "Where's Lupe?"

"She kept interrupting me for something to do, so I sent her home to make us some tamales."

"Mmm—nice call," I said.

"How did the deposition go?"

"Pretty good, I think," I said, then turned toward the living room and saw my hubby and Highsmith playing checkers there. "Jack, I thought you were working at the church."

"I was, and I'm done, so I asked Bill over until it's time to run the lines—do you mind."

"Bill is always welcome in our home."

"Thank you, ma'am," Bill said cordially.

"I am actually glad you all are here because I need to discuss something," I said, and my serious tone did not escape the three of them. "It's about Nelda's case, we are set for trial in thirty days and we may need some divine intervention."

"Any progress on settling?" Jack asked.

"No, but since the doctor's deposition went well, I was hoping that would change. When it ended I asked Shiras to revive the negotiations, but he wanted no part of that and made it clear that no further offers are forthcoming."

"Do you think he means it?" Dot said.

"I'm certain of it."

Jack grasped my hand, and said, "I know the offer at mediation was a low ball figure, but call him up and take it."

"It is withdrawn," I said and felt tears beginning to well in my eyes.

"People always say things like that in negotiations," Highsmith said. "I used to handle some of the labor disputes at the cotton mill and saw that tactic all the time. I bet a dollar to a donut hole they're just imposturing."

I shook my head. "It's definitely off the table and we have no choice but to shut the case down."

"Shut it down, as in dismissing it?" Jack said.

"I'm sorry, but I do not see any other choice. I messed this thing up big time and it's all my own damn fault," I lamented.

"Didn't you and Nelda discuss taking the case to court?"

"Fleetingly, but I explained that the girls and I could not do that. We agreed instead to work up the case to see what would happen. I made it clear that the courthouse steps was as far as I could go with it, and that's where we are."

Jack put his arm around my shoulder, and said, "Honey, why not take a few extra steps?"

I stared at him curiously. "What are you getting at?"

"I'm talking about you trying the case."

"Oh Jack, I wouldn't know the first thing about it, plus I can't go to court impersonating a dead lawyer."

Jack responded solemnly, "I think you should reconsider, but if you want to shut it down get Nelda's permission, and do it."

"It's not just Nelda, it's also Dot and Lupe too. They have worked their butts off on this case," I said, as tears began to stream down my cheeks, and I turned to see a misty-eyed Dot approaching.

She patted me on the back, and said, "Speaking just for me, I say do what you want to do. I will stand by you no matter what … including going to court."

"Thank you Dot, but court is not an option," I said.

Highsmith weighed in. "Why not take a swing at it, Gertie? You've done a great job on the case up to now, so just go on over there and finish it."

"He has a point," Dot said staring hopefully into my eyes. "This is a solid case and I believe you *can* do this,"

Jack said, "You've done all the work up and spent the money so why not take a shot? Even if you don't win it, we're no worse off money wise than throwing in the towel now,"

"He's right, and you can fulfill your dream too," Dot added.

"What dream?" Highsmith asked.

"Tell him, Gertie," Jack urged.

I dabbed my tears, and said, "As a little girl all I ever wanted was to go to school and become a lawyer. When that failed to pan out I chose the closest thing to it, but all these years later I still harbor regrets. When Nelda asked the likes of me to handle her case I naturally resisted, but the more I thought about it, I began to see it as an opportunity. With that, and being fed up with toting regrets around, I ended up taking the case."

Dot said, "Gertie has spoken of her wish to stand up for someone's rights in court ever since I have known her."

"Well there you go," Bill said. "You can help Nelda Fay and fulfill a dream at the same time."

"He's right," Jack said, "and tell them that quote from *To Kill a Mockingbird*.

"Which one—I know a several," I said.

"The one you like about fightin'."

I nodded and recited Harper Lee's words, *Real courage is when you know you're licked before you begin, but you begin anyway and see it through no matter what. You rarely win, but sometimes you do.*

"That's wonderful, except for that getting *licked* part," Dot said, "but we're not going to let that happen, now are we?"

"Thanks, everyone, but this is foolishness," I said, but three sets of determined eyes descended on me. "Jack, do you really think I can do this?"

"I most certainly do. You might not know all of the technical ins and outs of a trial, but you know enough. You also have great people skills and that's the main thing you need in court. I have seen you deal with kids, old folks, and relatives that are fussin' and fightin'. You've always been able to say things to make it right, and that's all you got to do here."

"Thanks, dear, but this won't be dealing with relatives and old folks," I said.

"What do you mean?"

"Jack, it's a judge and a jury for goodness sake."

"What's the difference? After all they're just people too. The two juries I served on were made up of folks of all colors, old and young, weak and strong, poor and well off. All you have to do is be yourself—with a different name—and tell Nelda's story."

"I agree," Highsmith said. "Hell, if I had a case, I'd rather have you two on my side than that old rummy Louise."

I relented by saying, "Well Dot, it wouldn't be like *To Kill a Mockingbird*, but perhaps we can clip the wings of a smirking old popinjay."

"So you'll do it," she asked eagerly.

"Are you in if I do?"

"Absolutely," Dot said. "I'm no closer to finding a job than I was the day Louise died, plus I'm *very* excited to see this play out."

I struggled for reasons to oppose the notion, but with the exception of fear, I could not muster a single rationale. "If Nelda still wants us to, I suppose we should," I said, and everyone nodded enthusiastically and patted me on the back. "I certainly didn't expect this kind of support, and I especially appreciate it from you, Jack," I said, and leaned over, threw my arms around his neck and planted a big, prolonged kiss right on his lips.

"Hell, do you two want us to leave y'all alone for a while?" Highsmith said.

I spent the rest of the afternoon alternating between working on the case and tending to five pies—three for Dr. Scotty and one each for Jack and Bill Highsmith.

When the girls arrived at our house the next morning, I convened a strategy meeting, conducted over plates of delicious pork hot tamales. With Dot already onboard, I began by and explaining to Lupe, in Spanish, the decision to go to court and she cheerfully endorsed the plan.

"I also spoke to Nelda," I said. "She is on board with this, in fact, she seemed thrilled by the prospect."

"You sure seem at peace with this now," Dot said.

"I'm fretting about it some, and didn't sleep so well last night, but Nelda was right. We *are* a hell of a team and have worked hard on this case, and I think we can give it a good go. That said, we have less than four weeks to work it up, and I have a mission for each of you, starting with you Lupe."

"Jes Miss Gertie."

"Here, take this map I printed," I said handing it to her. "Tengo tres pasteles—I have baked three pies, and they need to be delivered to Dr. Scott Strong at the hospital. Yo marce la ruta—I highlighted the route on the map and wrote the name of the hospital and the address at the top, comprende?"

"Jes Miss Gertie."

I removed a five dollar bill from my pocketbook and handed it to her. "This is for gas money and la pasteles are, en la caja," I said, pointing to the box containing the pies resting on our kitchen counter. "As for you Dot, I need some trial subpoenas issued, including one to serve on Jesus. I know he said he would be there when we need him, but the subpoena will assure it and it may help him get paid if he's taking off from work."

"Got it," Dot said. "I will get Tony Kennedy to serve it."

"Good idea," I said, and explained to Lupe in Spanish what the subpoena was for and instructed that when she returned from delivering the pies to call Jesus. "Tell him it is coming and explain why. No quiero asustarlo Jesus—I don't want to frighten him," I said, and Lupe nodded her understanding.

"Dot, I also want one served on the foundry CEO, Waite Morrison."

"Don't you think the defense will bring him to trial?"

"I am sure they will, but I want to signal that we are working up the case, serving him will get straight back to Shiras."

"Makes sense," Dot said, "and Tony can find him most every night at the Oasis Club, drinking it up with his buddies."

"Perfect, have him serve Morrison right there in front of his big shot friends and he can explain what it's about."

"You got it," Dot said eagerly. "What else can I do?"

"Get directions to the courthouse so we will know how to get there. I don't want to be driving around looking for it on the first day. Also find out how the parking works and learn what floor our court is on, and if it is accessible by stairs."

"Why are the stairs important?" Dot asked.

"That's a long story," I said. "I also need you to put together a trial notebook, like the one you did for Louise last year in that car wreck case. It needs to have the pleadings, deposition transcripts, all discovery responses, and our exhibits.

"And four copies of each exhibit, correct?"

"Yes—good memory. Then comes the attire, how do you think I should dress for the trial?"

"You have some wonderful dresses, many as nice as or nicer than anything Louise wore to court," Dot said. "I think you ought to wear that blue polka dot A-line with the white bow."

I shook my head. "I can't go to court dressed like Little Bo Peep. I have to dress … you know … lawyerly."

"Mi gots un bueno dress from mi quinceanera," Lupe offered.

"Honey—I wish more than you know that I could fit into your clothes, but I can't," I said, and Lupe nodded and turned to retrieve the pies from the kitchen.

Dot said with a wry grin, "I'm sure I can let it out a little if you want to wear it."

I leaned close to her, and whispered, "Very funny. I can't go to court looking like the hostess at the Ranchero Vista Buffet."

"Sorry, I couldn't help myself," Dot chuckled, "So what do you have in mind?"

"All I know is that I have to dress in a whole different way than I do for church or my usual office garb, but need to do it on a shoestring budget," I said, as Lupe returned carrying the box.

"Why don't you try that resale shop over on Kauffman—you know the one where Clarence went to book his cruise," Dot said.

"Martina Marshall's place?"

"Yeah, that's the one. Word is she hobnobs with the upper crust and is supposed to have some really nice things there."

"Despite being a notorious old maid, she is very pretty and does dress well," I said.

"Some say there's a reason she's an old maid," Dot said confidentially.

"Oh?" I said, as Lupe sat the box on the table and looked on curiously.

"Rumor has it she's lesbian," Dot whispered, though it was just us girls in the room.

"Martina from Lisbon?" Lupe said excitedly. "Mi gots un amiga from Portugal."

I glared at Dot, then turned back to Lupe. "It's nice that you have a friend in Portugal, but that's not—"

"She very good friend to me, jou think Miss Martina know her?"

Dot intervened, "I said Lesbian, not Lisbon." Lupe cocked her head like a hound hearing a dog whistle. "It means that she ... well uh ... she likes other—"

"Let it go," I said, "but I think you have got a good idea with Martina's store. I have looked through the window there a time or two, but I never went inside. I always assumed that even at re-sale prices, the clothes there would be both out of my league and price range. Under the circumstances though, I think it's worth a try—will you two come with me?"

"What about our assignments?" Dot said.

"This shouldn't take long, and y'all can get on them after we are done, okay"

"I'm in," Dot said and Lupe nodded.

"Good, I can use extra sets of eyes to help me decide," I said, and we walked out to my car and I drove us over to Kaufman Street.

I angle parked in front of Martina's boutique, named *Bel-Esprit*, and led the way to the front door. Once inside, I realized why I had never seen much beyond the items in the window. The place was dimly lit, but I nevertheless marveled at its size and decor. The dusky ambiance meant I needed my reading glasses to check the price tags and found the figures on each impressive in their own right.

"There is certainly some nice things here, don't you think?" Dot said while flipping through one of the chrome circular racks featuring skirts and blouses.

"There sure is," I said.

"They're mighty pricey for used clothes, though," Dot added under her breath.

"I noticed that, but I bet some of these outfits cost five times the price new," I said. "The question for us is what exactly does a female lawyer dress like? I know what Matlock and Perry Mason wore, but how is a post-middle age woman supposed to look?"

"You've watched that program *L.A. Law* haven't you?"

"Sure, I've seen it," I said.

"There were women lawyers on that show, including that lady that used to be on the Partridge Family—that's the way you need to dress."

"Dot, this isn't Los Angeles and I am twice as big as any woman on that show. No, I don't think I'll be squeezing into any silk miniskirts and sheer blouses to go to Waco."

"This one nice," Lupe said, pointing to a glistening silver ball gown. "Mi likes plata."

"I like silver too, but I am going to the courthouse, and not the opera."

"What about this one?" Dot asked, holding up a red dress with matching velvet trim.

"That would be fine if the trial was held at a French brothel," I said, and Dot giggled. "Come on now—help me out a little."

"Hello ladies," came a voice from behind.

I turned to see the proprietor herself approaching, and said, "Hi, do you remember me?"

"Sure I do, Gertie," Martina Marshall said smiling.

"These are my colleagues from the law business, Dorothy and Lupe."

"Welcome to Bel-Esprit ladies, can I be of some assistance to you?"

I said, "I hope so, you see Martina I need to purchase a—"

"Oh, you Martina?" Lupe interrupted excitedly. "You the one that is lesb—" Dot put her hand over Lupe's mouth in a nick of time.

I continued. "I need to get a business suit. Preferably something that I can mix and match with other blouses and scarves to change the look a little."

"I understand, but if you don't mind me asking is this because you need to find another job?"

"Something like that—you must have heard about Louise."

"Oh sure, I saw the obituary in the paper and it was quite a shock."

"Did you know Louise well?"

"I guess you could say that. We attended some of the same parties and played pinochle a few times. Me and my circle of friends quit asking her to things because of well … you know …"

"I know," I said. "Did Louise buy her dress clothes here?"

"She bought a couple new outfits and some accessories here and there, but she wasn't about to stoop to buying what she called *hand-me-downs*."

"So you sell both new and used clothing?" Dot said.

"We do, but instead of saying *used*, for our evening wear we prefer *previously enjoyed* and for our business suits we go with *previously successful in*.

"I need future successful in," I said facetiously.

Martina grinned, and said, "I can dress you for success, but achieving it is on you."

"Understood, what do you recommend?"

"We have plenty to choose from in your size and just know that the pre-owned outfits have been thoroughly inspected. Each have been mended as needed by a skilled tailor and expertly dry cleaned. Are you looking for professional casual or professional dressy?"

"I'm leaning toward dressy, but not too much so—if that makes sense."

"It does, come with me," Martina said, motioning us to follow. "I have some very nice business wear right back here."

She led us to a section toward the rear of the boutique and I got my first glimpse of her travel office. There was a glass topped desk there, three chairs and the surrounding walls featured framed posters depicting lovely tropical scenes. Martina directed us to a long rack of clothing and true to her word there were some wonderful choices. She showed us several worthy options and I selected three to try on. I modeled the first two and received favorable comments, but the hands-down winner turned out to be the third. It was a gray outfit with a long skirt and a conservative matching jacket and a white blouse. When I pushed aside the dressing room curtain, the three women looked at me, then to each other, then back to me with their mouths agape.

"Well?" I said.

"It's perfect," they said simultaneously—well, it was actually two *it's perfects* and one *esta perfecto*.

We next turned the focus to footwear, but the majority of the shoes Martina stocked that would go with my outfit were high heels—some very high. I knew better than to select anything like that knowing well that I would be walking and standing a lot, and that my feet were sure to swell. With no way to elevate them, I feared I would be miserable, if not hobbled, by the end of the first day. I likewise had not walked in high heels in years and doubted that I could without twisting an ankle and risk ending up in a cast. I settled on a pair with low heels that matched the suit well and with the addition of three versatile blouses and two scarves we wrapped up the sale.

9
CHAPTER

The Sunday before the commencement of the trial found me at our home office tying up loose ends. Not wanting to leave any stone unturned I reviewed everything Dot included in the trial notebook and worked on my questions for each witness I expected to encounter. That night, with my mounting anxiety and all of the information buzzing around in my head, I hardly slept a wink. I finally managed to doze off, but it was not until the wee hours of the morning, a time when the utility of the sleep is often outweighed by the bizarreness of the dreams.

I awoke for good before the alarm and deactivated it so as not to disturb Jack. I rose from our bed, showered and got breakfast started all before sunup. I was loading my tote bag with the trial notebook, supplies and our lunch for that day when I heard Jack stir. He entered the kitchen sleepy headed, took a seat at the table and I handed him his breakfast plate. I walked to the bedroom, traded my flannel nightgown for my new business suit and slipped on my dress shoes. When I returned moments later Jack was busy eating, until I cleared my throat. He wiped his mouth, turned in my direction, did a double take, followed by a wolf whistle, and said: "Wow babe, you look terrific."

"Oh my, any outfit that will get you to look up from scrambled eggs, ham, and grits must be special."

"You look special, *very* special in fact," he said, then struggled to his feet and delivered a peck to my cheek. "Gertie Chase, you get on over to Waco and knock it out of the park."

"I will do my best and I want to thank you for all of your support—I could not have gotten this far without it."

"I ain't done nothin', but are you doing okay? You seemed awfully fidgety last night."

"I'm just a little edgy, and sorry if I kept you awake."

"You didn't, but say, would it bother you if Bill and me went over there and watched some of the trial?"

"That's fine, I don't see how I could get any more nervous than I already am."

I loaded my car and headed out to pick up my trial team. Once all were on board we embarked on our forty mile drive with Mickey Gilley's *Super Hits* playing in the background. Despite leaving much earlier than the trip should require, a work crew blacktopping the right lane of highway 84 squandered most of our time cushion. Once beyond the work zone, I picked up the pace, but not so much so as to risk a speeding ticket.

Though I had visited Waco countless times over the decades, I had never seen the McLennan County courthouse and relied on Dot to navigate. I spotted it well before we got to it and the mere sight of it only heightened my anxiety. It is a long multistory building that looks a lot like the pictures I had seen of the U.S. Capitol in Washington. It had a big, bright white rotunda in the middle and tall flagpoles stood on each end, one featuring old glory and the other the flag of the Lone Star State.

I pulled into a parking spot on the side of the building and the four of us hustled up the walkway, past an area featuring war memorials, and toward the entrance. We ascended a long set of steps leading to large wooden entry doors and with that exertion, coupled with my nervousness, I commencing to perspire.

Once inside I paced over to a metal framed glass protected case hanging on the wall. It had a black velvet background featuring slotted ribs which held white plastic characters giving the court numbers. Next to each was the corresponding name of the judge and the floor on which each courtroom was located. Our destination was the 170th

District Court and I confirmed what Dot had researched, in that it was located on the third floor.

Nelda scanned the same board from over my shoulder and did so with more than a passing interest. When she saw the floor we needed her face showed concern. I tugged her jacket sleeve and pointed her to the two curving stairways in the center of the building under the rotunda. Those stairs led up to the second floor and a matching pair reached from there to the third. She nodded, exhaled with relief, and I checked my watch. Despite the delay presented by the road work we were on time, but only barely so.

To access the stairs we were required to pass through a security checkpoint. This area included a metal detector and a conveyor belt that ran items and accessories through a scanner. Next to it stood a sign listing the items that were *unconditionally forbidden* from entering the courthouse. This included cameras, recording devices, knives, and guns.

Policing this area were three uniformed officers, one monitoring the belongings passing through the scanner and the other two handled those traversing the metal detector. The latter maintained the orderly flow of the visitors and assured that each relinquished belongings that could trigger the metal detector. Once divested of such items they were placed on the conveyor and sent through the scanner.

Concerned about time I motioned the girls toward the checkpoint. In line in front of us were a man and a woman, each dressed in business suits and with them was a bearded man in black jeans and a denim shirt. They seemed to know the drill and I watched on carefully as they emptied their pockets into separate plastic bowls. Next, they removed accessories, such as belts, watches and cell phones and placed them, along with the woman's purse and the man's briefcase on the moving conveyor. Once done, they were motioned through the metal detector and as they reached the other side each reclaimed their surrendered belongings.

It was now our turn and I led the way by removing my belt and watch, then placed them, along with my tote bag and purse, on the conveyor. As they entered the scanner, I glanced anxiously at the officer sitting on a high stool on the other side. From the light reflecting off of his eyeglasses, I could tell he was seeing X-ray images of my items as they passed. Though I was certain I had nothing that would violate the stated policy, I had the same sensation you get when being pulled over by a traffic cop. It made me anxious and I sighed with relief when the officer on the other side of the metal detector motioned me forward. I passed tentatively through the detector without incident, gathered my belongings and looked to my left and saw Shiras and his assistant near the twin stairs waiting for an elevator.

I turned back and watched as Dot placed her purse and bag on the conveyor. Nelda Fay added her purse and they each joined me on the other side. Bringing up the rear was Lupe and since she had no purse, she stood next to the conveyor emptying the pockets of her intricately embroidered quinceanera dress. Though I could not see what she was removing and placing into the plastic bowl, she finally reached the bottom of her pockets and was likewise motioned through the detector.

As Lupe's belongings passed through the scanner I was drawn to the change in expression of the officer viewing the X-ray images. It was apparent from his lenses that he had the ability to start, stop and reverse the conveyor, and my dread rose as the images lurched back and forth several times as the line of visitors behind us grew.

The scanner officer rose from the stool, motioned to the other two guards, and said, "She's got a knife."

"A what?" I said urgently.

"A knife," the guard repeated harshly.

"Listen—there must be some sort of mistake," I countered.

"It's a mistake all right—one that carries jail time too," he responded.

"Voy a la carcel!" Lupe wailed.

"Of course you're not going to jail," I said.

"Not so fast—this is a zero tolerance checkpoint," one of the officers informed while the other seized Lupe by her upper arm. She was now trembling, bawling out loud and I noticed the sizable crowd behind us looking on with interest. I rechecked my watch and glanced back to Shiras, and he and his assistant stood witnessing the unfolding fiasco until the elevator door opened and they entered.

When the plastic bowl containing Lupe's belongings emerged from the scanner the officer not detaining her snatched it from the conveyor belt. He rifled through its contents and out came a pack of Juicy Fruit gum, a set of keys, a necklace that I would later learn were rosary beads, some loose change, and last, but not least, was a purple velvet Crown Royal pouch.

"It's in there," the scanner guard said, pointing.

The guard lifted the pouch, tugged at the strings to open it and removed what looked like a shiny silver knife. It was about five inches long and toward the bottom, it had a cross piece extending an inch or two on each side serving as a hilt.

"Lupe—why are you carrying a knife?" I asked.

"No, no," she said hysterically, "no knife-no knife."

"I beg to differ," the officer said, as he handed it to his partner.

"It's definitely a weapon, but it ain't very sharp," the other officer said, as he ran his fingers along its edges.

Lupe turned to me, and sobbed, "Es un crucifijo!"

I nodded, extended my hand toward the officer, and said, "May I?"

"May you what?"

"Can I see it for a moment?"

"This is evidence," the officer said.

"Please, I think I can clear this up." The officer looked to the scanner guard who nodded, then reluctantly handed the item to me. I examined it, turned it a hundred and eighty degrees, handed it back, and said, "It's a cross."

"A what?" the scanner officer asked.

"It's a crucifix," I said and pointed to the etched words on it reading *Christo nuestro Salvador*. "That means *Christ our Savior* in Spanish," I said, and the crowd behind us released murmurs of laughter.

The officer holding Lupe's arm released it, blushed and said, "Very sorry, ma'am."

"Esta bien … es okay," Lupe whimpered and dried her eyes on the sleeve of her dress.

"Since we took her into custody we have to fill out a report," an officer said, as Lupe reloaded her pockets.

I explained, "Respectfully ... sir ... we are already late for court and don't have time to fill out paperwork."

"Are you four together?" he asked and I nodded. "Then why don't you three go on up, while we get the information from the young lady?"

"That's a good plan in principle, but there may be some language issues," I said.

The scanner officer walked around the conveyor with a clipboard in hand, and said, "Here, just fill out this top part and we will do the rest."

I took the form and found the inquiries largely rudimentary. While those waiting behind us began to be processed through the checkpoint, I filled in the blanks that I could, called on Lupe for the remainder, and handed the clipboard back to the officer.

"Y'all can move along now, sorry for the delay," the officer said.

"Let's go, girls, it's past the top of the hour," I said, and we gathered our things and paced rapidly toward the rotunda.

"Gertie—you just passed the elevators," Dot said as we walked.

"We are taking the stairs."

"Why, especially since we are already late?"

"Trust me on this, it's going to be faster this way."

Once we reached the third floor, we were all winded, but we trudged on and followed the signs to the 170th court. We entered through the double entry doors and the first thing that caught my eye was the judge's bench. It was faced with hand carved, darkly stained wood, and it stood wide and tall along the back wall of the room. There was a long thin adjustable microphone on top of it and behind it sat a high-backed brown chair and some bookshelves. To its right was the witness stand and around it was a wooden railing on three of the four sides and further to the right was the jury box. I found the whole environment intimidating and spying an armed bailiff pacing the floor with a stack of papers in hand did nothing to help.

I led the way down the center aisle which had church pew like benches on each side. We passed through a swinging gate and I noticed two long tables facing the bench, each with a plastic tray with a water pitcher and cups atop it. Shiras and his crew of six had set up shop at the table nearest the jury box, so we defaulted to the other.

"The guy in the black suit is Shiras," I whispered to Dot while nodding toward the defense table.

"You're right, he is a buzzard," she whispered back. "By the way, the guy behind him is Waite Morrison."

"Oh, I see," I said. "I wonder why they have him sitting in the first pew instead of at their table."

"Look at him, he can't fit in one of those armchairs," Dot said, and I thought *Highsmith was right.*

Since there were only three chairs at our table, I asked Lupe to have a seat on one of the audience pews and she actually seemed eager to return to the other side of the gate. With Dot seated to my left, and Nelda at Dot's left, I opened my tote bag and pulled everything from it except for our frozen lunch. I reviewed my notes and the room was eerily quiet until a voice startled me.

"You're late."

I looked to my right and saw the imposing figure of the bailiff looming over me. I glanced eye level at his holstered gun, and then to the gold badge glinting on his chest from the overhead lights. I looked up to his chiseled lantern jaw and then to his stern face sporting a less than a charitable expression. "The judge has already come out here twice looking for y'all and considered entering a default judgment."

"You see sir, we got here on time—ahead of time actually, but we ran into a little problem downstairs. Would you please ... sir ... um, let the judge know that we *are* here and that we are very sorry."

"Bailiff, I can vouch for the fact that they arrived timely," Shiras said, much to my dismay. "When my paralegal and I went down to the newsstand, we witnessed that one of their team members got caught with contraband at security and that's what caused the delay."

"Is that true?" the Bailiff asked, turning back to me.

"Yes sir, but it was all just a misunderstanding."

"Oh, if that's so, where's the girl that got detained?" Shiras said.

I turned to the defense table. "If you must know, she is seated right over there," I said pointing toward the back of the courtroom.

"If she didn't do anything wrong, why was she detained?" Shiras said.

The bailiff added, "Yeah, explain that."

I addressed only the bailiff, saying, "You see sir, the security guy manning the scanner saw something from her pocket that caught his eye," I said and motioned to Lupe, and she displayed the cross. "He thought it was a knife, but as you can see it is a crucifix."

"That makes sense because if she had actually had a knife she wouldn't be sitting in here—at least not without handcuffs," the bailiff said glancing scornfully at my tattletale opponent. He then walked behind the bench and knocked on a tall wooden door then entered. When the bailiff returned, he stopped at our table, and said, "You got a reprieve. The judge had to attend to a medical issue and we won't start any sooner than the bottom of the hour."

"Oh my—I hope it's nothing serious," I said.

The Bailiff leaned over to me, and whispered, "Between you and me it's just the green apple trots. He's taken some medicine and as quick as it kicks in he will be in here."

"Gosh, I haven't heard that said since I was a little girl."

"Green apple trots?" he said, and I nodded. "I'm surprised you've ever heard it—where are you from?"

"I was born at Lost Prairie, but was raised in Mexia, how about you?"

"I grew up in Hubbard."

"Really?"

"That's right, are you familiar with Hubbard?" he asked, and his once stern expression had vanished.

"I sure am," I said. "When I was a young girl my mom used to drive me and my brother to the city swimming pool there."

"Oh hell, I spent most of my summers in that pool," he said, smiling for the first time. "But that's over a twenty-mile drive each way, and didn't y'all have your own pool there in Mexia?"

"We did, and I frequented it too, but far too often ours was not working. They regularly had a pump conk out or some knucklehead kid would go number two in it and they would shut it down."

The Bailiff belly laughed, and said, "That last part also happened some in Hubbard."

"I'm afraid that's a universal truth when you allow kids in," I said. "I was also creeped out by that poor Pendleton boy's drowning in our pool."

"I heard about that, but always thought it was an urban legend," he said.

"It's true all right. The men were draining the pool and the kid snuck in for a quick dip and got sucked down the drain and out to the slough."

He asked, "Did you know the family?"

"No sir, that happened in the forties well before we moved there."

"The story was enough to have you favor our pool?"

"That was a part of it, but the real attraction was that your pool had that high dive."

"I loved it too—did you ever dive off of it?" he asked.

"I really wanted to, but never worked up the nerve. I jumped feet first from it a jillion times though, and can still feel the chlorine burning in my sinuses."

He smiled, and said, "My name is Charlie Story. You ladies make yourselves at home, and the judge will be out here soon."

Shiras rose from his table, and said, "Bailiff, our crew has arrived and we have a lot of technology out in the hall—can they get started setting it up?"

"Fine by me," Charlie said.

Shiras signaled toward a pair of eyes peering in from the hallway through the left entry door windows. Both doors flung open simultaneously and I could not believe what I saw next. Three large flatbed carts, like the ones at the home improvement stores, came rolling down the center aisle. They were being pushed by men in grey coveralls, the type movers wear and the carts were carrying equipment, and plastic bins containing tools, materials, and supplies.

They commenced hooking up computer towers, monitors, laptops and other equipment that I did not recognize. They used spools of black cable and electrical cords to rig it all up, including connecting their electronics to each of the four large video monitors present. Soon the men exited with their empty carts, leaving behind a network of wires all carefully taped to the floor to avoid trip hazards.

I sat staring enviously at the extent of the resources on and around their table, considering that ours consisted of the notebook, three legal pads—one blank and two with my witness questions—some paper clips, sticky notes and spare fountain pens.

The next sound I heard was Charlie the bailiff bellowing, "All rise."

I almost jumped out of my skin, but we all followed the lead of the others present by rising from our chairs. The judge emerged from his chambers followed by a thin well-dressed woman. As he ascended to the bench, I saw that the judge was a squatty man with a large round belly concealed under his calf-length pleated black robe. He was bald except for a line of graying wavy hair around the sides and back and wore half glasses balanced on his bulbous, slightly red, nose.

"You may be seated," the judge said, and all present complied as he assumed his high-backed chair. He flipped through his file for a moment, then positioned his microphone in front of him, tapped the foam tip to assure that it was on, and said, "All right folks, I am Judge Robert Cushing and my bailiff over there is Charlie Story," he said, pointing to the officer now seated at his desk. "This nice lady setting set up shop by the witness stand is my court reporter, Blair Pitney. I am calling the case of _Nelda Fay Blatchford, individually and as Representative of the Estate of Clifford Blatchford, Deceased versus the Waite Morrison Foundry, Incorporated_. Is everyone in attendance that needs to be here?"

Shiras rose and responded, "Yes Your Honor, all parties are present and represented."

"Good, who are you, sir?"

"Your Honor, I am Alexander Shiras, Baylor School of law nineteen seventy-three and counsel for the defendant."

The judge made a note, turned toward our table, and asked, "You must have the plaintiff?"

"Yes sir, she's right here," I said pointing to Nelda.

"I can't hear you," the judge said and his humorless expression had me petrified.

"She's right here," I said louder, and reached around Dot and patted Nelda's shoulder.

"I can't hear you," he said even louder, and I glanced to Shiras who sat smirking.

Thinking the judge was hard of hearing I cupped my hands on each side of my mouth and yelled, "The plaintiff—Nelda Fay Blatchford—is right here—sir."

"Madam, you will rise when addressing the court, until you do, I cannot hear you."

I bolted to my feet and cleared my throat. "I am very sorry judge. I represent this lady here uh … Nelda Blatchford … the … um, plaintiff."

"And you are?" he asked.

"I am uh … Louise Barbour," I stammered.

"Good to know you," the judge said and jotted another note. "Now, how do you announce?"

"I already said who I am—do you need my school information like he gave?" I said, glancing toward Shiras.

"No, I don't need that from you and didn't need it from him for that matter," the judge said, "I'm only taking announcements at this time and need to know yours first?"

"I see … um … I announce that the foundry killed Nelda's husband."

"I read that in your petition, but I still need an announcement," he insisted, and I must have had an awfully blank expression on my face because he added, "Lady, are you announcing *ready* or *not ready?*"

"Oh, that," I said with a phony chuckle, why of course we're ready."

"What says the defense?"

"We are *very* ready," Shiras said smugly, "and judge, since Ms.Barbour introduced her client I would like to acquaint you with mine. Seated directly behind me is the third generation CEO of this family-owned foundry, Mr. Waite Morrison."

"All right—now that we've dispensed with the unsolicited introductions, counsel y'all come on up," the judge said motioning us forward. I rose and met Shiras at the bench, and the judge asked, "Have you all been discussing settlement?"

Shiras spoke first. "Your Honor referred us to mediation and we complied, but the case did not resolve."

"So, you *and* your client here attended it?" the judge asked almost accusingly, and I sensed Bernie Van Devanter had come through on his pledge.

Shiras cleared his throat, and said, "I was there on behalf of the insurance company and as the representative of my client."

"So you attended without the CEO?"

"That's right."

"My order said that *all* parties had to attend, was any representative of the foundry there?"

"Just me."

"Did you read my order, Mr. Shiras?"

"Yes, of course, I did, but I just—"

"Disregarded it?" the judge finished.

"I regarded it, but as Your Honor may recall we opposed mediation. We knew that the case was unlikely to settle so I represented my client and had full access to the insurance adjuster while there."

"I suppose it's water under the bridge at this point, but for future reference, I take my orders seriously and I expect the parties to do the same."

"Yes, Your Honor," Shiras said contritely.

"So back to my question—are you two still talking settlement?

This time I spoke first. "I tried to, but they say they are not interested."

"Is that true?"

"Judge, we presented a *very* generous offer at the mediation."

The judge addressed me. "Your side turned it down?"

"We did that day, but subsequently tried to accept it."

"I made it abundantly clear at mediation that it was a onetime offer, and it would be revoked if not accepted that day," Shiras added.

"And you and your client are sticking to that position?"

"Those are my marching orders, Your Honor," Shiras said.

"All right then, you two may be seated," the judge said, then addressed the bailiff, "Do you have the questionnaires?"

"Yes judge, they're right here," Charlie said, lifting the two stacks of papers from his desk, "do you want counsel to have them now?"

"Yes, we are ready for Voir Dire."

I returned to our table where Dot was busy making notes on a legal pad, and she whispered, "What was that he said?"

"Who?"

"The judge—what was that term did he just used," she said, looking down at her notes, "it sounded something like *for diarrhea?*"

"The judge does have the runs," I whispered back, "but I am pretty sure he said *voir dire*. If I recall correctly from Louise, that term has something to do with getting the jurors seated."

The bailiff handed Shiras one of the stacks of papers and delivered the other to our table, then addressed both sides, explaining, "As you can see, each potential juror has completed a form and been assigned a number. They will be seated in the gallery in numerical order from left to right, starting on the first row. The judge allows fifteen minutes to look over the forms and while you do that, I will retrieve the panel from the jury assembly room downstairs."

When Charlie left the courtroom, I leafed through the handwritten questionnaires and made notes on some of them. Once the time expired, the judge asked if either side had any questions. With none forthcoming, we sat in silent nervousness until Charlie entered. Trailing him was what seemed to be an endless stream of people and he arranged them in their rows and they took their seats. I noticed that Shiras had turned his chair around to face the audience, so I did the same. The judge greeted the new arrivals and made the introductions of the parties. He then quoted Thomas Jefferson on the importance of the jury system, then said, "Ms. Barbour, you may examine the panel."

I looked back at him curiously. "Examine them?"

"Yes."

I turned back to the audience, scanned them briefly, and said, "They look fine to me."

There were murmurs of laughter in the room and Judge Cushing grinned, and said, "A little levity at the start of a serious trial is always a good icebreaker—you may question them now."

"Thank you, sir," I said, then rose, took a deep breath, and walked with the questionnaires in hand over to the rail separating me from the folks. "As the judge said my name is Louise Barbour, and I am from over in Mexia. I imagine some of you know where that is, right?" Several of them smiled and nodded. "I am here for Nelda Fay Blatchford, the nice lady sitting at our table in the lovely white blouse and brown jacket. Unfortunately, her husband Clifford is dead so he's not here with us today—at least not in person," I added, and several present glanced upward and around.

"It is our contention that the defendant, the Waite Morrison Foundry in Mexia, caused Clifford's death. The fellow sitting on the first pew over there is Mr. Waite Morrison the tur uh ... the third, that is. He is not the Waite Morrison that the place was named after— that was his granddaddy. The late Mr. Blatchford used to work at that foundry and did so for a very long time. He was a welder at first, but they eventually made him a pipefitter in the 1970's, and that promotion proved deadly as he—"

"Objection," Shiras said, rising from his chair, "she's being argumentative."

"I will overrule the objection, but Ms. Barbour I do urge you to get to more about the questioning of the panel and less about discussing the details of your case."

"Yes sir," I said and turned back to the people. "It is our contention that Mr. Blatchford's work at the foundry put him in contact with some awful stuff called asbestos. He was never told it was dangerous and years later—a period the experts call *latency*—Cliff came down with a cancer called mesothelioma."

Shiras rose. "Objection, she's still arguing her case."

"This time I'll sustain the objection," the judge said. "Ma'am, you've given an overview of your case, and will get to make an opening statement, so *please* get on with your examination."

"Yes sir," I said, and as I headed toward the left side of the room, I added, "I suppose I am expected to ask you all a bunch of questions, but I have all the information you each gave on these forms. That should be enough snooping for most of you, but I do have a question or two after studying them."

I stopped in front of juror number three, and said, "Ma'am, I noticed that your last name is Minton."

"That's right," she uttered.

"Are you any kin to the Minton's over in Fairfield?

"Sherman and Maggie?"

I smiled, and said, "Yes, are y'all related?"

"Yes ma'am," she said eagerly, "I am their niece."

"Mr. Minton was my biology teacher in high school."

"Oh my, what a small world," she said, "you do know my Uncle Sherm passed, don't you?"

"Yes, and I was saddened when I saw that in the paper a while back. Was it the demon alcohol that did him in?"

"That's right—he was eat-up with the cirrhosis," she said grimly.

"I thought so," I said, shaking my head.

"So you knew he was a tippler—even way back then?"

"He was a good man and a terrific teacher, but those frogs in the biology lab weren't the only things there that were pickled," I said, and she grinned and nodded. I placed a big check mark on Ms. Minton's page, then approached juror number eight.

"You are Connie Davis."

"Yes ma'am, but it's actually Connie Todd now. I just haven't changed my voter's registration since my wedding last April."

"Congratulations on your marriage," I said.

"Thank you, ma'am."

I pointed to her questionnaire, and said, "I see from this that you work at a restaurant over in West."

"That's right."

"Does it happen to be Buck's Bar Be Que?"

"Yes ma'am, Buck's is our family business."

"I thought you looked familiar," I said. "So you are Buck Davis's granddaughter?"

"No, you charmer, you—I'm his daughter."

"At the risk of being accused of jury tampering, I find that hard to believe," I said, and turned toward the bench. "Your Honor, may I ask this nice lady a *very* important, but non-case related question?"

"Make it brief."

"Yes sir," I said and turned back to Connie. "Y'all have three sauces at Bucks, right?" I asked, and heard a sigh from the defense table.

"Yes, ma'am—original, sweet and spicy."

"Right, and by the way spicy is my personal favorite."

Shiras rose and said, "Judge, I don't see the relevance of—"

"Spicy is my favorite too," the judge blurted, and Shiras returned to his seat.

Connie blushed, and said, "That's actually my own recipe."

Inspired by that disclosure, I said, "I have tried to replicate that sauce for years, but I can't quite get it. There's a secret ingredient, isn't there?" She nodded, and I pressed on. "You don't have to, but I would be most grateful if you would share it with me."

The judge lifted his pencil and notepad and leaned forward attentively. Connie, on the other hand, glanced around at all of the other sets of ears present. "I'm willing to say, but I would appreciate it if I could just tell it to you only."

"Fine with me," I said, thrilled to be on the precipice of gaining the holy grail of bar be que sauces, but the judge would have no part of it.

"Ms. Barbour," he said sternly. "Mr. Shiras, my court reporter and I must hear all responses from the jurors."

"Understood," I said. "I won't ask her say it out loud in front of all of us, but anyone that can make bar be que and sauce like that, is welcome on this jury," I said and made a big check mark on her page and moved further down rail.

"Juror number thirteen—Mr. Quintus," I said to a well-dressed, and may I add handsome, Latino gentleman on the second row. "Hola Senor, como esta usted?"

He immediately frowned. "Miss—I will have you know that I am a fifth generation American. I graduated from the University of Texas with honors and I run my own company. I find your attempt to curry favor with me with pigeon Spanish to be—well—insulting."

"Hasta la vista, Mr. Quintus," I said, and placed a giant X on his page.

I questioned a few others, then told the Judge I was done, and then it was Shiras's turn. He strutted over to the podium proud as a peacock, and said, "Ladies and gentlemen, I must say that it is truly great to be back here in Waco where spent five of the best years of my life at my alma mater, Baylor University."

"It took you five, huh?" I asked, and Shiras glared at me.

"That's enough Ms. Barbour," the Judge said, "it's his turn to speak now."

"Yes sir," I said.

Shiras continued. "The first thing I want to know is if there's any reason why one or more of you might not be a good fit to sit in judgment of this case. You should know that this case could last from a couple of days to as much as a week or more. So my question to each of you is whether there is anything going on with your job, or at home that would make you a better candidate for service at some other time on some other case."

A woman raised her hand, and said, "Me and my husband have a vacation we've been planning for quite a while. We are leaving Wednesday and I would really hate to cancel it."

"Where are you going, if you don't mind me asking?" Shiras said.

"To Paris, sir."

"Lucky you," Shiras said. "The missus and I have traveled to France several times and I must say Paris is *very* beautiful this time of year."

"That's good to know sir, but we're going to Paris, Texas," she informed, and several giggled. The red-faced Shiras looked back to the Judge.

"We'll excuse her."

Shiras returned to the panel. "Anyone else?"

A young man on the third row raised his hand and in a quavering voice said, "Well sir, um ... you see ... me and my wife are about to conceive a baby."

"Conceive?" the Judge said with raised eyebrows.

Shiras added patronizingly, "I am sure the lad intended to say they are about to *have* a baby."

"Either way, I think he ought to be there," I said.

"Agreed," the judge said, "Young fella, you are excused from jury service and good luck with the arrival of your child."

"Any other conflicts?" Shiras asked. With no response, he commenced questioning the folks individually, and I must say the man did not mind prying. He delved into their private lives, including the details of what they did for a living, and if they had ever been on a jury before and if so, to what result. He asked their opinions on lawsuits, their stance on politics, and the depth and breadth of their education. Though they did not seem to mind it at first, the more Shiras probed, the more irritated some appeared.

His next target was Connie Todd of Buck's Bar Be Que fame. "For some reason, my opponent elected to consume the court's time discussing your sauce recipes. During that exchange the location of your family's restaurant was mentioned, wasn't it?"

"Yes, sir."

"I assume you live in the same town as that establishment."

"That's right. The front door of me and my husband's house is about a quarter mile from the restaurant."

"Tell me the name of the town," Shiras said.

"West."

"That's what I wrote down, but West—what?"

"Texas."

"I know it's in Texas, or you wouldn't be on this jury panel," Shiras said, "but what town in Texas?"

"West," Connie repeated, now seemingly unnerved by the interrogation.

"I get that, but is it West, as in West Texas—like Kerrville, Bandera or Boerne?" Shiras asked, oblivious to the fact that West is a quaint town located a short drive north of Waco.

"No sir, it's not way out there," she said. "It's just plain ol' West."

"No, no, no," Shiras said, shaking his head and wagging his index finger toward her. "As a lifelong resident of Dallas, I know well where Plano, Texas is located. It's nowhere near McLennan County and there's no such place as Plano West."

"Sir, you don't under—"

"Ma'am, you do realize that you *must* be a resident of McLennan County to be on this jury?"

"I do know that sir, and I do live in this county—I wouldn't lie about that," she said on the verge of tears, and some of those on the panel began to grumble amongst themselves. I glanced toward the bench, made eye contact with the judge, and he simply rolled his eyes.

"I think there's something going on here," Shiras asserted. "You already admitted in open court to having a faulty voter registration, and you and Ms. Barbour seemed awfully cozy. Now I demand to know *exactly* where you live!"

"You need to calm down, Mr. Shiras," the judge admonished. "I don't know how they do things in Dallas, but I don't allow verbal outbursts in my courtroom."

Shiras nodded, then said, "Let's try this. If I wanted to mail you a letter to your house, tell me precise wording I would need to put on the envelope to get to your town?"

"West—comma—Texas."

"Now we're getting somewhere. In what county is West Common?"

"Comma, not common," the beleaguered Connie said.

"Counsel, y'all approach," the judge demanded.

Shiras headed toward the bench, I rose to follow and when I walked by the audience, I winked and said, "He ain't from around here."

When I arrived at the bench the Judge addressed me first, "Ms. Barbour, you know better than to address the jury out of turn like that."

"Sorry sir," I said contritely.

"As for you, Mr. Shiras, that nice lady lives in the town of West—W-E-S-T."

"West is the full name of the town?" Shiras asked dubiously.

"Yes, and it's just a few miles up the interstate from here, and how in the hell did you attend school here for five years and not know that?"

"I guess I studied too much," Shiras said.

When Shiras completed his interrogation, Charlie ushered the folks back into the hallway. Lawyers do not *pick juries* as the saying goes, but rather they strike potential jurors to complete the panel. Each side was allowed six such strikes to eliminate those they found undesirable. I just wanted regular folks on the panel and all were fine with me, except for Mr. Quintus of course, so I struck him and that was it.

I handed my form to Charlie, and he looked at it and whispered, "What about your other strikes?"

"I only have the one," I said.

"You know you get six, don't you?"

"Yes sir, but since I made him mad he's the only one that concerns me," I explained.

Charlie shrugged, then walked to the defense table and collected Shiras' strikes. He reconciled both lists and soon enough we had seven men and five women under oath and in the jury box. Connie and Ms. Minton must have been struck by Shiras as they remained seated in the audience. The unchosen were thanked and dismissed by the judge and they rose and began to file out of the courtroom. Connie Todd approached me, wished us luck with the case, and snuck me a scrap of paper. It was her handwritten spicy sauce recipe, and I thanked her earnestly, folded the note and placed it in the pocket of my tote bag.

After each side gave their opening statements, the Judge informed us that he had a function to attend that afternoon and instructed all present to be back at nine o'clock the following morning. I did not know if the judge truly had a function or if it was his stomach's *malfunction* that prompted the postponement, but either way, I was glad to have an extra half day to prepare.

Since I brought lunch, and we all wanted to eat it before heading home, we consulted Charlie about a place in the building where we could heat our food. He explained that there was a room called the *lawyer's lounge* on the second floor that not only had a microwave but, also a refrigerator with an ice maker.

"That sounds perfect," I said, "but can these ladies go there too?"

"Sure, since they're with you it should be fine, and if anyone gives you any lip about it, you just let me know."

"Thank you, Charlie," I said.

We grabbed our belongings and headed down the stairs to the second floor, and located the lounge. Once there, I unloaded the plastic ware and paper plates and a baggie holding my hand-kneaded garlic yeast rolls. Then came the Tupperware bowls, one containing my partially frozen homemade spaghetti and another had a batch of my special spicy meatballs and marinara sauce. After I nuked it all in the microwave, we dined to our heart's content before heading to my car.

As we drove out of Waco, we listened to Hank, Jr. and at my request, Lupe agreed to get Jesus to the courthouse the next morning. Once home, I first got our meal started for the following day and refined and re-refined my questions for Jesus. At bedtime, I was concerned that I would have a tough time going to sleep. The stresses of the day must have taken its toll, as I conked out before Carol Burnett sang her *I'm so glad* ditty at the end of her show.

10
CHAPTER

I woke the following morning and I readied myself for day two of the trial. I remained nervous, however with a day—or should I say a half-day-under my belt, I felt a modicum of confidence. We embarked on the drive to Waco and with no road crew to impede our progress we arrived early.

Once inside the courthouse, we were carful that Lupe had nothing on her person that could cause us problems. We cleared security without incident, and with time to spare, I made our first destination the lawyer's lounge. We trudged up the steps to the second floor, entered the lounge and I placed our lunch in the refrigerator. When we returned to the hallway I saw the Judge emerging from an elevator car carrying a white plastic sack and whistling as he walked.

"Good morning judge," I said.

He seemed startled and jerked his head up toward us. "Oh … it's you. How are you ladies on this fine morning?"

"We are right as rain," I said. "What are you doing on this floor?"

"Same as you I suspect—storing my lunch," he said pointing to his bag.

"Sorry about yesterday, I guess I'm a little rusty."

"Your approach is a tad unconventional, but you're holding your own—say, I have to know what was on that note."

"Note?" I asked.

"Yeah, the one that lady from Buck's Bar-B-Que gave you. I saw her hand you a piece of paper and hoped it was the sauce recipe."

"Indeed it was," I said, and he grinned. I pulled the note from my tote bag and recited, "It starts with Ketchup, of course, then some finely minced fresh garlic—"

"Ha, I thought so. What else?"

"A pinch of cumin, paprika, brown sugar and cinnamon per pint," I said and handed him the note to see for himself.

The judge perused the ingredients, then said, "I can understand the cumin and garlic for some kick, but am surprised by the cinnamon."

"I would have never have guessed it."

"Well—I can't wait to take a stab at it, would you mind jotting it down for me?"

"I'll do better than that, you can just keep the note," I said.

He looked at me curiously. "Don't you want to try to make it?"

"Desperately," I said, "but the first thing I did when I got home yesterday was to write it down verbatim in my recipe catalog."

"Oh ... I see," he said, then folded the note and slid it into his shirt pocket. "Thank you for that and I will see you ladies in the courtroom," he said and entered the lounge.

We walked up the steps to the third floor and I was relieved to see a Hispanic gentleman sitting on a bench just outside of the courtroom. Lupe confirmed that it was Mr. Cardozo and he appeared much younger than I expected. She introduced me to him and through the combination of his English, my Spanish and Lupe's translation, we discussed the foundry and his work there with Cliff Blatchford.

When the trial reconvened, the judge greeted the jury, then turned to me, and said, "Who's your first witness?"

I stood and said, "We call Jesus Cardozo."

"Jesus, J-E-S-U-S?" the judge asked.

"Yes, sir."

"I thought so, but does he pronounce it jeez-us or hay-zoos?"

I wasn't sure, so I turned to Lupe sitting in the audience, and said, "Which is it?"

"I ask," she said and scampered to the courtroom door. She opened it, craned her neck through it, posed the question, and then addressed the judge. "He say both okay."

"So be it," the judge said. "Fetch him in Charlie."

The bailiff retrieved Jesus from the hallway, and as the two men walked down the center aisle toward the witness stand I spied another man walking in behind them. Though he looked a tad older and grayer, I recognized him from the video deposition as Brockholst Livingston, Shiras's slick, handsomely paid, British expert.

As he assumed a pew in the audience, the judge noticed him and asked, "Sir, are you a witness in this case?"

"I beg your pardon," Livingston said, like a true Londoner.

"I asked if you're a witness if so you'll need to wait in the hall," the judge said.

Shiras turned, and seeing who the judge was referring to, said, "He's one of my experts, Your Honor."

"Fair enough, you may be seated sir."

Blair swore in Jesus and as he took his seat on the stand, he seemed less nervous than me and sat bright-eyed and smiling.

My first question was to ask if he spoke English and his reply was, "Poquito."

The judge looked over his glasses at me. "If he answers your question about knowing English by giving a Spanish response, I think we may have an issue. Did you arrange for a certified translator?"

I rose and said, "No sir ... I did not."

"Don't you think that's going to be a problem?"

Sensing I was about to lose my first witness, I blurted, "Though not certified, I may have the next best thing," I said motioning Lupe to come forward from the back. I could tell she was frightened and though she looked as if she was walking the Bataan Death March she made her way through the gate and over to our table. "Judge, this is my assistant Lupe—I mean Guadalupe, and earlier she translated my conversation with Mr. Cardozo just fine."

"For Blair's record, I will need her full name," the judge said.

"Oh, my ... get ready for it," I said. "She is Guadalupe Maria Sylvia-Sotomayor, right?" I asked, and Lupe nodded rapidly. "She knows Spanish and English—well her English isn't that great, but her Spanish is excellent."

"We will need both for this to work."

"I realize that judge, but I am convinced she can get us through this just fine."

"What do you think?" the judge asked of the defense table.

Shiras stood, buttoned his suit Jacket, and said, "I don't think it's proper. You can't just select someone from the gallery and have them translate."

"Mr. Shiras, under the rules you have an absolute right to object that she is not certified and I will sustain it if you do," the judge explained. "Just know that I am going to allow Ms. Barbour time to engage a qualified interpreter. If we have to do that, it's going to waste as much as a half day of the juror's time."

"There's a couple of issues as I see it," Shiras said. "First off, Ms. Barbour should have thought about bringing a translator if she needed one. Secondly, the young lady apparently works for her."

"I fully understand all of that, but all I want to know from you is whether you are lodging an objection or not?"

"Well—I myself am fluent in Spanish and could—"

"There you have it," the judge said. "You can monitor her work, and if you contest any of the exchanges we will take it up at that time—so what do you say?"

The defense entourage conferred like a football team huddling, and when Shiras emerged from it, he said, "No objection at this time, but we reserve the right to assert one as we move along."

"Fair enough," the judge said and turned to Lupe. "Come on up young lady and be sworn."

Lupe eased cautiously toward the witness stand, stopping next to stenography machine, and Blair said, "Raise your right hand." Lupe complied, but not by raising her hand with her elbow bent at a forty-five-degree angle like normal. Instead, she extended her arm all the way into the air like an elementary school student would do to ask a question or signal the need for a bathroom break. "Do you solemnly swear to perform all the duties and obligations of legal interpretation and translation?" Blair said.

"Jes." Lupe said.

"Oh my lord," Dot uttered under her breath.

"You may proceed," the judge said.

I addressed Lupe. "Ask him his name."

"Whoa!" the judge said loud enough to make me flinch and for Lupe to duck. "It doesn't work that way. Ms. Barbour, you ask Mr. Cardozo the question and she … what's her name again?"

"Guadalupe, but she goes by Lupe."

"Right. So you ask the witness a question like normal, and … uh … Lupe here, will ask the witness the same question in Spanish— got it so far ladies?"

"Yes, sir," I said and Lupe nodded, but I was beginning to regret my suggestion.

"Good, now when the witness responds in Spanish, Lupe here will repeat his response in English, okay?"

"We're all on the same page, judge," I said, turning my attention back to the witness stand. "Would you state your name, please?"

Before the question was translated by Lupe, Mr. Cardozo said, "My name is—".

"Oh, Jesus!—" the judge said.

"Yes?" Mr. Cardozo said.

"I didn't mean you—I meant the Bible version."

Mr. Cardozo smiled and spoke a phrase to Lupe in Spanish.

"What did he say?" the judge asked.

"He say *no worry, that happen all the time.*"

"I bet, but the point is that Jesus … I mean Mr. Cardozo may know enough English to understand where some questions are going, but he has to let her … um … Lupe here, say it entirely in Spanish before he responds back in Spanish."

"Got it, Lupe?" I asked.

"Jes," she said.

"Good," the judge said, "now please explain that to Mr. Cardozo."

Lupe rattled off a few sentences in Spanish, Jesus nodded his understanding and I returned to my questions. For the next few exchanges, Lupe effectively interpreted my questions, then repeated Jesus' answers in her poor, but serviceable, rendition of English. Through this process, I managed to get a good deal of information about Jesus' background before turning my focus to his time at the foundry. During that line of questioning we learned that in the late 1960s, as a mere teenager, Mr. Cardozo began working at Morrison's. He knew Clifford and explained that they did not work together at first because he was a laborer and Cliff was a welder.

"Was there ever a time when you and Mr. Blatchford did work together?" I asked and Lupe repeated the question, and the translated response was, *Jes, it was in early seventies as Senor Cliff's labor worker.*

"Was this when Mr. Blatchford was a pipefitter?"

Lupe looked back to me curiously. "I not know no word for pipefitter, Miss Gertie," she said, and I couldn't believe my ears.

"Gertie?" the judge asked.

"It is ... uh ... it's just a nickname Judge," I stammered.

"Fine, but for the sake of clarity, and to avoid any further confusion, let's confine our references to each other with real proper names, shall we?"

"Yes sir," I said and through gritted teeth added, "Guadalupe, *please* call me Louise or Ms. Barbour, okay?"

"Jes Miss ...uh ... Barbour," she giggled.

"Excuse me, judge," Charlie said pointing toward the back of the room. I turned to see Jack and Highsmith entering and noticed several others now seated and watching the proceedings.

"Are any of you witnesses in this case?" the judge asked.

I intervened. "Not those two judge, one's my husband and the other is his friend."

"Fine," the Judge said, and the boys took seats in the gallery. "What about the rest of y'all?" the judge said to the others, and they too claimed no connection to the case.

Then the judge addressed me. "What are we going to do about pipefitter?"

"I know pipefitter," Jesus said.

"Problem solved," the Judge said. "Please proceed."

"Did you work with Mr. Blatchford when he was a pipefitter?" I asked and Jesus responded to Lupe, and she translated, "He says *Jes, he on his crew long time.*"

"Did Mr. Blatchford work around pipe insulation?" I asked.

Jes—much of it, Lupe recited.

"About the insulation—what did it look like?"

Jesus spoke and Lupe translated, "Senor Cardozo say *it came in big long boxes, with white pieces, and were...how do you say... luna media.*"

"Half-moon?" I asked.

"Yes, half-moon shaped," Jesus said directly to me, "and they were in three feet long pieces."

"Hang on a second Jesus, uh … Mr. Cardozo," the judge uttered, "you are answering before the interpreter again."

"And in English," Shiras added.

"You're right," the judge agreed, and added, "this whole translation thing isn't working worth a damn!"

Dead silence prevailed until permeated by a soulful whimpering. We all watched as poor little Lupe slumped her shoulders, placed her head in her hands, and sobbed aloud.

The judge stood, and said, "What's wrong, Miss?"

Lupe lifted her head, directed those big, brown, tearful Latina eyes to him, and said, "I sorry … I so sorry—I try so hard to terpret," she wailed.

I walked around the table and put my arm around her shoulders, and said, "There, there Lupe. You did just fine—didn't she judge?"

"I think …uh … I mean … yes, yes indeed. It's not your fault—no, it's not your fault at all," the judge stammered and turned to Jesus. "Just how good is your English, anyway."

"Not perfect, but pretty good—if I say myself."

"Why didn't you tell us you didn't need an interpreter?"

"You say I need one, not me. Besides, Senorita Lupe is cute, don't you think judge?" Mr. Cardozo said, grinning.

The judge cleared his throat and looked to me, and then to Lupe, and said, "Why yes … she is cute … very pretty I'd say."

The combination of the judge's comments, and being referred to as *pretty,* halted Lupe's tears like shutting off a faucet.

"Despite her being a *very* good interpreter, I sense Mr. Cardozo can handle the questions and answers on his own," the judge said, then addressed the defense, "Agreed counsel?"

Shiras said. "It's worth a try."

"Ms. Barbour?"

"I agree," I said and nodded to Lupe and she eagerly scurried back to the rear of the courtroom.

"Are you ready to continue, Mr. Cardozo?" the judge asked.

"Yes—but my throat is very dry, may I have a drink of water?"

"Of course," the Judge said. "Charlie, please get the Jesus here a cup of water."

Charlie poured a cupful from the water pitcher on our table, and as he handed the cup to Mr. Cardozo, Highsmith said, "Watch out, he may turn it into wine."

"No comments from the gallery, understand?" the judge said.

"Yes sir," Highsmith replied.

Jesus took two gulps from the cup, handed it back to Charlie, and the judge said, "You may proceed, Ms. Barbour."

"Let's get back to the insulation, explain to us how it would be installed."

"First you take off the old," Jesus said, and described how they would remove the existing insulation by prying it, sawing it or pounding it off with hammers or wrenches.

"Did you yourself do this?"

"In the early days, yes. Later batement companies did it."

"Batement?" the judge asked.

Shiras said, "I think he's trying to say abatement, as in asbestos removal contractors."

The judge asked, "Is that right?"

"Yes, batement contractors."

The judge addressed Blair. "Let the record reflect that when the witness says *batement* that he is meaning *abatement*."

I asked. "Would removing the insulation create dust?"

"Most definitely."

"Would the pipefitters be around when that occurred?"

"Yes, and sometimes they helped remove it, but only in the early days," he explained.

"Once the old insulation was off, what then?"

"They put the half-moon pieces around the pipe and hold it on with wires. Then the labor workers like me mix the mud to seal the insulation."

"Describe that mixing process for the mud."

"We pour powder from big sacks into a five-gallon bucket, or sometimes a wheel … a wheelbar … how do you say?"

"Wheelbarrow?" I said.

"Right, we pour the powder and mix in water and pipefitters spread it on."

"What was the air like when you mixed the mud?"

"Dusty—very, very dusty," he said, and I decided to pass him to the defense team.

When Shiras, marched over to the witness stand, Jesus' smile disappeared and he reacted as if the grim reaper himself was approaching.

"Sir, you don't know what the products you just described would have been made of, now do you?"

"It was bestos," Jesus responded.

"Bestos?"

"Yes, it was definitely bestos."

"Sir, do you mean asbestos," the judge asked.

Jesus nodded, and said, "Yes sir."

The judge turned to Blair, and said, "Let the record reflect that when Mr. Cardozo says *bestos* he means *asbestos*."

"I object to that, judge," Shiras said.

"Based on what?"

"Based on the fact that the witness is not saying the word *asbestos*."

"Do you maintain that Mr. Cardozo is referring to something other than asbestos?"

"No, but shouldn't he be required to say the actual word if he knows enough about it to be testifying in this trial?"

"We all know what he means, and simply because he says it a

different way than you and I, is irrelevant. I overrule the objection, now let's get on with it."

Shiras returned his attention to Jesus. "You have no actual knowledge that the insulation products and mud at the foundry contained asbestos, do you sir?"

"We were told it was."

"Objection, Your Honor," Shiras barked, "non-responsive and hearsay."

"Sustained, as to the hearsay," the Judge said and addressed Jesus. "Sir, please confine your answers to matters you know and not what you were told by others, understand?"

"As you wish," Jesus said.

Shiras continued. "Mr. Cardozo, where were you born?"

"Juarez."

"In Mexico?"

"Si—yes, Juarez Mexico."

"Did you attend grade school there?" Mr. Cardozo looked perplexed. "Grade school," Shiras repeated, then added in Spanish, "la escuela primaria."

"Oh, yes I did."

"What grade did you complete?"

"Four," Jesus said.

"Fourth grade, huh?" Shiras smirked while glancing toward the jury. "Can you read English?"

"Some, but not all."

"Can you read an English language newspaper?"

"Most words I know—some not."

"You can't tell this jury what was written on those bags of mud or the boxes of insulation, now can you?" Shiras asked.

"I never look."

"Thank you," Shiras said, and lifted a document from his table, and handed the judge and me a copy. It was a photograph of a cardboard box of thermal insulation and conspicuously stenciled on it in bold letters was *Asbestos-Free*. "I offer into evidence defense exhibit number one."

The judge stared at the document, then looked to me, "Any objection?"

I rose while struggling for a response. I glanced back at the photo, then muttered, "Yes sir ... I uh ... I don't know where this came from."

"I tend to agree," the judge said and turned to Shiras. "You're not saying that this is of a photo of a box at the foundry, are you?"

"No Your Honor. I only offer this for the limited purpose of establishing that there existed non-asbestos versions of the insulation."

The judge looked to me for further response, but I simply shook my head and sat down. "I will allow it, for that limited purpose only, and not as evidence of what the foundry did or did not have—defendant's one is admitted."

Shiras nodded to a member of his tech team, and in an instant, the same photograph sprang to life on all the courtroom monitors. "Mr. Cardozo, can you see this photograph," Jesus nodded. "I need a verbal response."

"Yes, I see it."

"Do you likewise see that the writing on this box that describes the insulation as *asbestos-free?*"

"Yes."

"Since you did not pay attention to the writing on the boxes you worked with, they very well may have had these same words on them, right?" Jesus glanced toward our table seemingly aware of the importance of the question, then turned back to Shiras and nodded. "Verbal response, please."

"Yes."

"Thank you," Shiras said. "Now about the removal of the old insulation products, the outside abatement contactors started doing that in the early seventies, true."

"Yes, it was required by Government."

"Right, and pipefitters like Mr. Blatchford would not do that during that time, right?"

"That's right, but he put on the new insulation."

"I object to the non-responsive portion for everything after *right.*"

"Sustained."

"To sum it up Mr. Cardozo, you cannot testify that Mr. Blatchford was exposed to asbestos at the Morrison foundry, now can you?"

Jesus hung his head, and uttered, "I not know."

"Pass the witness."

"Anything further, Ms. Barbour?" the judge asked.

"No judge."

"You may stand down, sir."

Mr. Cardozo stepped away from the witness stand, but instead of exiting the courtroom he took a seat next to Lupe in the gallery. Shiras, on the other hand, requested a conference to make a motion. We met at the bench, and the judge asked Charlie to take the jurors on a break. When the door to the courtroom closed, the judge said, "We're back on the record without the jury for a motion on behalf of the defense—let's hear it."

"I move to strike Mr. Cardozo's testimony in its entirety," Shiras said. "The only source of knowledge he has about asbestos content was from speaking to others. It is rank hearsay, and is neither competent or probative."

"I already sustained your hearsay objection."

"I understand judge, but with that ruling the rest of his testimony is irrelevant."

"I disagree," the judge said. "His description of the foundry, the work they did there and the dustiness of the products is pertinent."

"Only if they prove asbestos content," Shiras countered.

"I see your point," the judged said and turned to me. "I realize it is early in your case, but if you don't find some way to prove asbestos was in the stuff the plaintiff used, your case is in real jeopardy."

"I understand, sir."

"I will grant the motion to strike in part. Mr. Cardozo's testimony will be stricken, but *only* the portion concerning the materials having asbestos, and I will so instruct the jury. This ruling is made without prejudice and it can be re-urged at a later time. If in the end, there's no probative evidence that the materials the plaintiff used contained asbestos, I will strike the testimony in its entirety."

I did not fully comprehend the ruling, except that it was bad for us and walked dejectedly back to our table. When Charlie retrieved the jury, I realized I had another dilemma. I had not planned on needing more than the one witness that morning and had to act fast. I considered calling Nelda, but I had left the notepad with her questions in my car. What I did have, however, were my notes for Shiras' slick expert.

Once the jurors were seated, the Judge said, "Ladies and gentlemen, some of the testimony you heard from Mr. Cardozo was based in part, on what others told him. The portion about being told that the materials they used contained asbestos is hearsay, and thus inadmissible. Accordingly, I instruct that you each must strike that testimony from your mind. You should give it no weight unless and until asbestos content is proven, understood?" They all nodded and he turned to me. "Call your next witness counsel."

I rose, and said, "I call Brockholst Livingston."

"Wait!" Shiras said rising to his feet.

"Yes?" Mr. Morrison said, staring up at Shiras.

"Not you—Waite, I'm talking to the judge now," Shiras said. "Your Honor, I object—Doctor Livingston is my witness."

"Ms. Barbour?"

"It's his witness all right, but I want to question him."

The judge nodded, and said, "I see no reason why she can't question your witness in her case."

"I take exception to that."

"If you did not want him called, you should not have let him sit in this courtroom."

"As an expert, he is allowed to monitor the testimony," Shiras argued.

"I know that, but having a designated witness sitting in here makes him vulnerable to being called. I overrule the objection," the judge said and motioned Livingston forward.

Shiras grumbled under his breath as he returned to his seat, and Livingston passed him as he strolled toward the witness stand. Like Shiras, Livingston too was dressed to the nines and I had never seen a suit so shiny or an expression so smug.

Once seated, and under oath, I said, "State your full name, please."

He leaned forward in the witness chair, turned to the jury, and in his polished British accent said, "I am Doctor Brockholst Livingston, and I go by Brock."

"I can't blame him for that," Highsmith said under his breath.

"Mr. Livingston, I first want to know—"

"Doctor," he interrupted.

"Excuse me?"

"I said ... *doctor*. I have earned that title and expect to be referred to as such."

"Pardon me," I said with feigned contrition. "So ... *doctor*, what kind of patients you treat?"

He sighed. "I am sure you have my credentials in your file and know well that I am a Ph.D., not an M.D."

"Oh ... I see. Well, I will go ahead and call you doctor anyway, if you wish."

"How very kind of you," he sneered.

"What's a Ph.D.?" Jack asked.

"It means *post hole digger* to me, but I can tell that dude ain't never hit a lick," Highsmith said loud enough to be heard.

"That's enough sir," the judge warned. "I see from the cap you are holding that you're a service veteran so I'm going to give you deference—but cut the commentary."

"Yes sir," Highsmith said.

"Please proceed, Ms. Barbour."

"Doctor, I am sure the members of the jury have detected this by now, but you ain't from around here, are you?"

"You're right ... I *ain't* from around here," he mocked.

"Truth is—you came all the way over from jolly old England, didn't you?"

"Correct, but I have spent the past seven years living here in the states."

"Once here, you began hiring yourself out to lawyers like Mr. Shiras in order to help them win their cases, right?"

"Objection, your Honor, it's harassing, and I fail to see the relevance," Shiras said and the judge turned to me for a response.

Though I had studied up on objecting, I had nary a clue about responding to them, and said, "Um ... I will ... uh, I'll change the subject."

"Very well," the judge said.

"What do you get paid per hour to do all of this testifying?"

"I am certain you have that too, but my rate is three hundred and fifty dollars per hour."

A couple of folks in the jury box gasped, and Charlie the bailiff blurted, "Jesus!"

Those present instinctively turned to the audience, and Mr. Cardozo smiled, and said, "I used to it."

"Three fifty, huh?" I said rhetorically. "That's a lot for an hours' worth of work—how did you arrive at that price."

"As with any *price,* as you call it, it is based in part on my experience and what the market will bear. I assure you it is well within the range of what others in my métier fetch."

"What's métier?" I asked.

Highsmith answered first, "I think it's a town near New Orleans."

The judge glanced at Bill, then turned to Livingston, and said, "Is he right? Is it a town in Louisiana?"

"No, it is a French noun, not a town, and it means *occupation,*" Livingston explained condescendingly.

"That's very interesting, but we are having plenty of language issues in this case without adding another," the judge said. "So let's try to stick to English or Blair here might ask your rates to take the testimony."

"I'd settle for half," Blair joked.

Livingston responded, "I will cheerfully substitute the word *job* if that would please the court and plaintiff's counsel,"

"How very kind of you," I said, "but that hourly rate seems awfully steep, what do you say to that?"

"The fact is madam—and I use that term without the *e* at the end," Livingston said glancing toward the bench. "While in some circles my rate may seem excessive, I feel certain it is commensurate with what your experts are charging you."

"Mr. Livingston, I have—"

"Doctor," he corrected.

"Pardon me ... doctor, but my expert, who by the way is a *real* doctor, actually testified for free."

"Well, I guess you get what you pay for," he smirked.

I asked. "Just how many times have you testified for Mr. Shiras or his law firm?"

"I am not sure of the exact total, but quite a number of times by deposition and a few in trials."

"You have studied quite a bit about asbestos, haven't you?"

"You caught me ... the answer is *yes*."

"It is a poison, isn't it—I mean this stuff is toxic and can kill people, right?"

"It is convenient to refer to asbestos as a *poison* or to call it *toxic* for some sort of effect and to get a rise out of this jury. The truth is, virtually every substance we encounter in life has a poisonous potential," he said, then instinctively shifted in his chair to directly address the jury. "You see, there is a basic tenant in the field of toxicology which states *dose makes the poison* and that is accredited back to Paracelsus."

"I had an aunt that caught a dose of that, and it damn near killed her," Highsmith said, but thankfully not loud enough for the judge to hear.

"What are you getting at with this dose-poison thing?" I asked.

"Simply stated, it means that most anything at a high enough exposure can cause harm to human health. This includes everyday substances such as water, vitamin D, table salt and even alcohol."

"Alcohol?" Bill said urgently, but the judge did not hear it.

"What does this have to do with asbestos and Clifford Blatchford's death?"

"As a naturally occurring mineral, asbestos is in the ambient air. We all breathe it on a daily basis to one degree or another, but not in a dose that creates a risk to our health. If you breathe asbestos or countless other agents on and around planet earth at certain elevated doses it can result in disease."

"In terms of asbestos illnesses, that includes mesothelioma, the disease that took Clifford Blatchford's life."

"Asbestos can cause it, in rare instances."

"As such, the government banned it from products in the seventies, didn't it?"

"OSHA phased out some products then, but thankfully allowed others to continue until substitutes were found."

"You seem mighty pleased about that last part," I said.

Shiras rose. "Objection-harassing."

"Overruled, you will answer."

"The mere fact that a substance or a product can cause harm in extreme situations is not a justification for eliminating it."

"Are you telling this jury that asbestos materials are okay, and should be on the market today?" I asked.

"No, not necessarily. Manufacturers have developed suitable substitutes for most of the historic needs for asbestos," Livingston explained.

"Needs?"

Livingston returned his gaze to the jurors and lectured, "Asbestos was acid resistant, heat resistant and had excellent insulating values. It provided superior fireproofing qualities and delivered vital viscosity properties to the plastics industries. If we overreacted, snapped our fingers and made all substances that could possibly have a deleterious effect disappear, it could destroy civilization as we know it."

"I don't understand," I said.

"Dear lady, how did you make your way to this courthouse this morning," he asked.

"Highway eighty-four," I said.

The witness chuckled. "I was referring to your mode of transportation—was it an auto with a combustion engine?"

"That's right."

"Did you know petrol is toxic?"

I asked, "Are you referring to gasoline?"

"Correct."

"I have seen the warnings on the pumps, if that's what you mean," I said, having ceded the role of questioner to my witness.

"Right, but we don't eliminate it and do you know why?" Livingston said.

"No, but I bet you will tell me anyway."

"The reason that as a society we do not ban it is because the exposure to the motorist is minuscule. It is also a vital commodity for travel and industry and to ban it, without suitable substitutes, would be highly detrimental."

"That's all well and good, but exposure to asbestos can cause mesothelioma," I countered.

"True, but while asbestos is a cause of that malady, it's not the only cause. For example, therapeutic radiation treatments can cause mesotheliomas. Some say that the polio vaccine is a culprit, but that is not confirmed. There is also a mineral called Zeolite that may trigger the disease."

"What's that last one?" I asked.

"Zeolite, it is a substance found in Turkey."

"The bird?" I asked.

He sighed, and said, "No, the country across the Atlantic,"

"You are not aware of Mr. Blatchford being exposed to any of that Zeolite, are you?"

He grinned. "I know of no mesothelioma inducing agents to which he was exposed."

"My question to you is, you can't say that any of that stuff from Turkey or radiation made Cliff sick, can you?"

"That's not my problem," Livingston said. "I am sure that you are well aware that the law requires *you* to exclude all other potential causes."

"I will instruct on the law in this courtroom," the Judge admonished.

"I am sure you will," Livingston said.

"If asbestos is not the culprit, how do you explain Cliff Blatchford getting this terminal disease?"

"It is likely what is referred to as *idiopathic*," he said, and I recalled that term from Dr. Scotty's deposition. "I have seen no evidence that Mr. Blatchford was occupationally exposed to asbestos. That coupled with the fact that people sometime get this disease for reasons unknown, I conclude that it was idiopathic and not asbestos-related."

"Are you saying that *nothing* caused it—it just happened?" I asked.

"I am simply saying that there is no evidence that asbestos caused it. It is like people that contract lung cancer having never smoked cigarettes. There are genetic factors and perhaps other causes of this disease that we do not fully understand. The bottom line for this case is that there is no proof that this poor chap's illness was caused by his work at the Waite Morrison Foundry."

It seemed the more I asked, the worse things got and I decided to cut my losses. I passed the witness to Shiras, who elected to hold his questions until his case.

"Counsel, that's going to be it for this morning," the judge announced. "Ladies and gentlemen of the jury, you are now dismissed for lunch. Remember not to discuss this case amongst yourselves or with anyone else and we will see you back here at one o'clock."

Charlie ushered the panel to the jury room where they retrieved their belongings. He then escorted them out of the courtroom and when the doors closed the judge summoned me to the bench.

"Ms. Barbour, I take it you haven't tried an asbestos case before."

"You're right," I confessed.

"To tell you the truth, neither have I, but this is a very complex case."

"It is, and I promise to do better."

"Don't get me wrong, you still have a shot, but this better get moving in the right direction and fast."

"We do have other witnesses," I said, and he nodded.

I walked out of the courtroom and found that Jack and Highsmith had joined the ladies in the hallway. Jack informed that he and Bill were off to the Waco farmer's market and then back to Mexia to seine a pond for crawfish—half of the haul to bait their trot lines—the remainder for a future batch of my Cajun etouffee.

The girls and I retreated to the second-floor lounge and once there I removed the Tupperware bowls from the fridge. I pulled the lids off the containers, placed damp paper towels over them to avoid spatter, and each took a turn in the microwave. Once heated, the small dining area was filled with the fragrance of my home cooking.

Lupe was setting the table when the door of the lounge opened and in walked Judge Cushing. He removed a tin can from his lunch sack, pulled a can opener from one of the kitchen drawers and nodded as he passed us on his way to the refrigerator. He retrieved his soft drink, turned, tilted his nose upward and took a couple of sniffs.

"Is that greens I smell?"

"Yes sir," I said.

Dot added. "Judge, she's hands down the best darn cook in Limestone County."

He turned to me. "You're the one responsible for this wonderful aroma?"

"I am."

The judge stared admiringly at the containers on our table and took an inventory, "Black-eyed peas, collards and cornbread to boot."

"Don't forget the ham," Nelda said, lifting the damp paper towel to reveal the stack of thin red slices.

"Are those green things in the cornbread Jalapenos?" he asked.

"Yes, it is," I said, "and Lupe here grew the peppers."

"Oh ... so not only are you a swell interpreter, you have a green thumb too," the judge said patting Lupe on the shoulder, and she looked curiously at her hands. "Are they pickled or raw?"

"Raw," I said, and the judge grimaced.

"Don't worry," Dot said, "with them being cut into slivers and with the heat from the baking, they deliver only a mild punch—if don't happen upon a clump of them, that is."

"I always mix the batter well, but there's always a chance," I cautioned.

"Well, it certainly looks and smells terrific," he said, then began to open the can. It was then I noticed the Chef Boyardee label and said, "Judge, don't open that."

"Excuse me?"

"I would hate to see you eat out of a can with all this fresh food here."

"I ... uh ... I like SpaghettiOs," he said.

"I do too," I fibbed, "but save that for later and please take a plate of this instead."

"I'm tempted, I really am, but I—" he said, but stopped in mid-sentence and stared down at the table. "What's that in the collards?"

"It's just an extra ingredient I favor. You see, I use a little fatback instead of bacon."

The judge nodded, and asked, "And the little white pieces?"

"Minced onions and sautéed garlic," I said.

"We all know that part judge, but ask her what else she adds," Nelda said, with a sly grin.

"What about it?" he said.

I glared at Nelda, then addressed the judge, "I put in a little bit of thyme and a dash of sage."

Dot shook her head. "We know that part too, but what about—"

"At least have a taste," I said, trying to head off the interrogation.

"Are you sure?" the judge asked.

"It would hurt my feelings if you don't," I said, extending a plastic spoon to him. He hesitated for a moment, then sat the can and can opener on the counter. He took a scoop of the greens, placed it in his mouth, but did not immediately chew. For a moment his eyes were as round as saucers, then they rolled back in his head, and then he finally chewed.

He was savoring it for sure and when he swallowed, he said, "That's terrific, but there's something else in it that gives it a little kick, right?"

"There sure is and we sure would like to know what it is," Nelda said.

I explained. "Judge, that particular ingredient is not just secret, it is super-duper double secret."

"Make her tell you, judge," Dot urged.

Nelda nodded her encouragement, and explained, "She has won

six blue ribbons out of the last eight Limestone County Fairs with her collards."

"Very impressive—is this secret ingredient the reason for that success?" he said.

"Yes," Nelda blurted.

I explained, "She's right, and because of that I would uh … you know … like to keep it to myself."

"Just tell it to me, and it'll be our little secret," the judge said.

"You promise?"

"Ms. Barbour, as officers of the court we are both under oath in this building."

I did not know that, and immediately regretted my SpaghettiOs endorsement, but his comment was good enough for me. "Fingers in your ears ladies," I demanded. They complied and I whispered, "The kick comes from a couple of dashes of vodka. Once the greens cook down, you sauté them in a pan and douse it with the hooch."

"Oh my, so the alcohol is the key?" he whispered back.

"Yes, but don't worry about the vodka. It cooks off—so no alcohol remains, but it leaves the kick," I said and motioned for the girls to remove their fingers.

"I'm going to try that—thanks for confiding in me," he said cheerfully.

"You are very welcome, and you're also welcome to share in our lunch."

He shook his head. "That's awfully kind of you, but I … um … I don't think I should."

"You really do want some don't you and remember that we are both under oath," I said, wryly.

"Of course I do, but there are four of you and I hate to take food off your table."

"I made plenty to share, so please help yourself," I said handing him a partitioned Chinet plate and a fork to go with his spoon. The judge relented and scooped and forked eagerly and left the lounge with three slices of ham, a helping of greens, a pile of peas and a sizable wedge of the cornbread.

After we finished our meals and tidied the lunch room, I said, "Nelda, I am going to go to my car and get my other notepad—are you ready to testify?"

"Sure, I'm actually tired of fretting about it and would like to get it over with."

"Good, I would have told you earlier, but I didn't want to spoil your lunch," I said.

"The lunch was a real treat, and thank you for it," Nelda said.

"I second that," Dot added.

"Mi tambien," said Lupe, happily.

"You are all very welcome. Dot, please take my tote bag back to the courtroom and I'll meet y'all there."

Dot agreed and I proceeded down the stairs, out of the courthouse and to my car. I retrieved my notes and headed back inside and since I was unaccompanied I made use of the elevators. When I entered the courtroom I noticed more bodies present in the gallery, each seemingly there only as spectators. I joined the girls at our table and soon the jurors were back in the jury box and the judge asked for my next witness.

I rose and said, "We call Nelda Fay Blatchford."

The judge nodded and Nelda stood, walked cautiously to the witness stand and took her oath. She eased down into the witness chair, pulled a package of Kleenex from her purse, and laid it on the rail in front of her. She sat stiffly erect and to ease her into the questioning, I began with her background.

"Tell us your name and where you are from."

"I am Nelda Fay Blatchford and I was born in Mexia, Texas."

I knew well the answer to the next question, but asked anyway, "What doctor and in what hospital?"

She smiled, and said, "That would be midwife and my parents' bedroom."

"You are the widow of Clifford Blatchford?"

"That's right."

"Tell me about when you and Cliff first met."

I noticed her brace herself by gripping the wooden railing. "We actually went to the same church when we were just kids, so we had known each other as far back as my memory goes."

"Were you two sweet on each other back then?"

"Heavens no," she said with a nervous chuckle. "At that age, Cliff, and all the other boys for that matter were still in the *cooties* stage. He was also two years older than me so we were not in the same Sunday school class. However, I would see him at preaching and at the potluck dinners. Later, his parents moved to Navarro County and I was not around him for quite a while."

"Why did his folks move away?"

"Cliff was from a family of pickers, and I don't mean guys driving around in an air-conditioned van buying antiques," she said to the amusement of the attendees. "They were crop pickers and when Cliff and his siblings were old enough they, too became pickers. When the peach crop suffered in Limestone County they took a tenant farm opportunity and moved away."

"Where did they go?"

"To a cotton farm located east of Corsicana, but after several years with no crop rotation, the soil become poor and lied fallow. Fortunately, they had not sold their house in Mexia so they were able move back."

"When did you next see Cliff?"

"We did not cross paths until one afternoon at the Dairy Queen."

"The one in Mexia?" I asked.

"That's right. My girlfriends and I were in a booth eating ice cream when Cliff walked in with a couple of his buddies, but I did not recognize him right away. They ordered hamburgers and malts and took a table across the dining area from us. When he passed us on his way to get some napkins I saw his name embroidered on his Dunbar High School letterman's jacket. He was much bigger and more mature and looked so handsome. We made eye contact and I nodded and smiled, and he smiled back. As he ate and talked to his friends, he kept glancing over at me and I was glad for it."

"Was this while you two were still in high school?"

"Yes, I was a freshman and Cliff was a junior," she said, and the tension seemed to drain from her voice and she eased her grasp on the rail. "I had heard that he was a fullback on the football team. I did not know what that even meant and still don't to tell you the truth, but I was impressed by it just the same."

"May I approach, Your Honor?" I asked.

"Yes, you may."

I rose and walked around our table with a photograph and two copies of it in hand. I gave Shiras and the judge theirs and proceeded to the witness stand.

"Want me to mark that?" Blair whispered. I looked at her curiously and she added, "As an exhibit?"

"Oh—yes, thank you," I said handing her the original.

"Should the sticker go on the front or back?" Blair asked and we both glanced to Nelda.

She said, "I have duplicates, so it doesn't matter."

Blair placed the exhibit sticker on the bottom right corner of the image, handed it back to me, and said, "Plaintiff's one judge."

"Thank you, Blair," the judge said, "any objection from the defense?"

Shiras glanced up from the photo, rose and said, "No, Your Honor."

"Plaintiff's exhibit number one is admitted."

"So who are these two young folks depicted here?" I asked handing the photo to Nelda. No doubt she had seen the black and white 8x10 countless times, but nonetheless gazed at it fondly.

She slowly lowered it, sighed, and said, "That handsome fullback is Clifford and the gangly old thing next to him is me."

"What year was it taken?" I asked.

"This was the first photo of us together, so let's see," she said, pausing to make a mental calculation, "it had to be in nineteen sixty-six or seven."

"He has on the Dunbar letterman's jacket, but it looks like your corsage steamers are the colors of the Mexia Black Cats. Were you two attending different high schools?"

"Yes, Mexia High was integrating and I chose to go to there instead of Dunbar."

"That must have been awkward for you."

"It was, but I had little help," Nelda said with a wink and a smile.

Returning to the photo, I asked, "Whose truck is that in the background?"

"That was his father's nineteen forty-eight Ford pick-up."

"He let Cliff drive it?"

"On occasions, at least up until the day Cliff wrecked it," she said, shaking her head.

"How did he manage to do that?"

"He and his friends were out goofing around in it and they got challenged to a drag race. Cliff accepted and they took Belknap east until it turns into that dirt road and they had at it. Clifford won the race, but as he passed the finish line he lost control. He braked hard, but still managed to crash into the stump of an old sycamore tree."

"What did Cliff do?"

"Objection, Your Honor," Shiras said. "This little trip down memory lane has been charming, but it has nothing to do with the case."

"We've gone this far with it, so we might as well see it through," the judge said. "I overrule the objection—please proceed, Ms. Blatchford."

"Though banged up pretty bad the truck was still drivable, but Cliff dared not go straight home. Instead, he drove to our house and my family happened to be on the porch churning a batch of homemade ice cream. When he pulled up in front he motioned toward me through the driver's side window. I could tell by his expression he was troubled and when I walked to the roadside, he explained what he had done. Clifford knew he had to tell his dad, but he was scared and wanted me to come with him, believing he was less likely to *be killed* with me there. With a promise to have me back in thirty minutes my folks let me go along. When we arrived, Cliff called his father outside and led him around to the other side of the truck. He showed him the mangled fender and explained hitting a tree stump—with no mention of the drag racing."

"How did his dad react?"

"He was upset, but not overly so and was most thankful that Cliff wasn't injured. He did ask how fast he was going, and Cliff fudged by saying *ten miles per hour*. Cliff's dad said …uh … he said oh, I can't say it," Nelda said shaking her head.

The judge, now invested in the outcome, urged her on saying, "Go ahead, we can handle it."

"Okay," she said and cleared her throat. "His dad looked at the damage again and asked *if you were only goin' ten, how fast was the damn stump goin'?*"

I next explored how they began dating and where they went and what they enjoyed doing as a couple in love. She described how Cliff proposed to her and worked up the nerve to seek her father's consent to marry.

"What did your dad say?"

"After committing Cliff to some promises and agreements, my dad consented."

"What were these agreements about?" I asked.

"I wasn't privy to them at the time," she explained. "I was busy in the kitchen helping my mother when that private man-to-man conference took place on the back porch. I later learned that it involved things such as treating me like a lady, working hard and being a good provider, bearing children and never—ever—laying an angry hand on me."

"Did Cliff live up to those promises?"

"In each and every respect," she said firmly.

She next described how they embarked on a traditional courtship and that eighteen months later they tied the knot at their church. The exchanging of the vows was followed by a simple punch and finger sandwich reception in the fellowship hall. Avoiding the timing of said births, we discussed the delivery of their two sons, and then the arrival of the twin grandchildren and the impending birth of the third.

I transitioned to Cliff's career and Nelda described his post-crop picking work including that of a carpenter and roofer. She explained that he enrolled in an industrial program where he learned welding and once done scoured the want-ads daily for an opportunity to ply his newly learned trade.

"When he happened upon an ad for an apprentice welder position at the Morrison foundry he was overjoyed," Nelda said.

"Why was that?"

"He was excited in part because he was tired of nailing shingles in the Texas heat. He was also anxious to fulfill the *good provider* part of his pledge to my dad. Landing a job in Mexia, one only a few blocks from our house would be a true blessing ... we thought," she said and her joyful expression changed.

"Did he apply for it?"

"He did and though it was for a bottom rung position to be sure, Cliff knew that if he got his foot in that door, and worked hard, that he would thrive there. He hand-delivered the application, got a date for an interview and I remember vividly just how nervous he was when he left the house to meet with Mr. Morrison," she said glancing to the defense table.

"How did it go?"

"I knew the result the moment he bounded through the door. He was grinning from ear-to-ear, and he grabbed me, lifted me up and spun me around—I uh ... I was ... a lot lighter then," she added.

"He was excited, but were you?"

"Sure I was," she said. "Though the starting pay was meager, and he had to begin on the graveyard ... I mean ... the overnight shift—we saw it as a great opportunity."

"What were his hours?"

"Ten at night to six in the morning."

"When was he promoted from welder to pipefitter?" I asked.

Nelda thought for a moment. "It had to be in the early seventies"

"Can you narrow it down to a year?"

"I know it was when all that Watergate mess was going on."

"How do you connect it to that?"

"When Cliff made apprentice pipefitter, he had to return to working nights. I remember him being home during the day when those Watergate hearings were playing on TV—all three channels I might add. I was ticked off that my daytime stories weren't being played, but Cliff actually liked watching the hearings, and said that the scandal was more interesting than my soaps."

"How long did he have to work nights as a pipefitter in training?"

"It wasn't a full year, but it was several months. After that, he switched back to the first shift and had to adjust to working days again."

"Did Cliff like pipefitting?"

"He did, but he also commented on the difficulties of it. Don't get me wrong, welding is by no means a clean job, but pipefitting is downright filthy. Though it was a higher pay grade, if I knew then what that job would do to him, and what would happen to him, I'd ... I'd ... I'd never let him do it," she said and reached for a Kleenex.

The judge said, "Do you need to take a break ma'am?"

Nelda shook her head. "No sir—I'm all right."

The judge nodded toward me, and I continued, "Tell us about Cliff's daily work attire."

"The foundry required him to wear heavy steel-toed shoes with protective spats to guard his feet and ankles from the molten metals. His uniform was dark gray pants, white socks and a light grey long-sleeved shirt with his name embroidered on it."

"What would he do when he got home?"

"Assuming we did not have company Cliff would go from the garage straight to the laundry room and strip down to his underwear."

"Why would he do that?"

"He didn't want to get the dust and dirt from the foundry all over our house."

"Describe how he looked when we arrived home on a typical day."

"His clothes were always sweaty no matter the time of year and very dirty regardless of what he did that day. Dust would be all over his uniform, and where he had sweated it would be caked on. It would often be in his hair, his eyebrows and nostrils."

"I object to the nonresponsive portion," Shiras said.

"Response?" the judge said to me.

"I object to his objection," I said. "Nelda's answer was very responsive—he just did not like it."

"Objection to counsel's sidebar," Shiras added.

"Then I object to—"

"Whoa, y'all calm down," the judge said, with his gavel raised. He pondered, then said, "I … uh … I overrule the responsiveness objection. I overrule the objection to the objection and sustain the sidebar objection. Blair, did I get them all?"

"Yes, sir—at least I think so."

The judge nodded, and said, "Carry on Ms. Barbour."

"What would you do with Cliff's clothes once he removed them?"

"If the weather was tolerable I would carry them out the rear door of the laundry room and into our backyard. I would set them on the patio table and shake out each article one by one."

"What if the weather was not tolerable?"

"I would shake them out over the laundry room garbage can. The dust that got on me, or fell to the floor, I would brush off and sweep up once the wash was started."

"How often did you do this laundering?"

"Every weekday and during turnarounds it could include weekends as well," Nelda explained.

"Did Cliff work shutdowns and turnarounds?"

"Oh yes, he did. There were some shutdowns where outside contractors came in to handle it, but other than that Cliff took all of them that he could."

"Good overtime?"

"Yes indeed, Cliff never turned down time and a half if he could help it."

"Why did you do laundry so frequently?"

"Cliff's work clothes were expensive," she explained. "As a result, he only had two full uniforms at any given time so I did a load a day to keep up."

"The foundry made the workers buy the clothes that they mandated."

"Yes, but they had a program where they would deduct the payments out of each check and we would replace items as they wore out."

"About the dust that you have described, what did Cliff tell you it was from?"

"Objection—hearsay," Shiras blurted.

"Overruled," the judge said. "I believe the rules allow her to describe conversations she had with her husband—you may answer, ma'am."

"Cliff said that most of the dust was from the insulation at the foundry."

"Did he ever tell you the dust was asbestos?"

"Objection, Your Honor," Shiras bellowed. "There is no foundation for Ms. Blatchford to answer that and the question calls for speculation and hearsay."

"Ms. Barbour?"

I rose, and said, "Judge, you just said yourself that she can testify about what they discussed."

"This is different," the judge said. "I am going to overrule the hearsay and speculation objections, but what about the lack of foundation?"

I knew what was on the line, but tensed, then uttered, "I uh … I … don't understand."

The judge looked disapprovingly at me, and said, "You two approach please." Shiras and I returned to the bench and the judge said, "Ms. Barbour, he is saying there is a lack of foundation for her to give an answer your question. Mr. Blatchford may have told her that it was asbestos, but what was *his* basis for saying that?"

"Sorry judge, but I'm still confused. You let Nelda give his description of the dust from the insulation and she—"

"That was different," the judge said. "Him telling her about the dust from the insulation was is his own personal perception, but what it was comprised of is not—any response to that?"

"No sir," I sighed.

The judge addressed Blair saying, "I will sustain the foundation objection until a proper predicate is laid."

I swallowed my disappointment, returned to our table and pressed on. "When did Cliff retire from the foundry?"

"On his sixty-fifth birthday."

"Did he become a couch potato after that?"

"Lord no," Nelda said emphatically. "He remained very active in retirement."

"What did he like to do?"

He was a true sportsman and loved to fish and hunt, and spent a lot of his time doing that with our boys. He also maintained our house, inside and out. He mowed the grass and we tended our garden together. He also did woodworking and had his own shop, and he was especially good at it."

"What did he make in his shop?" I asked.

"He could make most anything, including bookcases, cabinets, tables, chairs and the like."

"What did he do with his finished pieces?"

"He rarely kept anything for himself, giving most items away as gifts to friends and family. He donated pieces for fundraisers at the church, and on occasions, he gave furniture to families that had suffered a fire or had theirs stolen."

"What else did he like to do?"

"He did handiwork for people at church, mostly the elderly, and for some folks around our neighborhood."

"Did he charge them anything?"

"No, but some insisted on paying him which would help with our household expenses."

"When did Cliff start having signs that something wrong?"

"It was seven, maybe eight months before he died. He had gone hunting on the last week of deer season and returned home complaining of tightness in his chest and a cough. Cliff was always healthy as a horse and I knew that if he complained he was truly feeling bad. I was worried that it might be bronchitis or some form of respiratory infection—God knows now I wish that was all it was."

"What was done about his symptoms?" I asked.

"He took over the counter medicines and I urged him to get some rest and to not to exert himself. After a couple of days with no improvement, I was getting worried and nagged him to go to the doctor."

"Did he agree to go?"

"Of course not," she said with a nervous chuckle, "but things changed one chilly morning when Cliff went out to check the mail. He said he was *stir crazy*, so I let him do it and though he did not realize it, I was watching him through the front window. On his way back up the driveway, I noticed he kept stopping and bending over and putting his hands on his thighs. He was taking deep breaths, and I had never seen him do this before, at least not without extreme exertion. Since he was not improving I demanded he see Dr. Ginsberg—our family doctor at that time."

"Did Cliff agree?"

"Yes, and with minimal resistance and that, more than anything else, proved to me he was troubled," Nelda said and proceeded to describe the details of the physical exam and the doctor's order for chest x-rays.

"What did they show?" I asked.

"That he had fluid around his lungs and the doctor thought it was pneumonia. They treated it with antibiotics and that helped some, but a few days later the shortness of breath returned. Dr. Ginsberg eventually referred Cliff to a specialist in Temple."

"What did the specialist do?"

"They first drained off the fluid to give him some relief and to help him breathe. Following that, Dr. Patel did a biopsy and sent it off to a lab for testing and it showed—" Nelda's voice fell off, and her emotions took hold and she dabbed tears from her cheeks.

"Are you okay to go on?" I asked.

She nodded, and said, "Yes … yes … I'm all right."

"Then tell us about the biopsy."

"Three days later we were asked to a meeting to discuss the results. I had always gotten my test results over the phone or by mail, but this time they would not do that. I tried to stay positive, but even Cliff knew he was in trouble. We headed over to Temple that morning and I don't think either of us said a single word during the drive. When we entered the office, both Doctor Patel and Doctor Strong were there and I could see it in their eyes."

"What did they tell you, hon?"

"They were sure he had a rare form of lung cancer."

"How did Cliff react?"

"He didn't, at least not then, but I could see it in his eyes," Nelda whimpered

"Fear?"

"Yes, and in a way, I'd never seen before."

"What kind of cancer did they say Cliff had?"

Nelda took a deep breath, paused then said, "We were told it was that meso ... uh, mesothe ... dang it."

"Mesothelioma?" I said.

"Yes—that's it all right," she said. "I had heard that term on TV, but I could not imagine Clifford having any bad disease like that—one that we couldn't even pronounce."

"What were you two told about it?"

"Doctor Patel said that it was ... it was ... oh God—"

"Take your time, sweetie," I said and paused until she gathered herself. "The doctor said it was what?"

"Incurable—six to nine months," Nelda gasped, then slumped forward with her head in her hands. She was trembling and sobbing, but the room remained respectfully still and quiet. Soon she calmed, raised her head, and wiped her now bloodshot eyes with a tissue.

"We can take a break if you like, ma'am," the judge offered.

"Please go on ... I want to get through this," she sniffled, "0and I'm very sorry for all the blubbering."

"It's quite all right, we all understand," the judge said.

I continued. "In your last answer, you were saying that Cliff had six to nine months to live, right?"

"Yes, that's all they gave us."

"How did he take the prognosis?"

"Clifford never wore his emotions on his sleeve. On that day and beyond, outwardly he seemed to take it well—until one particular evening. I had been over at the church for devotionals, and when I returned home I could not find Cliff. At that time of the evening, he would normally be in our den watching television, but he was not. I walked down the hallway, checked the bathroom and the light was off. I finally found him in our bedroom and what I saw floored me."

"Please explain," I said.

"Though the bedroom door was slightly ajar, Cliff apparently did not hear me come home. When I reached to open the door to enter, I stepped back when I heard him. I peeked in through the opening and into our bedroom and there he sat all slumped over on the side of our bed. He was clutching my pillow with his head hung down toward the floor and sobbing. In four decades of marriage I had never seen or heard him cry, and it broke my heart."

"What did you do?"

"Not wanting to embarrass him, I moved away from the bedroom and quietly backtracked toward the front door. Once there, I pretended to enter, and this time I made enough racket that he was certain to know I was there. I called his name from down the hall and though it took a second or two, he answered me. I took my time making my way back to the bedroom, and when I entered he had straightened up and my pillow was in its place. I asked him if he was okay and he said that he was *just tired*."

"How did your family react to Cliff's diagnosis?"

"The grandchildren didn't understand it, but our boys and their wives were devastated. They were all so close to Cliff and it seems silly now, but they did not think their daddy would ever die."

"Did his mesothelioma cause Cliff to curtail his activities?"

"Not too much—at least at first. As it took hold though, he laid off of the yard work and helping with the garden. Later he stopped going to his woodworking shop, but quitting the church choir hurt him the most."

I smiled, and said, "He had a great singing voice, didn't he?"

"He did indeed, four octaves worth."

Nelda next provided details of the progression of Cliff's illness and how his health rapidly declined. She described that within a matter of a month and a half, he lost over fifty pounds leaving him weighing barely a hundred and twenty.

I decided to use two additional photographs from those selected from Nelda's family album. The first was from the December before the diagnosis and it featured a cheerful and robust Clifford on the floor next to their Christmas tree. He was surrounded by the whole family and was wearing a red and white Santa hat. A fake cotton beard drooped on his face and he was passing out presents to eager recipients. The second picture showed him after the weight loss, weak, gaunt and lying in bed with their twin grandkids. The contrast between the two images was stark and I had Blair mark them, and each were allowed into evidence. I handed the photos to Nelda and she described them and I asked her to explain how the grandkid's reacted when they were brought in to see Cliff.

"They did not recognize him at first and were actually a little frightened. Once they heard his voice though, they perked up and hugged him," she said, then sighed, "turned out to be the last time they would see their Granddad—alive that is."

"What was Cliff's physical condition at this point?"

"He was weak and confined to our bed most of the time, and then came Hospice."

"Tell us about getting them involved," I said.

"I had heard the term, but knew little about them or what they do. Since both Doctor Patel and Doctor Strong urged us to involve them, I did some research."

"Like what?"

"I spoke with some folks at our church that had, unfortunately, experienced similar episodes with loved ones and to a person they highly recommended Hospice. I learned that they actually come into people's homes and when I explained that to Clifford he was skeptical, to say the least. As a private man the notion of having strangers in our house, especially with him sick, was not a concept he readily embraced. Ultimately we agreed to reach out to them and it was the best decision we could have made."

I said, "For those of us fortunate not to have needed their services, tell us what Hospice does."

"They are so helpful and knowledgeable and the nurses are nothing short of angels of mercy. The first thing they did was to have a team of movers bring us a full-size hospital bed. It was so big that it had to be brought into our home in pieces and assembled inside. Since it could not fit in our bedroom, it was placed smack dab in our living room. My boys and I, and the nurses all pitched in to move the furniture out of the way to make room for it. The movers put the bed together, the nurses adjusted it and we all teamed up to move Cliff from our bedroom to the living room and place him on it."

"How did Cliff take that?"

"Not so well, but the nurses explained to him that this was a way to let this all play out at home and not in a hospital room. That was important to Cliff and to further ease his mind I brought one of our camping cots into the living room and set it up next to his bed."

"To sleep on?"

"That's right," she said.

"Wasn't that uncomfortable?" I asked.

"Somewhat, but it was a small sacrifice considering I was not going to get much sleep no matter where I laid my head."

"Did the Hospice nurses make regular visits to your home?"

"Yes, and though it was awkward at first, we quickly adapted to their presence. Later, the visits per week increased as you know … uh … as Cliff declined. It was then that the nurses were most helpful to me and our whole family."

"How so?"

"There is no other way to put it except to say that they teach the process of dying. This included the signs to watch for and what to expect at different stages. They monitored Cliff's vital signs and assisted with keeping him clean and most importantly comfortable. Cliff's comfort was our biggest concern and when he would complain, the nurses wasted no time in medicating him."

"What kind of pain did Cliff experience?"

"Oh God … it was just plain awful. He would wince in pain and occasionally moan out loud. Sometimes he would be in such anguish that he could hardly draw a comfortable breath, and one of us, or when the nurses were there, they would get his medicine in him. It would eventually help, but the time between him getting a dose and

Cliff receiving relief seemed like an eternity to us. I can only imagine what it was like for him and all I could do was hold his hand and talk him through it."

"Was he conscious at this point?"

"Sometimes, but other times it was difficult to tell. The nurses warned us though, about saying distressing things around him, even if he seemed unconscious. Apparently, patients in Cliff's state can perceive things and depending on what is being said it could add to the anxiety or it could comfort him, and I will give you an example. One morning the nurse arrived and she took a seat in a chair next to the hospital bed. Cliff appeared completely out of it as she took his blood pressure. After she recorded the results, she sat at his bedside tending to him, while I put on a CD of our church choir performing Cliff's beloved hymns. Included were *How Great Thou Art, When the Roll Is Called up Yonder* and Cliff's personal favorite, *Amazing Grace* which he performed as a solo on the recording. When the nurse was done swabbing his lips, she re-checked his blood pressure and it had dropped by twelve points on the first number and eight on the second."

"You mentioned swabbing Cliff's lips, what was that about?"

"We both signed those papers, you know the ones with the *do not revive* clause in it. As such, when Cliff declined to the point where he could no longer eat or drink on his own there would be no IV to provide him nourishment. I uh … I wanted so much to … to … oh God," she stopped and grabbed another Kleenex.

"Take your time Nelda," I said.

She cleared her throat, and sobbed, "It was only natural to want to feed him and nurture him, as I had done for all those years. The nurses explained that giving him anything would just prolong the uh … the … the inevitable and I just prayed that he would not think I was neglecting him. Since all they allowed him to have was ice chips, his mouth would dry out and his lips would crack. As a result, when any of us gave him the ice we also tended to his lips and mouth."

"How would you go about that?" I said.

"On the nurse's recommendation, we bought a supply of those little plastic paint brushes, the ones with the grey foam sponges on the end. We kept a bowl of water on his rolling hospital tray and would dip the brushes in it and used them to wet and swab his lips and the inside of his mouth."

"It was all about his comfort at that point."

"That's right, and toward the end when he was most always unconsciousness we could not tell if he was in pain or not. That worried us greatly considering that above all we did not want him to suffer. The nurses would keep up with his vital signs and from things like his heart rate they could tell if he was hurting or not and that would guide them on when to give the morphine."

"If he had no IV and could not ingest it, how did he receive the pain medication?" I asked and immediately noticed that the question disturbed her.

"I pray Cliff will forgive me for telling this," she said, glancing upward. "Toward the end, the nurses administered the pain medicine on a schedule and used suppositories. When they weren't there—I did it."

I said gently, "Tell us how it all ended."

Nelda set up straight, took a deep draw of breath, and exhaled. "I got up that morning and started the laundry and made some toast for breakfast. Cliff had not been conscious for the better part of the past four days and I knew from my own instincts, and through Hospice that he was nearing the end. The nurses were due to arrive shortly, so I was tidying up the house. As I did, I walked through the living room a few times and on one such pass, I looked over at Cliff. All of a sudden his eyes blinked rapidly several times then popped wide open. I could tell that the overhead light was bothering him so I raced over and switched it off. I then sat on the cot next to him, grasped his hand and stared into his eyes and I was amazed."

"About what?" I said.

"They were his normal eyes and not his dying eyes," Nelda said.

"Can you explain what you mean by that?"

"If you have never ushered a loved one through the process of dying it's difficult to explain. In the beginning, they have scared eyes, ones that are filled with fear and dread, but as they diminish in weight and function their eyes change. I saw it with my father when he was near the end and it was no different with Clifford. I think the military calls it the *thousand yard stare* and when someone has it, the eyelids are no longer droopy and partially closed like normal. Instead, they are wide open, so much that you can see the entire pupil. When Cliff was at that stage he would look at me, but he seemed to stare right through me. It was as if he was looking well beyond me and toward some faraway place. I thought he just might be staring straight into heaven, but at this time and on this morning it was different. There was no anguish, no fear, and no thousand yard stare. They were *his* eyes—the eyes I had known every day of our life together staring straight into mine. For the moment he was just like he was before he got so sick and though no words were coming out, I could tell that he was mouthing, *I love you.* He gently squeezed my hand, then shut his eyes, and I did not need vital signs or any doctor to tell me that he was leaving me. He gave one little gasp of air and then one big one and then *it* happened."

"What?" the judge said before I did.

"Cliff's face had a slight grin and tears filled his eyes and streamed down the side of his face. I know they were tears of joy as he left us to commence his next journey. Now I have read up on this and some articles explain that fluids can come out of a person when they die. They say it's *natural*, but I know in my heart that they were tears—his tears—and not just some so-called *bodily function*," she said, laid her head on her folded arms on the rail of the witness stand and wept.

Others present shared in the emotional moment, including three jurors and several spectators who dried their own eyes. The judge reacted by swiveling his high back chair 180 degrees and plucking a book from the shelf and pretending to read it.

I resumed my questioning by discussing Cliff's funeral and the expenses of it and his burial. I then turned to the difficulties of life following Cliff's death. Nelda described resorting to family members, neighbors or hiring handymen to perform the tasks that Cliff had customarily handled.

"You depended on Cliff a lot, didn't you?" I asked, and noticed Charlie handing a note to the judge.

"That's an understatement," Nelda sniffled.

"How important was family through all of this?"

She sighed, and said, "I can't imagine going through this without their support. I am so very, very lucky to have them."

I nodded and said, "That's all from me, thank you Nelda."

Shiras bolted to his feet and walked eagerly around his table, but stopped on a dime when Judge Cushing held up his hand and said, "Whoa—we're done for today."

Shiras frowned and consulted his Rolex. "It's only a quarter to three."

"I'm fully aware of the time Mr. Shiras, but I was just informed that I have an emergency TRO hearing at three-thirty in a sequestration case," the judge said displaying the note from Charlie.

"Why can't I question the plaintiff until then?"

"I would like to review the motion and exhibits before the parties get here—if you don't mind," the judge snapped.

"Understood," Shiras relented.

Then the judge addressed the jurors. "I apologize for this, but a temporary restraining order is an urgent matter, otherwise I would not delay this trial for it. You are dismissed for the day, so we'll see you all and the parties at the same time in the morning."

We packed up, exited the courthouse and as we drove away, all I could think about was just how anxious Shiras was to get to Nelda.

11
CHAPTER

When we arrived at the courthouse the next morning, we followed the same routine by visiting the lawyer's lounge before heading for the third floor. Once in the courtroom, I glanced to the defense table and noticed Shiras seated there. He was biding his time reviewing what likely represented his slate of questions for Nelda, inquiries that he had undoubtedly honed with the extra time afforded by the Judge's emergency hearing.

We idled at our table until the judge entered and the court came to order. Once the jury was seated, Blair motioned Nelda forward and she walked anxiously back to the witness stand. She took her seat and Blair reminded her that she remained under oath.

The judge nodded to Shiras, and said, "Your witness."

Shiras rose and made a beeline to Nelda. "Ms. Blatchford, your husband smoked cigarettes during his lifetime, did he not?"

"Yes sir, he smoked some back when he was in the service and for a few years into the seventies."

"You know that cigarettes are harmful to human health, don't you?"

"Yes, sir. They are bad, in fact, they are terrible. I never liked a single moment that he smoked them, but men, especially servicemen and blue-collar workers smoked a lot back in the day."

"Judge, I object to the responsiveness and move to strike everything after the word *terrible*," Shiras said.

"Sustained."

"Your husband also suffered from high blood pressure and had early stages of diabetes, didn't he?"

"I don't see what that has to do with anything," Nelda replied defensively.

"Objection, non-responsive," Shiras said.

"Sustained," the judge said, then instructed, "ma'am, please just answer his questions and nothing more."

Nelda nodded, and said, "Yes, Cliff did have early stages of diabetes, but he was exercising and watching his diet for that."

The judge beat Shiras to the punch. "Ms. Blatchford, counsel asked if your husband had diabetes, and not how it was handled. Just answer Mr. Shiras' question as asked, and if any response needs further elaboration your counsel can do that on re-direct, okay?"

"Yes, sir."

Shiras continued. "Now, tell us your husband's blood pressure history?"

"It was a little high, but was always well controlled with medicine, and now he has no blood pressure."

"Objection, nonresponsive."

"Overruled," the judge said. "You asked for the blood pressure history and you got it."

Shiras sighed, then asked, "How old was your husband when he died?"

"He was sixty-eight."

"Truth is, he was only a month or so away from sixty-nine, wasn't he?"

"That's right. Cliff died in late August, and his birthday would have been in October."

"Do you understand that risk factors like smoking, diabetes and high blood pressure tend to shorten one's life?" Shiras said.

"I suppose that's true, at least in some instances."

"Are you familiar with the term, *life expectancy*?"

"I've heard of it," she said.

"Do you know what your husband's statistical life expectancy was?"

"No sir, but I don't think that—"

"Would it surprise you to know that with all factors being

considered, your husband's life expectancy was between age sixty-nine and seventy-one?"

"I don't understand," Nelda said, seemingly unnerved by the line of questioning.

"It's simple," Shiras said staring directly into Nelda's eyes. "According to mortality data, your husband was due to die as early as age sixty-nine. Consequently, he had statistically lived to his life expectancy when he did pass on."

Nelda said, "How do you calculate that?"

"I don't, but experts do," Shiras smirked. "Statisticians arrive at these scientific projections based on certain factors. In the case of your husband, they would take into account his family history, ethnicity, his cigarette abuse, and the aforementioned life-threatening diseases. Do you dispute these statistics Ms. Blatchford?"

"Sir," Nelda said, as she leaned forward, grasped the rail with her left hand and pointed the index finger of her right hand at Shiras. "My husband was not a *statistic*. He was a man—a kind, robust and loving man—your client made him a *statistic*," Nelda said, and her anxiousness evaporated and was quickly replaced by outrage. "Now, you have told us *your* expectancy for my husband's life, now let me tell you mine."

"Your Honor, the witness is yet again being non-responsive," Shiras said.

"Overruled—I will let her complete her answer," the judge said with an amused expression.

"It may seem silly to you Mr. Shiras, but my expectation was to have many more years with my husband. Precious time together to eat out on occasions and to travel some—not to places like Paris, France—but towns we could drive to and enjoy. Like traveling to Palestine to see the dogwoods in bloom, or to Tyler for the rose festival. To drive to the Hill Country to visit Enchanted Rock and walk the streets of Fredericksburg. I expected to sit at our breakfast table each morning and read the paper, sharing sections of it with Cliff and helping with the word search puzzle. Instead, I am all alone and I hurt, and I—"

"Thank you," Shiras interrupted, "now are you claiming—"

"I'm not done—damn it!" Nelda said, and immediately placed her hand over her mouth.

"That's quite all right," the judge said, "please proceed, Ms. Blatchford."

Nelda returned her focus to Shiras. "You came into this courtroom armed with so-called *data* that states that my Clifford had as little as a year or two left to live. I don't believe a word of it, but let's assume you are right and that's all he had. You need to know that I would trade everything I possess, and all of my own tomorrows to have that time with him. Instead, in the morning before I leave to come here, I will be at that same breakfast table, with one cup on it instead of two, and no desire to even touch the newspaper."

"Are you through?" Shiras asked.

"Yes, sir."

"Good. Now, are you claiming loss of income in this case?"

Nelda turned to me and I shook my head, and she said, "No sir."

"I ask only because yesterday you and your lawyer discussed money your husband earned doing odd jobs. Because of that, I feel compelled to ask if you and your husband claimed that income on your tax returns."

The judge glanced to me, but I did not know what to say or do leaving Nelda to fend for herself.

Nelda thought for a moment, then said, "Gosh, I'm not sure, but I doubt we claimed it since it was usually paid in cash."

"Is that the deciding factor? It being paid in cash?"

"I don't understand what you're getting at," Nelda said.

"If you failed to claim it as income and you signed the tax returns, you committed the crime of tax evasion."

Nelda flopped back in her chair, and with a strained expression, said, "It was just a few bucks here and there."

"It's a federal violation and did you know that tax evasion is how the feds got Al Capone?" Shiras asked and the judge glared at me urgently.

I rose and said, "I obj—"

"Sustained," the judge said. "Since they aren't claiming a loss of earnings this line of questioning is irrelevant and harassing, so move along."

"Counsel did not state an objection," Shiras argued.

"I said move along Mr. Shiras," the judge growled.

Shiras shook his head, lifted a document from his table and after having it marked by Blair, walked it to the witness stand. "Let me show you a certified record that was obtained straight from the Limestone County Sherriff's Department," he said, handing Nelda the single sheet of paper and she perused it. "Are you familiar with this document?"

"I have never seen this, but I know what it's about."

"It involves your husband, right?"

"It does," Nelda said.

"Yes indeed," Shiras said, and handed both the judge and me a copy, and I first noticed that document was titled *arrest report*.

"I move to admit defense exhibit one."

"Any objection Ms. Barbour?"

I rose, then stammered, "I ...um ... I ... no sir."

"Defense exhibit one is admitted," the judge said, and Shiras wasted no time in having his tech team display the image on all of the court's television monitors.

"Take a look up here Ms. Blatchford," he said, pointing her to the nearest screen. "This document clearly shows that your husband committed the crime of assault in nineteen seventy-eight."

Nelda stared up at the image, and said, "That's what it says, but he didn't—"

"Do you recall answering my interrogatories in this case?" Shiras said, lifting our thick set of responses.

"I do, and it's a half day of my life I will never get back," Nelda said.

"Sorry for the imposition, but when you file a suit claiming my client killed your husband—we get to ask questions," Shiras sneered. "Now during that *half day*, you may recall that we asked if your husband had ever been charged with or convicted of a crime, and you said *no*, didn't you?"

"That's right."

"You knew about this assault, but chose to conceal it from us?" Shiras accused.

"I didn't conceal it, I simply—"

"You swore to the truthfulness of the—"

"Objection, he keeps cutting off Nelda's answers," I said.

"Sustained. Mr. Shiras, you have a right to question the witness, a right no superior than her right to respond. Please proceed, but only in a question *and* answer exchange."

"Yes judge," Shiras said, then homed in on the witness stand. "The point is, you lied in these responses by denying the late Mr. Blatchford's criminal act, with an oath no different than the one you have taken in this courtroom."

"I signed them if that is what you mean."

"It was an oath—in front of a notary, subject to the pains and penalties of perjury, true?"

"I guess, but you don't under—"

"Why didn't you tell us the truth about your husband's criminal history?" Shiras pressed.

"One reason is I had forgotten about this incident, but Cliff didn't—"

"That's it? You forgot?" Shiras interjected and glanced toward the jury with feigned disgust.

"Yes, I had not thought about this in ages."

"You expect us to believe that you verified these false responses, because you could not remember your own husband's crime, yet simultaneously this jury is supposed to believe all of your other ancient recollections?"

"There was no crime," Nelda implored. "I can explain it if you'll—,"

"I want you to answer my question first," Shiras said.

I rose and said, "He's at it again, judge."

"I agree," the judge said. "Counsel, quit cutting her off and let her fully answer."

"She is not being responsive to my questions," Shiras protested.

"There is an objection for that, and at this point, we all know you are acquainted with it. Plus, I think she's trying to clarify this incident, right ma'am?"

"Yes sir—desperately," Nelda said.

"I thought so, go ahead and finish your answer."

Nelda explained, "I know exactly what this is about, and Cliff did get arrested, but he wasn't charged with anything."

Shiras countered, "Charged, arrested, what's the difference? The fact is we asked for this information and you failed to disclose it, now didn't you?"

"Yes sir, but I—."

"So you lied in those responses," Shiras charged.

The judge looked over to me and I rose and said, "Mr. Shiras is—"

"I agree, and I sustain the objection."

"Wait!" Shiras barked.

"Yes?" Mr. Morrison said.

"Not you Waite," Shiras said, then turned back to the judge. "Your honor, counsel didn't make an objection."

"I believe she was going to object you continuously interrupting and badgering Ms. Blatch—"

"But she didn't say that."

"Now, you're interrupting me," the judge blurted rising to his feet.

"Sorry, Your Honor, but I think I'm entitled to know her objection and have a chance to respond to it."

"Fine," the judge said turning to me. "Ms. Barbour, what's the basis of your objection?"

"I object to him cutting Nelda off and badgering her."

"I sustain the objection."

Shiras grumbled, then said, "Ms. Blatchford, let's get to the bottom of this once and for all. Do you deny that your husband assaulted a man in nineteen seventy-eight?"

"I guess that depends on what you call an assault."

"Well, let's see here," Shiras said, staring up at the document. "Did your husband, a one Clifford Eugene Blatchford, and I quote, *use his fist to inflict bodily harm* on a man named Curtis Rehnquist?" Shiras asked, and Waite Morrison bolted straight up on his pew and tried to gain his lawyer's attention.

"He most certainly did," Nelda said firmly.

"Well ... you sure seem awfully proud of your husband being charged with a crime," Shiras said sarcastically.

"Ahem," Morrison said, to no avail.

Nelda responded, "You don't understand, he wasn't—"

"He committed a very serious offense, didn't he?" Shiras said.

"Objection," I said rising, "he's already back at it."

"Sustained. Counsel, *please* let Ms. Blatchford fully answer, or we will be taking a break from the trial for a contempt hearing."

"I understand," Shiras said.

"Good," the judge said, then turned to Nelda. "You may continue with your *full* answer, ma'am."

She nodded and said, "I *was* proud of what Cliff did back then, and still am today. Do you *really* want to know why?" Nelda challenged with raised eyebrows.

"Psst!" said Waite Morrison, seemingly desperate to gain Shiras's attention.

Oblivious to his client's entreaty, Shiras continued, "We would all love to hear about it, so take us all back to the ... scene of the crime, will you?"

"Gladly," Nelda said. "It all happened at the foundry's annual company picnic and Mr. Morrison could confirm what I am about to tell you, assuming he was sober enough at the time."

"Objection, nonresponsive," Mr. Shiras said.

The judged paused, then said, "I'll overrule the objection, but please get to the assault thing or whatever it was."

"Sorry judge, but drinking was a big part of the picnics the foundry hosted down at the Confederate Reunion Grounds. You see, Mr. Morrison, and some of the other men, drank a lot at these events, and there were various competitions."

"Competitions?" The judge asked.

"Yes sir, they had things like the sack race, tossing washers and pitching horseshoes, but the grandest of all was the awarding of the *Golden Bottle Cap* award."

"The what?" Shiras asked.

"The *Golden—Bottle Cap—award*," Nelda repeated slowly and distinctly. "There was actually a wooden plaque with a big plastic gold colored cap—like the cap off of a beer bottle and it was given to the biggest beer drinker at the picnic."

Shiras glanced down to his ashen-faced client, then said, "Judge, I object to all of this. It has nothing to do with Mr. Blatchford's assault."

"Overruled, please proceed, ma'am."

"But judge," Shiras blurted.

"Mr. Shiras," the judge said sternly, "your outbursts have become a pattern. The next time you sense the need to interrupt or shout like that in this courtroom, I strongly suggest that you take a deep breath and count to ten."

"Sorry, judge. I'll … uh … I'll do just that."

"Good, otherwise, you better start bringing a toothbrush to court, as Charlie here just might be escorting you over to one of the holding cells on the other side of that door," the judge said, pointing to the wall opposite the jury box. "As for this line of testimony, you opened the door to it by accusing Ms. Blatchford of lying and she is going to get a chance to explain herself," the judge said and signaled for Nelda to continue.

"Each year the foundry provided catered bar-be-que, snacks and soft drinks to the employees and their families. They also furnished some wine and several kegs of beer would be tapped out there for both the casual drinkers as well as those participating in the contest. Each time a competitor filled and finished off a plastic cupful, they would turn it upside down in front of them on their picnic table. They continued mounting them up until they formed a tower and the one with the tallest stack at the end of the picnic, that was still conscious, was declared the winner. On this particular day, Mr. Waite Morrison himself was the reigning champion, having won a close contest the year prior," Nelda said, and Shiras glanced to the CEO who simply nodded.

"Mr. Morrison competed hard to retain the plaque, but try as he might he petered out. That year the trophy was awarded to Cliff's superintendent, Curtis Rehnquist. Curtis hailed from Baton Rouge, Louisiana and was a mean, sawed-off Cajun, known by everyone as *Coon Ass*—sorry Judge."

"I have relatives in Lake Charles—I have heard the term," the Judge said, "but for future reference, let's go with C.A. or Curtis, shall we?"

"Yes sir," Nelda said. "C.A. was known to all as a hard drinker and he once boasted that he was entitled to the *lifetime achievement award from Budweiser*. As the day drug on and the beer kegs were being emptied, Coon … I mean Curtis, had consumed more than a little too much. Despite having already been crowned the champ he continued drinking well into the evening. He was definitely tight and could barely walk."

"You are not trained in law enforcement, are you Ms. Blatchford?" Shiras asked.

"That's true."

"What qualifies you to comment on his, or anyone else's sobriety?"

"Nothing, other than good common sense. Considering the height of his cup stack and his behavior, I did not need to go to the police academy to know he was smashed."

The Judge intervened. "I think we have the intoxication picture painted, so can we please get to the altercation?"

"Coming right up judge—I promise," Nelda said. "Toward the end of the picnic, I was standing over where Cliff and the guys were pitching horseshoes. Curtis staggered over to me and with slurred speech asked if he could kiss me—he actually said *smooch* as I recall. Anyhow, Cliff overheard him and came to my defense. It was clear that Curtis was out of his mind and knowing that, coupled with C.A. being Clifford's boss, he did not want to be too froggish."

"What did your husband do?" the judge asked.

"Cliff politely, but firmly told C.A. to leave me alone. Curtis grumbled something unintelligible, then staggered over to the kegs for a refill. Unfortunately, he returned about ten minutes later and that's when things came unwound. Curtis struck a stance in front of me and was staring at me with those glassy bloodshot eyes. Though swaying from side to side he tried to kiss me. I pushed him aside and when I turned to walk away, he pinched me on an area where a lady ought not to be pinched by any man not her husband and mine saw it and cold-cocked him."

"Your husband punched him?" the judge asked.

"Yes sir," Nelda said. "He laid him out cold as a wedge and he just laid there motionless."

"Did someone call an ambulance?" Shiras asked.

"Lord no," Nelda said dismissively. "Coon ... uh I mean C.A. was already about to pass out, Cliff just expedited it a little."

"Did someone at least call the police?" Shiras said.

"This was before cell phones so there was no way to do that. However, Cliff managed to flag down an officer making a routine pass through the park."

"Your husband was the one that involved the authorities?" the judge asked.

"Yes sir, and when the patrolman got out of his car Cliff told him what had happened and the officer handcuffed him. By then Curtis had come to, but was too drunk to answer any of the officer's questions. The patrolman took them both away—Curtis for public intoxication and Clifford for assault.

"Aha—assault!" Shiras crowed.

"Hold your horses," Nelda chided. "When the police learned the whole story, which was confirmed by several co-workers from the picnic, they turned Cliff loose. That was the end of it and Cliff was never charged with anything."

Shiras seemed to have had enough and passed her as a witness, and since I had no further questions we broke for lunch. The girls and I headed out into the hall, down the stairs and straight to the second-floor lounge. The fare on this day featured Texas red chili, saltine crackers, a small jar of Lupe's pickled jalapenos and a jug of sweet tea.

While I began microwaving the large container, Lupe removed the plastic bowls and spoons to set the table and Dot was placing paper napkins by each place setting. Once done, we joined hands and thanked the Lord for our meal, and for Nelda's nice job on the witness stand. She was relieved to have it behind her, but appeared as exhausted from the experience as she did after her Dallas deposition.

We were chowing down when the door opened and the judge entered, and he made his way past us and into the kitchen. He opened the freezer door, pulled out a box and I got a glimpse at it. It was one of those frozen TV dinners and the featured entrée was Salisbury steak. The writing on the box boasted, *Regal Cuisine-a Dinner Fit for a King.* He opened the box and removed the rock hard, frosty compartmentalized plastic plate of the meat, green peas, and mashed potatoes. When he reached to place it in the microwave, he stopped, raised his nose, sniffed twice, wheeled around, and asked, "Is that chili I smell?"

"Why yes, it is," I said, pointing toward the centerpiece of our table.

The judge marched to our tableside, gazed at the bowl, and said, "My dear wife—God rest her soul—used to cook it for me. I have tried to make it myself, but it's never been fit to eat."

"Did she have a recipe?" Dot asked.

"Oh yes, a very good one, but the problem is she knew it by heart. She tried to show me a time or two, but it was always *a pinch of this* and a *smidgen of that,* and try as I might I could never duplicate it. I truly regret not getting her to write it down for me but, how was I … um … supposed to know what would happen," he said misty-eyed.

"I am sorry for your loss," Nelda said for all of us.

"Thank you," he said, "and I'm sorry for your loss too Ms. Blatchford—y'all seemed like a wonderful couple."

"That we were, judge."

"Please put that so-called *Regal Cuisine* back in the ice box and have some of this," I offered, but the he seemed hesitant. "Really judge, we have plenty to share. I also have more of this batch in my freezer at home—but just know that this is two days old."

"You took the time to make chili during trial prep?" he asked, and I nodded. "I see, well I'm not at all deterred by it being a couple of days old. I have always felt chili is best after congealing for a day or two."

"It's a good batch, taste it for yourself," Nelda said, offering the judge a spoon.

He accepted it, dipped it in the steaming bowl and raised it to his face. He sniffed it in the manner of a wine connoisseur checking the bouquet before tasting it. He placed the spoon in his mouth, removed it, closed his eyes, then chewed and swallowed.

"Mmm—that brings back such great memories. It tastes just like Linda's, and you *have* to write down the recipe for me—if it's not a secret of course."

"It's not and I will be glad to share it," I said. "Now, fix yourself a bowlful and take all you want."

"Are you sure? I don't want to impose."

"I'm positive," I said, and the judge wasted no time in re-boxing the frozen dinner and placing it back into the freezer. When he returned to our table Lupe grinned as she handed him his own bowl.

Spooning eagerly, he said, "This is very nice of y'all, and thank you for it."

"I hope you enjoy it and if you do, let me know and I will bring you one of the frozen bowls that you can take home to heat up during the next cold snap," I said.

He nodded and headed for the door with his soft drink in one pocket, saltines in the other, the bowl of chili in his right hand, and a big smile on his face.

After we finished our lunch and tidied up, we returned to the courtroom. As we entered, I was pleased to find Jack and Bill among the growing number of onlookers. I gave him a rundown of the events of the morning, including the details of the drunken escapade at the foundry picnic. They were amused by the tale and took seats next to Lupe to watch the resumption of the trial.

When asked for my next witness, I decided to go right after the foundry, by choosing to question Mr. Waite Morrison. The selection seemed to rattle the defense team, but Morrison rose and waddled toward the stand.

Once seated on the armless witness chair and sworn, I said, "Tell us your name, please."

"I, I, I am, uh ... uh ... Waite Morrison, th, th, th—"

"The turd," Highsmith murmured, and Lupe giggled. The judge glanced in their direction but thankfully did not catch the comment.

"You were saying that you are Waite Morrison, the third right?" I said, and he nodded. "You are the current owner of the Morrison Foundry aren't you?"

"I am... uh ... I am the, the, the, majority owner and CEO, and my, my, my two brothers own minority shares."

"Sir, you have worked at that foundry all your life, haven't you?"

"No, no, not all of it—yet," he said, drawing some laughter.

"Let me ask it this way, you have worked there your whole adult life, true?"

"I uh, I guess you, you could, could say that. When I, uh, uh, returned from prep school to go to Baylor here, here in you know ... right here in, in—"

"Waco," I finished.

Shiras rose, and said, "Objection, counsel is testifying for the witness."

"Someone has to," Highsmith said, and the judge again glanced suspiciously his way, then overruled the objection.

"Let's do it this way, when did you start working at the foundry."

"That, that was in, in, in nineteen sixty-seven."

"Do you remember Clifford Blatchford?"

"Why, yes, yes—I do—I mean I did. He was a fine, fine, fine man indeed, and a good worker."

"Do you remember the particular company picnic we discussed this morning?"

Springing to his feet, Shiras blurted, "Objection, Your Honor. I truly do not see the relevance of continuing this line of questioning."

The judge peered at me over his glasses, and I rose and said, "They started it."

"She's right. Mr. Shiras, you kicked that hornet's nest over, so I will overrule the objection," the judge said, and then turned back to me, "but Ms. Barbour, I do ask that we not relive every sordid detail of the affair."

"Yes sir," I said. "Mr. Morrison, about that particular company picnic, you do remember it, don't you?"

"Yes, yes ... bits and pieces," he said, and Shiras lowered his head.

"Lots of libations served there that day?"

"We did ...uh ... you know ... we, we, we—"

"All the way home," Highsmith said.

"Sir?" the judge said.

Highsmith responded, "Are you talking to me?"

"Yes, did you say something?"

I turned and made eye contact with Bill and shook my head reproachfully. "Uh ... it was nothing sir," Bill said.

I returned to Morrison, "About the booze, you were saying?"

"We did furnish some, some beer, beer, beer, and wine. We just wanted everyone to have, have, have a good time," Morrison said as he ran his right index finger between his shirt collar and his thick neck to loosen it.

"Did you witness Curtis Rehnquist getting slugged?" I asked, and heard Jack and Highsmith cackling under their breath.

"I did not actually see it, at least I don't think so—but it happened all right."

"You know C.A. was bombed and that he assaulted Nelda, don't you?"

"Well, er uh ... I ... uh, like I say, I know, know the altercation occurred, but I would not call what Curtis did an, ass, ass, assault."

Jack chuckled and whispered, "He said *ass assault.*"

"That's pretty accurate, ain't it?" Highsmith said.

"No more comments from the peanut gallery," the judge scolded, and the boys nodded contritely.

I continued. "You heard this morning that Curtis twice tried to kiss my client and then pinched her on the butt."

Morrison's face flushed red. "Yes, yes that was the claim."

"Claim? No one denied it including Curtis, right?"

"That's, that's true," he conceded.

"I see by your ring finger that you are a married man?"

"Why, yes, yes, I am. Forty-four years' worth," he said proudly.

"If not an *assaulter*, what would you call a man that did the same thing to your wife?"

"Blind," Highsmith said.

"By golly, I think you're right," Jack added, and Lupe chortled.

"That's an outrage!" Shiras said, turning his head toward the gallery.

"I've seen her—have you?" Highsmith defended.

Shiras turned to Morrison, who simply shrugged, then Shiras bleated, "I demand he be removed from the courtroom!"

"Sir," the judge said removing his glasses and pointing them toward Bill. "I will have you held in contempt if another audible word is spoken by you in this courtroom, understand?"

"Yes sir," the scorned Highsmith responded.

Before I could pose my next question, Shiras rose and said, "Mr. Morrison does raise a salient point, judge. I object to the continued use of the word *assault*. Unlike what Mr. Blatchford inflicted on that Curtis character, what Ms. Blatchford described doesn't constitute an assault at all and—"

"Wait," the judge said.

"Yes, sir?" Mr. Morrison said from the witness stand.

"No, not you sir," the judge said. "Charlie, let's give the jurors a break while we hash this out."

Once the panel was out of the room, the judge addressed Shiras. "As I understand your objection, you do not believe the term *assault* is an appropriate description for what occurred to Ms. Blatchford?"

"That's correct."

"We're still on the record, so let's hear your argument."

"Even if everything Ms. Blatchford testified to actually happened, it is not an *assault*. Now granted I haven't seen my penal code in a long—"

Lupe giggled. "He say his *penal cold*."

"Code, code!" Shiras declared. "C-O-D-E as in my *penal code!*"

"He say it again," Lupe chortled, and the boys snickered.

"Shush Lupe," I said, and she put her hand over her mouth to muffle her laughter.

The judge cleared his throat, and said, "For the duration of this hearing, I suggest calling it the *criminal statutes* instead of the … uh, the … you know what, okay?"

"Fine," Shiras said, then continued with his argument. "As I was saying, I have not studied … um … the criminal statutes since law school, but I seem to recall an element of *severe bodily harm*."

"I just happen to have my penal …ahem … criminal statutes right here," the judge said, reaching behind him and pulling his paperback version from his bookshelf. He flipped through the pages, then said, "Ah, here it is. For the record, I am reading from section twenty-two point one regarding *assault*. Though the first two subsections do mention *bodily injury*, the third says, and I quote, *intentionally or knowingly causes physical contact with another when the person knows or should reasonably believe that the other will regard the contact as offensive or provocative*. Mr. Shiras, the use of the word *assault* is appropriate unless you intend to argue that what ol' coon … I mean what C.A. did was neither *offensive* nor *provocative*."

"I withdraw the objection," Shiras said, returning to his seat.

When the jury returned from their break, I continued questioning of the CEO. "Sir, do you agree that Curtis was drunk when he assaulted Nelda Blatchford?"

"I do recall that he had, had, consumed quite a bit."

"Enough so to out drink all of his fellow competitors and take home the award, right?"

"He was the, the, the champ that year, but I did not give him the plaque until Monday."

"You neglected to bring it with you to the picnic?"

"I did not, not, expect to lose," Morrison said, and Shiras sighed aloud.

Shifting topics, I asked, "Mr. Morrison, do you admit that after Mr. Blatchford became a pipefitter he worked with asbestos insulation materials?"

"No, no—I don't think that's, that's that's the case at all."

I looked over at Nelda and she stared back at me with a stunned expression. I turned to the defense table and saw Shiras' wry grin.

"Are you telling me that Mr. Blatchford was not exposed to asbestos while working at your foundry?"

"That's, that's, exactly what, what I am saying?"

"It's not true!" Nelda blurted.

"Wait!" the judge said, then beat Morrison to the punch, "Not you, sir." Addressing Nelda, he said, "Ma'am, I know the emotions are high here, but you can't just interject yourself into the proceedings like that."

"Sorry judge," she said.

"Carry on, Ms. Barbour."

"Mr. Morrison, are you saying that as a pipefitter that Mr. Blatchford would not have worked with insulation?"

"He, uh, uh he worked with insulation, for, for, for sure, but it did not contain asbestos."

"Did it ever?"

"Certainly, but not, not at the time Mr. Blatchford was pipefitting."

"When did it stop having it in it?"

"In the, the, the, the early seventies. You see ... uh ... when Mr. Blatchford made pipefitter it, it, it was around the time OSHA went into effect. We stopped buying the asbestos-containing, ver, ver, versions at that same time, be, be, because, it was being phased out. So, so, no, I do not believe Cliff Blatchford was ex, ex, exposed."

"What about the old asbestos insulation, wouldn't he have encountered that?"

Morrison sat up in his chair, and said, "No, no, no. As Mr. Cardozo said, we had abatement contractors do that."

"Why?"

"The reg, reg, regulations required EPA cert, cert, certified abatement contractors to remove and dispose of the old, old, old insulation. So, so, we were forbidden from doing it in-house."

"No more questions," I said and, I sank back into my chair.

"Your witness," the judge said.

As Shiras rose, I noticed that the photo of the asbestos-free insulation box used to question Jesus returned to all screens. Through Shiras, the CEO explained that though the image was not from a box at the foundry, that it was nevertheless identical to those in their inventory in the seventies. He then described the various sources from which they purchased the non-asbestos insulation. Shiras then took him through their *loss prevention* programs and emphasized the foundry's safety policies and their compliance record with both OSHA and the EPA. They covered the awards that the foundry had received from the National Safety Council and other trade associations. Once Shiras was done, I had no more questions and was relieved when the judge told us that we would adjourn for the day.

The boys joined us in the hall, and Jack said, "Honey, I thought you were great."

"Yeah, you really put it on 'em in there," Highsmith added.

"Thanks, guys," I sighed.

"What's the matter, honey?" Jack said.

"Didn't y'all hear Mr. Morrison?"

Jack nodded eagerly. "We sure did, and you had him back on his heels with all that company picnic stuff."

"Maybe, but that's not what I needed to prove through him. Morrison's testimony that the insulation was non-asbestos guts our case."

"Morrison's full of crap," Bill scoffed. "That place was full of asbestos and if it wasn't, how else did poor Cliff get sick?"

"They have an answer for that too with the *idiopathic* theory?" I lamented. "Boys, I *have* to find a way to prove Morrison is wrong—assuming he is."

"What about that Jesus fella, he helped didn't he?" Jack said.

"Some, but he did not know if the insulation had asbestos."

"He said it had it—we both heard him, didn't we?" Jack said, and Highsmith nodded.

"He had no basis for it and the judge threw that part out," I said and my emotions caught up with me. I put my arms around Jack's shoulders and whispered, "Oh God—I'm losing this thing and a hefty chunk of our savings along with it. I've made a mess of this and I am so, so sorry."

He placed his thumb under my chin, raised my head and stared into my eyes, "Come on babe, you can pull this thing out."

"We're circling the drain and I'm out of live witnesses," I sniffled.

Lupe and Nelda were out of earshot, but Dot was sitting on a nearby bench staring on with a strained expression. I used a tissue to dry my eyes and nose and turned to Bill. "The wisecracks are amusing, but they're going to get me in hot water with the judge."

"Sorry—I'll try to be good," he said.

"What about the other guy that worked there?" Dot said, as she rose and walked to my side.

"Romeo?" I asked, and she nodded. "He never worked with Cliff, so I left him off the witness list."

"Have you talked to him?" Jack asked.

"No, not directly, but I guess it wouldn't hurt," I said.

"By golly, I think you're right," Jack said.

12
CHAPTER

We grabbed our belongings from the courtroom, and Jack and Bill escorted us down the stairs and through the courthouse exit. I bid farewell to the boys and the ladies and I headed directly to my car. As we drove out of Waco, everyone was quiet and seemed exhausted and I filled the silence with a Best of Marty Robbins CD. His songs always put my mind at ease—except for *El Paso*—that one always made me nervous. We dropped Nelda off at her house and I agreed to pick her up at the same time the following morning.

As we drove away, Dot said, "I didn't want to get into this in front of Nelda, but what's the plan for tomorrow?"

"We're sunk," I said. "All I have left is reading in the deposition of Dr. Scotty."

"Won't we have extra time to investigate while the other side puts on their case?"

"Iredell told me that if we have not made our case by the time we rest, the foundry can make a motion and win without doing a single thing."

"Oh no," she said urgently, "so what are we going to do?"

"You raised a good point about Romeo—he may be our only hope," I said, and addressed Lupe, "que Senor Catron dijo sobre el insulation—what did Romeo say about the insulation?"

"I not ask Miss Gertie," she said, as we pulled to stop in front of her small apartment.

"Lupe girl, I really need to find out what he knows. Can you call him and see if he will meet with me, and if so can you come along?"

"Jes, Miss Gertie. I call him and remember where he live. I sure he meet with you—he a nice man with familia bueno."

"See if you can reach him now," I said handing her my cell phone.

She pulled a scrap of paper from her dress pocket, placed the call, and all I heard was some friendly Spanish being spoken so rapidly that I could only discern an occasional word. She returned my phone and informed that Romeo had agreed to meet, but only if we came for dinner.

"Dinner?" I said staring back at her incredulously. "Don't I have more to do tonight than dine with Romeo?"

"It sounds funny when you say it like that," Dot said, with a chuckle. "I can't help picturing you speaking down to him from a balcony."

"If we don't turn this case around this may be my own, real life, Shakespearian tragedy."

Dot asked, "Are you going to do the dinner thing?"

"I don't have a choice."

"Well, since you are doing that, what can I help with?"

"One of the things I planned on doing this evening was marking up Dr. Scotty's transcript with the parts I want to read in court—can you do that?"

"Sure, I did that for Louise several times."

"I recall that. Be sure and put *post-it* notes on each of the pages with the good questions and answers. Highlight the passages in yellow, and include the discussion of his background, the diagnosis stuff and how the Blatchford's reacted to it. Do the same thing with the photocopy so there will be an exact duplicate. This will allow me to read the questions and you to recite the answers."

"You want me to read the answers … *in court?*" Dot asked as a wave of fear washed over her face.

"Yes, I would look real silly reading both questions and answers and having to trot back and forth between the witness stand and our table."

"It would be good exercise," Dot lobbied.

"Cut it out, will ya," I said playfully. "You'll do fine, and the whole thing will only take a few minutes. Grab the copies from my tote bag and make doubly certain they are both marked the same way."

"I will have them ready for tomorrow. I can also provide our lunch if that will help?" Dot offered.

"I am planning on making gumbo, but if this dinner lasts too long I will just bring a casserole I have in the freezer."

"What kind?" Dot asked.

"King Ranch Chicken."

"Mmm," Dot purred, "that's what I hoped you would say."

I turned to Lupe. "Did Mr. Catron really insist on discussing this over dinner?"

"Jes—it's the thing they do, Miss Gertie," she said and opened the rear passenger side door. "He happy you help Señora Nelda and thank you with dinner."

"Why can't he thank me on the phone?"

"Es importa for Mexicanos to talk with food."

"I thought it was the Italians that did that."

"Italianos, Guatemalans, Mexicanos, Cubanos—all Latinos," Lupe stressed. "He say be there at seis."

"Six, huh?" I asked, and Lupe nodded. "All right, I will pick you up here at five forty-five and we will go there together, okay?"

"Jes, Miss Gertie."

"What do you think they'll serve for dinner?" I asked.

Lupe shrugged. "I not know—guess we find out together," she said, shutting the door and leaving me with even more apprehension.

I dropped Dot off at her house, then headed straight home. Once at our kitchen table, I worked on my closing statement and wrote and re-wrote it several times. Soon the metal trash can next to me was half full of wadded yellow pages from my notepad.

Hearing Jack entering through the front door, I asked, "Anything on the lines?"

"Two pollies and one of them damn hissin' turtles snagged by the shell—scared the hell out of me."

"That's it?"

"Yeah, we think Sanford's tank is fished out, so we might move the lines back to Lake Mexia for the weekend," he said, taking a seat across the table from me.

"I think it was just bad luck," I said. "There have always been big channel cats in that pond, so don't give up on it."

He nodded, and said, "You seemed mighty low at the courthouse, are you feeling any better?"

"A little, but I am taking your advice on speaking with Romeo," I said, then explained my impromptu dinner engagement. "I plan to smother some liver and onions for you before I go."

"You've got better things to do," Jack said. "I'll just heat up a chicken pot pie."

"I want to do it, plus you don't need all that sodium."

"What are you workin' on?" he asked staring down at my legal pad.

"Since the trial could end as soon as tomorrow, I thought I should get my closing argument down."

"Any luck?"

"About as much luck as your fishing trip, as you can see," I said pointing to the trash can. "I don't have a clue as what to say and regret not getting some samples from Iredell."

"I don't think that would help," he said.

"Oh … why do you say that?"

"Each case is different and what you say has to fit your personality. For that it doesn't come from here," he said patting his head, "it has to come from there," he said pointing to my heart.

"Just stand in front of them and wing it?"

"Jot down some notes if need be, but don't read from a long flowery script, and by all means don't tell the jurors what they already know. On my juries, the most common complaint, for both sides, was that the lawyers kept repeating things over and over. They treated us like we were deaf, stupid or both. Each side spent most of their argument rehashing everything we already heard. Just stand in front of the people, make the case short and simple, and it will be fine."

I smiled, and said, "By golly, I think you're right—to coin a phrase."

That evening I met Lupe at her appointment and she guided me toward Romeo's neighborhood. Soon we were in a rough area on the southernmost outskirts of town, adding to my mounting trepidation. However, my angst eased when we pulled up to the address and I saw that their home was a modest, but well-maintained single story bungalow. I looked toward the windows in the front of the house and there seemed to be no lights on inside, causing me to wonder if anyone was home.

We parked along the curb and exited my car and it was then that I noticed a large dog chained to a mesquite tree in the front yard. It was a male bull terrier and he was there for a purpose. The chain connecting his collar to the tree seemed short enough to keep him off the sidewalk but close enough to make you wonder. He growled through his bared slobbery teeth as we entered the yard, then barked aggressively as we passed him and made our way up the sidewalk and to the front door.

The barking must have alerted someone from the inside as the porch light illuminated before I knocked. Constrained by a security chain, the windowless wooden front door opened slightly, and all I saw was one eye peering out at us.

"Estamos aqui para la cena con senor Catron," Lupe said.

The door closed, the chain was disengaged and then opened fully. A lovely woman in an auburn dress invited us inside with a sweep of her arm, and said, "Bienvenidos."

"Señora Catron say *welcome*," Lupe said, as we entered.

"I know that word," I whispered back, then said, "Buenas tardes, usted tiene una buena casa."

She smiled and ushered us from the entry into the living room of their small, but very pleasant home. This room was dimly lit and the only ambient light emanated from a series of flickering votive candles on a long, thin, sofa table. The walls in this area were adorned with framed family photographs, old and new, and in color and black and white. Also, present was the largest collection of crucifixes I had ever seen and numerous framed depictions of Jesus, including walking on water, Jesus with the leper—I think, and a large panorama of the last supper.

We were then led into a dining area which was well lit. There was one long table and a smaller one was placed in the opening between the dining area and the laundry room. I surveyed the table and noticed several ornately painted covered ceramic pots sitting in the center, and my mind naturally wondered their contents. Also, present were multiple stacks of flour and corn tortillas, and I thought *if nothing else I can eat tortillas—those I know I like.*

It was then that I got my first glimpse at who I felt sure was Mr. Catron. He was a short but stocky well-dressed man who possessed a commanding air about him. His bearded face was dark brown and his skin was leathery and featured deep inset lines on his cheeks, forehead and around his eyes. He had a thick head of graying hair, combed straight back and held in place by an abundance of hair gel.

"I am Romeo Catron, and I welcome you both to our home," he said.

"I thank you all for inviting us," I responded.

He bowed slightly, and said, "You are most welcome."

Lupe and I were introduced to the family—all of them. Included was an adult daughter, grandchildren of varying ages, two aunts, one uncle and an elderly great-grandmother, and I must say I do not recall ever meeting a kinder bunch people.

Anxious to get to the matters at hand I turned to Romeo and asked, "How well did you know Mr. Blatchford?"

He shook his head disapprovingly. "I am sorry, but we do not discuss business at our table."

"I thought they *only* did business at the table," I whispered to Lupe, and she simply shrugged.

"Enjoy," Ms. Catron said, in Spanish and motioned us to sit. The youngsters stood patiently at the small table, as did those surrounding the larger table, and each were staring at Lupe and me. We took adjacent chairs at the big table, and only then, did the others take their seats. Following Mr. Catron's lengthy blessing, Ms. Catron placed a bowl on my plate. She ladled from one of the pots and into my bowl what looked like soup. I covertly examined it and the first thing I noticed was that the broth had corn, rice, and cilantro. *So far so good* I thought and used my spoon to roil the soup and noticed other ingredients, including beans and some type of meat.

I glanced around the table and everyone, including Lupe, began lapping it up. I, on the other hand, made a shallow dip with my spoon taking only broth. I raised the spoon to my lips and with all eyes on me I sipped from it. I was relieved to find that the soup was warm, flavorful and tasty, and said, "Esta bien." The family nodded enthusiastically and I dipped up a deeper spoonful which included some of the vegetables, sipped it and swallowed. I felt at ease now and dipped boldly into the bowl and retrieving more vegetables and a piece of the meat. I placed it in my mouth and though the texture of the meat was a little slimy, I chewed it and swallowed.

Curious as to its source I asked, "Señora Catron, como esta la carne en aqui?

"Intestino de cabra," was her response.

I turned to Romeo. "Beg pardon, but I did not understand."

He wiped his mouth with his napkin, and said, "Some call it tripe, but it is goat intestines."

I broke out in a sweat and though I tried to conceal it I felt on the verge of heaving. I helped myself to the tortilla and managed to eat the remainder of the soup without touching any additional solid pieces.

Once done I placed my spoon in the bowl, and said, "Delicioso."

"Gracias," Ms. Catron said graciously.

"Would you like more?" Romeo said, and I could tell by his expression that my true reaction to the goat guts had not escaped him.

I smiled and said, "Gracias, pero no mas."

He winked, and whispered, "It is an acquired taste."

Ms. Catron made a gesture that signaled a bashful young granddaughter into action. The girl approached, removed my napkin from the table, followed by my plate and bowl. Once all were done with their meals, more youngsters teamed up to clear both tables, while others began to wash the dishes and utensils in the kitchen sink. Lupe and I offered to help, but Mrs. Catron would have no part of that.

Instead, we were escorted by Mr. Catron back to the living room, where Lupe and I took a seat on one of two tweed couches there, and Romeo assumed the other. Separating us from him was a large square coffee table, and he killed the dimness by switching on the brass floor lamp next to him.

"Now may we discuss Mr. Blatchford?" I asked.

"Not until we enjoy an after dinner drink," Mr. Cardozo said, then signaled toward the kitchen. One of the older granddaughters approached and placed a tray on the coffee table. Atop it sat three green goblets and a matching pitcher containing a dark liquid with ice and slices of fruit floating in it. The ice cubes rattled as the girl slowly and carefully filled each glass to near the rim. Once done, Mr. Catron motioned to us to take one and Lupe and I claimed a goblet, then Romeo took his, raised it to eye level, and said, "Salud."

"Salud," we repeated, and I took a gulp of the beverage, and I must say it was good.

"Do you like it?" Romeo said.

"It is very tasty, what is it?" I said.

"Sangria wine."

I had never had that particular variety and though it was a little sweet for my untrained palate, I found it flavorful, smooth and soothing. The more I sipped, the more at ease I became and soon we began discussing the foundry. Mr. Catron freely answered my questions, and when I reached the bottom of my goblet, he asked, "Would you like another?"

"Si, gracias," I said, and returned my empty glass to the tray. He filled it by draining the remainder of the pitcher, except for the ice and the fruit slices, into my goblet. I lifted the glass to my mouth and before I could sip from it, Mr. Catron's granddaughter swapped the depleted pitcher for a full one.

"I am pleased that you are helping Señora Blatchford," Romeo said. "I admired Mr. Clifford very much and though we did not work together, I know that he was a good man and a hard worker. I was very sad when I learned that he was sick and my family prayed for God to heal him, but the good Lord had other plans."

"So, tu no trabajar directly with Cliff?"

"No, and the word is trabajar," he corrected. "Your Spanish is good, but in your sentence, it would be *Trabajaste*."

"Got it," I said, then thought *why in the hell am I speaking in Spanish anyhow?*

"To Senor Cliff!" Romeo toasted, then lifted his glass, had a sip, and I took a gulp.

"Lo viste, I mean … did you ever see Clifford performing his job duties?"

"I am sure I did considering I walked through the plant on many occasions. Regretfully, though I have no specific recollection in that regard."

"I see," I said, taking another drink. "Do you recall any interaction with Cliff?"

"Oh, yes," he said. "Quite often he would get things from me at the tool room and we would talk."

"Que hablar, what did you two talk about?"

"Family mostly. He kept up with my children and I did the same with his."

"So, the tool room a place where los hombres got things they needed for their jobs?"

"That is correct. We had some parts and tools there, but we had much more than just that. It was more like a warehouse—they just called it the *tool room.*"

"It was a grande space?" I asked.

"Very much so, almost as long as a soccer field."

"Que mas—what else did you store there?"

"Most everything the plant needed to operate except for large equipment. We had small pumps and valves, gaskets and packing, rope and twine. There were refractory bricks and mortar for the furnaces and insulation and insulating cement for the piping," he explained, as Lupe sat silently nursing her first drink.

"Can you give me the name of the los hombres that ordered the products?" I asked as I polished off my second serving and marveled at how rapidly my glass was refilled.

"Pete O'Conner, is one. He was the purchasing manager in the later years. Before him it was Fred Warren."

"Como obtuviste mas—how did you get supplies reordered when you needed it?"

"I filled out paperwork called a *requisition*. It would detail products we were running low on, and how much we needed to order, and I would deliver it to the purchasing manager."

"Do you recall ordering asbestos insulation?"

"Most definitely, I did it for many years. It came in long boxes and the labels said *asbestos* right on them."

"Do you remember a time when it came without asbestos?"

"Yes I do," he said, as he drained the remainder of the second pitcher into his glass and motioned toward the kitchen. A third arrived and while I sipped Romeo described the process of converting from asbestos to asbestos-free insulation. "You see, OSHA was coming and word got out that asbestos was not good to one's health."

"Si, muy malo—that means *very bad* Lupe," I hiccupped, and polished off my drink. "When was this?"

"It was in the early nineteen-seventies," he said, and I hiccupped again. "Are you all right?"

"Estoy bien—never felt better," I said. "About the non-asbestos insulation, how ... how, uh ... how did you know to start ordering it?"

"It started with a memo straight from the desk of Mr. Morrison. It instructed that we were no longer to purchase asbestos insulation and attached to it was a list of vendors that sold the non-asbestos type."

"Was that before or after the time Senor Blatchford was a pipefitter?"

"It was before."

That was not what I wanted to hear, and asked, "Are you sure about that?"

"I am positive," he said.

Oh God, we're sunk, I thought through my increasingly hazy mind. It seemed that Waite Morrison was telling the truth, however my most immediate concern was my empty glass. I glanced back to the kitchen and seeing none of the daughters, I helped myself to another goblet full from the pitcher. I took a gulp, turned to Lupe and asked, "Want another?"

"No gracias."

I turned back to Romeo and now saw two of him. "Are y'all saying that Senor Blatchford would not have worked with asbestos?"

"No," he said, taking a sip from his glass.

"No he did, or no he didn't?" I slurred, took another gulp and closed my right eye to return to the Romeos to one.

"Mr. Cliff was definitely exposed to it."

"No comprendo, pero me gusta—Lupe that means *I don't understand it, but I like it*," I said as I rose unsteadily to my feet. The room started spinning, and I sang, "Ai yi yi yi, we—have—a case now."

"Salud," Romeo said raising his glass.

"Salute to you too!" I uttered and transferred my drink to my left hand and brought my right hand up to my forehead in salute, but struck it so hard that I staggered backwards and everything faded to black.

13
CHAPTER

"Wake up Miss Gertie, wake up," was the next sound I heard. I blinked my eyes several times struggling to discern where I was and what was happening.

"Who is it?" I said.

"It's me, it's me," the voice repeated.

"Lupe?"

"Jes!"

"Where are we?" I asked.

"Su casa," she said.

I glanced around and realized that I was fully reclined in the passenger seat of my own car which was parked on our driveway. I laid my head back down and dozed off again until I felt movement and heard Jack's voice. I roused enough to know that he and Lupe were on each side of me struggling to walk me up the steps and into our house.

Once inside, they guided me over to Jack's reclining rocker, and when they eased me down to it, the teetering back and forth sent me to gagging. Jack instinctively grabbed the metal trash can and dumped the wads of my discarded closing argument notes on the floor. He then positioned the can between my knees—in the nick of time—if you get my drift. Once that lovely episode ran its course I again dozed off.

The next thing I knew, Jack was standing over me gently shaking my shoulders. I opened my eyes and saw through the patio window that the morning was dawning, but that the sun had not fully risen.

"Here, take this," Jack said, and I wiped my eyes with my fingers and saw his outstretched hand holding a cup of coffee. He placed the cup to my lips, I blew two breaths across it to cool it, and took a couple of small sips.

"What time is it?" I asked.

"Almost seven."

"Where is Lupe?"

"At her house, but she'll drive your car back over when—"

"Lupe has my car," I interrupted urgently and raised my head so fast that I winced from the resulting pounding.

"Don't worry," he said, "she'll be back here between seven-thirty and eight to pick you up."

It was all Jack could do to help me to my feet and guide me, aching head and all, into our bathroom. I turned on a hot shower, stripped down and eased into the tub. With the hot drops pelting my skin and the steam engulfing me, I closed my eyes and tried to piece together the events of the evening prior. The last memory I could recall was something Romeo said about the insulation, but I lacked retrievable details. Consequently, I did not know if I would have him at the courthouse to question or what he would say if I did.

After my shower, I dried off, took some aspirin and dressed for the day. I walked to the kitchen, sat my tote bag on the counter and opened our freezer. I placed my casserole in the tote and added the frozen bowl of chili and the recipe I promised the judge. I sat mentally preparing myself for the difficult day ahead until I heard a horn honk.

Jack, who had been pacing between the kitchen and the front door said, "That's her."

I rose slowly to my feet, grabbed my purse and thanked Jack for taking such good care of me. Keeping my head as dead level as possible, I walked gingerly out the front door and to my car. Lupe was standing by the open driver's side door and her concerned expression told me plenty.

"Jou okay, Miss Gertie?"

"No."

"Want me to drive?"

"Yes," I said, and opened the passenger side door, adjusted the seat, and eased down into it. Once buckled, I leaned my head back and closed my eyes. I felt modicum of relief until Lupe turned the key to start the car and Tejano music blared from the speakers.

I nearly jumped out of my skin, and cried, "Please turn that down."

"But its Selena," she pleaded.

"I am begging you in the name of all things good and decent," I snapped.

"Okay," she said and mercifully lowered the volume—not to zero—but enough to make it tolerable.

As Lupe guided us toward the highway, I said, "I am sorry I raised my voice with you."

Lupe said, "No problema. I hope jou feel better."

"I guess I got pretty snockered last night."

She glanced at me. "I not know snocker, but you muy barracho."

Concerned about our punctuality, I glanced to my left wrist and realized that I had left my watch at home. I leaned toward the center, looked at the dashboard clock, and said, "No acelerar-don't speed, but we are cutting it close on time."

"Jes Miss Gertie," Lupe said, pressing harder on the gas pedal.

I pulled down the lighted mirror on the visor above me and turned my head in multiple directions. I noticed my ashy complexion and bloodshot eyes, and said, "Thanks for driving me home last night."

"Es de nada, me likes jour car," Lupe said.

"What about Dot and Nelda?"

"I call them last night and they meet at court."

"What did you tell them?"

"I say jou drink mucho sangria—sorry I told truth."

"That's all right, they are going to figure that part out anyway," I said. "How did I … I mean you … I mean how did we leave things with Mr. Catron?"

"He worry 'bout jou and hoped jou to feel better."

"That's nice, but about the case—what can he say about Senor Cliff and the insulation? I recall something that was bad, but something I was glad about … I just don't know what it was."

"No comprendo that, but he did say he weetness for you," Lupe said.

- Brian Clary -

"He's coming to the courthouse?" I asked and she nodded. "But, you don't know what is he going to say?"

"I not know—guess we all find out at court."

When we arrived and parked, true to his word I spotted Mr. Catron. He was standing on the courthouse lawn near the war memorials, well-dressed and feeding pigeons with small pieces of bread. When he spotted me he rushed over, and said, "Are you all right?"

"I'm making it, but I'm very sorry that I—"

"Please—no apologies," he said, gently patting my shoulder. "It was my fault, I should not have served so much wine."

"That's very kind of you to say, but you did not make me drink it," I said. "But listen—we need to go inside, will you please come with me?"

He agreed and followed Lupe and me up the stairs to the courthouse and as we walked we discussed the insulation issues. We cleared security and took the elevators to the third floor and made our way toward the courtroom. As we neared it, I saw Dot pacing the floor in the hallway with a distressed look on her face.

When she caught sight of me she rushed over, and said, "Oh, thank the lord you're here."

"I'm very sorry about all of this," I said.

"Don't worry—everything's fine, but are you okay?"

"Do I look like okay?"

"No," she said, shaking her head sympathetically, "are you able to do this?"

"I can get through it," I said. "Dot, this is Mr. Romeo Catron, Mr. Catron, this is Dorothy Swayne."

"Pleased to meet you," he said, bowed slightly, and shook her hand.

"Excuse us for a moment," I said, and pulled Dot aside and whispered, "Did you fix up the doctor's transcript?"

"Yes, its ship shape," Dot said. "Did you remember to bring the lunch?"

"Did I what?"

"You mentioned bringing King Ranch Chicken, but I don't see your tote bag."

"Fiddlesticks. In all my stupor I must have left it on the kitchen counter along with my watch."

Dot said urgently, "If you don't have that, you don't have your notes—what are you going to do about questioning witnesses?"

I leaned toward her, and confided, "I don't have any more notes. I'll have to wing it with Romeo and improvise my closing argument."

"Do you want to start with Doctor Scotty's testimony to buy some time?"

"I don't want to make Mr. Catron wait around, so we'll put him on first. Is Nelda in the courtroom?"

"Yes, and she is very worried."

"Is that the right time?" I said pointing to the clock on the wall. Dot glanced at it and then to her watch, and nodded. "Mr. Catron, you'll need to stay out here until we need you, okay?"

"Most assuredly," he said.

Then a thought hit me. "Is Shiras and Morrison already in the courtroom?"

Dot said, "Shiras and his team are, but I saw Morrison go into the men's room a couple of minutes ago."

"Then scratch that," I said, and addressed Romeo. "I don't want you near the courtroom until we are ready for you. Please wait downstairs on the second floor and the bailiff will come get you when it's time."

He agreed and as he walked away, Dot asked, "Why did you do that?"

"Morrison will recognize Romeo, and I don't want them to see what's coming until the last possible moment."

"You think of everything Gertie—is he going to help?"

"I think so, but I'm not sure I can call him since he was not on our witness list. Can you look at the evidence rules and see what you can find—I may need a loophole?"

"Sure thing."

When we entered, Nelda heard the door and turned anxiously

toward the back of the courtroom. I nodded her way and her tense expression eased. The three of us walked down the aisle, through the gate and Dot and I took our seats at the table and Lupe, now less timid, perched on the pew behind us. The judge was on the bench talking on the phone and I glanced right and saw Shiras sitting and frowning. I then noticed that the number of casual onlookers in the gallery had grown to the largest presence yet.

The judge ended his call, then remarked facetiously, "Nice of you to join us."

"Very sorry judge, I got uh … a little hung … I mean held up," I said.

"You're only a couple of minutes late, but it is the second time."

"I promise it won't happen again."

Shiras rose, and added, "That's not much of a commitment, considering the case is likely to end today."

"How many more witnesses do you have, Ms. Barbour?"

"I just have—" I started, until headache pangs pulsed through my head causing me to cringe and for my eyes to water.

The judge stared at me curiously. "Are you okay?"

"I'm just a little woozy, that's all," I said. "As for witnesses, I just have one live and I need to read in some of Doctor Strong's testimony."

The judge turned to Shiras, "How many for your side?"

"At this point I am not sure we are going to call any. I have asked some of my questions during her case, she gave me a lot of what we needed from Doctor Livingston during her examination, and I frankly don't think they can meet their burden of proof."

"I didn't ask for your commentary on the merits of the case, you can take that up with proper motions after we have wrapped up," the judge said. "I would just like to let the jury know if this is going to be over before the weekend."

"I think that's safe to say," Shiras said, smugly.

"All right then, we're ready for the panel," the judge said.

Charlie knocked on the jury room door, eased it open and motioned the jurors out of the room and to their now all too familiar seats. The judge informed the panel that the case would likely conclude before the weekend, and most seemed relieved by the prediction.

"Ready counsel?" the judge said to me.

"One moment please," I said, and eased over to Dot, "Find anything?"

"Not yet, but I am in the right section."

"Keep trying," I whispered.

"We're waiting," the judge urged.

I turned back to him, and said, "Your Honor, we call Mr. Romeo Catron."

Judge Cushing motioned Charlie into action, and as he walked by our table I gained his attention, and whispered, "You will find him on the second floor. He's a Hispanic gentleman with greying hair and wearing a purple shirt." Charlie nodded and passed the returning CEO on his way out the courtroom door. Mr. Morrison joined the defense team and they immediately convened a huddle. All I could discern were faint, but heated exchanges and moments later Charlie returned with Mr. Catron and showed him to the witness stand.

"Your Honor, may we approach?" Shiras asked.

The judge nodded, and I met Shiras at the bench. "What do you have?"

"Judge, we object to them calling this man since they have not included any such person on their witness list."

"Is that true counsel—is he not listed?" the judge asked.

"That's right," I said, glancing back to Dot and when our eyes met she nodded rapidly.

"Then what's your response to the objection?"

"I will respond, but may I have a moment with my assistant?"

"Yes—briefly," the judge said.

I darted back to our table, and asked, "Did you find something?"

"I think so, look at this part here," Dot whispered, and handed me the evidence book. She pointed me to a highlighted passage, and added, "They call it a witness to rebut."

Lupe giggled, and said, "Miss Dot say weetness butt."

"Shush, Lupe," Dot said.

"What kind of weetness— I mean witness?" I said.

"One to rebut, or as they also say in this section, a rebuttal witness.

As I understand the wording it means that you can call an unlisted witness when you need to put on testimony to counter something the other side's witness has said."

"Ahem," the judge prompted.

I glanced back over my shoulder. "Just one more moment, sir," I said and returned to Dot. "Like rebutting Morrison saying the insulation contained no asbestos?"

"That's the way I read it."

"Thanks, I'll run with it," I said and eased back over to the bench with the rule book in hand.

"Let's have it," the judge said.

"Your Honor, I am calling Mr. Catron for ... for... uh ...," I muttered as my compromised brain went blank. I glanced down to the marked page, and uttered, "I am calling Mr. Catron to counter Mr. Morrison's testimony from yesterday."

"Fine, but what about his objection to you not having him on your list?"

"Your Honor, he's my re-butt witness," I said, and heard Lupe chortling from behind.

The judge asked, "Are you saying you want to call him in rebuttal?"

"Yes sir—that's the trick," I said, and the judge turned to Shiras.

"It's a trick all right, a dirty one at that, and we vehemently object. The case law is clear on this type of sneak attack witness, and he must be disallowed."

"He has a point, Ms. Barbour. What's the nature of his rebuttal evidence?"

"I am calling him to counter the testimony of the foundry from yesterday. As you will recall, Mr. Morrison said Cliff Blatchford never used asbestos insulation. We never anticipated such a false denial and want to counter it with this witness."

"Sounds like rebuttal to me," the judge said to Shiras.

"It's only rebuttal, because they failed to serve us with discovery, nor did they bother to take Mr. Morrison's deposition. Now she wants to be rewarded for that incompetence with this drastic form of relief?"

The judge frowned, turned to Blair and announced, "Based on

Ms. Barbour's representation concerning the expected testimony of the witness, and Mr. Shiras' ad hominem attack on Ms. Barbour, I will let Mr. Catron take the stand."

Shiras slammed his fist on the bench, and blared, "That's a per se abuse of discretion."

"Mr. Shiras, I have warned you about these outbursts and you agreed to count to ten—remember?"

"Yes ... my apologies to the court," Shiras said and tromped back to his table.

Romeo settled into the chair, and I stood next to him using the rail of the witness stand to steady myself. As Blair placed him under oath I heard the courtroom door open and turned and saw my hubby and Bill Highsmith entering. Jack was carrying my tote bag and he raised it, pointed to it and I smiled and nodded.

The judge pushed aside his microphone, and asked, "What did you bring today?"

"King Ranch Chicken," I whispered, and he smiled and repositioned his mic.

I began my questioning by taking Mr. Catron through his background, including his family history. I then asked what he recalled about Clifford Blatchford, and he discussed Cliff's best attributes and how he admired him and his work ethic. We next turned to his own career at the foundry and he detailed his duties from starting as a trainee to his tenure in the tool room.

"For a number of years, you actually managed the tool room, right?"

"Yes ma'am, for the last twenty years of my career," Romeo said proudly.

"And the tool room was essentially a warehouse for storing products and equipment?"

"Objection, leading," Shiras said.

"Sustained, please rephrase your questions without suggesting a response."

"Yes judge," I said. "Mr. Catron, can you describe the tool room?"

"Yes, it was a warehouse that stored products and equipment," he said, grinning and Shiras sighed.

"Describe it, please."

"It was and still is, a large metal building with a railroad spur and loading dock in the back. Inside, it has several rows of shelves for product inventory and there is a service counter in the front that I manned."

"If a laborer or a pipefitter like Cliff Blatchford needed products from the warehouse, would they come to your service counter?"

"Laborers would not do that, but pipefitters would."

"Would this include requesting insulation materials?"

"Yes, of course."

"Mr. Catron, you are acquainted with Mr. Morrison seated over there, aren't you?"

"Yes, ma'am, he was the big boss—the *el hefe*, as we called him."

"Did he say El Hefty?" Highsmith said.

"Don't start sir, I'm not in the mood," the Judge said, and Bill nodded contritely.

I continued. "You were not here yesterday when Mr. Morrison testified, but I want to ask you about something he said. Assume with me that he told this jury that you all were under orders not to buy any asbestos-containing insulation products while Mr. Blatchford was a pipefitter—was he telling the truth?"

Shiras bolted to her feet. "Objection, he can't—"

"Yes, that is true," Romeo said, Nelda gasped, and murmurs permeated the room.

"Objection, withdrawn," Shiras said, returning to his seat.

"How did you learn of this order?"

"Mr. Morrison issued a memo to that effect."

"I see, does that mean Mr. Blatchford could not have been exposed to asbestos after that memo?"

"Certainly not," Romeo said firmly, and the murmurs became a commotion.

"Silence," the judged bellowed and rapped his gavel until the room returned to calm. "You may proceed Ms. Barbour."

"Please explain how Cliff Blatchford would be exposed," I said.

Shiras stood and barked, "I object, Your Honor."

"What is it now?"

Shiras seemed speechless for the moment, then uttered, "Lack of foundation and the question calls for speculation."

"Overruled, you may answer the question, sir."

Romeo explained, "You see ma'am, we kept a large inventory of products in the warehouse."

"Including insulation, right?" I asked.

Shiras, now red-faced, rose and shouted, "I object! She's testifying for the—" He stopped in mid-sentence when he saw the judge's expression and Charlie walking around his desk toward him. "Uh ... can I count to ten?"

"I doubt it," Highsmith said, and Shiras and the judge glared at him.

"Go ahead," the judge said, and we all waited as Shiras counted silently.

Once done Shiras said, "Okay, I'm ready now."

"Fine, but before you proceed, I want to issue a final warning," the judge said addressing both Shiras and Highsmith. "I want you, two men, to listen to me very carefully. The courthouse is a public place, but as evidenced by the security station you two passed through to get up here, that access has its limits. This little corner of it is mine and I make the rules and enforce them with my powers of contempt. I demand a professional decorum in my court for both participants and guests—understood?

"Yes sir," Shiras and Bill said simultaneously.

"Good," the judge said. "Mr. Shiras now that you have sufficiently calmed yourself, what is your objection?"

"I object to counsel leading the witness."

"Hell, through all if this I forgot the pending question," the judge said. "Blair, would you please read it back?" She complied and the Judge said, "I'll sustain the objection— you'll need to restate your question, Ms. Barbour."

"Mr. Catron, were there insulation products in your warehouse?" I asked.

Shiras rose, and said, "That's still leading."

"It's a close call, but I will overrule it. You may answer, sir."

"There was always insulation in my inventory."

"What was the insulation for?"

"There were miles and miles of steam lines in the plant, and the pipefitters insulated them with pipe covering and sealed it with asbestos cement.

"And the cement was also referred to as mud?"

"Yes, insulating mud."

"Did your warehouse have an inventory of insulation and mud when Mr. Morrison issued that memo you just described?"

"Yes, a very large inventory."

"Did any of that insulation contain asbestos?"

"I, I, I object," Waite Morrison said rising to his feet, and Shiras sighed, and shook his head.

"I'll uh, overrule it ... I guess," the judge said awkwardly.

"Let me re-ask it," I said. "Mr. Catron, when Mr. Morrison's memo reached your desk, was there any insulation in your warehouse that contained asbestos?"

"Yes ... all of it did," he said, and I heard Nelda squeal with excitement.

"So, asbestos insulation was used *after* OSHA?" I asked.

In a voice drenched with desperation, Shiras said, "Objection leading."

"Sustained," the judge said, "you'll need to rephrase."

Wanting to ask an objection-proof question, I chose my words carefully, "What happened to the asbestos insulation after the memo?"

"The men used it all up."

I crossed my fingers, and said, "Including Cliff Blatchford?"

"Definitely."

"How long did it take to use it all up?"

Romeo pondered, then said, "It was three, maybe as much as four years, and it was not until we got close to running out that we ordered the non-asbestos type."

"Did Mr. Morrison know about the men using up the asbestos materials first?"

"Objection—speculation," Shiras said.

"Good point," the judge said, and addressed Romeo directly, "how is it you can testify about what Mr. Morrison knew or didn't know?"

"He's the one that ordered it done," Romeo said.

"Ordered it, as in him requiring the asbestos version to be used up first?" the judge asked.

Waite Morrison rose hastily, anxious to make another objection, but Shiras reached around and jerked the CEO back to his pew by his suit jacket.

"Yes," was Romeo's response.

"Why did the foundry keep such a large inventory of insulation?" I asked.

"It is important to know that when we ran low on most any item it was my job to request more. I would prepare the requisition and the purchasing agent would order replacements—in very large quantities."

"How come so much?"

"It is like anything else, the more you buy the cheaper the price. When we would run low on pipe insulation they bought so much that it arrived by the rail car and that is why we had the railroad spur in the back. We had received a large shipment of asbestos insulation just days before the word came out that it was dangerous. Mr. Morrison did not want to waste the money by discarding it, so he instructed us to use it all up before ordering the safe insulation."

"Mr. Catron, were the asbestos insulation products dusty?" I asked.

"Yes, ma'am, they were *very* dusty," he said. "They were dusty in the warehouse, but were even worse out in the foundry where Mr. Blatchford used it."

"How was it dusty in the warehouse?"

"Some of the bags of mud and boxes of insulation would break open on the train or get damaged by our forklifts. The dust would come out every time it was moved and it would get all over the floor and on us workers too."

"Did you breathe any of that dust?" I asked.

"I am afraid so," Romeo lamented, "it would have been impossible not to especially when sweeping it up."

"You mentioned the dust was worse for pipefitters, how so?"

"A lot of the pieces of insulation had to be cut in order to place them on the pipes. Sawing it was extremely dusty," he explained.

"Did you witness that happen with your own eyes?"

"Yes, ma'am and the mixing of the mud was just as bad, if not worse. They had to pour the powder from the bag into a bucket or a wheelbarrow to mix it with water. When they did it released clouds of dust."

"Mr. Morrison testified that mixing the mud was not Mr. Blatchford's job, was he right about that?"

"Correct, it was not his job … but he did it," Romeo added with a flourish.

"Pipefitters sometimes mixed the mud?" I asked.

"Yes ma'am, especially when the crews were short on laborers. In that instance, and in order maintain the pace, pipefitters like Mr. Blatchford would mix it. Even when the laborers did the mixing the pipefitters would be right there breathing it. Any man that did it or was around it being mixed would look like *Frosty the snowman* at the end of the shift."

"Nothing further," I said.

"Anything from the defense?"

"Yes, but one moment, Judge," Shiras said and had what appeared to be a heated conversation with Waite Morrison. When the red-faced men separated, Shiras walked over to Mr. Catron and stood in front of him akimbo. "You are not a chemist, are you Mr. Catron?"

"No sir, I am not."

"And, you're not a materials analyst?"

"What is that?"

"I'll take that as a *no*," Shiras smirked. "You never had any of that pipe covering or cement tested for asbestos content did you?"

"Me?"

"Yes, you," Shiras said tersely.

"I did not."

"Did anyone there test it that you are aware of?" Shiras asked.

"No, sir."

"You can't swear to this jury that you ever saw Mr. Blatchford mixing the mud or sawing pipe covering and looking like *Frosty the snowman*, now can you?"

"No, not specifically."

"Do you agree that when Mr. Blatchford was a pipefitter that he would not have removed old insulation from the pipes?"

"Yes, I agree with that," Mr. Catron said.

"That's because abatement contractors did that, true?"

"That's correct."

"So, Mr. Blatchford's only potential for exposure would be applying new insulation products, right?"

"Yes."

"You have no basis to say that the pipe covering Mr. Blatchford used contained asbestos, do you?"

"I already said it was my job was to fill out the requisitions, and that we received that big order of the asbestos insulation."

"That's it? Just a faint memory of one of countless requisition forms you saw from decades ago?"

"There's that, and I recall *asbestos* being written on the boxes."

"You recall, huh?" Shiras scoffed. "Is it possible that you are remembering it wrong?"

"It is always possible," Romeo conceded.

"Right," Shiras said gleefully. "I pass the—"

"That's why I brought this," Romeo said lifting a photograph from his shirt pocket. He handed it to Shiras who looked at it, and shoved it back into Mr. Catron's pocket.

"Pass the witness," Shiras said, and walked back to his table.

"You may stand down sir," the judge said, and Mr. Catron stared at me urgently.

Rising to my feet so fast that it made me dizzy, I said, "Wait!"

"Yes ma'am?" Mr. Morrison said.

"Not you sir," I said. "Judge, I want to see that picture."

"You two come up," the judge said, and Shiras and I complied.

"Let's see it, Mr. Catron," the judge instructed and Romeo retrieved the photo from his pocket and handed over. The Judge stared at it, grinned and then handed it to me. I examined the photo and found that the old Polaroid snapshot featured two men and a much younger Romeo being handed a plaque. Behind him sat stacks of boxes with *asbestos pipe covering* stenciled on them.

"I assume you want to use this Ms. Barbour?" the judge said.

"I sure do."

Shiras said, "I object."

"Imagine that," the judge muttered, "Charlie, let's give the jury a coffee break while we sort this out." Once the jurors were out of the room, the Judge said, "Are you ready, Blair?"

"Yes, sir."

"We're back on the record without the jury, and still under oath on the witness stand is Mr. Catron."

"You may call me Romeo."

"If it's all the same to you I will stick with Mr. Catron," the judge said.

Romeo grinned. "As you wish, sir."

"All right, let's hear your objection, Mr. Shiras."

"First off, this photo was not produced in discovery."

"Ms. Barbour?"

"Judge, this is the first time I've laid eyes it."

The judge turned to the witness stand. "Mr. Catron, this is quite an interesting photo, where did it come from?"

"After Ms. Barbour left my house last night, I recalled that on my final day at the foundry I took an empty box to work. At the end my shift I filled the box with my personal belongings from my desk. This morning I went to my garage and located that box and found this photo. I thought it would be helpful to justice so I brought it with me."

"Describe everything and everyone depicted in it?" the judge said.

"This is me, thinner and with less gray hair," he said pointing, "and this is Mr. Morrison giving me my twenty-year plaque—I still have that too if you want to see it."

"That's all right, who is this," the judge said pointing to the third figure in the photo."

"He was a supervisor named Curtis Rehnquist."

"That's C.A.?" the judge asked.

"I don't know a C. A., but we all called Mr. Rehnquist *coon ass*."

"Yes—we know," the judge said. "When would this photo have been taken?"

"With this being the twenty year anniversary and since I started there in nineteen fifty-five, it should have been approximately nineteen seventy-five."

"It has the exact date right there," I said pointing at the white border at the bottom of the photograph and to the dim green dotted characters reading: *3-19-1975.*

"Well there you go," the judge said. "So Mr. Shiras what's your objection to it, other than it stinks up your case?"

"I claim surprise and it's not proper rebuttal evidence."

"Ms. Barbour just saw it for the first time today—so it wasn't unfairly withheld," the judge reasoned.

"How can we be sure of that? First, we get the sneak attack witnesses, then this photo pops up out of nowhere, and according to the witness Ms. Barbour was at his house last night."

"So what? Isn't a lawyer allowed to meet with a fact witness?"

"Judge, all I'm saying is it reeks of collusion."

"Do you contend they're both lying under oath?" the judge asked.

"He's the only one under oath," Shiras said, nodding toward Mr. Catron.

"Don't you know that we are both under oath in this courthouse?" I said with mock indigence.

"It just seems awfully convenient that we're winning the case, and all of this new evidence mysteriously surfaces."

"I'm quite sure Ms. Barbour wishes she had this picture months ago, am I right?" the judge asked.

"Absolutely," I said

"Anything else counsel?"

Shiras looked flummoxed. "Yes, um … the … uh … the exhibit has not been authenticated."

"I think Mr. Catron just did that," the judge said. "I am sure, Ms. Barbour can lay the proper predicate on the record if you would like."

"That's not necessary," Shiras conceded.

"Anything else?" the judge asked and Shiras shook his head. "I overrule any and all objections."

"You do want this marked, don't you?" the judge asked.

"Indeed I do," I said.

"I'll take care of it," Blair offered, and I handed her the photo. She placed the exhibit sticker on the white border, numbered it and handed it back to me, and said, "Plaintiff's exhibit number two, Your Honor."

"Plaintiff's two is admitted," the judge said, "get 'em back in Charlie."

When the jury returned to their seats, I spent several minutes questioning Romeo about the photo and how it proved asbestos insulation was available at the foundry at least until March of 1975. I passed him and was walking back to our table examining the photograph when something caught my eye. "Your Honor, on second thought can I ask a couple of additional questions?"

"About what?"

"I want to clarify something in the photo."

"That's fine, but make it brief."

"I promise it will be, but I would like to reflect this exhibit on the TV screens, if Mr. Shiras will have his people do it for me."

Shiras stood. "No way! This is our equipment and cost us a fortune to have it set up here."

"I can't make you do it," the judge said, "but just know we have an Elmo projector in the back. If you won't put it up, I will personally retrieve my projector and rig it up for her out here."

Shiras sighed, then said, "Give it to me."

I extended the photo to him, he snatched it from my hand and gave it to a member of his tech squad. Soon the cheerful face of Mr. Catron receiving his plaque was on all screens and the jury got a good look at it.

"Mr. Catron, please tell us what Mr. Morrison has around his neck and Mr. Rehnquist has in his right hand."

Shiras said, "Objection—relevance."

"Overruled, you may answer sir."

"Those are what is known as canister respirators," Romeo said.

"What are they for?"

"You wear them on your face to avoid breathing dust and fumes, and these men took theirs off for the camera."

"Did they always wear them?"

"Anytime they were off the carpet, they did."

"What do you mean by that?"

"I mean whenever they were out of the carpeted offices and in the plant. All in management wore them when they were in the foundry itself."

"This photo was taken in the plant, wasn't it?"

"Yes, it was."

"Where is your respirator?" I asked.

He smiled and said, "I never got one those."

"Do you know why?"

"It's hard to say, but probably because of the cost. I saw those requisitions too and the canister type masks were very expensive. Another reason is that to wear that type of respirator you need to be clean shaven every day. Like me, most of my co-workers had facial hair."

"You preferred having the facial hair?"

"Yes, and still do as you can see," he said grinning.

"Did the foundry provide the rank and file any type of fume and dust protection?"

"Only those cheap paper masks like people allergic to grass use when they mow their yard."

"Did you and your co-workers wear those?"

"Sometimes we would. If it was a real dusty, enough so that you could choke on it, the men would use a paper mask or tie a bandana or handkerchief over their nose and mouth."

"Those you wore over your facial hair, right?"

"Correct."

"Mr. Catron, would you have been willing to shave your face every day to wear a canister mask if you had been told breathing dust at the foundry could cause a deadly form of cancer?"

Shiras stood. "I object, she's—"

"No," Mr. Catron answered, and I was taken aback.

Shiras looked equally surprised, and said, "I withdraw that objection."

Romeo turned and stared at Waite Morrison, and added, "If I had known that, I would have quit my job the very day I was told."

"I pass the witness," I said, and Romeo was allowed to stand down.

As he passed our table on his way to the back of the courtroom, he patted my shoulder, and said, "I hope you feel better."

I smiled and whispered, "I'm feeling fine now—thanks to you."

To cap off our case Dot and I read into the record the portions of Doctor Scotty's testimony. Dot had done a fine job excerpting the questions and answers and though nervous at first she read her parts well. Once done, I was fortunate that the judge took a break so I could assess if there was anything we had forgotten.

I conferred with Dot and we reviewed the trial notebook and she reminded me about the medical records and bills. With Doctor Scotty's testimony proving them up as *reasonable and necessary,* all I needed was a little help from Blair. She separately marked each set from all individuals and facilities that treated Cliff and the invoices for the funeral and burial expenses.

When the judge returned to the bench he approved all of our records and we rested our case. Shiras rose and informed the judge they too rested. A part of me was relieved that there would be no more evidence, but I also knew that by them doing so that they felt I had not made our case.

Shiras consulted his Rolex, and said, "Judge, it is only eleven o'clock, are we going to get the jury in and do closing arguments?"

"I um … well … I think we need to break for lunch first," the Judge responded with a furtive glance toward our table.

"Fair enough," Shiras said. "We are planning on going to the Hereford House for steaks if you want to come along?"

"That's kind of you, but I already have lunch plans."

Charlie left with the jury and I thanked Jack for bringing my tote bag. I offered for the boys to lunch with us, but they opted to drive to West for Buck's Bar-B-Que. The girls and I headed directly to the lawyer's lounge and once there I began microwaving our food. Lupe set the table and in anticipation of having company, she included an extra bowl.

By then I was feeling better from my hangover but was far from well. I hoped that getting a hearty meal on my stomach would help me along, but the mere smell of it heating affected me negatively. I grew leery about eating anything, especially a dish as rich as King Ranch Chicken, and opted for a few saltine crackers instead.

We were not in the lounge more than five minutes when the judge bounded in. No longer timid about partaking in our fare, he walked empty-handedly passed us and straight to the microwave. He peered through the window and watched the bowl slowly rotating, and said, "Smell's great, reckon there's enough for little ol' you know who?"

"Certainly," I said reaching into my tote, "and here, take this."

"Is that the chili?" he said, examining the bowl.

"Yes, judge, and inside here is the recipe for it," I said handing him the sealed envelope.

"Thank you, and please call me Bob ... at least when we're in here. Did you make the dish yesterday?" he asked as the oven dinged.

"No sir, I made it a while back and froze it," I said, and used an oven mitt to remove the steaming Pyrex dish from the microwave. I placed it on a trivet resting on the tabletop and began crumbling more tortilla chips on the bubbling surface of the casserole. "I was going to make my seafood gumbo last evening, but I ... well ... let's just say—something came up."

"Have you ever had King Ranch Chicken?" Dot asked.

"Oh yes I have and I love it—mind if I have a little taste?" the judge asked, grabbing his own spoon.

"Not at all judge—I mean Bob," I said, "help yourself to all you want and I also have chili cheese Fritos to go with it if you like."

He nodded, took a spoonful, placed it in his mouth and savored it. "Oh my, this is fantastic. My Linda was an excellent cook, but she could never quite master this dish. It always came out … kind of … well—"

"Pasty?" I said.

"I was thinking gloppy, but yours isn't like that even after being frozen and reheated."

"I'm glad you like it," I said. "You see Bob, I do mine a little different than most recipes."

"I would love to know how, do you need to tell me in secret?" the judge asked glancing toward the other ladies.

"That's not necessary for this one," I said, as Nelda eased an ink pen from her purse and placed a paper towel in front of her. "Unless I am in a real hurry, I don't use canned products or cream for the foundation. As with this batch, I prefer to make the base from scratch and it's a cross between a roux and a mole sauce."

"I would really like to make it someday, but it sounds complicated."

"It's not that hard, but it requires several spices that you probably do not have in your kitchen cabinet."

"That's a safe assumption considering all I have is salt and pepper."

I flashed him a sympathetic expression, and said, "Well Bob, you are just going to have to add some more to your repertoire," I said, and he laughed. "The most important step when making the base is you don't want to scald it in the saucepan or it will have a bitter taste. Just keep whisking it as it cooks and add the flour and spices in slowly, instead of all at once."

"I see," he said. "Can you jot the full recipe down for me … Gertie?" I was taken aback by the reference, until he added, "that is your nickname, isn't it?"

"Yes of course, and I would be delighted to send you the full recipe, even if I have to mail it."

"It is truly delicious, but you only have the one dish and there's four of you, and I just can't—"

"We have plenty," I said.

"Are you sure?"

"Positive," I said handing him his bowl. "As you may have detected I am a little under the weather and am not very hungry."

"Sorry to hear that, but your loss is my gain," he said cheerfully, trading his spoon for the ladle. He dipped out a heaping bowlful, covered it with a handful of crushed Fritos, and then headed to the door whistling up a storm as he exited.

When we returned to the courtroom, Shiras and his entourage sat confidently at their table and we bided our time until the judge entered. Charlie brought the jurors in and once seated, the judge said, "You may proceed with you summation, Ms. Barbour."

I walked to the podium with only a cup of water in hand and focused on Jack's advice. "You each have already given the better part of a week of your lives to be here, so I will be brief in my comments. You have been very attentive throughout this trial, unfortunately, that was true even when I was blundering," I said and noticed that Bill and Jack had made it back from West. "Because you have paid such good attention, I am certain you know the case facts as well as I do and will not waste your time explaining what you have already heard."

I took a sip from the cup of water and continued. "None of us are guaranteed tomorrow—we all realize that, and all the prayers in the world do not prevent some tragedies. Good people—sometimes young people or persons in great health die suddenly and we often wonder why. I remember a time when a cyclone struck a small Pacific island and devastated it from coast to coast. The storm took the lives of countless innocent men, women and precious little children. At our church services the following Sunday, we were taking up a collection to go to the relief effort and a deacon asked the pastor *why does God let things like this happen?* Our pastor gave the best answer I have ever heard when he said, *I don't know.*"

"There are plenty of situations in life that we do not understand and so many things are beyond our control and we often feel lost. That said, there are many tragedies that *are* preventable, including those in the workplace. Engaging in work and holding a job is an honorable and fulfilling endeavor. It provides those that pursue work, in home and out of the home, with a purpose and a sense of dignity that is superseded in importance only by faith and family. Employers owe a responsibility to their workers to provide a safe place for them to do their job. It is a covenant, an unspoken promise—an obligation no less important than the duty they owe to their customers and shareholders. When employers fail to uphold their end of that bargain and workers are hurt, get sick or as in this case even die, it is a rank betrayal of that trust."

"Those affected by such tragedies include grandchildren, both born and yet to be born, that will know their grandfather only through stories and photographs. A grieving wife that takes most meals by herself and lays down alone each night inches away from where her loving husband slept for decades. A widow that stares into the darkness knowing that if something confronts her, such as an intruder, a plumbing leak, or a dangerous thunderstorm—she is on her own. Once she manages to calm herself and close her eyes, her mind naturally drifts to things that might have been. She reflects on the man of her dreams and the dreams that died with him. This includes all the trips that will never be taken and the morning conversations that are now just faint memories. She mourns the loss of companionship and the silencing of a four-octave voice," I said, and heard a whimpering from behind me.

"Then there are the damages. It speaks the obvious to say that you as jurors and good men like Judge Cushing can't return Clifford to Nelda. All the system of justice can do is try to make it right in some measure. The concept of *justice* can be elusive and it may mean different things to different people. This morning I looked up the definition and *justice* essentially means to be *fair*. I suppose I am expected to suggest to you a dollar amount to write on that form you will take to the jury room, but I am not going to do it. I don't envy you in having to arrive at that number, but we all trust that you all will be *fair* and deliver *justice*," I turned, grabbed my cup and returned to our table.

"Mr. Shiras, it's your podium,"

"May it please the court," Shiras said as he rose, buttoned his suit jacket and paced over to the jurors. "Ladies and gentlemen, I too appreciate your service, but your sacrifice this week was rewarded by sitting in judgment of a wholly unmeritorious case. We all feel bad for Ms. Blatchford and her loss, but we disproved many of the elements of their claim—aspects that the written charge from the judge will instruct are necessary for their side to prevail."

Shiras began pacing. "Ms. Barbour shied away from the evidence in her summation and I would say for very good reason since the facts are not her friend. No one here denies that my client owed Mr. Blatchford a duty to provide reasonably safe working conditions and for a variety of reasons I say that they did just that. At this point, do we even know if Mr. Blatchford ever used the asbestos version of the insulating materials? They brought that Catron character here this morning and he said it was possible Cliff Blatchford never worked with it at all. Despite being very cozy with my opponent Mr. Catron admitted he never saw Mr. Blatchford using it and a grainy old photograph and speculative recollections are not enough to sustain plaintiff's burden of proof."

Shiras struck a stance along the rail separating him from the jurors, and added, "Even if you make the leap of faith that Mr. Blatchford used asbestos insulation, it is undeniable that my client was in the foundry business and not the insulation business—so whose fault is it? How was this family owned business supposed to know that this stuff could cause cancer all the way back in the nineteen seventies and beyond? Did you see or hear any evidence from plaintiffs about my client having that knowledge or that the insulation companies ever provided warnings on the products they shipped to the foundry? You sure didn't see a warning on the insulation boxes in Mr. Catron's mysterious photo, did you? So why aren't the companies that made the insulation and the so-called mud present in this courtroom? After all, if plaintiff became sick from their products aren't they the true bad guys? This was *their* business, and *they* were the experts on their own products—not my client. But they're not here and you ought to ask yourselves why."

"The judge has provided specific instructions and you have taken an oath to follow them. The most important among them demands that you each reach your decision based *only* on the evidence. Though we all empathize with Ms. Blatchford, you are duty bound to deliberate according to the written charge," Shiras said lifting his copy of the judge's instructions. "It says in here that you must decide the case, and I quote, *without bias, sympathy or prejudice.* I am confident that if you fulfill that duty, you will return a verdict in favor, my client."

"In the unlikely event you find for plaintiff let's discuss damages. We established that based on Mr. Blatchford's age and his myriad of serious diseases that his death was statistically around the corner. This means that even if everything they alleged, in this case, were true, a notion that you know we strongly deny, it would have had little impact on Mr. Blatchford's lifespan. I am sure that's why Ms. Barbour was too embarrassed to address that fact and was unwilling to offer a figure for the damages. Since she was reluctant to do it, I will suggest a number ... I recommend a nice round figure called zero."

Shiras returned to his table, the judge retired to his chambers, and Charlie ushered the panel to the jury room.

I asked the girls to follow me into the hallway, and once there, Nelda said, "Gertie, you were nothing less than fabulous."

"I agree, you nailed it," Jack said and Dot, Lupe, and Highsmith nodded.

"Thanks for that, but you all heard his argument—he sure pointed out plenty of my failures."

Highsmith shook his head. "Oh hell, I was watchin' those jurors and they weren't buying any of his crap."

"I hope you're right," I said. "How was the bar-be-que, boys?"

"Delicious—as usual," Jack said. "We brought you some brisket and it's on ice out in the truck."

"That's real nice of you fellas," I said. "Well, I guess we better get back in there and ride this thing out."

With the exception of a couple of coffee breaks, the jury stayed behind closed doors well into the afternoon and I began to wonder if we would have a verdict that day. I had no way of assessing the implications of the length of the deliberations, in terms of whether it was good or bad for us, but I noticed that those on the defense team seemed smugly confident.

At our table, Nelda sat knitting baby booties, Dot worked a word search puzzle and Lupe was reading a Spanish language tabloid she purchased from the newsstand downstairs. I, on the other hand simply sat, often with my head on my folded arms dozing intermittently. I was exhausted and still experiencing occasional waves of nausea. When the buzzer from the jury room rang I jerked my head up so fast I almost fainted.

As Charlie passed our table I asked, "Do they have a verdict?"

"No ma'am, if they did the buzzer would have gone off twice," he explained. "They probably have a question or need another break."

The judge emerged from his chambers sans the robe and took the bench. He instructed Charlie to discover what the panel needed and when he returned, he had a note in his hand.

"What is it?" the judge asked, as I joined Shiras at the bench.

"They have a request," Charlie said and handed the paper to the judge.

The judge read the note, grinned and said, "They want to know if they can use a calculator," he said displaying the note. "Any objection, Mr. Shiras?"

"No ... uh ... we have no objection," he uttered.

"Since they can't use their cell phones, we will need to provide one."

"I have this one judge," Blair said, with her pocket calculator in hand.

"Perfect," the judge said, and Charlie took the calculator and walked it into the jury room.

Twenty-five minutes later the buzzer sounded—not once—but twice and my stomach knotted. The judge returned and while the jury entered, Nelda and I rose and locked arms.

Once seated, the judge asked the jury, "Do you have a verdict?"

The foreman, a well-dressed man from the second row, rose and replied, "We do."

He handed the paperwork to Charlie who in turn delivered it to the bench. The judge silently read all of the questions and answers and all we could do was watch and wait. He finally began to recite them aloud, saying, "Negligence? *We do.* Proximate cause? *We do.* What sum of money, if any, do you award plaintiffs as damages in this cause," the judge paused, and looked over to me, then said, "two-point-five—million—dollars."

"Wahoo!" Highsmith yelled, and a raucous commotion from the crowded gallery ensued. The judge employed his gavel for the second time that day to return the room to silence. I turned to see Bill's grinning face and Jack sitting next to him slack-jawed. I tried to use my trembling right hand to write the verdict figure on my legal pad, but with my excitement, I did not know how many zeroes to put. Consequently, I dropped my pen and used my legal pad to fan myself.

Nelda released my left arm, hugged me tight and whispered in my ear, "You did it, girl, you really did it."

The judge thanked the jurors, then dismissed them from their service. We all rose as they filed out, once gone we thanked the judge, Blair, and Charlie. The defense team would have no part of exchanging farewells and busied themselves in yet another huddle as the men in the coveralls returned and began packing up the boxes and unplugging all of the electronics.

I urged the girls out to the hallway where we were able to greet some of the jurors. We thanked them for blessing us with such a wonderful result and some shook my hand and others tearfully hugged Nelda. Two asked for my business card and I explained that I was *getting out of the business*, then Jack began regaling them with his own jury service tales.

All was glorious until something caught my eye. I turned and saw Charlie peeking through the door and motioning us back inside the now near-empty courtroom. As we filed in he informed that Shiras requested that he retrieve the judge to hear a motion. As the movers pushed the loaded rolling carts past us, I noticed a fellow at the defense table that I had not seen before. He was not wearing a suit, but rather was clad in tan slacks and a golf shirt and was holding a file folder.

We all stood when the judge entered, and he asked, "You have a matter for the court, Mr. Shiras?"

"Yes, Your Honor. It's an oral motion for a new trial."

"Counsel, we haven't even entered a judgment in this case. Once we do that, file a written motion and set it for hearing on my Monday motion docket," the Judge said and turned to leave.

"Judge," Shiras said urgently. "I think this needs to be brought to the court's attention—*now*."

The judge nodded and assumed his high back chair. "All right, what's the basis for your motion?"

Shiras pointed directly at me, and said, "This lady is *not* Louise Barbour." My legs went wobbly and I collapsed back in my chair. "Your Honor, her name is actually Gertrude Chase and she's not a lawyer at all," Shiras added while accepting the file from the fellow in the slacks.

"That's a very serious allegation."

"I realize that judge, but I have the evidence right here," Shiras said, raising the file in his right hand.

Eschewing Shiras' proof for the moment the Judge stared over at me, and asked, "Is what he said true?"

I did not know what words to use but knew well not to lie. I slowly struggled to my feet, looked the judge squarely in the eye, and said, "Everything Mr. Shiras just said is true. I am not Louise Barbour, I am Gertrude Chase and I am not a lawyer."

The judge sat speechless for what seemed an eternity. I felt as I did as a little girl when I had misbehaved and sat in my room awaiting my dad's punishment. The judge scratched his head and sighed a couple of times, then broke the silence by asking, "Mr. Shiras, how did you come to discover this?"

"It was fishy from the beginning and it started the day my firm was assigned the case to defend. There is a small community of firms that file asbestos suits and we had never heard of Ms. Barbour. We did what we normally do with any unfamiliar opponent and commenced an in-house investigation. We wanted to learn about her experience, including if she had ever tried any cases and if so to what result. When we asked for Ms. Blatchford's deposition, they allowed it to occur at my office and I thought that too was odd. During the deposition, I noticed that the plaintiff and Ms. Chase seemed to be pretty chummy with each other, and then there was the manner in which Ms. Barbour—I mean Ms. Chase comported herself."

The judge said, "What about it?"

"It was conducted like ... well ... as if she had never done a deposition before. On the heels of that, we received a notice to forward future filings to a P.O. Box."

"A post office box?" the judge said, glancing over to me and I simply nodded.

"We saw it all so peculiar that we retained this man here beside me—private investigator Robert Grier. He managed to gather quite a bit of information on Louise Barbour, but it didn't seem to add up. Ms. Chase appeared too young to have been Ms. Barbour and bore no resemblance to the photos in the law school annuals he accessed. At my request, Robert drove to Mexia, and asked around and gathered most of the information contained in this file, including Ms. Barbour's obituary."

"Obituary?" the judge said, returning his eyes to me. "Are you dead, I mean is the real Ms. Barbour deceased?"

I nodded, and said ruefully, "Deader than Elvis."

"Please continue, Mr. Shiras," the judge said.

"While in Mexia, Robert located Ms. Barbour's son, Clarence Vanderbilt," Shiras said, turning and pointing toward the back of the room. I swiveled my head around and sure enough, it was Clarence in the flesh, craning his neck to look through the window in the courtroom door. "Your honor, we would like to put Mr. Grier on the stand, followed by Mr. Vanderbilt."

"I'm not sure that's necessary," the judge said. "Ms. Barb ... I mean ... Ms. ... um ... what's your real name?"

"Chase, Gertrude Chase," I said.

"Yes, yes thank you," the judge said and jotted a note. "The point is Mr. Shiras she has already admitted the veracity of your assertions."

"With all due respect, I *really* think we need make a record of this," Shiras urged.

"You might be right, but before we consider that let's try to get to the bottom of this," the judge said, then addressed me. "What in the world were you thinking?"

"I guess I wasn't thinking, at least not clearly, but I want you to know up front that this was all my idea—not theirs," I said, nodding to the other ladies. "This all started a few months ago when the real Louise Barbour died suddenly right there in our office. You see judge, Dorothy here and I have been in the law business all of our adult lives and had worked for Louise for the past eighteen years. She was a decent woman in a lot of respects, but in many ways, she was …well … let's just say not so kind. I know it's not godly to speak ill of the departed and just know that what I'm about to tell you is not intended as an excuse—but rather as an explanation."

"Duly noted," the judge said.

"Louise was *really* hard on us. She didn't pay us very much, even by Mexia standards, but it was our job and we poured our hearts into our work. We took great care of the clients and despite our bosses cruelties we never complained … we could not afford to."

"Y'all were afraid of her, weren't you?"

"Yes sir, but our biggest fear was being unemployed. So we put up with the abuse, her erratic behavior and drinking habit in order to keep working."

"She had the monkey on her back?" the judge asked.

"He must mean Clarence," Highsmith said, and the judge glared in Bill's direction.

"Yes she did, and in a bad way too," I said.

Then Shiras weighed in. "This is all very touching, but I object to—"

"Hush, for god's sake," the judge scolded. "We're not even on the record and I believe it is important to have some context to this whole affair—if you don't mind."

Shiras returned to his seat and I proceeded, "Louise's drinking problem escalated greatly over the past few years and the worse it got, the more duties we assumed. Toward the end, Dot and I were truly running the office. We interacted with the clients, prepared all of the documents and did virtually everything, but the court appearances. When Louise died, we encouraged the man that you saw googling through the door to get another lawyer in to run the firm. We held out hope that if he did we could stay employed, but it was Clarence's decision and he wanted no part of that. He demanded that we wind up all of the firm's business, including getting the files assigned out to other law offices. Though once done we knew we would be kicked to the curb, we made sure every file was updated and placed in capable hands."

"Why did y'all agree to do it considering you were essentially fired?" the judge asked.

"Principally because we cared about the clients and did not want their cases to slip through the cracks. Considering the slim prospects of being hired anywhere else, we each needed the extra two weeks' pay."

"I get the dilemma, but what's that got to do with you ending up in my courtroom impersonating a deceased lawyer?"

"While referring out the inventory of cases we happened upon Nelda's file, and it came as a surprise to us all. We knew nothing about it, but later learned that Louise met with Nelda one weekend, when we were not there, and signed her up. She stuck the file in a filing cabinet and never did anything more on it. When I reviewed the file the first thing I noted was just how close we were to the running of the statute of limitations and it spooked me."

"How close?" the judge asked.

"Just over three months."

The judge's eyebrows narrowed. "You mean to tell me that the real Ms. Barbour signed up this wrongful death case and let it get that close to being time-barred?"

"That's right, so we needed to get it placed, and placed rapidly. Since we were already referring everything out to other lawyers I figured we would find a firm close by to take her case. I quickly learned that no one around Central Texas does plaintiff's asbestos work, and I was getting alarmed. I contacted a friend of mine at one of the big firms in Dallas to see if they would run with it. Turns out they do handle asbestos matters, but they're on the same side as Mr.

Shiras and could not take it. I learned, however, that the defendants most always settle these cases, so I—and I alone cooked up the grand plan to handle it. I figured that I could file the case and work it up for Nelda, and it would resolve short of trial—boy was I wrong."

"Did the son uh ... Mr. um—what's his name?" the judge asked.

"Clarence Vanderbilt," I said.

"Yes, was he aware of this?"

"Sure, I didn't hide anything from him," I said, and explained the details of my agreement with Clarence. "Judge Cushing, I want you to know that I am awfully sorry for deceiving you and Mr. Shiras. I only wanted my friend, whom I have known since I was a teenager, to be compensated for the death of her husband and for us girls to make some money too. When the case did not settle and considering that a sizable chunk of personal savings wrapped up in the case, I decided to plow forward."

"You funded the case?"

"Yes, sir—me and my husband over there, that is."

"I see," the judge sighed. "Ms. Blatchford, did you know coming into this that Ms. Chase was not a lawyer?"

Nelda rose, and responded, "Yes sir, I did, and though she would never tell you, this is all *my* idea."

"That's all right Nelda," I said. "You don't have to—"

"I want to Gertie," Nelda demanded. "You see judge, it was me that planted the seed of handling the case in her head. She told me *no* at first, but I kept pestering her until she gave in."

"Why would you want a non-lawyer to handle such an important case?"

"I have always had the utmost faith in Gertie, and wanted her by my side through all of this. Judge, she is the kindest and most knowledgeable person I have ever known and that's why I asked her to do this for me," Nelda said, and we all stood teary eyed and held each other's hands in solidarity.

"Did you two have a fee contract?" the judge asked.

"Yes sir, we used the one I originally signed, but Gertie reduced the fee percentage," Nelda said.

"You negotiated a reduction?"

"No sir, Gertie insisted on it over my objection."

"Oh, I see," the judge said. "The first thing I will tell you is that your contract is void. A fee agreement with a non-lawyer is unenforceable, and anything you get from this case, beyond out of pocket expenses, is yours and yours alone."

"That's not fair," Nelda said.

"Maybe, but that's the law," he said, and leaned forward in his chair, and turned to the defense table. "Mr. Shiras, when did you learn that Ms. Barbour—I mean Ms. Gertie ... I mean, Ms. Chase was ... not a lawyer?"

"As I stated earlier we received bits and pieces of information over time. We had to put it together and that took a—"

"Whoa," the judge said, raising his right palm and facing toward Shiras. "I want to know one thing and one thing only. What is the precise time that you knew, for a fact, that this lady was not an attorney?"

Shiras hesitated, then said, "Well—judge, it's tough to say a specific time with precision."

"Do you want me to put you and your investigator on the witness stand?" the judge asked.

"I'd like to see that," Highsmith said under his breath.

Shiras' eyes darted about, then he conceded, "I guess we knew for certain about a month, to a month and a half ago."

"Let me make sure I have this straight. You knew of this charade long before you stepped foot in this courtroom, but you and your client let this case go forward to trial?" the judge asked, and Shiras simply stared at his wing tips. "I guess if you had won the case you would have never said anything about this."

Shiras remained mute and the judge leaned back in his chair and stared at the ceiling. You could have heard a feather fall and I glanced back to Jack and his expression only heightened my own fright.

Eventually, the judge broke the silence, saying, "This is the damnedest thing I've seen since the two-headed dog at the carnival. With thirty-seven years in the practice of law, including sixteen on this bench, I have never even heard of anything like this—not once. There is one thing for certain—no one here has clean hands," the judge added, and Lupe inspected her fingers curiously. "We have this subterfuge by the plaintiffs, the defense side learning of it and sitting on it. Then there is the questionable sworn testimony from the foundry."

"You, you mean me, me, me?" Waite Morrison said with his voice cracking.

"Yes, you," the judge said, then returned his attention to our table, "I can tell you one thing Ms. Blatchford, your case has been tried and it will remain tried. I am not granting this motion and your verdict stands. Anyone that wants to challenge me on that can take it right on up to the Court of Appeals. That said, I'm going to offer a one-time opportunity to the parties, one that must be accepted by all, in its entirety, before leaving here today. I am offering to reduce the damage verdict to an even one million dollars. If this remittitur is acceptable then an agreed judgment signed by all parties will be entered accordingly. I want an additional agreement that in doing so all parties waive any right of appeal and that all of this remains confidential. I do not see that last part as much of a sacrifice since I doubt either side would want any of this to be a matter of public record or worse to spill out into the newspapers—do you two follow me so far?"

"Yes, judge," Shiras said.

"Ms. Chase?"

"I understand it, sir."

"Good, but we have another problem here. Ms. Chase, you have engaged in the unauthorized practice of law, which is more than frowned upon in this state, in fact, it can be charged a crime. As such, I can't just ignore what has happened here this week and there must be consequences—serious consequences." I felt faint again and struggled to catch my breath. "I want a further agreement from both sides that there will be no action taken with the State Bar. In exchange for that, I will handle the punishment aspect of all misconduct with my powers of contempt."

"That part is a little tricky," Shiras said. "As Your Honor is well aware, the rules require a member of the bar to report ethical breaches. For me to fail to alert the State Bar of her felonious conduct is, in and of itself, an ethical violation."

"They do require that Mr. Shiras and I might add that they require it to be reported *promptly*—not after a month and a half and only when you need it as leverage after losing a jury trial," the judge said, and Shiras returned to staring at his shoes. "Each side has a bona fide problem and the only question for you two, and your respective clients is how you want it handled. I am asking you all to consider my offer and the defense side can to go to the jury room and the plaintiff's team can meet out in the hall and ponder it—you have twenty minutes."

The judge rose and disappeared into to his chambers and the defense team scurried toward the jury room. Our squad exited the courtroom, followed by Jack and Highsmith and I asked the girls to wait at the end of the hall. "Jack, did you get the gist of judge's deal?"

"Yes, and I am all for it if the ladies agree. This way we at least get our expenses back, but what do you think's going to happen on the punishment thing."

"I don't know, but I trust the judge on this more than a bunch of strangers in Austin."

"He's pretty stern," Jack said.

"He seems to like me, but I have certainly gotten on his bad side in the last half hour," I said, "but we're on the clock so I better get with the others."

I approached the ladies and began discussing the judge's proposal. I started with the money aspect and explained in English and then in Spanish roughly what each would net after fees and expenses.

"You left out your cut,' Nelda said.

"You heard the judge, it's not legal."

Dot said, "If it isn't legal for you, it isn't for me and Lupe."

"You guys didn't practice law without a license," I said. "Look, let's worry about that later—is the deal okay everyone?"

Nelda spoke first, saying, "Gertie, you three did a wonderful job and put more effort into this than I could have ever hoped for. Even at the reduced amount, it is far more than I ever thought I would get from the case."

"So you'll do it?" I asked.

"Sure I will, but only if we can settle your portion after the fact."

"Don't worry about that," I said, and addressed Dot and Lupe, "You girls on board?"

"I'm in," Dot said, and Lupe nodded eagerly.

"Good, let's see what Shiras and his bunch have to say," I said.

"What do you think the judge is going to do to you?" Nelda asked grimly, and I shrugged. "I hope he doesn't do anything bad," she said tearfully and hugged me. When I opened my eyes I saw from over Nelda's shoulder Clarence waddling toward us.

I separated from Nelda and addressed him. "What do you want?"

"My fair share of my mama's case, that's what," he demanded, as he folded a slice of pizza the size of a home plate and started in on it.

Sensing the looming confrontation, Jack and Highsmith stood, but I waved them off, and turned back to Dot and whispered, "Look— this could get ugly, so would you get Lupe and Nelda back to our table, and come get me if the judge comes in?"

"Sure thing," Dot said and urged the women to follow her.

I scowled at Clarence, and said, "You helped the foundry's lawyer, didn't you?"

"Well, I uh —" Clarence stammered.

"Tell me the truth, damn it!"

"I did, so what?"

"Why would you do that?"

"I thought they would pay me something if I did," Clarence said, and a long string of cheese dangled from his chin. "Y'all tricked me, and if I don't get something out of this, none of y'all should either," he added in his pathetic, whiney voice.

"I am only going to say this once so you better listen carefully. We earned this fair and square and in case you have forgotten, we had a deal."

"There's nothin' in writing."

Now I was mad as a hornet and he knew it. "Honorable people

don't need an agreement in writing—not in Texas at least. Decent people transact business on a hand shake and consider their word to be their bond."

"What does that even mean?"

"I would not expect you to understand, but listen up. There's no telling what's going to happen to me when I go back in there, but I can promise you one thing. If you throw a monkey wrench in this deal I am going to tell the judge, the bailiff and anyone else who will listen about your gambling operation," I said and pointed to my own chin to alert him to the swaying string of cheese.

"Gambling operation—are you kidding? I just do a little bookmaking," he scoffed and addressed his mozzarella issue by twirling the cheesy string around his index and sticking it in his mouth.

"It's illegal," I said.

He mumbled between chews. "All I have to do is deny it and it'll be your word against mine."

"I'll put your lard ass on that witness stand and place you under oath."

"You wouldn't."

"Try me," I said, "and on top of that I will subpoena your customers and they will save their own skins by dropping you in the grease."

"Who cares, it's just a misdemeanor," he defended, but I could tell he was as nervous as a long-tailed cat in a room full of rocking chairs—so much so he stopped eating.

"You've done pretty well for yourself bookmaking, right? I mean, I've heard you brag about the money you have made."

"I make okay money at it."

"What about your taxes?"

"What about 'em?" he asked.

I eased closer to him and whispered, "I bet you've never claimed a dime of that income on your tax returns."

"So?"

"It's the IRS Clarence," I said. "Failing to report income is a federal crime and do you know that tax evasion is how the feds got Al Capone into Alcatraz."

"That's bull."

"Look it up yourself," I said.

Clarence transferred his pizza to his left hand and used his right to retrieve his cell phone. He pecked in a search query and as he read, the color drained from his face—and sweat beaded on his forehead. Since he looked as if he was going to vomit, I took a couple of steps backward, and said, "So you just get on back to Mexia and leave well enough alone and your little tax evasion scandal stays between us, all right?"

"Fine," he said, turned and headed back down the hallway. Then a miracle occurred when he tossed his partially eaten slice of pizza in the garbage can before vanishing into an elevator car.

I walked over to the fellas, and Jack asked, "What did you tell Clarence, he looked as if he had seen a ghost?"

"I made him an offer he couldn't refuse," I said in a poor Italian accent.

Jack laughed, then asked, "What did the ladies say about the judge's offer?"

"We're all in, we just need to see what the other side wants to do."

"I'll keep my fingers crossed."

"Throw in a prayer too," I said.

We walked through the courtroom door and back to our table, just as the defense team was emerging from the jury room. Charlie retrieved the judge and when he took the bench, he nodded toward Blair to go on the record. He recited the details of his proposal, and then said, "Starting with the plaintiff, what did y'all decide?"

I rose and said, "We discussed it judge, and we are all on board."

"Including the reduction of the verdict, no appeal, and no publicity?"

"Yes, sir—all of that."

"And I handle the punishment for both sides?"

I swallowed hard, and uttered, "That's fine too."

"What about Mr. Vanderbilt?"

"That has been handled, sir."

"What do you say, counselor?" the judge said to the defense.

Shiras rose, and said, "The insurance company has been consulted and they are in agreement. My client and I likewise accept the proposal," I grabbed Nelda Fay's hand and gave it a squeeze. "For the record, we waive all rights to an appeal, no publicity, no state bar and we will rely on you for any consequences."

"Let's get to that part next," the judge said. "Regarding Mr. Morrison's ... ahem ... iffy insulation testimony, I chalk that up to a senior moment—a simple memory lapse, and no punishment is forthcoming."

Morrison rose and said, "Thank, thank, thank—"

"Don't mention it," the judge said, and Highsmith cackled. "As for your problem Mr. Shiras, during the break, I contacted the State Bar. I learned that you have a spotless record and considering your longevity in the practice you are to be commended for that," the judge said, and Shiras nodded. "With that record and taking into account the nature of your perceived ethical slip up, I see the likely outcome with the bar to be a private reprimand. Consider this as me privately reprimanding you, but I do find you in contempt of this court. As a sanction, and in order for you to purge yourself of the contempt, I order you or, alternatively your firm, to donate within the next thirty days five thousand dollars to the cancer research charity, Golfers Against Cancer."

"Fair enough," Shiras said. "I am familiar with them and know that they do good work."

"Indeed they do," the judge said.

Shiras added, "We will timely make the donation and send you a copy of the receipt."

"Fine," the judge said, then turned to me. "Sadly, Ms. Chase I do not believe the State Bar would be so charitable with your situation and would most assuredly punish you aggressively," he said, and I placed the palms of my hands on the table to brace myself. "You did a real bad thing here, do you understand that?"

"Yes sir, I sure do."

"I believe you do and that's why you so willingly confessed everything to me. I admire the fact that you did not put on any pretense about your conduct. I will also say that for someone who has never been in a trial before you handled this case in a very capable and professional manner. It wasn't always pretty and I give you only small kudos on style, but all in all you were very effective. However, the fact that you did a good job and ultimately prevailed, does not excuse what you did. You are *not* a lawyer and should have *never* been in this courtroom presenting yourself as one. As such, I must find you in contempt of this court. For the record, I further rule that your fee contract with the plaintiff is null and void. Ms. Blatchford, all net proceeds from the verdict is yours to do with as you see fit. Finally, Ms. Chase, I believe that there must be a proper punishment—a strong punishment—one that includes confinement."

"Jail?" Nelda asked, and the judge nodded.

Lupe wailed and collapsed backward onto her pew with her face in her hands. My nauseous feelings from that morning returned and I pulled the trash can over in front of me and took deep breaths. Though she too was sobbing, Dot began fanning me with the plastic water pitcher tray.

"Mr. Shiras, I'm going to determine the length of the sentence and need to ponder that, but you all are free to go."

Shiras nodded and glared at me as he and his crew left the courtroom. Once the door closed behind them, the Judge asked me to approach. I glanced back to Jack as I walked slowly to the bench and could tell he was as frightened as I was. I stood awaiting my fate, and the judge said, "Ms. Chase, I did not want Shiras and his coterie to know this, but your so-called *confinement* is going to be one day in jail. Don't worry—it won't be at the County Jail, but rather in one of our holding cells right through there," he said pointing to a wooden side door.

"Oh thank God," Nelda gasped, and my own tension eased.

"There is a reason for this leniency and I will gladly explain it," the judge said. "Historically, the term *lawyer* was simply defined as someone who is capable of assisting another in need, in certain matters. Take Abe Lincoln, for example, he did not go to law school. Instead, he read some books, took an oral exam, was admitted to practice and the rest is history."

"I would also, add that in this state we used to allow long-suffering legal secretaries to sit for the Bar Exam without going through law school. This was because they had extensive on the job training working on most every aspect of prepping cases. They had encountered an array of legal matters, and many knew as much about the law and procedure as the lawyers that they labored for. I sense that you and the nice lady next to you fall into that category. Unfortunately, they don't allow that anymore and I think it's a pity. The only way one can get a law license now is to incur the tremendous expense of graduating from an accredited law school. Then you have to pass the bar exam and many that achieve that won't have as much knowledge as you two already possess. I have witnessed some fine lawyering in this courthouse, both as a litigator and as a judge, and have seen many who had far less skills and resourcefulness as you, Ms. Chase.

"Amen to that," Blair said, and Charlie nodded.

"That said, I want you to report here tomorrow morning for your one day in confinement. Charlie won't even lock the door to the cell and you won't have to spend the night. You just have stay there from eight to five—that constitutes a *day* in my book. Though the stay entitles you to meals, the food here is pretty bad, so you may want to bring your own nourishment—hopefully enough to share," he said with a wink. "During your time of confinement, you may purge yourself of contempt and gain your release by writing out all of your home cookin' recipes, including for chicken and dumplings, biscuits, cream gravy, every pie you make, gumbo, casseroles, including King Ranch Chicken, yeast rolls, and jalapeno cornbread, agreed?"

"Yes sir," I said, exhaling.

"Good, see you in the morning. Any other questions?"

"I have one, Your Honor," Nelda said.

"All right, let's have it."

"When you say that all of the proceeds are mine to do with what I want, does that mean *anything* I want?" she said, glancing at Dot, Lupe and me.

The judge smiled, and said, "Yes, anything your heart desires."

We began gathering our belongings and as Jack and Highsmith headed for the exit, the judge said, "Excuse me, sir."

The boys stopped and the judge pointed to Highsmith and motioned him toward the bench with one finger.

EPILOGUE

Well, now you know how I ended up here in a jail cell in McLennan County. I appreciate you listening to my story and I hope you enjoyed it. I have to go now since I have a hell of a lot of recipes to write.

"Bill, can I borrow a pen, mine seems to have petered out."

"Sure, Gertie," Highsmith said, handing me his through the bars of the adjacent cell.